Thicker than Water

The Tenth in the Murray of Letho series

by

Lexie Conyngham

To Shiart,

for
Lexie Conyngham.

Thanks for coming!

First published in 2017 by The Kellas Cat Press, Aberdeen.

Copyright Alexandra Conyngham, 2017

The right of the author to be identified as the author of this work as been asserted by her in accordance with the Copyright, Designs and Patent Act, 1988.
All rights reserved. No part of this publication may be reproduced, stored, or transmitted in any form, or by any means, electronic, mechanical or photocopying, recording or otherwise, without the express permission of the publisher.

ISBN: 978-1-910926-30-7

Cover design by Helen Braid at ellieallatsea.co.uk

Lexie Conyngham

DEDICATION

To the ladies and now gentlemen as well of University Hall, St. Andrews: two happy years in Lumsden and two in Old Wing, and many friendships made!

Dramatis Personae

Charles Murray of Letho
Henry Robbins, a manservant with a plan
Mary Robbins, his wife
Carlisle, Letho House's long-established gardener
Cosmo Gordon, an artist
Dr. Archibald Lindsay, temporary physician at Letho
Grisel Fenwick, a forceful aunt
Sundry servants

Professor David Shaw
Mrs. Shaw, his culinarily-talented wife
Flavia Shaw, a young lady just out
James Shaw, her brother, a scholar of sorts
Walter Fenwick, another scholar, of rather better sorts
Pennie, a sensitive manservant

Mr. and Mrs. Bogue, a clothier and his wife, going up in the world
Sandy Bogue, their musical son
Sarah Bogue, their less musical daughter
Wee Dod, their talented servant

Thomas Swanson, silversmith, perhaps also ascending in the world but not so quickly as he might like
Jack Swanson, his son, a clerk
Victor, a valued member of the family

Rory McArthur, another clerk
Janet McArthur
Rosina McArthur, an infant
Mrs. Loudoun, their neighbour
Nathan Houston, her brother, a travelling trader

Constable Round, late of the 42nd. Regiment of Foot

Lexie Conyngham

Chapter One

'What colour would you call that waistcoat of yours?'

Daniel peered down at it, puzzled.

'It's a kind of grey, I suppose,' he said, lifting his chin again to try to reconstruct his pose. The artist contemplated Daniel's midriff from a few yards away.

'I'll maybe need to get more of that paint in,' he said, and retired to his easel with a frown. The gardener, who was pacing in the shadows at the back of the dining room, grinned.

'I tellt you often enough you've too much fat on those bones, Daniel Hossack. Too much of your wife's good cooking and too much sitting around doing nothing while others are working.'

Daniel blushed, and sighed, then tried to assume a superior air.

'Mr. Carlisle, I'm an indoor worker. It's hard to get the kind of exercise you do all day.'

'Aye, there's no doubt, it's a healthy life in the gardens,' said Carlisle with satisfaction. Then he scowled. 'And a busy one, at this time of the year. Any chance I could get back to it soon, Mr. Gordon, sir?'

'Just let me …' said the artist, dabbing irritably at something on the canvas that had not gone well. He grabbed a cloth that dangled from the pocket of his own rather fine waistcoat, and wiped vigorously before applying the brush again. His gaze flickered up to Daniel and down again.

'I dinna think I'd ever be set up on a canvas, mind,' Carlisle went on thoughtfully. 'Me, arranged in my finery in a grand dining room!'

'I want to paint you in a hothouse, if you have such a thing,' said Gordon the artist absently. 'And no finery, Carlisle: your working clothes will be perfect. Give me a minute, and I'll just take a look at your face.'

The sound Carlisle made might have been one of disappointment, or derision. He was a well-established servant, one of the last who had already been in post before Mr. Murray's father had died, and that was a dozen years ago. The half-hour he had been standing waiting on Cosmo Gordon's artistic pleasure might have been the longest time anyone remembered him being indoors, except for sleeping, for twenty years. It did not suit him: he smelled of earth and foliage and new prunings, carrying a web of the outdoors with him even as he paced the good Turkey carpets and eyed the unfamiliar silverware on the sideboard. A pair of great oak log buckets by the fireside caught his attention: perhaps he remembered the tree they came from.

'Try to stop wriggling, Daniel,' Cosmo Gordon murmured.

'He's distracting me,' said Daniel petulantly, nodding at Carlisle.

'I need to be off,' said Carlisle, unapologetically. 'It's a busy time, March. And I've permission from the laird to be away off to St. Andrews the day: there's a gentleman there with purple peas to sow, and I heard I could have some if I went to see him. If I dinna go soon I'll no be back the night.'

'Of course you will,' said Gordon, soothing, though his mind was still mostly on the acreage of Daniel's waistcoat. 'I'm off to St. Andrews myself later, we can go together, if you will. And if you do end up being late, no doubt my landlady can find you somewhere to sleep.'

Both Daniel and Carlisle knew the tone of that phrase. 'Somewhere to sleep' in this case did not mean a cosy bed in a well-warmed chamber: it meant anything from a few worn blankets and a chair by the embers of the kitchen fire, down to some straw shared with the family pig. Daniel did not raise his eyebrows as he would have liked to, as Gordon was studying his face, but Carlisle grinned with deep irony, his gaze on Cosmo Gordon's well-fitted back.

Carlisle turned when the door opened, and straightened when

he saw that the laird himself was among them. Charles Murray was tall, dark-haired, in his thirties, and edging eagerly out of the mourning he still wore for his dead wife: it would be a few months yet before he was properly free of it. However, his mood was light on this brisk spring morning, and he nodded to Carlisle in his usual friendly fashion before glancing over at Daniel and Cosmo Gordon.

'Oh, Daniel!'

'Yes, Mr. Murray?' Daniel was torn: should he stand respectfully and spoil his pose, or sit and be thought rude to his master?

'Just stay there, Daniel,' said Murray, with only the least touch of sarcasm. 'Where's Robbins? Have you finished him already?' His gaze darted around the dining room, as if expecting to see a finished canvas propped somewhere nearby.

'Robbins said he was busy,' said Cosmo Gordon, turning to Murray at last. 'He suggested I paint Daniel here first.'

'Oh, that's a shame,' said Murray. 'I was hoping he would lead the way. Where is he, Daniel, do you know?'

Daniel gave a tiny shrug.

'He said he had something he needed to do in the attics, sir.'

'In the attics? What on earth is he doing up there?'

Daniel made a face, and Cosmo Gordon frowned at him.

'He didna say, sir.'

'I hope it's not a leak. Carlisle, weren't you going to St. Andrews today?'

'Aye, sir, but I'm waiting to see Mr. Gordon here first. Though it's a busy time and all,' he could not resist adding.

'Indeed. Well, if you need to go tomorrow, or stay overnight, you have permission, of course. I need to go there myself today, to see Walter, and I just wanted to tell Robbins that I might stay overnight myself.'

'I could tell him, sir,' said Daniel, eager for responsibility.

'Yes, yes, you do that, Daniel, thank you,' said Murray. 'But I'll just see if I can find him anyway, just in case it is a leak.' Or in case you forget, he did not add, though both he and Daniel knew the words were in the air. 'You're heading back there yourself this evening, aren't you, Mr. Gordon?'

'That's right, Mr. Murray,' said the artist, still working on the canvas. 'I'll be back not tomorrow but the next day, I think.'

'Of course: whenever you can fit us in,' agreed Murray. He was rather excited at the thought of having portraits of all his servants, and he hoped that they were, too. Cosmo Gordon came quite well recommended and seemed a respectable sort of person, though busy. Perhaps that in itself was a recommendation.

'I see Davie Shaw's student is out in the garden again,' said Thomas Swanson, smoothing down his coat with care. His son glanced up from his desk at the parlour window, watchful to lift his pen away from the paper as he did so.

'Why should he not be?'

'What on earth does he have them do out there?' said his father, not expecting an answer. 'Poking in thon wee pond he has dug, and taking measurements round trees. And drawing.'

'Natural philosophy, I suppose,' said Jack, who had completed his bejant year at United College, and knew something of the life. His father snorted.

'What use would that be to a minister? Does it help him to preach a sermon?'

'Maybe he doesna want to be a minister,' said Jack dangerously. His father eyed him.

'He wouldna be the first, would he, then?' he demanded.

'University degrees arena just for ministers,' his son replied, as he had done many times before.

'You wouldna ken: you didna stay long enough to find out.'

'I kent fine I wasna fitted for the Kirk,' said Jack, already regretting his rashness. 'And maybe the lad next door has other plans, too. Is he the one with the thick brown hair?'

'That's the one. Walter, I think his name is.' His father seemed happy enough to turn the conversation back, too, thank goodness. 'Ken, I found him the other day down by the Cathedral, trying to find his way home. How long has he been next door now? Six, seven months? And he canna find his way back from the Cathedral.'

'Aye, well, his brains are maybe in a different bit of his head,' said Jack, not unkindly. 'Father, I've to finish this bond for the end of the day, if you don't mind.'

'Oh! Oh, aye, of course,' said Thomas Swanson. He smoothed

his coat again, and adjusted his wig ever so slightly on his forehead. 'I'll be in my workshop, then.'

'Aye, aye,' said Jack, his head already bent over the document again. His father allowed the least little smile of pride to creep over his face, then turned and left the room without another word.

'Will you fetch me some muslin when you're out, Rory?'

He remembered Janet's words with a start, but still stood, hands in his pockets, pressed against the wall he was staring over. The rocks between the Castle and the harbour lay layered and flat, like the scales of a mighty defeated fish, its head crushed by the cliff.

Eider ducks bobbed, cushioned on the shallow waves, perpetually appalled, while around them were cormorants busy in flight or patient on the edge of a rock, waiting to be served. A little flock of eight or ten eiders slid into the sea between rocks, and hurried off. One lazy, foamy wave closed over them and they emerged, busily flapping off the excess water. By the third wave they had their balance, rode it supremely, and headed out to join their colleagues in the bay, a fishing flotilla with purpose. Over to the east, a fishing boat slipped out of the harbour in the shelter of the pier, and carved a smooth path towards Kinkell Braes, the long land fingering down to meet it.

The wind bit at his face and chilled his shoulders. He should fetch the muslin: after all, it was not Janet's fault that she could not go out to fetch it for herself, and indeed he would not encourage her to try. And it wasn't as if she was asking for anything fancy this time: she needed the muslin for the bairn. If he could get that position with the council, now, maybe they could afford something that would bring a smile to Janet's face – but Jack was up for it, too. Was Jack a better clerk than he was? Maybe, maybe not, he decided fairly. But with his father a burgess, Jack might have a wee bit more influence over the decision. Which of them would get it? What need did Jack have for more money?

Aye, he should fetch that muslin and not have Janet tempted to go out for it herself. Particularly not now ... For a while there he had allowed himself to relax, to forget all about it, but now it seemed that the danger had returned – had followed them to St. Andrews. Even he should be careful, never mind Janet. But he had work to do, and the muslin needed to be fetched. He pushed himself away from the wall, drew out his hands and shook them to get the blood back into his fingers, and headed back into the town. The eider ducks swam on, regardless.

Murray ducked his head to squeeze through the attic door at the top of the back stairs. He had not been up here since he was a boy, he thought, and it gave him a little thrill, wondering what mysteries might be up here, as if he were a boy again, playing amongst the old clothes and discarded furniture with his brother, emerging coated in sooty-scented dust to be told off by the housekeeper. The door was not large, but the rooms beyond it were a reasonable size, if cluttered: they fitted oddly around chimney breasts and the shape of the roof, and they had no windows, but otherwise he could walk about them without hunching despite his height. Robbins was smaller than he, a little less than the middle height, and would find this remote accommodation perfectly accessible. Murray turned away a little with his candle, trying to work out where Robbins might be from any light he had with him. Fresh bootprints marked the dusty floor and he followed them on a circuitous path through piles of boxes to find, at last, his manservant perched on one trunk and polishing another with vigorous movements, his eyes shining in the light of the candle secured beside him. He jumped when Murray appeared.

'Sir! I am sorry, sir, I did not hear you. I must have been in a dwam.' He stood carefully, one eye on the candle.

'I think you were, Robbins: you were miles away,' said Murray, pleased with himself nevertheless that he could still creep up on someone unheard. 'What are you doing up here? I feared you might have found a leak in the roof.'

'No, nothing like that, sir, though I like to inspect it around this time of the year, after the gales have died down a little.'

'Of course. You did say.'

'And when I did so, sir, I noticed that some of these old leather trunks need a polish: they're very dry, and they might crack.'

'I thought you were to be painted this morning, before the other servants.'

'I beg your pardon, sir, I believed this was more urgent. And

Daniel was very eager to go ahead and have his turn.'

'I'm sure.'

'I'll go next, of course, sir,' Robbins added.

'Good, good. I particularly want him to take your likeness, Robbins – and Mrs. Robbins, too, even if she is no longer on the official staff here.'

'Mary, sir?' Robbins blinked in surprise.

'Of course: and if you like them both, I'll have copies made for you to have at home.'

'Ah, thank you, sir.' Robbins did not sound quite as pleased as Murray might have expected, but he chose not to follow this up at the moment. Robbins straightened out his polishing cloth, and adjusted a brush beside him. 'Was there anything else, sir?'

'Oh, yes. I'm off to St. Andrews shortly to see Professor Shaw, and I might, if invited, stay overnight. No doubt his wife will feed me well at dinner time, so even if I do come back tell Mrs. Mack I shan't need much in the way of supper.'

'Mrs. Shaw's puddings, sir?'

'Mrs. Shaw's puddings, indeed. I hope I survive the experience.'

'You'll see Walter?'

'That's part of my purpose, certainly. Have you any message for him?'

'Just that I hope he's working hard and not losing the advantage of all this privilege, sir.'

'I'll tell him,' said Murray with a smile. Walter, the grandson of Robbins' predecessor as butler at Letho, had shown little promise as a servant himself, but after a favour he had done for Murray he had been allowed to pursue his education with Murray's old university tutor, with a view to studying at the university himself in due course, and continue his interest in natural science. He was a solemn boy.

'And I think his aunt had a parcel for him, when anyone was to go. A suit of flannel, I believe,' Robbins added tight-lipped.

'Oh, thank you. I shall go through the village and collect it, if I can.'

Walter's aunt was a formidable woman, but grateful enough to Murray for offering to take the parcel that Murray suffered no ill effects from his brief visit to her cottage in Letho village. As he walked his horse slowly down the roadway to the right-hand side of the sloping, triangular green, wrestling to find a comfortable way to carry Walter's bulky new undergarments – along with, the aunt had explained, two pots of decent jam - he nodded to Mrs. Feilden, the doctor's wife, who was talking to a young man with a rather fine looking horse. Intending his slow pace to allow him time to spot anything untoward in the village for which he was responsible, he instead took in every detail of the black stallion, from its alert ears to its well-polished shoes, and knew a degree of envy. It was a lovely beast. With a sigh, he pulled the strap tight on Walter's parcel and mounted his own perfectly adequate mare, patted her neck perhaps out of a sense of guilt for his infidelity, and trotted down the road past the inn to the main highway for St. Andrews.

He would have liked to give his mare her head a little on the smooth road, but it seemed to grow busier every month these days, mostly with carts plying to and fro with goods to and from Cupar and beyond. Time was, he reflected, indulging himself, that a journey to St. Andrews meant you were there for a week at least, resting, making the most of the long and difficult journey. Now, with better roads, people seemed to pop over to the place just for the fun of it, and think very little of it – and, he admitted, on a fine chilly spring morning like this one, why not? In the fields to either side the March sowing was almost complete, and miniature calves suckled their small black mothers. Sheep too were pursued by lambs of limitless energies and nerviness, and crows in dancing pairs made mad black columns for a moment above the grass, before tumbling back to the ground to reassemble their dignity. The sky was blue-white and startling, and the new leaves pressed against it by the trees were an almost indecent shade of green, determined to wake up the world to the new season.

The road held plenty of memories, too, of his journeys to and from St. Andrews as a student. He had not been there since he had delivered Walter into the care of his old tutor, Professor Shaw, six months before, but he did not expect the old town to have changed much. There were three main streets, up on the headland, running east to west and converging gently on the ruined cathedral on the eastern tip: North Street held United College amidst old cottages and modern houses; Market Street was where the traders worked and, inevitably, the market was held; South Street, with the arches of the Pends at one end and the West Port guarding the other, had the gateway to St. Mary's College on its south side. South of that again, along part of the street's length, was the mill lade that flowed down to the harbour, and by its side lived, in an ancient and rambling house, Professor Shaw, his wife and daughter, and whatever students had chosen to lodge with him for this session. More normally, professors would choose their lodgers, but Professor Shaw was the kind of person to whom life happened – charitably, up to now, for the most part, but very much in complete disregard for his feelings on the subject.

Murray smiled: he was very fond of his old tutor, and hoped that Walter was doing well there. He would soon find out.

He negotiated the queue of carts waiting to cross the bridge over the Eden at Guardbridge, distracting his horse carefully from a noisy quarrel occurring by the side of the road. One carter was gesticulating with a coin to another man: the coin was bright, reflecting the light over the water, and in a moment Murray was past the altercation and trotting into the sharp breeze coming off the broad estuary to his left. It was cold but fresh, tingling across his face and snatching at his breath, and he took the opportunity of a momentarily quiet road to break into a quick canter. The mare enjoyed it too, for a few minutes, then they willingly drew up at the side of the road to gaze over the hedgerow at the silvery waters beyond.

Immediately he heard hoofbeats following him at a smart pace, and glanced round behind him. It was the lovely black stallion he had last seen in Letho, with its rider.

'Good day to you, sir! I am sorry you stopped: I thought you might have fancied a little race!' The rider, raising his hat politely, revealed a head of curly fair hair, a nose that a kindly friend would have called aquiline, and a pair of blue eyes glinting with good humour.

'I fear my horse, though reliable, is no match for that fine mount of yours,' Murray admitted. He kept the mare clear in case she found the stallion as handsome as he did. 'He's a beauty.'

'I'm extraordinarily lucky in him, it's true,' said the man modestly. 'He was a gift from my brother, when I graduated M.D.'

'You're lucky at least in your choice of brother!' said Murray. 'Have we met? My name is Charles Murray of Letho.'

'I'm Archibald Lindsay,' said the man, and they made what bows they could in their saddles. 'I'm from Perthshire, but if you're the laird of Letho then I'm lucky again, for I shall be staying in your village for a few weeks. You know your local physician has taken a tumble?'

'Dr. Feilden? Yes: he fell down from a hayloft on my neighbour's estate when he was tending to an injured farm worker. Mrs. Feilden said he had broken his leg.'

'That's right, poor fellow. He wrote me to come and help with his patients until he is up and about again: his son and I studied together, and while his son has his own practice I am a dilettante, I'm afraid, and therefore free to follow my fancy.'

'Are you set for St. Andrews just now?' Murray asked, as both horses were growing impatient. 'Shall we ride together?'

'It would be a pleasure.'

They set off again, side by side, with Murray trying not to dwell too much on the perfections of Dr. Lindsay's horse. The physician, it transpired, had attended St. Andrews a few years after Murray, then gone on to Edinburgh to complete his medical studies, and they had a few acquaintances in common.

'Are you off to see one of your tutors in St. Andrews, then?' Lindsay asked.

'Yes, Davie Shaw. He's teaching natural philosophy these days, and I have sent a boy from the village to stay with him to prepare for university. I want to see how he's getting on. What about you?'

'I had no one particular in mind, though I should be happy to see Professor Shaw again. This is the closest I have been to St. Andrews for some years, so it will be enough to see all the sights and revisit my memories, to walk about the cathedral ruins, to gaze out from the cliffs above the harbour, to sit for a little in the quadrangle and imagine myself in my red gown again ... It goes all too quickly, does it not?'

'Far too quickly,' Murray agreed. 'If one only visits now and again, it is a very efficacious way to feel ancient. Today's students seem so young, and yet so established: it is their place now, not ours.'

'You are determined to cast a gloom over my visit!' said Lindsay, laughing. 'but I refuse to be deterred! I shall make you a wager,' he said, drawing a silver coin from his waistcoat pocket. 'I shall wager you that before we part in the town, I shall have met someone of my acquaintance, and will straightaway feel at home again!'

Murray laughed, too.

'That is not a wager I can accept,' he said. 'How can I tell where you will feel at home?'

'You are right, I suppose,' Lindsay sighed with a grin, and went to replace the coin in his pocket. 'Doubly so, since I am not at all sure about this coin. What do you think?'

He tossed it over, and Murray caught it. It was a silver shilling, very shiny, not darkened with use, and the images on it looked authentic. Yet Murray knew what Lindsay meant: there was something not quite right about it. Was it the weight? The colour? He could not quite put his finger on it.

'Where did you come by it?' he asked.

'From a man in Letho: what was his name, now? Yule, that was it.'

'Francis Yule? His children have been ill.'

'That's the man.'

Murray frowned.

'He's a decent man: and not overly bright. I doubt he would have given you a false coin on purpose. I wonder where he found it?'

'The innkeeper in the village – I'm staying there – he warned me there were a few about.'

'False coins? That's not good. I must send word to the sheriff, though no doubt he knows.'

'Nevertheless, no doubt he'll be happy to know that the laird is keeping an eye open, too,' said Lindsay. 'Keep that one, if you wish, for evidence.'

'Thank you, I shall.' Murray slipped the coin into his own waistcoat pocket, and frowned as they rode on up the sharp little hill into St. Andrews.

Chapter Two

Murray left Archibald Lindsay at the head of North Street, having ridden with him from its foot at Lindsay's insistence to accompany him through the ghosts of his past. Lindsay dismounted at the gate to the cathedral precincts and found a boy to mind his beautiful horse (several clamoured for the privilege), and Murray bade him farewell and rode on round the sweeping corner to join South Street. A few more minutes brought him to Professor Shaw's irregular house by the mill lade, and the little professor came himself to greet him at the front door. A sensitive-looking manservant led the mare off with delicacy to the little stable, and Murray was hurried inside where the family was waiting eagerly to see him.

'Charles, dear boy, how good to see you again! And still in mourning, dear, dear,' murmured Professor Shaw. The tutor was short and wide – Murray always felt he was arching over him, like a pallmall hoop over a ball - his face that of an amiable frog, and with his habitually flying neckcloth he resembled nothing more than one of his wife's famous puddings, tied up in a clout for boiling. Mrs. Professor Shaw and their children, now fast approaching adulthood, were almost as comfortable looking, rounded and shining and content. Mrs. Shaw curtseyed to Murray's bow, and as her daughter had come out since Murray's last visit, presented her. Flavia Shaw, cherry-faced and berry-eyed and with a nervy habit of batting at her own hair with the back of her hand, wobbled a little as she bobbed her curtsey and giggled at herself, and her brother James, a couple of years younger, shook his head in mock despair. Murray made a very proper bow to Flavia and everyone relaxed, their duties done. Mrs. Shaw led the way along a narrow dogleg passage into the familiar parlour, warm with a lively fire in the grate, and Walter, who had been sitting at the window with a book, ostentatiously rose and bowed to his erstwhile master.

'Walter! I am glad to see you looking well. Are you still enjoying your studies?'

'I am, sir.' Walter's cap of chestnut hair glowed healthily in the firelight, and he waved his book at Murray. 'See this, sir? It's a fellow by the name of Ausonius, and he writes all about trees and fish on some foreign river. Well, he did: Professor Shaw says he's dead the now.'

'I believe he has indeed gone to his eternal rest,' Murray acknowledged. 'I remember reading that, too. How do you find your Latin?'

'It's no too bad, sir,' said Walter after a moment's thought.

'He's doing very well, Charles,' said Professor Shaw kindly. 'His Latin and Greek are coming along prodigiously, though perhaps he is less naturally inclined towards the ancient philosophers, would that be fair, Walter?'

Walter frowned, and nodded.

'They're gey hard to understand, sir. All that about stokes and stuff makes no sense to me.'

'Think of it as something you have to learn now to get on to the interesting stuff,' said Murray helpfully. 'Later you might find it makes more sense. Even the Stoics.'

'Aye, sir,' said Walter dubiously. James poked him hard in his side, and Walter scowled at him.

A maid brought in a tray of tea and generous slices of Mrs. Shaw's black bun. Murray tried to take a small slice, knowing how things would go for the rest of the day, but there was no such thing in that household as a small slice, and he resigned himself to doubling his weight on his short visit.

'You're engaged to stay here for dinner, Charles, of course, but perhaps you'll agree to stay the night, too? There is a recital this evening by a string quartet that you might enjoy,' said Professor Shaw.

'Oh, yes, Mr. Murray! We're all going to it,' said Flavia eagerly. 'They're very good! Well, I'm sure you've heard better in Edinburgh,' she added thoughtfully, 'but if you can put such memories from your mind, sir, no doubt you can find it in you to enjoy it.'

'Have you been to Edinburgh yet, Miss Shaw?' Murray asked, amused.

'Not yet, certainly,' said Flavia, 'but James and I have an invitation for some time soon.'

'A colleague at the college there,' Professor Shaw explained. 'I have little wish to go, I must say, but the children are excited and I daresay it will lift Mrs. Shaw and me from our slumbers, don't you think, dear?'

Mrs. Shaw, who had been Professor Shaw's cook housekeeper when he had had a parish, blinked in awe at the thought of the sophistication of Edinburgh.

'I have never been! I have no idea ... Mr. Murray, you must tell me what people wear in Edinburgh!'

'Much the same as people wear here, Mrs. Shaw! Don't be the least concerned: you will be welcomed wherever you go where there are people of sense.'

'And are there people of sense in Edinburgh, Mr. Murray?' Flavia asked cheekily. Walter, taking the conversation seriously, said:

'Very few, Miss Shaw, in my experience. Begging your pardon, sir,' he added belatedly to Murray.

'Well, I'm sure you will all enjoy it, and then return home to delight afresh in St. Andrews,' said Murray reassuringly. 'It will be a great experience.'

The Shaws exchanged glances, all in their own ways excited about the prospect. Murray, made quite at his ease amongst these easy, familiar people, sat back in his armchair and allowed his gaze to wander around the parlour, noting the usual cushions embroidered at various stages of Flavia's needlework education, the stuffed birds peering from their domes on the bookcase, the slightly scuffed furniture well loved and used, until he lit on an unfamiliar portrait which hung next to the door.

'I had no idea you had had your likeness taken, Professor!' he said in surprise.

Professor Shaw blushed and choked a little on his cake, waving his napkin in deprecation.

'No, no, not at all! Well, yes, it is my likeness, I suppose, indeed I'm told it is a good one, but I did not choose to sit for it. A kindly student ... well, a former student ... so good of him, but really, he could have spent his money much more wisely. But he is a generous soul, and would not take no for an answer, bless him!'

'May I look? Is it recently done?'

'No, not really: a few years ago, I suppose. It has not hung there before,' Professor Shaw explained, as Murray rose to take a closer look. 'We had it upstairs, but my dear wife insisted ... I do not think it causes too much offence, over there, though surely no one who visits here really needs to see two of me!'

'It is a good likeness, and well done, sir, I believe,' said Murray. He bent to examine the signature. '"C. Gordon" – is that Cosmo Gordon, by any chance?'

'It is, it is! That's very clever, Charles.'

'Not at all: he is at Letho at the moment, painting portraits of the servants.'

'Oh!' said Walter suddenly, and a look of something that might have been envy passed swiftly across his face. Murray smiled at it.

'I would not leave you out, Walter, even though you are no longer in my employ. If Professor Shaw can spare you tomorrow I shall take you back to Letho and have Gordon paint you, too.'

'Sir!' Walter frowned, not sure whether he was entirely pleased or not. Any new situation was a minor challenge to Walter.

'This is a fine recommendation. Has Gordon been in St. Andrews long?' Murray went on, still studying the painting.

'A few years, I believe. He hails from somewhere in the Highlands, but I think he is here permanently – when he is not travelling. He lives at the top of Market Street, in lodgings.'

'Yes, that was where I wrote to him, I believe.' Murray took a last look at the portrait, and returned to his seat. 'What was he like to work with? Was he a pleasant, easy fellow? For I confess I have hardly seen him so far.'

Professor Shaw frowned anxiously, thinking back.

'He was perfectly pleasant,' he concluded. 'Quite gentlemanly, in fact: I don't think he was one of those painters who considers himself a tradesman. The only thing was ... well, no doubt he is a very busy man. I thought he gave the impression that there was somewhere else he had to be. Somewhere rather more important: and indeed there may well have been, for who is less important than a dusty old professor?' He smiled as he said the words, but it was clear he took them seriously.

'Then he's a fool, Father,' said Flavia abruptly, 'and you need pay no more attention to him.'

'Hush, now, dear!' said her mother gently, a hand on her arm.

'I scarcely have much chance to pay attention to him,' her father admitted, 'for he pays no attention to me. I thought he might at least recognise a face he had painted when he met its owner in the street, but he must paint so many.' It was unusual, Murray thought, for Professor Shaw to feel slighted by anyone, for he had so low an opinion of himself that it would have been hard for anyone else to undercut it. 'But dear, remember that Mr. Murray has employed him, and Mr. Murray might not want to think that he has employed a fool.'

'I'm not sure I have, but if he dismisses someone like you so casually then I fear I may have to dismiss him, too,' said Murray loyally. 'Who was the student that paid the painter? How does he regard him?'

'Oh, I think he was after your time, by a few years, Charles,' said Professor Shaw. 'He hailed from Perthshire, where his brother has an estate now. Lindsay is his name, Archibald Lindsay: I believe he has entered medical practice now, though he would have little need of the money, I should have thought.'

'Archibald Lindsay? Fair hair and a prominent nose?'

'That's the fellow. Do you remember him?'

'I should, for I rode into St. Andrews with him this morning and left him at the top of North Street, not that I had ever met him before this day! I daresay he'll be along to see you before long!'

'Well,' said Professor Shaw, turning slightly to look again at his portrait, 'that will be a pleasure, I'm sure.' There was a moment's silence, as awkward a one as Murray had ever felt in that house, but the professor broke it before it could grow too far. 'Walter, will you show Mr. Murray what we have been doing in the garden? And all your excellent work in the business. Charles?' he said, rising from his cosy armchair and constraining Murray to rise, too. Walter set his tea cup down with self-conscious care, and followed them out of the parlour. James Shaw, with a light of mischief in his eyes, went too.

Up steps and down and round corners and Professor Shaw

showed Murray out into the garden of his property. When Murray had last seen it, it had simply consisted of some rose bushes, a patch of vegetables and a row of well-kept bee skeps against the stone wall, and these features had been retained. However, the lower part of the garden, which had been, he thought, a decaying orchard, was now completely different. In fact, it reminded Murray of nothing more than a model of Venice, dug up and brought to Fife and left to its own devices. A waterway flowed from a grid in the garden wall, down a pebbly runnel and via a number of pools of different sizes and presumably depths, their surfaces mostly wrinkled in the light March breeze. The pools were fringed with willow, alder and hawthorn, and prickly with the spring growth of herbaceous plants at the water's edge, though each, Murray noticed, had one place where the bank was a bare flag of stone, with a small stone seat. Here and there stone slabs also formed simple bridges so that every pool was easily accessible, and so was the wind gauge set up with a thermometer attached on a post in the centre of the complex. Murray stood and stared in wonder, while Walter, with a proprietorial air, took a notebook and pen from his pocket and advanced on the nearest pond, peering into the water and making notes. It was clearly the centre of some fascinating scientific experiments, but besides that, it was a most attractive prospect, designed to delight the eye as well as the mind.

'So what do you have here, then?' Murray asked.

'The water is diverted into the garden from the mill lade. A very nice man who works for the council helped with that, I have to say, and I had to show them that it would not emerge any the dirtier for my little experiments in here – though I believe Mr. Swanson next door was a little concerned at first. The pools contain fish, of course, and a few other species, arranged in such a way that we can easily observe them while they can live happily in the belief that they inhabit a normal river or pond. Here, for example, we have some rudd – see that little shoal there?' The light flashed on a movement heading in under the bank's leafy shelter. 'There are minnows, too, and sticklebacks, and one or two chubb.'

'Lazy, greedy lumps,' Walter murmured.

'True, true: they will eat anything as long as they do not have to run too far to do it,' Professor Shaw agreed with a smile. 'A little like young James: where is he now?' But James had absented himself from the scholarly party, and was seen disappearing in the direction of the stables. Professor Shaw frowned briefly. 'How is your puddock's gener, Walter? He's a most observant boy, Charles, and assiduous in his notes.'

'The crud, sir?' asked Walter, rising and brushing off his knees. 'Aye, a few of the wee kail ladles are out already, though I think it's a wee thing cold for the rest yet. Do you see, sir?' He beckoned Murray over to show him a thick mat of frogspawn, flecked with wriggling black dots, then pointed to one or two tadpoles darting about the pond. Murray sank his hands on to his knees and let himself be absorbed by the busy life already under the surface, and occasionally on it, screws and water baillies and unnameably tiny squiggles of movement that crowded the whole pond, if one looked closely enough.

'What's the Latin word for chubb, then, Walter?'

'Leuciscus, sir,' said Walter straightaway.

'And rudd?'

'Scardinius.'

Murray straightened, and met Professor Shaw's eye. They both nodded: Walter seemed to be finding his feet.

'Do you know Mr. Bogue?'

'I don't believe so.'

Murray and Professor Shaw stood patiently in the hallway, while Mrs. Shaw and Flavia flapped about perfecting their evening attire and Walter and James Shaw compared notes on their Greek translations for the next day, seated together about five steps up the stairs. As far as Murray could see, comparing notes for James meant copying the right answers from Walter.

'He's a burgess now, quite successful. He bought a house at the other end of South Street,' Professor Shaw waved in a generally easterly direction, and knocked a candle out of the sconce beside him. Fortunately Murray caught it before it fell, and replaced it carefully in its holder. 'His son is quite musical and the family generally enjoy music, and they have taken to hosting – it's remarkably good of them, though of course some of the professors won't attend because he is only a clothier, but who is to say that his music – or his kindness – are any the less for that?'

'They host musical soirées?' Murray clarified.

'That's right. A real pleasure,' said Professor Shaw with satisfaction. 'And his son has a little string quartet, which will play for us this evening. My dear, I should hate to miss the beginning!' he called to his wife in slight reproof. Flavia skidded to a halt beside them.

'Well, *I* am ready,' she announced, as though everyone else were holding her back. Mrs. Shaw hurried up with Flavia's shawl, and the boys were chivvied from the stairs, leaving their books on the step where they had been sitting, and the party managed at last to leave the house and set off towards South Street.

The house at the eastern end was old, and an unpromising stone entrance with worn initials carved over the gateway led, up some shallow, dipping steps, to a surprising barrel-vaulted drawing room of a very respectable size. The grand piano at one end seemed only reasonable in the circumstances, and a selection of chairs and sophas, thoughtfully arranged, allowed the visitors – already numbering around thirty – to sit in their parties or separated, by the fire blazing in the generous fireplace in one long wall or in cooler corners further away. Professor Shaw and his party were on the point of entering by the double door when a young man pushed past them to go out, turning as he went to call back into the room.

'I'll away and look for him, Gordon.'

'Dinna bother, Rory,' came another voice from behind the grand piano. 'Wee Dod'll play, will you no, Wee Dod?'

Someone else, possibly Wee Dod, added,

'You'll need to tune your fiddle, Rory, not go chasing off.'

The young man paused awkwardly in the doorway, and Professor Shaw waited without comment. The man Rory's close-cropped red hair caught the rich candlelight from inside the drawing room as if his skull had been finished with gold leaf: his eyes, deepset, pondered his decision while his fingers twitched as if they should have a coin to toss, and his nose was scrunched-up, though whether that was in thought or was his natural expression it was hard to tell. It was not, Murray thought, the face of a man at ease with himself.

In a moment he gave a little sigh through his teeth, tinged with exasperation, then pushed back into the drawing room again, making his way through the visitors to the front. The man at the grand piano nodded slightly and continued to float his fingers lazily across the notes, unconcerned. Rory snatched up a fiddle and bow from a table, and began to test the strings.

'You'd like to be near the front, wouldn't you, Charles?' asked Professor Shaw.

'Only if it does not inconvenience anyone else, sir,' said Murray. 'Perhaps the ladies would like to be near the fire?'

'I'd like to be at the front,' said Flavia promptly.

'I shouldn't like to be too near the fire,' said Mrs. Shaw meekly, 'if no one else minds. But if anyone wants to be warmer that is perfectly nice, too. I should be happy to sit by the fire. But Mr. Murray, of course, you're musical: you'll want to be near the front.'

'Mrs. Bogue!' Professor Shaw interrupted.

'Oh, Mrs. Bogue! Thank you so much for inviting us,' Mrs. Shaw joined with her husband. 'May I present one of my husband's old students, Mr. Charles Murray of Letho? He is our guest at present.'

Mrs. Bogue, a woman of stiff attire but pleasant demeanour, welcomed them all shyly and suggested that they might indeed like to take a portion of the seats nearest the grand piano. They made their way through the other seats, the Shaws nodding happily to various acquaintances all around, and arranged themselves on two small sophas and two low stools, for the boys, in what seemed to be the front row of the stalls. The red-haired violinist was still fidgeting with his fiddle, and the boy at the piano, who could not have been more than twenty, lounged back perilously as he gave Rory the various notes he demanded. A slim, fair-haired man who had been bending over a violincello case, stood up and turned as he lifted the 'cello clear, and caught Murray's eye with surprise.

'Mr. Murray, sir,' he said with a bow.

'Mr. Gordon.' Murray nodded back. 'I had no idea you played, as well as painted.'

'Only a little, as you will no doubt hear,' said Cosmo Gordon with a little laugh. 'And we are a man short this evening.'

'Aye, Jack,' muttered Rory ominously.

'Never mind McArthur, sir, he doesn't like things not to go according to plan.'

Rory McArthur snorted and turned away, not expecting to be introduced.

'You will of course remember,' Murray felt mischievous, 'Professor Shaw, whose likeness you painted some years ago.'

Gordon's eyes widened the very least in surprise, but he had the grace to bow.

'Of course, Professor. It was a pleasure.'

'It has been much admired,' said Shaw politely.

The artist made another little bow of thanks, but rose from it giving Murray a little twisted smile. Murray looked away, trying to think why the expression was familiar to him. It reminded him of nothing more than the occasions on which his father, a man always most observant of the stations in life of his fellow men, felt that Murray had introduced him into a social situation in which he was likely to be embarrassed. Yet how could that be? Murray glanced back at Cosmo Gordon but the man was already seated with his 'cello propped gracefully against his legs, drawing the bow across the strings in a sweep of music, eyes on the music stand in front of him.

It had been Cosmo Gordon then, who had urged Rory McArthur to tune his fiddle: Wee Dod, instead, turned out to be one of the Bogue family servants who was about Walter's age and took up the extra violin place with mannerly care. As guests continued to arrive and be arranged, the four players tuned their instruments, the boy at the piano lifting a viola to his shoulder and giving himself the notes, too. At last, he nodded to his companions, and caught the eye of a middle-aged personage of chiefly conical shape who was standing conversing by the fire. The personage, who expanded from his old-fashioned, high-fringed wig down to his weightily tailored posterior, adjusted his waistcoat and stepped forward, and the audience fell silent, knowing the sign.

'Ladies and gentlemen,' said the personage, apparently Mr. Bogue, 'welcome once more, and thank you for attending our musical evening! You will no doubt have heard this ensemble before: Mr. McArthur and Wee Dod on the violins, Mr. Gordon on the violincello, and my son Sandy on the viola, when he can drag himself away from his beloved pianoforte!'

Waving cheerfully at his father, young Sandy Bogue rose at last from the piano stool with a final trill on the high notes, and took his place with the other three. At the last moment a very pretty young woman, with Sandy Bogue's colouring, stepped amongst the players and stationed herself to turn some of the music: Murray's anticipation of the evening brightened.

'They plan to start this evening with Mr. Mozart's string quartet for Mr. Haydn called 'Spring', in honour of the fine weather. So if you're all quite ready?' He gazed out at the audience, eyebrows raised, then back at the players, waved a hand resignedly, and moved out of the way. Cosmo Gordon lifted his bow and caught the eyes of the other players, and they began.

For an amateur quartet in a small town, Murray was pleasantly surprised – more, he thoroughly enjoyed the music, though each of the players had his own strengths and weaknesses. Cosmo Gordon, for example, shone in the allegro and the minuet, the lively notes dancing from his strings. Rory McArthur and, unexpectedly, Wee Dod the boy servant, were more impressive in the slower movements, Wee Dod because he was careful and gave every note its true value, technically flawless, particularly for a last minute stand-in, but perhaps lacking in maturity. McArthur, on the other hand, played with fractionally less accuracy but with every ounce of his heart and soul, scowling all unawares into some unseen space between him and the audience, knuckles and fingerpads pale as they worked to their utmost. And young Mr. Bogue, the son of their host, was equally skilled throughout, though by contrast to Rory McArthur for him it seemed effortless, a joke, almost, with flourishes and trills simply skipping out of the instrument for the sheer joy of it. They played the Mozart and then, to Murray's delight, a Haydn piece, almost with the same skill, then allowed the audience a pause for refreshment before returning, vigour renewed, to play some Scottish airs that set feet tapping all around the room. The audience seemed most satisfied with their evening's entertainment and the thanks that were expressed to their host and hostess as they queued to leave were to all appearances heartfelt, Murray's among them. But again, just as they reached the door, someone impatiently squeezed past them.

'For pity's sake, Rory, what's the matter with you?' Murray heard young Sandy Bogue demand with a sigh. Rory, again, turned briefly to call back into the drawing room.

'I'm away to look for Jack Swanson the now. He'll have to

answer to me for his absence, unless something's gone badly wrong!' With a glint of light like flame across his red head, Rory slipped past the guests, fiddle case in his hand, and disappeared into the night.

Chapter Three

'So what did you think of our little ensemble?' Mrs. Shaw asked Murray, a trifle warily, as they returned along South Street. The air was brisk, though the evenings were noticeably lighter now, and the audience, once outside, were dispersing quickly. Rory McArthur had vanished completely.

'I thought them prodigiously good,' said Murray quite truthfully. Sometimes it was a bit of a burden to be thought musical. 'I have indeed heard much worse in Edinburgh,' he added, exchanging a grin with Flavia.

'That does not bode well for the delights of our visit there, then,' she said with a moue of mock discontent.

'The young lad, Wee Dod, is very talented for his age,' Murray went on. 'Is the missing player just as good? If so they should try a few quintets.'

'Jack Swanson? He's the son of our neighbour. A fine young man,' Mrs. Shaw added innocently. Murray caught Flavia rolling her eyes, but she made no comment.

'He's a good fiddle player, though nothing brilliant,' said Professor Shaw kindly. 'An able enough scholar and a good clerk, I believe.'

'He's at the college?'

'No, no, not any more. He did his bejant year, oh … he would have left in the year '14? He and Rory McArthur and Sandy Bogue were all in the same year, but Jack and Rory just did the one year. Sandy graduated A.M. last summer. So yes, '14 it would have been. How time flies!'

'That was Sandy at the pianoforte? The viola player?'

'The same.'

Murray smiled.

'He seemed too relaxed to have committed himself to any depth of study,' he admitted. 'What are his prospects? Mr. Bogue is a cloth merchant, I think you said?'

'Yes, and as you might guess, a wealthy one these days. Sandy is supposed to be looking for a schoolmaster's post, or a place as assistant to a minister, but, well …'

'Sandy's in no great hurry,' Flavia finished, cynically.

'That's certainly the impression he gives. But there, if his father is wealthy – poverty, or the threat of it, is a great instiller of energy in new graduates, I seem to remember,' said Murray, smiling again. He himself had done his time as secretary to a peer, when he was newly graduated, and was not unfamiliar with the threat of poverty. 'But Jack and Rory have to work for a living?'

'They are clerks – good ones, but journeymen as you might say just now, both of them,' explained Professor Shaw.

'But a post has come up with the burgesses,' Flavia added, 'and both of them want it!'

'Flavia, don't gossip so!' admonished her mother. Flavia scrunched up her button nose in protest and batted her hair with the back of her hand.

'It's not gossip, it's true,' she said.

'But –' began her mother.

'It can be both,' said her father gently. He turned back to Murray with a shrug of his little shoulders. 'The two friends are competing, yes. I wondered, in fact, if Jack was off trying to take some advantage in the competition this evening, for it is the kind of thing he might do, and it is not like him to miss an ensemble.'

'Is that why Rory was so cross?'

'That's what made me wonder.' Professor Shaw nodded. 'Though I cannot think what it could have been: most of the high heidyins that might have influence were at the recital, anyway.'

'We rise quite early, Charles, as you'll remember,' had been Professor Shaw's last words to Murray the previous night. They had taken a small glass of punch together in the professor's study as the others retired for the night, talking gently over Walter's satisfactory progress and the evening's music. Murray had climbed content up a narrow stairway to a guest room which he knew from earlier overlooked the garden. The shutters were now firmly closed against the cold, a hot brick had been tucked under the bedclothes and his nightshirt had been wrapped around it, no doubt by Mrs. Shaw's own kindly hands. The fireplace in the room was so tiny that to light anything larger than an egg cupful of fuel would have caused a conflagration amongst the bed-hangings, so it had been left bare: the hot brick was most welcome, as was the cup of hot spiced milk which the cook had pressed into his hands as he left the hallway.

He slept well, with Mozart's rondo spinning delightfully in his head, and woke refreshed in the morning to see chinks of light already slipping around the shutters' ancient woodwork. He slid quickly out of bed, gasped briefly at the cold floor and creaked the shutters open. It was still early, but you could see it was promising faithfully to be a beautiful day, the long sunlight sliding sideways across Professor Shaw's neat garden as if testing the faint folds of the haar that still lingered there. Murray managed to persuade the old casement window to open, and the breeze bounded up like an eager puppy, bringing the gift of spring in its jaws to play with and carelessly dropping it at his feet. He grinned and inhaled. Resistance was useless, and in a few minutes he was washed in cold water and dressed and tiptoeing down the crooked stairs, boots in his hand, towards the back door.

On the first landing he met Walter, who gazed at the boots as though trying to calculate what his old master might possibly be up to now. He himself had his boots firmly on, a muffler around his neck and a slate in his hand.

'Good morning, sir,' he said without emphasis.

'Good morning, Walter.' Murray found himself whispering, but Walter was talking in normal tones so he spoke up. 'Off to carry out your early morning observations?'

'Aye, sir. At first light, every morning.' He tilted his chestnut head with some pride.

'May I accompany you?'

'Aye, sir, that'd be grand.'

Walter led the way through the passages they had followed yesterday, past the kitchen where a scent of firewood and cooking was starting to issue forth, and out into the fresh, biting air. Murray took another deep delicious breath, but Walter was already off, inspecting thermometers and wind and water gauges where the sunlight had only just reached them, and studying the cloud formations in eight precise directions. Murray grinned at the sight with deep satisfaction: Walter was a terrible servant, but he had the makings of a scientist as long as he didn't lose his way between here and the college too often.

He left Walter to his scribbling and stretched, rubbing his long fingers vigorously through his hair and allowing the birdsong to fill his ears. A blackbird, thrushes, tits and woodpigeons all joined the chorus, wrens sounding out from the low bushes, crows and gulls adding percussion high in the blue sky. Mrs. Shaw's hens murmured an accompaniment, and even the bee skeps, when Murray put an ear to them, were humming along. The whole garden was alive with sound: it seemed almost rude to interrupt.

'Do you want to come and see the ponds, Mr. Murray?' Walter asked, suddenly reappearing beside him. 'We have a wee thing you can use to see the fishes better: it's gey clever.'

'I'd love to, Walter,' said Murray with just a degree of resignation.

It passed quickly: the lower half of the garden, the water garden, as Murray thought of it, was even more charming in the morning light than it had been yesterday afternoon. The sun glinted on water moving and still, and made the shades of green in the foliage draped into the ponds more vibrant than ever. Murray noticed that the runnels had been arranged more cleverly than he had first thought, with one rill taken off the main stream at a height of three feet or so, and run in a wooden trough over and around the other pools.

'Different kinds of fishes in that one,' Walter explained, 'with the shallow stream and the faster flow, and the Professor doesna have to get down on his hands and knees to keek at them. I love this place,' he added unexpectedly, with a sigh. 'Now, I'll show you this wee thing for looking at them. You can get down on your hands and knees fine, can you no, sir?' He seemed a little dubious, so Murray quickly knelt and Walter handed him a wooden bucket. When Murray looked inside, he found that the base of the bucket had been replaced with glass. 'Set it intill the water, sir, and sink it a wee bit, and then keek in: you can see under the surface as if it was magic!'

Murray did as he was bid, and at once a shoal of rudd slipped by at the bottom of the bucket, clear as day, his view unimpeded by any reflection across the water's surface. He pushed the bucket a little lower, and saw sticklebacks and minnows, water snails and a great black toad in the midst of bright green strap-like leaves. As he watched, the toad gave a great shudder, and was surrounded by a swirl of toadspawn in ribbons of gauze. The toad, relieved, rearranged herself. Newts rose and fell through the water, unconcerned.

'Aye, well, sir, I'll need it back some time the day,' said Walter, and Murray jumped. How long had he been staring into this underwater world? It had been a while since he had had the time just to sit and stare. He pulled the bucket back out of the water and handed it to Walter with an apology.

'Now the next pond,' said Walter, leading the way to a larger pool further downstream. He lay expertly on the bank and pushed the bucket in, then blinked. He sat up, took a long stick from nearby, and poked it into the pond, apparently at random, then tried the bucket again. 'That's no very good,' he remarked.

'What's wrong?'

'Well, take a look yourself, sir,' said Walter generously. 'Can you see a'thing moving on the bottom?'

Murray lay down and did as he had done before, waiting for a moment for his eyes to adjust to the changed perspective. There were fish here, down at the bottom of the pool which was mixed pebbles, grit and mud, but Walter was right: none of them was moving any more than with the water's gentle flow. They lay on their sides, a shoal as dead as in any fishmarket.

He moved the bucket slightly to see if he could find anything living, and pale weed brushed against the glass base. Then he stared, blinked, and stared again.

The pale weed had fingernails.

He sat up abruptly, pulling the bucket back on to the bank.

'How do we get round to the other side of this pond, Walter?' he demanded. The opposite bank was one of the leafiest parts of the whole system, bright with fresh ground elder, tangled with last year's brambles and uncut grasses under a hawthorn bush or two. Walter, blinking, led him around the pond to where one of the long stone flags formed a bridge across the main stream, and once across Murray strode ahead, then paused abruptly, wary of disturbing anything he should not.

'That stick, Walter, please,' he murmured. Walter skipped back and fetched the stick, his face wound into a frown. Murray took the stick and poked into the undergrowth in front of them, the pond to their right. In a moment he felt just the wrong kind of resistance, and stepping forward carefully, he pulled back the old brambles, trying not to snag his bare hands or his sleeves. Gradually they were able to see what lay there amongst them: a man's body, face down – face, in fact, in the pond, dark hair shifting just a little in the current – one arm trailed at his side and one in the pond, too, as if he had flung it forward to save himself in his fall.

'He'll be dead, then?' said Walter, flatly.

'I don't think he could be otherwise, Walter.'

'Och, for goodness' sake, sir, not again!'

Before Walter ran to fetch Professor Shaw, Murray tried to impress upon him the necessity to break the news gently, or not to break it at all and let Murray do it: he knew from past experience that the little academic was easily upset and he had no wish to do him any injury. It did not even fleetingly cross Murray's mind that his host might already have some knowledge of this man's death: it simply was not in Davie Shaw's gentle nature.

When Walter had gone, at a pace more stoical than urgent, up the garden to the house, Murray allowed himself the opportunity to study the corpse properly, before any local constable or sightseer or even grieving family came trampling in to destroy any possible marks that might solve any mystery here. The corpse was that, apparently, of a young man, by the build: the face, of course, was not at present visible. He wore brown breeches and a green coat, of a style consistent with respectable tradesmen, decent farmers at market time, or even, Murray reflected with a memory of his own wardrobe, minor gentry expecting a rough day. The hair was neatly cut short, the back of the neck pale, though even an outdoor worker would be peely wally enough after a hard winter. The arm that lay at his side was the one nearer Murray, the corpse's right arm. The hand still clutched at brambles, broken ground elder leaves crushed juicily amongst them, the skin torn and green from the brambles but also broken and bloody, he thought, across the knuckles – and beneath these recent marks Murray thought he could also see ink, black and layered, on the first and second fingers just as they bent towards him. A student, perhaps? Murray fleetingly hoped that if it was a student, it would not put Walter off his studies.

Could the death have been an accident? He sat back a little, trying to picture it. The body's odd posture, one arm forwards and one back, certainly did not suggest a planned self-killing: there seemed to have been some element of surprise. He could have tripped over the brambles, fallen head first, perhaps knocked himself out on something Murray could not yet see in the water. But then would he have clutched the brambles so tightly, if he had been unconscious? And all that left to one side the question of what the man was doing in Professor Shaw's garden in the first place – unless …? A shudder of pure dread passed over Murray for a moment, but in the end he was sure that it was not young James Shaw: this man was taller, more muscular, darker haired, though the hair was wet and it was hard to tell. It was not likely to be the Shaws' manservant Pennie, either, for he was thin and there was little chance he would have habitually ink-stained fingers, even in this household. There was no hat, but it could easily have been lost in the brambles, or removed by an assailant, or sunk in a pond – or left behind somewhere entirely different.

Murray's hands were still ungloved: he touched the body gently, at the wrist and at the back of the bare neck. It was quite cold. Had it lain there last night as they all went off comfortably to bed, dying or dead? That was not a happy thought. Had it even, he wondered, been someone who had enjoyed the recital with them, and been on their innocent path home when someone had attacked? Had he been taking a short cut through the garden – Murray made a mental note to ask Professor Shaw if people often did, or for whom it might be a short cut – or had someone for some reason brought him in here to be killed? Had he been killed elsewhere and brought here, or died here? So many questions: he knew that any medical examiner would be able to tell at least if the man had still been alive when his head had entered the water, for the poor fellow would have inhaled water and it would be lying in his lungs, easily found. There was no blood that Murray could see, no sign of external injury.

Someone at the recital … or someone who had been expected

at the recital, but had not appeared? Murray had no idea what Jack Swanson looked like, but if he were missing – and had Professor Shaw not said that the Swansons lived next door? That was someone who might well have used the elaborate garden as a short cut, and it would be easy to trip and fall in this network of waterways. Murder or accident? Murder or accident? Murray could not yet tell, but he was already determined to find out, to do his best for the young man lying there so cold.

He heard voices and heavy breathing before he saw Professor Shaw and Walter returning, with the manservant – so it was definitely not him – hurrying back down the garden. Professor Shaw had evidently dressed in haste: his neckcloth was untied and his waistcoat buttons askew, and his hair stood up like the spikes on a timid hedgehog. His eyes were wide.

'My dear Charles, surely Walter is mistaken? Begging your pardon, Walter, but you know –'

'I've seen plenty corpusses afore,' said Walter sourly. Murray had the distinct impression that Walter held him responsible for that. 'Yon one's as dead as the rest.'

'I'm afraid he's right, sir,' Murray confirmed, as gently as he could. 'The man is quite cold and dead. I have not wanted to move him until you were here, but we should lift him out of the pond and see if you know who he is – unless you would rather someone else was fetched for that purpose?'

Professor Shaw swallowed visibly, closing his eyes tight.

'No, no,' he said after a moment, 'I must do my duty to him. After all, he is dead in my garden, whoever he may be.'

'I wondered if it might be Jack Swanson.' Murray knew he was putting off the moment when they would have to look at the dead man's face. 'You know, because he did not turn up last night when he was expected, and as he lives next door he could perhaps have been using your garden as a short cut and tripped and fallen.'

'Then it would be my fault!' cried Professor Shaw.

'Hardly,' said Murray. 'You would not have invited him, I imagine, to walk through your garden, and he must have known that it was not a straightforward walk. But I suggest that because the alternative is worse, don't you see?'

'The alternative?' Professor Shaw's mind, usually quick, refused to recognise anything worse than a tragic accident. Murray sighed, and took firm hold of the dead man's collar.

'Are you ready?'

He heard more footsteps on the path behind Professor Shaw and Walter.

'Father? Mother says something terrible has happened – oh!'

Flavia stopped short, and so did Murray, letting go of the collar again.

'Is he dead? Who is it?' asked her brother James, who grabbed the arms of both Walter and Flavia in his excitement.

'We don't know yet, James. Take your sister indoors, will you?' murmured the Professor.

'I'd like to see who it is,' Flavia stated firmly. 'Otherwise I'll just wonder, and that would be much worse. Is it Jack Swanson, do you think? He has a green coat like that.'

'Lots of people do,' argued her brother. The boy was pale, paler than Walter, but interested. Flavia shoved him as only an older sister can do, and James shoved back, a little half-heartedly. The manservant, perhaps feeling the bank a bit crowded, came round over the slab bridge to lend Murray a hand. Murray waited to see if Flavia and James would go, but they seemed set to see the thing out. He grabbed the collar again, and the manservant seized him around the waist, and they pulled back, levering the dead man awkwardly up and out of the water and on to the bank.

'That's not Jack Swanson,' said Walter judiciously as soon as the face could be seen. 'That's Rory McArthur.'

Flavia let out a scream that raised the birds from the trees, and fled up the garden.

'Oh, no. Oh, no,' muttered Professor Shaw, watching her go but unable in all conscience to tear himself away from the soaking corpse of the young man he had known. He was shivering. 'Oh, that's terrible. But what on earth would Rory McArthur be doing in my garden, dead or alive? Jack Swanson one could nearly understand, but why Rory?'

By the time the town constable had arrived, the corpse's dark, wet hair had dried to its natural red and he was more clearly Rory McArthur. Murray had closed his eyes and draped a clean handkerchief over his greenish-white face, hiding his gaping mouth that would not be closed. Murray spent part of the intervening time poking around in the water where Rory had lain, but he found nothing but dead fish, and definitely no missing hat. While Professor Shaw and Walter sat grimly by the body, Murray paced around the garden, paying particular attention to the edges, where high brick and stone walls cradled the morning sunshine around the trees and plants within. Near the lowest part of the wall, not quite as far from the house as the curls of the stream complex, but close, he found a broken bush with a few ravellings of green woollen thread on it: he pocketed them carefully, intending to see if they matched McArthur's green coat. Around the base of the bush were part footmarks, as if someone had fallen into the bush and struggled to scramble out again – perhaps in a hurry. Again, he thought he might be able to match even the edges of the broken footprints to McArthur's boots. If so, it certainly seemed that he had entered the garden of – if not quite of his own volition, then at least on his own two feet. Was he being pursued by his murderer? Or was he running from who knew what, and tripped and fell, as Murray had suggested before that Jack might have done? The interesting thing here, though, was that however the death might have occurred, McArthur seemed to have been running from the house next door – the one that belonged to Jack Swanson's father. And McArthur had left the recital in a mood that was far from good, looking for Jack Swanson.

The arrival of the constable interrupted Murray's investigations, and he hurried back to where the men were gathered around the corpse, lest it should be removed before he had had the chance to compare coat wool and boot soles. Either Murray's reputation for discovering murders – and murderers – had preceded him, or the constable reckoned that gentlemen required humouring, for the man listened patiently to all Murray had to say and even padded over to the wall to inspect the bush and the partial footprints. The constable was an army pensioner, with the scar of an old burn covering one side of his face and a missing eye. His nose had apparently come into violent disagreement with more than one musket butt, and his upper teeth were wooden, but there seemed little wrong with his mind. He calmly fetched one of McArthur's boots, and matched it precisely into the sharp lines of the half print nearest him. Murray showed him the threads and where they had been found, and again the constable returned to the corpse and poked around, ignoring Professor Shaw's sympathetic winces, until he found a longish, jagged rip on one side, near the hem, just, indeed, where a man of middling height would have caught it on a bush of that size. He nodded at Murray, both satisfied. McArthur, for whatever reason, had come down off the garden wall at this point and blundered through the bush. More than that they could not immediately say. Instead, the constable commandeered the Shaws' manservant, and between them, with the use of some sticks and a blanket, they removed McArthur to the police room for one of the local doctors to examine. The sun blinked overhead as they went, a cloud darting across it like the back of a hand dashing away a tear. It was altogether a strange and unsettling start to the day.

It was not altogether helped when Murray turned round at the Shaws' front door to find Carlisle, his gardener, standing on the front path in a state of mild bewilderment.

Lexie Conyngham

Chapter Four

Carlisle removed his woollen cap and stood there, as awkward as Murray had ever seen him.

'What's the matter, Carlisle? Is something wrong at Letho?' It could not be a good sign if the easiest servant to send with bad news was the head gardener. Murray's heart twitched. 'There's nothing wrong with Miss Murray, is there?'

His daughter Augusta, eighteen months old and precious to him beyond all sense, was staying in Edinburgh with his old friends the Blairs.

'No, sir, not that anyone has tellt me,' said Carlisle, precise if not entirely reassuring. 'To tell the truth, sir, I wasna looking for you nor expecting to see you. I was looking for a Davie Shaw, as I understood it.'

'Davie Shaw?' The little professor heard his name, and turned at the doorway, frowning anxiously at the stranger. 'You're looking for Davie Shaw? I'm Davie Shaw.'

'Professor David Shaw,' Murray put in quickly, knowing that Professor Shaw would not until all kinds of social tangles had been created. The gardener raised his well-furnished eyebrows.

'I beg your pardon, sir, but I was tellt Davie Shaw. It was in connexion with some purple peas for planting.'

Professor Shaw frowned for another instant, then his face cleared into the smile of a happy brownie.

'Oh! Mr. Carlisle? I was expecting you yesterday, was I not?'

'You were, sir, and I'm that sorry. I was – ' he glanced at Murray, 'held back at the house.'

'Never mind, never mind,' said Professor Shaw cheerfully. 'It makes not the remotest difficulty. Come in!'

'Oh,' said Carlisle, with another glance at Murray, 'I'll just gang round the back, if it's all the same to you, sir.'

'Of course, if you prefer it,' said Professor Shaw, and to Carlisle's evident surprise, led him around the house. Murray felt he ought to follow.

'I can't remember where you said you were travelling from, Mr. Carlisle,' Shaw called over his shoulder.

'From the village of Letho, sir,' said Carlisle drily.

'From Letho! Oh, but – you'll know Mr. Murray here, then.'

'Carlisle is my gardener,' Murray confirmed.

'Oh, goodness! I am very slow, I'm afraid, Mr. Carlisle: you must excuse me. Now, this is the garden,' he began, with an anxious glance about it as if he feared there might be other dead bodies lurking in the bushes. 'Did you say peas?'

'That's right, sir. A friend of a friend said there were some for trying out, like.'

'That's right! That's right, there are. For the kitchen garden at Letho?'

'Aye, sir. I like to try new things, and Mr. Murray is kind enough to let me.'

As if I had much say in the matter, thought Murray, with a smile.

'I'll leave you to it,' he said aloud, then stopped. 'By the way, Carlisle, weren't you to travel here with Cosmo Gordon last night?'

'Aye, that's a fact, sir,' agreed Carlisle. 'But we didna arrive till gone seven, and though I came round to make my apologies for my lateness, I was tellt the family were not at home. I came back later but I timed it badly, for I think you were all asleep.'

'Oh, yes, of course, we were out yesterday evening,' said Shaw. 'I'm so sorry. I hope you had somewhere comfortable to spend the night?'

'Aye, aye, I have a friend is a nurseryman here in the town. He was the one tellt me about the peas, see.'

'Oh! the peas!' Professor Shaw had forgotten again.

'I'll definitely leave you to it!' said Murray, and went indoors to see if any breakfast had been thought of, in the midst of everything else.

There was indeed breakfast, with fresh rolls of sweet bread, and good coffee, and there were Walter and James, each with a book propped in front of them against solid old candlesticks, reading out odd bits to each other. Murray's arrival did not deter them in the least.

'I hope Miss Shaw is recovered from her shock?' he said as he spread a little of the end-of-year butter on his roll.

James peered at him in surprise.

'Oh, aye. I think so, anyway. Dinna ken what was wrong with her. Girls, eh? Oh, here, Walter – "*fideliter*".'

'Like fiddle-playing,' said Walter.

'Na. "Faithfully", said James, and they both laughed. 'Was Rory a faithful fiddler?'

'Or is Jack Swanson?' asked Walter.

'Aye, a good question,' agreed James, and returned without explanation to his book.

'"*Suaviter*",' said Walter after a moment.

'Something to do with pigs? Swine?' asked James, taking a bite from his bread roll without bothering to pause in his speech for the occasion. Walter gave a snort.

'It's "smoothly". Smooth pigs, though, eh? No hairy.' They sniggered again. Murray was a little disconcerted: Walter had not often been seen to laugh back at Letho, but now he seemed to have fallen very naturally into the character of a schoolboy learning his adverbs, as if he had done nothing else with his time for the last eight years.

The parlour door opened, and the Shaws' manservant Pennie appeared.

'The Professor, sir?' he said, looking about. He had a pared-down gentility about him that did not quite match the rest of the household.

'In the garden, with a visitor,' said Murray.

'Oh. May I ask you, sir, to let him know, as I was told to tell you, too: I'm just back from the police room, and the constable says to say that the doctor will not be available to look at the poor lad till midday at the earliest.'

'I see: thank you. I'll let the Professor know, when he's free.' The man bowed and left. Murray buttered another roll thoughtfully. He was not expecting anything strange or startling from the doctor. In his search in the pond for the hat, he had realised that there was no sharp stone or hard surface on which a man might accidentally have cracked his head before drowning, and indeed he could see no injury, broken or otherwise, on Rory McArthur's skull. There was no smell of alcohol about him, either, and he had leaned far too close to sniff around lips and nose to make sure. The front of his shirt and waistcoat, both correctly fastened, were whole and without tear, and though Murray had not gone so far as to pull them up to examine the dead man's chest and stomach, he was sure no fresh wound would be found. In short, he was convinced that Rory McArthur had drowned, and he was already fairly sure that someone else had had a part in that drowning.

James and Walter were both still playing with their adverbs.

'Walter,' Murray interrupted, 'do you know where Rory Mc Arthur lived?'

Walter's eyes widened in panic. Directions were not his best subject.

'James?'

'Aye, sir. He's in one of the closes atween South Street and Market Street. I think it's the one by the kirk. Aye, but anybody would ken, that you asked around there.'

'No doubt. Thank you.' Murray finished his coffee, and rose from the table without reluctance. 'Did he have any family here?'

'"*Fortiter*". Family? Well, he has a wifie there, and a bairn. Is that what you mean?'

'That would generally fall within the definition, yes. Thank you, James,' he said, and left the room for the most part unnoticed by either of the boys.

It was not the close by the kirk, the great mediaeval bulk of the town's church that sat between South Street and Market Street. It was, however, the next one along, and a couple of helpful neighbours were happy to direct him, suggesting to him that he was looking for Roderick McArthur for a clerking job he needed done. Murray did not argue, though the news would be flying sooner or later. In the next close, which was broadish at its south end but narrowed almost to extinction at the north end, he recognised the tiny building from the neighbours' description, tucked into a corner like a country girl embarrassed at the New

Town Assembly Rooms. He had almost to bend to knock on the door, and did so gently thinking he might, if he were not careful, simply break it.

There was a narrow window beside the door. When his first knock went unanswered, and his second, less tentative knock was also ignored, he risked a swift look and was at once quite sure that at that very moment someone had shifted quickly away from the inside of the window. Perhaps it had been a reflection of something elsewhere in the street? A gull flitting past overhead, perhaps? Then he heard a child crying, and was sure it came from inside the tiny house – though certainly the buildings were so closely stacked together here he might have been mistaken. He paused on the doorstep, not sure what to do.

'She's there, aye, aye,' came a voice. Murray looked round. On a doorstep opposite sat a woman of indeterminate age, spinning with a hand-spindle and rocking a small basket with her foot. From the basket came contented gurgles. The woman seemed equally settled.

'It's Roderick McArthur's house I'm seeking,' he explained. 'Am I at the right place?'

'Y'are,' admitted the woman. 'You'll be seeking him for a clerking job, nae doubt.'

'And I'd like a word with his wife, too, if I can find her.'

'Oh, aye?' The woman cast him a less friendly look, and Murray hurriedly shook his head, in denial of any harm to Mrs. McArthur's reputation.

'I have some news for her, that's all. You think she's within?'

'Aye, she is. I seen her half an hour since, and I've been here ever since. Forbye, she never goes out hardly at all.'

'But she came out half an hour ago?'

'She didna come out, no. I seen her at the windae, keeking down the close. I dinna think she's been out at all the day: sometimes she'll be out with the bairn's cloths, to put them over the line here,' she waved up at the communal lines that ran between the houses, 'but I've no seen her do that the day, and none of that lot's hers.'

There was a movement behind her in the shadowy doorway, and a man squeezed out past her. The atmosphere chilled immediately. He was a man who would have passed for something carved from stone, if stone could have that wedge of yellow hair perched on the back of its head, and those glassy blue eyes, one blackened by a recent bruise, and those steady, confident movements. He propped himself against the wall of their house, drew out a short clay pipe, and regarded Murray in a manner that clearly stated that yes, he could beat the dust out of Murray in a fair fight; no, it would not be a fair fight; and yes, it would not take much to start it. Murray bowed as a pre-emptive measure.

'A delightful baby,' he remarked, fortunately honestly. The infant gazed up at him in wonder. 'Yours, sir?'

'Naw,' said the man concisely.

'My grand-daughter,' said the woman hurriedly, with a glance at both of them, 'and this here's my brother, Mr. ...?'

'Murray,' said Murray, bowing again. The man nodded.

'Mr. Murray. My brother, Nathan Houston.'

'Are you come frae far, Mr. Murray?' asked Nathan Houston, with a little more than just polite interest.

'Not at all: I live at Letho, off the Cupar road.'

'Here in Fife?'

'That's right.'

Nathan Houston toed the ground in front of him thoughtfully.

'Did ye no bide some time in Perthshire, then?'

'In Perthshire? No, never. I've lived in Edinburgh, and down the coast here a bit for a while, and at Letho, and here in St. Andrews, but I've never stayed more than a few weeks in Perthshire in my life, I believe.'

'A few weeks?'

'Not more than that,' Murray assured him.

'And when would that have been?'

Murray stared at him, trying at the same time to remember when he had stayed in Perthshire, and to work out why on earth it should be of such interest to this individual.

'Come on, now, Nathan, leave the gentleman alone. He only wanted to get Rory McArthur for a clerking job. You dinna want poor Rory to lose a customer, do you?'

The look on Nathan's face in response to that was an interesting one to anyone who suspected that poor Rory might have been murdered last night: Rory's best interests, at least in job terms, did not seem to be close to Nathan Houston's heart, supposing he had one.

'I heard him say he had news for Mrs. McArthur, and all,' said Nathan.

'I do.'

'And what might that be, then?'

'It's news for Mrs. McArthur. If she wishes to share it with you afterwards, that is her business, but it is not mine to share it first.'

'Aye, that's only fair, Nathan,' said his sister. 'You wouldna like it if a'body kenned your business.'

Nathan, for a wonder, nodded slightly, just about conceding this point.

'But you're still no getting to see her,' he added suddenly, in case he should be thought to be weakening. 'There's a pair of pistols on the shelf by the door here, should you want to make a quarrel of it.'

'You're remarkably protective of your neighbour,' said Murray. 'Strangely so, if you ask me. Is there something – the matter with her?' He hesitated, trying not to allow any escape route for Nathan's denials. Was she ill? Dead? Peculiar? Dangerous, even? A simpleton, who might be more upset than the average woman, in particular by anyone who hailed from Perthshire? Or had she perhaps already heard the dreadful news of her husband's death?

'There's nothing the matter with her,' said Nathan at last. 'She's just a friend of ours, and we all look out for our friends around here.'

'So I see,' said Murray, and adjusted his hat. 'Well, you have protected her from receiving her news, but she will receive it, no doubt, sooner or later, from someone else if not from me. Good day to you.'

He had to walk very near to Nathan's protruding foot to leave the close: he concentrated on looking unconcerned, while at the same time tense in case of a last-minute attack, even of the foot-accidentally-in-your-way-I'm-very-sorry-sir type, but Nathan seemed satisfied enough at his retreat. Murray wondered if the constable would allow him to come back later with him, and whether or not they would reach the hermit-like widow before rumour did. A shame if the gossips got there first: he liked to see the news being broken, to judge the reaction for himself, if he could.

But there was another house he could try, and other information he could seek, before the town's doctor would proclaim on Rory McArthur's body at noon. He returned to South Street and crossed it back in the direction of Professor Shaw's house, but instead of walking as far as the Shaws' front gate, he stopped at the house before it. As far as he knew, no one had yet accounted for Jack Swanson's failure to play with the ensemble last night, and he might not even have been seen since: if nothing else, it should be ascertained whether or not he had been attacked last night, too, perhaps before even his friends had missed him.

The house, to judge from the outside, was of an age with the Shaws', but much plainer and more practical in construction, neat and symmetrical, with a black, shiny door with bright, shiny door furniture in the centre. Murray studied it for a moment: the shutters were open, on ground and upper floors, and there was no outward and visible sign of an inward and invisible grief. He approached therefore and was about to rattle the risp beside the shiny door when it opened, and a maid emerged. She jumped when she saw him, poised with one hand in the air, and almost dropped the cloth and brass ball she was carrying.

'Good morning!' Murray was equally taken aback. 'I see now how the metalwork is so well kept. Is Mr. Swanson within? Mr. Jack Swanson, I should say.'

'Aye, sir, he is. May I ask who is to be announced, sir?'

'Charles Murray of Letho is my name.' He handed her a card, and smiled encouragingly. 'I gather Jack was in late last night, was he?' He stopped short of winking, but he hoped he did not look too old to be a drinking partner for young Mr. Swanson. The maid, however, was not in a position to help.

'I dinna live in, sir. I was away to my ain place by seven when all was cleared after dinner. I only came back this morning.'

'Oh, of course.'

'Please step into the hall, sir: the parlour is just here.'

Murray expected to be shown into the parlour to wait for Jack to appear from some recess of the house, possibly hurriedly dressed, but to his surprise a young man was seated in the window, catching the good north light for what was evidently his habitual working table. He rose in surprise when Murray was announced, though he may very well have seen him approach the house.

'My father is in his workshop, sir: I am Jack Swanson, his son. Will you please be seated while I have him fetched?'

'That would be very kind, but it is partly you that I wanted to see.'

'Me?' Jack waited until Murray had taken a seat. The sopha was well upholstered, but harder than it looked and distinctly chilly. 'I beg your pardon, sir: what was your name again?'

'Charles Murray of Letho. Please forgive my arrival like this, but there was some concern over your safety.'

'My safety?' Jack was finding the whole encounter a puzzle. He sat down on the edge of his stool, and automatically picked up a steel pen without looking at it. He was not unlike the sopha, Murray though absently: well upholstered but hard, not flabby. His dark hair was receding prematurely, for he could not be more than about twenty, with a face that spoke of more time spent indoors than out, though otherwise healthy. His fingers were blotted with ink stains.

'You were not at the recital last night at Mr. Bogue's,' Murray began.

'Oh, that!' Jack relaxed a little. 'A muddle over the date, that was all. I realised too late. Did Wee Dod play in my place?'

'He did, and acquitted himself well.'

'Aye, it'll have done him good. He's nervous playing before an audience.'

'So presumably, then, you were here all evening?' Murray asked lightly, trying to give the impression that he, too, was now more at ease.

'That's right! I stayed here. Oddly, I was practising the Haydn – I thought the recital was tonight, you see. Foolish of me! I simply had the wrong date in my head.'

Murray had been inclined to believe him the first time he had said it, but somehow the repetition made it less convincing – that, and they way he had begun to fidget with the steel pen he was holding.

'Then presumably Rory McArthur found you here?'

'Rory?' Jack blinked.

'Yes, he went looking for you.'

'Did he?' Jack sounded uncertain. 'He never came here.'

'Yet surely this would be the obvious place to look for you, when you didn't turn up?'

'Well, yes ...' The steel pen was subject to some complex manipulation, as Jack stared past Murray. Murray let him be for a moment, and was about to start on a new tack when the parlour door opened with a bang.

'Ah, Mr. Murray! No, no, pray do not trouble to rise, sir! I am sorry to have detained you, but the maid has only just told me of your arrival.'

Mr. Swanson elder was clearly the pattern and design of his son's appearance: Murray wondered if Mrs. Swanson had had any input in her son at all. Thomas Swanson was perhaps a little less solid, a little more of a challenge to the security of his waistcoat buttons, and the receding hairline had been overcome altogether by a snug brown wig in whose manufacture Murray thought he could see the hand of one of the better Edinburgh wigmakers, Urquhart in George Street, perhaps. The skin of his face and hands was paler and less healthy than his son's, and missing the ink stains. He was accompanied by a bulldog, white with a brown head, an argument for the theory that people and their pets grow together in appearance. The dog sniffed Murray's knees proprietorially, then sat back to scrutinise the newcomer.

'Mr. Swanson.' Murray rose and bowed nevertheless, since he was in the man's parlour.

'What can we do for you, Mr. Murray?' Mr. Swanson beamed. 'May I say at once that I once had the privilege to be of service in a small way – a matter of replacing the top to a decanter – to Mr. Murray your late father.'

'Indeed? How very good of you.' It must have been an urgent repair, Murray thought: his father would have taken the decanter to Edinburgh if there had been time, not used a local silversmith. Yet it said something of Swanson's capabilities that Murray's father had risked him at all. 'But I'm afraid it is not as a customer that I am here. There has been – an unexpected incident at your neighbour's house -'

'Professor Shaw's? That's not that surprising,' put in Jack suddenly. His father gave him a warning smile that away from Murray's presence would undoubtedly have taken on a much more ferocious appearance.

'And I have come to ask you if you perhaps heard or saw anything out of the ordinary last night? You were in, were you?'

'Yes, yes, I was in.' Swanson was assured, but Murray glimpsed, out of the corner of his eye, a surprised twitch of the steel pen. As if he was aware that it was doing him no favours, Jack set the pen down exactly by his papers, and squeezed his hands tight between his thighs.

'And did you hear or see anything unusual?'

Swanson considered, and looked again at his son.

'No, no, I don't think so. Did you, Jack?'

'Nothing at all.'

'Were you generally at the front of the house, or at the back?' Murray asked.

'At the front,' said Jack at once. 'I was in here all evening after dinner. And playing the violin, as I told you – practising the Haydn.'

'I was in my workshop,' said Swanson smoothly. 'It's at the back of the house – an old-fashioned arrangement, I know, but this house was my father's before me and his before that, and though it might not be how we arrange matters these days, it has, as it were, a sentimental hold on me. Foolish of me!' He echoed his son's words earlier. 'Then I went to bed, which is just above here at the front. You have aroused my curiosity, sir: may we ask what on earth has occurred? I hope Professor Shaw and his family – and his student – are all in good health?' He flushed a little, perhaps aware that this was a rather belated enquiry.

'Yes, they are, though of course somewhat upset. I'm afraid that a dead body was found in the garden this morning.'

Father and son both gasped, in such a similar way that Murray found it hard to distinguish between them. The bulldog glanced from one to the other, concerned.

'What? Whose?' came from them at once like a chorus.

'I'm afraid,' he said, trying to watch both of them at once, 'that it was Rory McArthur.'

'Rory McArthur?' Thomas Swanson was the first to speak, though not to great effect. 'Rory McArthur?'

'The man who went looking for you last night, Mr. Swanson.' Murray turned to Jack. He was seated with his mouth open, staring past them both, his face blank.

'Rory McArthur?' Thomas Swanson repeated again, though the words seemed at last to be making a connexion in his mind. 'Went looking for me last night? Or looking for Jack here?'

'For Jack, Mr. Swanson. Jack forgot to go to the recital last night, and after it Rory set out to find him to see if he was all right.' Or to give him a piece of his mind, Murray added to himself, thinking from Rory's flushed and angry face that that had seemed much more likely at the time. 'Now, perhaps you'd like to consider again, both of you: did you see or hear anything out of the ordinary last night, and did Rory McArthur come here?'

Chapter Five

'I never saw him,' said Jack Swanson at last, though his voice seemed to have been crushed, somehow. He was trembling. 'I never saw him all night.'

'I was in my workshop,' Thomas Swanson repeated, flat, shocked. 'It's at the back, then I went to bed as I said. I didn't hear anything in either place.'

'What time did you go to bed, Mr. Swanson?'

Swanson considered.

'It would have been past ten, but not by much, I doubt.'

'And you, Mr. Swanson?'

Jack's eyes were still not looking at anything in the room.

'Before that, I think,' he croaked, then gave himself a little shake. He rubbed his eyes and focussed on Murray, though there was no colour in his face. 'We rise early, sir: I was in my bed when the bell struck ten at the town kirk.'

'And this workshop,' said Murray. 'You said it's at the back of the house?'

'Oh, aye, sir, aye. Come and see it, and welcome!' Swanson was regaining his composure faster than his son was: some part of him was probably always ready to pander to a potential customer, particularly one with land and money. 'Come just now, if you will!'

Thomas Swanson bustled out of the parlour, the bulldog at his heels, and Murray, pleased with the invitation, rose to follow him. But Jack, suddenly on his feet, laid an urgent hand on Murray's elbow.

'How did he die, sir? Do they know?'

'They don't know yet,' said Murray. 'But it looks as if he drowned.'

'Drowned!' Jack's voice was breathless, and his hand slipped off Murray's arm again, as if all strength had left it. He sagged back on to his stool, arms dangling.

'Mr. Murray?' Thomas Swanson had returned to fetch him, and Murray, with a backward glance at Jack, followed him. They left the house by a back door and crossed a small cobbled yard, neatly kept without a weed in sight.

'Not so convenient in the rain, of course, sir, but our new cobbles keep it dry underfoot, and the main thing is it diminishes the risk of any fire spreading to the house.'

'Of course.'

'I'm not using the furnace today, though. It can be awful cosy in there sometimes, sir! Victor – that's the dog – he's always beside me on winter days, keeping warm. Here, let me lead you in.'

He took a key from his belt and unlocked the door. The workshop was a single storey, thick-walled, spacious room, open to its shallow-pitched rafters. There were four shuttered windows, two to each side, and shelves along one wall containing, it seemed, moulds, half-finished pieces of silverware, and black iron strongboxes in various sizes. There were heavy stone jars, too, with labels painted on them: Murray noticed arsenic amongst them, which he knew was used by silversmiths, but boric and sulphuric acid were there, too, if his Latin was sound. Racks of tools stood on benches and elsewhere, well organised for easy use, their handles polished from years of handling. In a quiet corner was a blanket for Victor the bulldog – he immediately trotted across and made himself a nest of it, well used to keeping his master company as he worked. Swanson flung open the nearest set of shutters to reveal an unglazed space, with strong bars across it. A little fresh air fought its way in, which was a relief: the whole room stank of pitch.

'I'll show you what I'm working on at present, sir,' said Swanson, proud of his premises. The furnace, warm but not glowing, sat in the centre of the far wall, with a fine set of bellows attached to it, and before it, on another solid bench, was a large bag made of sacking apparently filled with sand or something similar. Snuggled into it, in turn, was a cast iron bowl, some eighteen inches across, filled with pitch but with something else glinting under the surface.

'It's cooling at the moment,' Swanson explained, 'and that's best done slowly. It's a big ashet, wanted by the Principal of United College, no less! I've been working on the repousse pattern, so the pitch is there to cushion the hammering and then I fill it again to set it, and when it's cooled I'll be chasing it with these.' He indicated a rank of little punches and chisels, their metal handles shiny and spread from years of being endlessly tapped. 'You have to do all of it a few times to finish the whole design. Then, of course, I have to arrange its transport all the way down to Edinburgh for the assay officer to dunt his wee thistle on the thing, then all the way back up again. That's the worrying bit.' He sighed.

'Complicated work,' Murray agreed. 'Do you make the designs yourself?'

Swanson showed him a sheet of paper, with a pattern on it of a round plate with a design of strange creatures and leaves. Presumably the Principal was not intending to donate it as an alms dish in the college chapel, then.

'There's a local artist was asked to draw this one, and I follow his pattern. I think it's a fine one, do you think, sir? Of course, with the repousse you're doing back to front.'

'That's when you hammer the design up, I suppose, from the back of the plate?'

'That's right, sir! And the chasing is done from the front: that's the detailed bit. We have some very popular designs that many of the local gentry have selected as being appropriate for their domestic use, though as you see, I am always happy to work with a talented artist on a commissioned pattern for something,' he breathed out reverently, 'unique.'

Expecting the man to offer him a price list at any moment, Murray forged on quickly.

'And does your son Jack work with you?'

'Ah, no, sir. Jack went to the College, you see, and so he has found work more suited to his tastes and skills. It's a strange thing when your only son doesn't want to take on your business – when it's been in the family since my grandfather's time – but there you are. He has some of the skills, but none of the interest, sadly.'

'Ah, yes: but I hear he is a very successful clerk, is that right?'

'A father is always delighted to hear praise of his son, sir,' said Swanson, beaming.

'And musical, too. I was sorry to have missed his performance last night.'

The beam turned to a frown, but more of puzzlement than anger. Murray left it: presumably Jack had not had the chance to explain his confusion over dates to his father.

'So last night you were working on the repousse here?'

'Yes, yes, that's right,' said Swanson, though the frown lingered.

'Would you have had the shutters open?'

'Yes, indeed, for it's hot work, and the pitch can give you a headache after a while.'

'So if something had happened in your garden, before you went to bed, you must have heard it?'

'Well … I was hammering, of course.'

'Oh, of course. May I look outside?'

'Aye, aye, by all means.'

Swanson closed and bolted the shutters, and came after Murray through the door. Victor lurched to his feet and hastened to follow. Beyond the workshop the garden extended as far as the Shaws' did next door, though it seemed longer as the house itself had not been allowed to ramble so freely within its grounds. The upper half, or thereabouts, was laid to grass, with a hen run to one side and beyond it a pigsty. The lower half appeared to have been intended as a kailyard, with paths through it that led to a gate in the end wall, but the ground was suffering from the winter's neglect and had not yet been cleared for sowing – Carlisle the gardener would not be impressed. Murray, still riding on the authority he seemed to have over Swanson by being a laird and a potential customer, paced down the gentle grass slope, taking in as much detail as the opportunity afforded. The high brick wall which surrounded the Shaws' garden was just as high on this side, and extended around the whole of this garden, too. Three or four trees stood a little aimlessly along the Shaw side of the garden, as if not quite sure what they had come for. Murray examined them one by one: the first and second were unremarkable, but the third had seen some exciting times recently: some of the bark was scraped off at about Murray's waist level, and several twigs were torn back. The damage was fresh.

'May I?' Murray asked, gesturing to the tree. He set his hat and stick down next to the wall. Victor watched with interest.

'Of course,' said Swanson, though it was clear he had no idea what Murray had in mind. Murray reached up with both arms, set a foot in the crook of the second branch up, and hauled himself with more ease than he had expected into the tree, amused at the little gasp of astonishment behind him. He could clearly see over the wall, and was not surprised to find that he was level with the bush he had found earlier, the one with broken twigs and footprints around it. Another small part of last night's story was told.

He was about to jump back down when he saw Professor Shaw in his own garden, staring sadly down at the fishponds. He looked lonely and despondent, and Walter, kneeling at his feet to poke at something in the water, seemed from this distance equally subdued. Murray sighed. He should go home, but he did not like to leave the Shaws quite like this. As far as he knew, Flavia had not even reappeared since her uncharacteristic outburst. He gathered in his coat tails and jumped back down on Thomas Swanson's side of the wall.

'Thank you so much for your time, Mr. Swanson,' he said. 'I should be going.' He picked up his hat and stick.

'Did I hear you tell my lad that Rory McArthur had drowned?' Swanson sounded at last a little less assured.

'That's what it seems to be, yes.'

Swanson touched his wig delicately.

'He and my lad – well, they had their quarrels, as any young men might. Young Rory, he was gey sensible, serious like, and Jack works hard but he likes a wee bit of fun, too, as any lad of his age might. But what I mean to say is, that they were friends. Always have been, since they met at the College. It was the music, maybe, brought them together, but they stayed friends.'

'I'm very sorry for your son's loss, then,' said Murray, not without sympathy. He tipped his hat back on his head, and bowed. 'No doubt we shall meet again before long, Mr. Swanson. Good day to you.'

He found as he had thought that there was a path back to the street around the Swansons' house so that he did not need to go back through it, and in a moment or two he was on the other side of the wall, in the Shaws' garden. The professor and Walter were pretty much where he had last seen them. He cleared his throat as he approached, hoping not to alarm them. Professor Shaw turned, looking old, but tried to smile when he saw Murray.

'I should not trespass any further on your hospitality,' Murray said, trying not to sound like a rat leaving a sinking ship.

'Oh, no, stay, Charles, please!' said Professor Shaw eagerly. 'If nothing else, I know how much experience you have had in horrid affairs like this one: I warrant you will not like to see a puzzle unsolved, never mind a young man dead before his time without any wrongdoer brought to justice.'

He was absolutely right on both counts, Murray had to concede: and the Professor's own clear distress was another motive. The Professor had cared for him like a son when he was a student, and he felt the same affection for him now as a son might. He would see it through if he could.

'Nevertheless, I should at least go and see that my household are all right before I abandon them. And I shall need clean clothes!'

'That at least is a valid reason. But if you must go, at least stay to dinner.'

'If you don't mind, Professor, I shall go before dinner and return tomorrow. We are still without a housekeeper at Letho and it is a busy time of year: I must at least see that all is in order, to reassure the staff.'

'Of course, dear boy, if you must you must. When one has responsibilities ... Which reminds me, I must see my tertian students in two hours! I had quite forgotten. It is the worry of all this business, I am sure!'

It might be, thought Murray fondly, but it would not be the first time the Professor had forgotten to teach a class, for whatever reason.

'Rory was one of your students, was he not?' he asked. 'You said he left the college in the year '14.'

'Oh, that's right. Poor boy: to think he would come to this!'

'Tell me about him.'

'Professor!' came a voice from further up the garden. They turned to see the town constable wandering amongst the rose bushes hunting for them.

'Down here!' Shaw called back, waving energetically. The constable spun round, squinted with his good eye, and nodded, before picking his way towards them.

'I thought you'd like to hear, sir, that the doctor's just been to look at the lad. He says he drownded, sir.'

'Is that all?' asked Murray. 'I mean, was he able to deduce anything else?'

'There was no wound on him, except for a bruise on his back, just below his neck. Maybe a hand's breadth below the level of the shoulder.' The constable spoke quite freely to Murray still.

'That would scarcely kill him,' said the professor thoughtfully.

'But it might knock him over,' said Murray. 'A hard enough shove, and he would have his head under the water before he knew what was happening. And he tried then to haul himself back with the hand that was on the bank – why not with both hands?'

''Cause,' came Walter's sombre voice from the edge of the pond, 'he couldna get that hand round with the wicked murderer on his hunkers the side of him, holding him down.'

There was a moment's silence, then all three men nodded.

'Aye, he could be right an' all,' allowed the constable. Murray struggled to suppress a completely inappropriate grin.

'Walter has assisted me in other investigations of this kind,' he explained to the constable.

'Aye, I'd heard tell you'd had dealings with a few unlawful killings, sir,' said the constable, eyeing him intelligently. 'The sheriff's man in Cupar's a cousin of my sister's man's stepmother.'

'I see.'

'So dinna think, sir, that I'm going to turn away any help you might like to offer in this matter.'

'That's very good of you, constable. I'm not sure I know your name?'

'Round, sir. Late of the 42nd. Highlanders.'

'Excellent.' Murray grinned, then grew more solemn. 'Did you know Rory McArthur?'

'I knew the young man to see, sir, but he'd never caused any trouble that I kent of, not even as a student.'

'Well, the Professor here taught him as a student, and he was about to say something of him, weren't you, sir?'

'Well, yes,' said Professor Shaw, 'what I can remember.'

'That'll be good enough for a start, sir,' said Round encouragingly.

'Well, then.' Professor Shaw sank on to one of the stone benches. Murray perched on a rock opposite him, and the constable arranged himself against his staff with the ease of a man used to long sentry goes.

'Of course, I have known him a little since he left the college, too,' the Professor began. 'Let me see. He was always a serious boy: clever enough, too, but not brilliant. A hard worker and, as far as one can ever judge, a good boy, I think. He was never any trouble.'

'That's a rare enough thing, sir,' remarked Constable Round with a respectful nod.

'Indeed!' Professor Shaw smiled slightly. 'He did not, I believe, have much of a sense of humour. I remember someone, a few of the other students in his year, trying some kind of trick on him once, and he did not take it well, flew at them in a rage, in fact. Of course that delighted them, and I remember thinking that he had set himself up for all kinds of teasing and fools after that, but it didn't really happen. I think that was mainly because he and Jack Swanson and Sandy Bogue took up together with the music, and Sandy and Jack were always popular lads. That protected Rory, I suppose.'

'Did he come here often?' Murray asked. 'Would he know your garden at all?'

'He stayed here a month or so when he first arrived, but I did not have the fish ponds then. He would have been here a few times, when he was studying natural philosophy,' Professor Shaw remembered. 'He liked to be out of doors. He was brought up in the countryside, up in Perthshire, and the town was not his natural place. I thought he would go home after leaving the college, and set up for a clerk in his local village, but perhaps there was not the work there for him. He and Jack were apprenticed instead as clerks to Sandy Bogue's father, in the clothier business. Mr. Bogue has a succession of apprentice clerks but he rarely keeps them more than a couple of years. He and Jack were no exception, and – oh, nearly two years ago now, it was, first Rory left and then Jack.'

'Was there a quarrel? With Mr. Bogue, I mean?'

'No, I don't believe so. They had just learned what they were there to learn, and Mr. Bogue would never pay them a journeyman's wage if he could pay them as apprentices. So Mr. Bogue no doubt found himself a couple of new apprentices, and Rory left St. Andrews.'

'He left? Where did he go?'

Professor Shaw scratched his nose, and looked at the constable.

'Home, I think. Do you know, Mr. Round?'

'That was the impression I had myself, sir, but I dinna ken that I'm sure.'

'Well, maybe home, then. Wherever it was, it wasn't long till he was back with his new wife and set up as a journeyman clerk, which was just what Jack had done, too, while he was away. So now they are in competition for much the same work.'

'And Rory had a wife to support, while Jack doesn't,' Murray commented. 'That will make a difference, too.'

'And a babbie,' added Constable Round. 'The wee lassie would be coming up for a year, nae doubt.'

Murray briefly remembered his own wee lassie at nine months, and suppressed a fond smile.

'Well, apart from a friendly rivalry – I take it it was still friendly?'

'I believe so,' said Professor Shaw anxiously.

'Apart from that, did he have any enemies? Someone left from those pranks in his student days? Sandy Bogue?'

'He and Sandy are always friendly.'

'Some family connexion? His or his wife's?'

'I dinna think there's a'body related to them in the haill town. Mebbe the haill county,' said the constable, shaking his head at what he clearly thought was a sad state of affairs. Murray tapped his stick on the side of his boot.

'Well, what do we know so far? He left the recital saying that he was going to look for Jack Swanson, to find out why he had not been there. He seemed to me to be quite cross, but perhaps that was just his manner. Then we have nothing, until he appears to have climbed over the wall from the Swansons' garden – there is a handy tree on the other side, Constable, with appropriate scrapes and scratches to it – landed in that bush, and drowned in your fish pond. The Swansons both say they were in, but neither says he heard anything. Is there a Mrs. Swanson, by the way?'

'Oh, she died years ago,' said Professor Shaw. 'No, the Swanson men live alone. I don't even think their maid lives in.'

'That's what she said. Well, it's not much to go on, is it?'

'Does that mean you canna help, sir?' asked Round.

'Not straightaway. I'll have to think about it, and I'd like to talk to Mrs. McArthur – she's not answering her door, and her neighbours are unusually protective of her.'

'Well, someone will have to tell her the bad news, sir. Will you come with me again the now?'

Murray frowned: he did need to get back to Letho, but the opportunity was a good one.

'All right, then: I can't spare too long, I'm afraid, but I do want to see her.'

The constable kept a constant two paces behind Murray all the way back to South Street and to the close where Rory McArthur had lived, his staff tapping solidly on the cobbles. When they reached the little door where Murray had knocked uselessly earlier, Round used the staff to rap with some authority.

'Mrs. McArthur? Constable Round here. Come out, ma'am, for we've news for you.'

Murray glanced around. The woman across the lane peeped through her window, then emerged to see more clearly what was going on. There was no sign of her brother at all. She nodded at Murray, not unfriendly.

'Is she still within, do you know?' Murray asked her, but just as he did he heard the door open a little beside him, and a woman looked out, her head on one side and an effort at a smile on her pale, pretty face.

'Mr. Round? What is it you want?' She flicked a glance at Murray, and he felt himself assessed – nervously, yes, but also, he thought (hoping it was not just vanity), appreciatively. He grinned at himself.

'This is Mr. Murray of Letho – just by Cupar. May we come in a wee minute, Mrs. McArthur?'

She hesitated, and seemed to look past them down the close. Then she nodded quickly.

'I suppose,' she said. 'But watch the wain: she's into everything.'

The constable stood back to allow Murray to go first, and they squeezed into the little house. It apparently consisted of not much more than the one room: there was a box bed, a fire with cooking implements around it, a shelf with some books, including a large Bible, a small clock and Rory's violin case, a table at the window which seemed to do service as both a dining table and a work bench for Rory McArthur's clerking, three stools and a long bench, and in another alcove a little bed made up for the girl now crawling off it towards them. Afraid of treading on her in the tiny space, Murray stooped and swept her up.

'Miss McArthur, I assume? How do you do,' he said politely, tucking the child into the crook of his arm as he had with Augusta when she was as conveniently sized.

'That's Rosina,' Mrs. McArthur nodded, as she went to swing the kettle over the fire. The child was bonny – as was her mother, though as pale as she - and must have inherited her red hair from both parents. 'If it's Rory you want – if it's Mr. McArthur you're wanting, he's no in – as you can tell. I dinna ken when he'll be back. But sit yourselves down the now.'

'When did you see him last, Mrs. McArthur?' Murray perched on a stool, and arranged Rosina on his lap, drawing out his watch for her to play with. The child liked the shiny case and after a moment's inspection, sucked it happily.

'Yesterday.' She squatted on the creepie stool next to the fire, and looked up at them suddenly. 'Is there something wrong?'

Constable Round exchanged looks with Murray, and sat slowly on the nearest stool.

'Rory had an accident last night, Mrs. McArthur.'

'An accident?' Her eyes were wide and very blue. She looked from Round to Murray and back, suddenly frightened.

'He's dead, Mrs. McArthur.'

'Rory? Rory's dead?' She shot to her feet, knocking the creepie stool hard into the wall. She snatched Rosina from

Murray's arms, and the child, trying to cling to the shiny watch, set up a wail. 'You'll have to go. I'll have to go.'

'Go where, Mrs. McArthur?' Murray asked in surprise.

'I'll have to go.' She balanced Rosina on her hip, and began to pull a bag from under the box bed. 'I'll have to go.' Then she stopped abruptly, and sank to the floor. 'Where will I go?' And she burst into tears, wrapped hard around her wriggling child.

'Why do you need to go, Mrs. McArthur?' Murray asked gently. 'What are you trying to run from?'

'Rory's dead!' she sobbed. 'Do you not see, whoever you are – do you not see, if they got Rory, they'll get me!'

Chapter Six

The trouble, they discovered rapidly, was that however much Mrs. McArthur sobbed and protested, she would not, or could not, tell them who it might be who was now threatening her life, and who might have taken her husband's. She almost smothered her daughter in her sobs, and the daughter continued to add both volume and emotion to the general hysteria until, inevitably, there was an urgent chapping at the door and when Murray, warily, went to open it he found Nathan Houston's sister, Mrs. McArthur's neighbour, outside looking furious.

'What in the name of mercy are you doing to that poor woman? Janet, Janet, come here!'

Janet did not move, but the woman pushed past Murray and knelt beside her on the floor, enfolding her in motherly arms and gradually easing little Rosina into an embrace less likely to suffocate her. Rosina's sobs subsided and Mrs. McArthur grew less noisy, but no more communicative.

'What is going on here?' the woman snapped again, managing to cow both men from her position crouched on the floor.

'It's Mrs. Loudoun, is it no?' asked the constable politely, adding, after a pause, 'Nathan Houston's sister?'

'That's right,' said Mrs. Loudoun fiercely, 'but Nathan had nothing to do with this.'

Interesting, Murray thought: Nathan Houston was evidently known to the constable, in that special way that those with a liberal attitude to local and national legislation seem to be known.

'I never said he had,' said Constable Round, attempting to soothe. 'We've had to tell Mrs. McArthur that her husband died last night.'

Mrs. Loudoun rocked back on her heels, eyes wide, but recovered quickly.

'Rory McArthur? Dead? How?'

'It looks as if he was likely murdered, Mrs. Loudoun. He was drowned.'

Mrs. Loudoun looked away, rocking Janet McArthur gently, taking a moment to absorb the information.

'That's terrible,' she murmured at last.

'Do you know of anyone who might have had cause to harm him, Mrs. Loudoun?' Murray asked, equally quietly. She glanced up at him, shaking her head.

'He was just a clerk. He was nothing special. He looked after his wife and his bairn, and he did his work, and oh! he played the fiddle awful well.' A controlled tear was released, and trickled down her lined face.

'He did indeed.' Murray nodded, and after a moment added, 'Mrs McArthur seems to feel that whoever killed her husband will now threaten her safety, too. Would you have any idea who that might be?'

Mrs. Loudoun blinked properly at that, and sat back a little, surveying Janet McArthur's face. Janet was still crying steadily.

'I have no notion. Janet, who would that be, dearie?'

Janet shook her head, squeezing her eyes tight shut as if that would ward off any harm.

'She hasn't been able to tell us,' said Murray carefully, 'but it will be difficult to protect her if we don't know who it is. And obviously we want to catch Rory McArthur's killer.'

'Aye, of course,' said Mrs. Loudoun, absently, still looking closely at Janet. 'Who are you feart of, Janet dearie? Who could it be?'

They waited, but Janet just shook her head again, tightly, like a child refusing to take its medicine.

'You said she rarely goes out,' said Murray, remembering his conversation with Mrs. Loudoun earlier. 'Why do you think that might be?'

'Well, she's no frae round here,' said Mrs. Loudoun reasonably. 'I thought she was maybe a bit shy. She's always seemed nervous, haven't you, dearie? They have no family hereabouts.'

Constable Round grunted acknowledgement of this strange fact.

'Where are they from?' asked Murray, then felt silly. 'Where are you from, Mrs. McArthur?'

There was no reply, only a wild glance at Murray like an unnerved horse.

'Rory McArthur said they were from Perthshire, some place,' said Mrs. Loudoun after a moment. 'And that's the way they speak, ken, both of them.'

'True.' Murray remembered Rory McArthur's words at the recital. He took a wary step closer, and crouched down next to the women. 'Mrs. McArthur, can you tell me anything at all about these people who you think killed your husband? Was it something to do with his work?' He tilted his head towards Rory's erstwhile desk at the window. She stared at him, and after a moment shook her head. 'Was it someone he knew socially?'

This time she frowned, puzzled.

'Maybe one of the other musicians? One of his friends?'

She shook her head again, as if he had said something ridiculous.

'Someone from the college?'

Another shake of the head.

'Someone from your home, perhaps? From Perthshire?'

She shook her head again, but this time he was not so convinced. She closed her eyes as she did it, as if detaching herself from the lie. He sighed, and stood up: he could not think of any more options at the moment anyway.

'So you didn't go out much, but he went to play his fiddle and to visit his friends, is that right?'

She was curled up comfortably against Mrs. Loudoun now, and at last ventured a small, squeaky 'Yes'.

'Did his friends come here?'

'Not very often. Sometimes.'

'Who came here?'

'Sandy Bogue came the one time. He was very nice. And – and Mr. Swanson.'

'Thomas Swanson? The silversmith?'

'No, no! Mr. Jack Swanson.' A faint flush coloured her pale face for a moment at the misunderstanding.

'Ah, yes. Anyone else?'

'Mrs. Shaw came to see me, after the bairn was born. And a

few times since, to see I was all right.'

'And you were, weren't you, dearie?' put in Mrs. Loudoun, with the least hint of defiance. Murray wondered if the two women had set themselves up as competing grandmothers of this baby with no local family.

'But the person you think harmed Rory,' Murray found himself using simple language, as if Janet McArthur was the bairn herself, 'they never came to visit?'

'Oh, no!' That was clearly a horrific thought: Janet scrunched herself under Mrs. Loudoun's protective arm and blinked up at Murray like a water mouse threatened in a riverbank.

'Why won't you just tell us who it is, dearie?' Mrs. Loudoun urged her gently. Janet scrambled to pull herself a little more upright.

'Because Rory told me never to tell. "You're no to say anything, Janet," he said to me all the time. "The less you say, the safer you'll be. The less you go out, the less chance of a'body spying you and finding where you are." That's what he always said. And he said "I'll be here to protect you, Janet, never you worry. I'll always be here. Just say nothing and bide indoors, and all will be well." Ah, but it's no, is it? Because they've got him, and now they'll be coming for me!'

Murray caught Constable Round's eye and turned away a little.

'We have to find somewhere safe for her to stay,' he said quietly, 'or she'll either run, and who knows where to or how safe she will be then, or she'll simply stay here and starve through fear of doing anything. I'd take her to Letho, but it's a bit far for you and she wouldn't know anybody.'

'Would Professor Shaw, do you think ...? He has room for them.'

'He does, but I wouldn't want to wish any threat on him, if she's speaking the truth – and we have to assume she is, for her own safety, for now at least. He's not a strong man, and his manservant is not much better, I think.'

The constable sighed.

'I could try to take her in myself,' he said, 'though with my ain bairns and my sister's family while her man's away in Canada and my brother's two since he died last year it's a wee bit cramped already. But if needs must …'

'She can stay with me, of course,' Mrs. Loudoun put in suddenly. They both jumped, and she gave a sharp sigh at their uselessness. 'If that suits you, of course, Janet dearie. It'd be a joy to have you and the wee one across the close. My grand-daughter's away hame again.'

'And you'll keep me safe?' Janet asked, gazing at her.

'I'll do my level best,' said Mrs. Loudoun, with brisk efficiency.

'Then that's where I'll go,' said Janet. 'Mrs. Loudoun will look after me.'

'Is yon Nathan Houston there just the now?' Constable Round asked, almost as if it did not matter.

'He's in and out. He's only staying while he's between trips, ken,' said Mrs. Loudoun, with a little more of that defiance.

'Wi' his pistols?'

'He doesna like the pistols,' said Mrs. Loudoun, neither confirming nor denying their presence. 'He only got them because he was attacked and robbed on his way down to Edinburgh twa-three weeks ago. He says they're gey unchancy things.'

'He'd rather use his fists, I daresay,' Constable Round agreed. Mrs. Loudoun drew breath to retort and Murray stepped in quickly.

'Where does he travel to?' he asked.

'Edinburgh, Glasgow, Perth sometimes. Wherever there's trade,' she said. 'He's no idle, my brother, not like some.'

'No, he's no idle,' agreed Constable Round without expression. Murray tried not to laugh.

'Well, can we carry anything across the close for you, Mrs. McArthur?' he asked.

'Och, you'll no need much,' said Mrs. Loudoun. 'You can always jook back when you need something. Well, Rosina, are you going to come with your mammie and stay with me a wee while?'

Janet McArthur stood and picked up her daughter, and Mrs. Loudoun refused assistance to pull herself up on to her feet. She busied herself settling the fire while Constable Round solemnly stepped outside and checked up and down the close for anyone behaving suspiciously, and then Murray followed the women out of the little house, closing the door behind them. He and the constable watched them disappear into the house across the way, and then headed back down the close to South Street.

'What did you make of all that?' Murray asked, when the busy street made them difficult to overhear.

'I dinna ken, sir. It's no much use to us unless she can tell us who it was that threatened him.'

'Maybe Mrs. Loudoun will winkle it out of her,' said Murray.

'Aye, but if she does she might not tell us. Och,' he sighed, 'she's no a bad woman herself, but that brother of hers is a fellow with a hand in all kinds of dealings.'

'I saw him earlier. On the bright side, he looked as if he would protect Mrs. McArthur against all comers.'

Constable Round laughed shortly.

'He might an' all. So you're for Letho now, are you, sir?'

'That's my plan, but I hope to be back tomorrow.'

'Then I hope we can talk again then, sir.'

The constable bowed, and Murray went to fetch his horse from the Shaws' house.

It was only later, as he set out for Letho, that he went over Janet McArthur's conversation again in his mind. Rory had told Janet to stay indoors and to speak to no one, but he had not followed that advice himself, not at all. Surely, then, from what she had said, the threat was not to Rory McArthur, but to Janet?

He had an easy ride of it, the day bright and chilly again, and at Letho Robbins met him in the hall.

'All well, sir,' he answered Murray's first question as he followed the laird into the library for their usual meeting. 'Carlisle went to St. Andrews not long after you yesterday, later than he had planned so he was going to stay last night with a friend there.'

'I saw him this morning,' Murray agreed. 'Turns out the man he was to obtain his purple peas from was Professor Shaw.'

'Indeed, sir?' Robbins' colourless eyebrows rose fractionally. 'The painter is back and already at work. He has made a start on Daniel, I believe, and is now begun on Iffy.'

'He was back early: he played in a very fine string quartet last night.'

'He arrived an hour or more ago, sir.'

'And how is Iffy managing?'

Robbins' lips twitched slightly.

'I took the liberty of watching at the door for ten minutes, sir, to assure myself that all was well.' Murray nodded: servants needed chaperones too, sometimes, and Iffy, stringy and daft though she was, seemed to attract a certain kind of male. 'Iffy was finding standing still a bit difficult, I believe. She was very excited, of course.'

'Of course.'

'She's not often allowed in the dining room.'

That was fair: other kitchenmaids might have been brought in as an extra servant at table from time to time, but Iffy was hopelessly clumsy and noisily nervous, and Mrs. Mack the cook had long since despaired of her improvement.

'And how was Gordon coping with her?'

'I believe artists often have quite, er, lively tempers, sir.'

'Oh, dear. Perhaps I should pop in later and see if his feathers need to be smoothed?'

'That might be helpful, sir.'

'Who's next on his list?'

'Mrs. Mack, sir, if he cannot get Carlisle. He wants to paint Carlisle in one of the hothouses, he says, but Carlisle maintains he is too busy in March to be painted.'

'That could be true. I should have thought of that. Oh, and I said to Walter that if he is able to come back from his studies for a couple of days, he is to be painted too. After all, it still feels as if he is part of the household, and it makes up in part for missing his grandfather.' Walter's grandfather, old Mr. Fenwick, had been butler to Murray's father, and had recently died peacefully in his retirement.

'Very good, sir. May I ask how Walter is? They'll all want to know.'

'He seems to have settled in very well, from what I could see. He is friends with Professor Shaw's own son who is about an age with him, though I'm not sure he'll be a great influence on him. He is learning his Latin and Greek, and all about fish.'

'Fish, sir?' Robbins looked a little sceptical.

'Yes: and in the course of that, this morning he discovered a dead body.'

'A what, sir?'

'A young clerk of the town, once a student of Professor

Shaw's, lying with his head in a fishpond.'

'Murdered, sir?'

'It seems so.'

'Aye, well,' Robbins nodded thoughtfully. 'Walter'll be in his element, then, no doubt.'

Having given instructions for what was to be packed for his return to St. Andrews the following day, Murray took a slice of cheese and a hunk of bread, had a fresh horse saddled, and set off for a ride around at least a little of his land to see how the sowing was progressing. There was no sense in inspecting the gardens, as Carlisle would still be in St. Andrews and the under gardeners would not want to talk without their master there: Murray sometimes thought the Roman tyrants could have learned a good deal from his gardener. Instead he went about to inspect the arable land, to check on the last of the willow coppicing, and to receive reports on the progress of new lambs and calves. Easter had been early: the Easter Communions last Saturday and Sunday had put everyone out, attending the preachings in a chilly church and a colder kirkyard, and the session had been busy the week before issuing tokens, so there was a sense all throughout the estate of hurrying to catch up before the weather warmed and the weeds made their first attack.

He finished with the village, his boots muddy and his coat flecked with straw, leading his horse so that he could stop to talk to people more easily as he went. He had had to bring his rents down after Waterloo, nearly three years ago, but at least that meant he still had tenants: one or two of the Collessie cottages were still empty, the tenants of the neighbouring estate evicted and no one able to pay the rents to replace them. Mr. George, Letho's third main landowner at Dures House, saw things as Murray did and had brought his own rents down, too: the village was still lively and growing prosperous again, where others were not.

He had just detached himself from an irritable Collessie tenant, when he noticed, first, the beautiful horse, and second, its rider. Poor Dr. Lindsay was not going to attract any attention to himself while he rode that splendid beast.

Murray hastened from Walter's aunt's cottage door, and went to greet the doctor. Dr. Lindsay swung himself down to Murray's level and bowed.

'I hope you found St. Andrews was still to your taste?' Murray asked, patting the black stallion on the neck then turning to do the same to his own horse, in case she felt jealous.

'Oh, very much so! And just as sociable,' said Dr. Lindsay with a wince. 'I have not risen this late, or this rough, since I graduated!'

Murray grinned.

'I had thought we might see you at a little recital I was invited to by Professor Shaw: four excellent musicians, in a string quartet.'

Lindsay laughed a little ruefully.

'No, we were not apt company for such delights! My host had some very fine claret just up from Leith and I'm afraid we made quite a dent in his supply. We would not have been in a fit state to appreciate anything more sophisticated than a military band, I think.' He paused, smiling at the memory. 'And Professor and Mrs. Shaw are well, are they?'

'For the most part, yes. I shall be returning to them tomorrow to help them with ... a small domestic matter.'

'They are gentle folk, are they not?' asked Lindsay sympathetically. Murray knew what he meant: the world could seem a very harsh place to the Shaws.

'Well, I shall see what I can do to assist them,' he said. 'In the meantime, would you like to join me for supper tonight? I'm afraid we are a bachelor household at present, but my cook is good.'

Dr. Lindsay made a face.

'I'm sorry: I am already engaged to – Dures House, is it? Miss George and her brother. Along with Mrs. Feilden: Dr. Feilden has told her to go and enjoy herself.'

'Ah, well, another time. Their cook is good, too!'

And it might be a wise move for the Georges, Murray thought, as he headed back to Letho by the field path. Miss George was an unclaimed treasure much in need of a husband, and Mr. George could appreciate a fine horse in his stables just as well as the next man.

Knowing his mare was too tired to be bothered jumping the haha, he worked his way round to the drive and headed straight up towards the low front doorway of Letho House, turning off to the left at the last minute to skirt the factor's house and make his way under the archway to the stable block. He left the mare in the capable hands of a stable boy, and struck by a sudden thought went, not back round to the front door, but in the other direction, further away from it, towards the walled gardens. An under gardener directed him to a hot house against one of the high brick walls, where even in March vine and fig leaves pressed against the windows. The smell inside was sweet and warm: the atmosphere was not.

'I'm only just back in the door!' Carlisle was complaining. 'And there's a thousand and one things to be doing!'

'Then find one you can be doing while I paint you!' Cosmo Gordon had an easel folded under his left arm, and in his right hand a bag containing, by its size and shape, a smallish canvas as well as the requisite paints and brushes. He still managed to gesture impatiently. Carlisle considered, then caught sight of Murray in the doorway.

'Mr. Murray, sir. Is there no other body in this establishment that Mr. Gordon here could paint before me? I'm gey busy.'

'What's your most urgent task?' Murray asked, knowing there was no use beginning with an argument.

'I've to get the yunyuns in, and thin the leeks,' said Carlisle at once. Murray was sure he had prepared some good outdoor tasks ready to deter Cosmo Gordon.

'Couldn't you do those indoors?' asked Mr. Gordon. Carlisle gave him a look he could have used on weeds to great effect.

'What about Professor Shaw's peas? Will you be sowing those indoors or out?'

'Well,' Carlisle considered. 'Indoors, I reckon, but that's no till later. Twa three hours maybe.'

'The light will have gone then,' snapped Cosmo Gordon. 'I'm afraid your gardener is being deliberately obstructive, Mr. Murray.'

'It is a very busy time of year,' said Murray soothingly. 'But he will have to sit to you some time soon. Why don't you do the peas late tomorrow morning, Carlisle, in here, and then Mr. Gordon can paint you while you're doing them?'

Carlisle snorted, but could see that he might as well take the defeat on his own terms.

'Aye, well, I suppose. Mind, I'm no sitting idle: there'll be a few jobs to be done.'

'Well, I'm sure you're well able to organise them to have them ready, Carlisle. Now, Mr. Gordon, do let me help you with that easel, and let's find someone else for you to paint. Have you done Mr. Robbins yet?'

'He's another one,' Cosmo Gordon complained, then made an obvious effort to calm down a little. 'He's a very busy man.'

Murray took the easel and led the way back across the gardens to the courtyard at the rear of the house.

'He is, I'm afraid. We have no housekeeper at the moment, as I'm sure you've noticed, and so a great deal falls on Mr. Robbins. Perhaps you could do Mrs. Robbins? Or Mrs. Mack, the cook?'

'I fancy doing Mrs. Mack,' Gordon admitted. 'She has a fine, interesting face. I don't think I've seen Mrs. Robbins. Is she on the staff, too?'

'She was, until she married Mr. Robbins,' Murray explained. 'But she's still part of the household.'

'Well, if you wish her painted …' They entered the hallway from the courtyard, and Cosmo Gordon paused. 'This is so like my own family's house, you know: just this hallway is so like it. In feeling, perhaps, more than in architecture.'

'Really? I thought you were from St. Andrews.' He had not much considered the painter's family background, but now he thought about it perhaps he did have something of a gentlemanly air.

'Oh, I live in St. Andrews, yes. My family had a house in Perthshire, though – well, a castle, really, I suppose you would call it.' His offhandedness over the distinction was, Murray thought, assumed. Cosmo Gordon stood all the straighter as he spoke of it.

'And what happened to it?' Murray asked sympathetically. One heard of so many large houses catching fire – and then there was the disaster that had happened to his own servants' wing.

'Oh, the family lost it. A financial misfortune.'

'Very sad,' Murray agreed. A financial misfortune was a phrase that really told him very little, but he did not press. 'It is then your good fortune to have such a talent as painting to support you in life.'

'Hm.' Cosmo Gordon did not look as happy about that as he

might have done. 'Yes, I have been fortunate so far.'

'And of course dedication to your work is always helpful,' Murray carried on, leading the way back into the dining room and ringing the bell for Robbins. 'Not every man would have hurried back here to work directly after a friend was found dead.'

'What?'

Cosmo's painting bag crashed to the floor.

'Oh, I beg your pardon,' said Murray, very slightly disingenuously. 'I assumed the rumour would have reached you before you left St. Andrews this morning. One of your fellow players from that excellent recital last night.'

'What? Who? Not Jack Swanson?'

'No, not Jack. Roderick McArthur.'

'Rory? Dead?' Cosmo Gordon tugged out a dining chair and slumped on to it, his head in his hands. 'I knew it!' he muttered. 'I knew it would come to this!'

Chapter Seven

Cosmo Gordon was clearly not hesitant about talking, so Murray stayed silent, still as Cosmo's portraits, waiting. He had the distinct impression that Gordon's pause was mostly for dramatic effect – he was after all an artist, and indeed a performer - so Murray could easily be patient. After a moment, Gordon heaved a deep sigh, letting his arms dangle between his knees.

'Roderick has always found it hard to control his temper,' he said, his voice sorrowful. 'And I have always been sure that one day it would bring him, or someone else, into danger. That's why I thought you must mean Jack: Roderick was angry with Jack when he left the Bogues' house, saying he'd let us down, not turning up like that. I let it go – let him go – sure that by the time he found Jack he would have cooled down: with Roderick it was a quick burn, but it could cool fast enough when he reconsidered.' He pushed his chestnut hair out of his face, displaying his fine cheekbones to some advantage, and leaned back in the chair again, staring past Murray. 'I assume he and Jack came to blows at last.'

'You mean you think Jack killed him?'

'Oh! It would have been in his own defence, no doubt: Jack and Rory were the best of friends, had been for years. The quartet was their idea, started when they played together as students, so they told me. But if Rory attacked him, Jack would have fought back. Different if it had been Sandy Bogue. Sandy lets the world slide by him, without a care. But Jack's temper is nearly as bad as Rory's and if he's roused he'll strike.'

'You've known them all for a while, then?' Murray asked, quietly prompting him.

'Oh,' the hand pushed the hair back again, 'two, three years? Since before Rory was married, anyway. Sandy was still a student, and Rory and Jack were apprenticed to his father but they'd all known each other as – what are they called, the first years? Bejants?'

'That's right.'

'Yes, bejants. And Sandy is one of those musicians that hardly has to try: he just picks up the instrument and off he goes. He's perfect, really, to play with Rory and Jack, because he never lets them ruffle him. Then when I turned up in St. Andrews and I met them they asked me to join in.'

'How did you meet?'

'I was doing some work with Jack's father – he's a silversmith, and someone had asked me to design something he was to make.' Cosmo Gordon leaned back further in his chair and eyed Murray suddenly. 'You're asking an awful lot of questions, there. What is all this to you?'

'I was there when the body was found,' said Murray solemnly.

'Oh, poor Roderick,' said Cosmo, and he seemed for a moment to shrink into himself. Then he cleared his throat. 'Where – where was he found?'

'He was lying with his head under the water by one of Professor Shaw's pools. Professor Shaw has a series of fishponds and rills in his garden: Rory McArthur was there.'

'Professor – oh, the little one with the face like a frog.'

Murray paused.

'Yes, Professor Shaw. You painted his portrait some time ago.'

A fleeting grin slipped across Gordon's face, and Murray wondered if the artist made Rory McArthur as cross as he was making him.

'So I did. Yes: a few of his former students wrote and asked me to do it.'

'It's a good likeness,' Murray granted him.

'It is, isn't it? I wonder what he's done with it: he didn't seem the type to have much art about the house.' He sighed, and pulled himself back to the point. 'But what was Roderick doing in this professor's garden?'

'We don't know yet.' Murray did not feel the need to remind Cosmo Gordon that the Shaws' house was beside the Swansons'.

'And what has poor Jack said? Have they taken him in yet?'

'They haven't, no. He has not admitted to having killed McArthur, as far as I know.'

Gordon whistled thoughtfully.

'He'd be better to admit it and show that it was in his own defence,' he said, anxiously. 'It's not going to do him any good when they find out it was him and he hasn't said. What's he going to do? Steal a fishing boat and flee the country?'

'There's always a chance,' said Murray, 'that it wasn't him.'

'What?' Gordon was taken aback.

'What do you know about Rory, and where he came from? About his marriage?'

'His marriage? I barely ever met his wife. Janet, isn't it?'

'That's right. Did he ever say where he had met her? How they came to marry? You knew him before his marriage.'

'I did.' Cosmo Gordon considered for a moment. 'Yes, I knew him then. It's only a couple of years ago. He said he was leaving now his apprenticeship was done, packed his things, left his lodgings, said goodbye to us – I remember Jack and Sandy walked him to the West Port to see him off. I didn't know him so well, I said goodbye to him at his lodgings. The next thing we knew he was back in the town with a wifie, in a wee hoose up a close by the town kirk there. He might have mentioned something to the others, but he never said anything about her to me – and Roderick was not the kind of man you asked about things like that. It wasn't that he refused to say anything: it was just something about him that told you not to ask him. Do you know what I mean?'

'Yes, I think so. Some people have a kind of wall up about them.'

'Aye, that's the very thing. Roderick's wall was a good high one, with maybe a thorn hedge in front of it, too.' He grinned, sadly. 'So no, I know nothing of his wife. But it wasn't – ah, how can I say it? He never looked happy. I don't mean he looked miserable, well, no more than was his nature. He wasn't naturally a cheerful type, ever. Oh, what do I mean? When a man's just married, and all's right in his world, his face shines and he walks with a lighter step – and I never saw Rory do that. I don't think he was ever in love. But maybe that was just Rory.'

'You say he never said much about himself – did he mention his home?'

'Somewhere in Perthshire, that's all I know. That wall and the thorn hedge were enough to stop any chatter about things like that.'

'So he never mentioned any threats?'

'Threats?'

'Any danger he might be in?'

'Roderick McArthur? In danger? Why on earth would he be in danger?'

'Oh, just something somebody said, that someone had threatened his life.'

Cosmo Gordon settled on his chair, head on one side, considering this puzzling new piece of information.

'I cannot imagine why or who,' he said at last. 'That makes no sense whatsoever. But as I say, that hedge and that wall: if he had a secret, it would be hard to spot it in the general silence.'

Murray sighed.

'Oh, well. I'm sorry for your loss, anyway.'

'Aye, aye. Me too,' Gordon agreed, nodding. 'He was a grand fiddle-player, if nothing else. And his wife and bairn will miss him.'

'Well,' said Murray, 'it must be time to change for dinner. You'll have to paint Mrs. Mack afterwards, if at all today.'

'Of course. I'll sort things out here, then go and take my own piece and be back later.'

But before Murray could cross the hall to climb the stairs to his bedchamber, there was a shriek and a crash from behind the doorway to the servants' quarters. It sounded as if a sizeable cat had been trodden on with force, and Murray was not the only one, it turned out, who ran to see what had happened. In the stone corridor between the main hall and the kitchens, Iffy was standing clutching her arm, broken glass all about her on the flagged floor, and a splendidly dramatic patterning of blood all up one wall and down her gown and apron. She was as white as a sheet. Daniel, ever keen to see what was going on, was the first to appear.

'Daniel, go and fetch Dr. Feilden at once,' snapped Murray, forgetting Dr. Feilden's broken leg. Daniel tore himself away and ran from the house. 'Iffy, step over the glass and sit down here before you faint.'

Iffy sagged against the wall and Murray pulled out his

handkerchief, ready to wrap the gash in her arm. Mrs. Mack bustled out from the kitchen.

'Merciful Heavens, Iffy, can you no carry one decanter from the kitchen to Mr. Robbins' pantry without flinging it about the place?'

'It just lepped from my hands, Mrs. Mack!' sobbed Iffy. Murray held her arm up above her head, trying to stop the bleeding, but there was a slice of glass protruding from the cut. It was awkward work.

'Here, let me, sir,' said Mrs. Mack, but she was not much better at it. Iffy's sobbing was growing fainter and her eyes were closing.

'Brandy,' said Murray. 'Where is Robbins?'

'In the parlour, sir, seeing to the table.'

Murray darted back into the hall. He had been dining in the parlour while the portraits were being painted in the dining room: he almost flattened Robbins coming out of the cosy front room.

'Brandy, Robbins: Iffy's had an accident.'

The front door crashed open, and Daniel fell through, panting. Murray thought fleetingly that he should really be made to run more: he was growing far too fat. Behind him, looking surprised, was Dr. Lindsay, blond curls ruffled at the removal of his hat.

'Mr. Murray?'

'That was quick!' Murray gestured him to follow and returned with Robbins to the corridor where Iffy slumped against the wall. Robbins fumbled with the keys for his pantry to fetch the brandy. Dr. Lindsay assessed the situation swiftly and knelt by Iffy, wary of the broken glass.

'Now, then, Miss,' he said, with brisk kindness. Iffy opened her eyes.

'Och, am I in heaven?' she said with vague astonishment. 'Are you an angel, sir?'

'Not in the least,' said Dr. Lindsay with a smile.

'Och, no,' said Iffy. 'Mrs. Mack said I'd never get to heaven, but I'd hoped …'

'Och, be quiet, lass!' said Mrs. Mack, more gently than was her custom. 'You're no dead yet: you'll have plenty time to sort out your destination.' She watched keenly as the doctor set to work, cleaning, easing the glass out, testing the wound for more pieces, then stitching across it. Daniel, still trying to catch his breath, made a nauseous noise and turned away.

'Well done, Daniel: you were very quick,' said Murray.

'I met the doctor on the drive,' Daniel explained. 'Lucky.'

'Very lucky,' agreed Dr. Lindsay, at last standing up. 'I was on my way here to apologise for my brusqueness earlier. I felt I had been rude to you, sir.'

Murray was surprised.

'Not at all: I am sorry to have given you the impression that you had been, except that your apology brought you here faster. Will she be all right?'

Mrs. Mack pulled Iffy to her feet, groaning.

'She'll need to lie down for a couple of hours, or she'll be light-headed. And I've dressed the wound, but you'll need to watch out for infection, of course.'

'Of course.'

'Mrs. Robbins will come over and see to it, if you wish, sir,' said Robbins politely. His wife had served her time as an army wife, and was well used to wounds.

'That would be very good of her, Robbins. Thank you. Dr. Lindsay, a drink before you go?'

'If I may wash my hands first.' Lindsay turned up palms red with Iffy's blood.

'Of course. We'll be in the library, Robbins.'

'Sir.'

Mrs. Mack and Daniel helped Iffy back to the kitchen and presumably the settle by the fire, and Murray led Lindsay over to the library where Robbins shortly joined them with a basin of hot water, soap and a towel. Daniel followed with brandy, more hot water in a jug, and glasses for punch.

'I cannot stay long – thank you,' Lindsay added to Daniel who removed the washing things. 'As I said I am promised to the Georges.'

'Of course – and I was not at all offended. I asked you at very short notice: I cannot ask you again for now as I hope to return to St. Andrews in the morning, but no doubt you will be here for a while and we can arrange something later.'

'I should look forward to that, sir.'

'Sit, anyway, for now, and take some brandy.'

They sat by the empty library fireplace, warmed instead by the brandy punch, and for a little while discussed the books on the shelves, much loved by Murray. Dr. Lindsay seemed then to feel he should finish his professional job for the evening.

'Your maid will have a nasty scar there for a while.'

'She is tremendously prone to accidents, I'm afraid. The cook is constantly complaining about her, yet I know she will look after her well until she is better. I have no housekeeper at present, unfortunately – and no doubt I shall have to find someone to come and help the cook. Bachelor households: I'm afraid this one is a little chaotic at present!'

'You have never married?'

'My wife died in the autumn before last. I have a daughter, Augusta,' Murray could not resist saying, 'who is but a year and a half old, but she is staying with dear friends in Edinburgh for another couple of weeks. I look forward to having her home.'

'I am sorry – I see you are indeed still in mourning. I beg your pardon.'

'Not at all.' Murray was used to his own feelings of ambivalence at this period of mourning. Another few months, now, and he would be quit of it.

'Well,' Dr. Lindsay rose and set down his brandy glass. 'I'm afraid I must be going.'

'I'll see you to the door,' said Murray, standing up too. He opened the library door and Dr. Lindsay preceded him to the front door, carrying his medical bag. 'Good day to you!' Murray stood and watched as Lindsay strapped the medical bag to the saddle of his spectacular horse, then waved the doctor off. As he turned and shut the door, ready once again to go and change for dinner, he pondered. Dr. Lindsay felt like someone he should be friends with, and superficially there was no animosity between them. Yet he felt a stiffness there which puzzled him: there had been no need for Lindsay to visit especially to apologise for declining his invitation, and no peculiarity about the invitation itself: as one of the local landowners Murray would be expected to ask the new doctor to dinner or supper soon after his arrival. And their conversation just now in the library: their discussion of the books had been full of agreement and mutual goodwill, and yet … He was still trying to put his finger on the exact problem as he turned, and saw, at the doorway of the dining room, Cosmo Gordon, white as a sheet.

'Are you quite well, Mr. Gordon?' asked Murray.

Cosmo Gordon blinked.

'Oh, yes, yes! Sorry, Mr. Murray: I felt a little wave of giddiness, there.' He held the doorpost in one long hand, steadying himself. 'I am in need of my dinner, as I said.'

'Of course. Don't let me detain you.'

Cosmo Gordon walked unsteadily to the door to the servants' quarters, and disappeared. Murray watched him go, hoped that someone had swept up the glass, and headed upstairs to change at last.

The evening had been quiet, after dinner, and given over to reading and writing several letters, a task he would normally have done in the morning when the post arrived, had he been there. It included a letter from his friends the Blairs and his reply, all concerning his darling daughter who was staying with them, and a couple of answers from friends to whom he had written regarding a replacement for his housekeeper and perhaps a maid or two, too. His servants' hall was badly depleted at present, and the manservants would go on marrying which took them away from Letho's direct concerns. He sighed. If he were desperate enough, he would have to contact an agency in Edinburgh, but he hoped it would not come to that.

On Friday morning he set out early again for St. Andrews, and this time completed the journey alone. It was another chilly spring day with the sunlight dancing on the waters of the estuary. He had left Cosmo Gordon apparently fit and well heading out to the gardens on his hunt for Carlisle, and wished him luck, and with that had put the concerns of Letho behind him for a little, and concentrated on the work ahead of him.

Whether Roderick McArthur had been killed by someone close to him in St. Andrews or by a visitor from his past was impossible to say at present, and there were plenty of people to question and plenty of things he wanted to discover. Where had Rory been between his departure from the Bogues' recital and his death in the fishpond? Who else had seen him? Where had he met his murderer? If the killer was someone from his past, what was their motive, and why had they attacked Rory and not Janet, who seemed, from her account, to be the intended victim? If Rory had really made Janet stay indoors, then it did look as if he was protecting her – or was he one of those men who are over-possessive of their wives, unwilling to let another man catch a glimpse of them if it could be prevented? Janet was not particularly to his taste, but she did have a fragile charm, Murray thought, and certainly it had been enough to make Nathan Houston protective of her, at the very least. Was Rory the jealous type, as well as short-tempered? He needed to find out more from those who had known him best.

He was greeted warmly at the Shaws' house and returned his mare to the stables, the manservant stroking her nose as if she was an old friend already.

'No, I know of no progress at all!' sighed Professor Shaw, taking him into the parlour for a welcome cup of tea. 'The constable has not been near us, which I take to be a good sign for us, and I have not seen him at the Swansons', either.'

'Cosmo Gordon was quite convinced that Jack Swanson had killed Rory McArthur – that is, when I told him who the victim was, for before that I believe he thought that Rory must have killed Jack. He said that Rory had a short temper: is that your recollection of him?'

Shaw frowned.

'It is, I'm afraid. He was one of those quiet men who suddenly bursts out, though I should not have said he was violent with it. He was more likely to do harm to himself. He could look quite apoplectic at times.'

'Cosmo Gordon thinks that Jack must have killed Rory while defending himself. I did not say that it had not looked like that to me. There was little sign of a struggle by the body: I should have thought more that he was taken by surprise there, though what he was doing in your garden is another matter.'

'Poor lad, poor lad,' Professor Shaw nodded, then shook his head, agreeing that he did not know either. Murray restrained a smile, though it would have been a fond one.

'Well, I shall go and find the constable and see what stage he is at. And then, all things being equal, I hope to go to see the Bogues.'

'Oh, that's a good idea! They are very nice people, Charles: so kind and generous with all their musical evenings. They will want to help, I am quite sure.'

Constable Round was out of his office, busy, a clerk said, with a dispute near the market place. Questioned further, the clerk was fairly sure that Constable Round had not yet been near the Bogues' house.

'He's a gey busy man,' he said, anxious to defend his colleague. Murray thanked him, and continued back to South Street and to the little close that led to the Bogues' unexpectedly grand old house. In the daylight Murray could read the marriage stone over the lintel, and noted the venerable date, 1596, but also that neither set of initials, bride nor groom, included a letter 'B': it was possible, therefore, that this was not an old family house but one more recently acquired. He rattled at the risp, thick with shiny black paint, and waited. It was not long before a maid came and let him in with a very proper curtsey.

'Are any of the family at home?' he asked.

'Miss Bogue is within, sir. I'll take you to her.'

The maid led the way, not to the fine barrel-vaulted room but to a much smaller and cosier parlour, perhaps what would once have been called the solar. A bay window with leaded panes overlooked a garden, and a small fire kept the room warm. On a window seat, stitching as if she had been perched there since 1596, was the girl who had turned the pages for the string quartet. She stood in surprise as Murray was announced.

'Forgive me for intruding like this,' said Murray at once, bowing. 'My name is Charles Murray of Letho, and I was privileged to be at the recital two nights ago.'

'Oh, yes! You were there with the Shaws, I remember. I hope you enjoyed the evening.' She had a deep voice, contralto, Murray thought at once, his mind on music. The southern light touched her toffee-coloured hair with a very pleasing effect.

'Very much: no doubt you will have heard the sad news of what has happened since.'

'Rory McArthur? Yes! A terrible shock. Poor Rory.'

Murray sat where she indicated, but declined an offer of tea.

'You must have known him for some time, Miss Bogue?'

'Yes, a few years, I suppose. He and my brother Sandy were at the college together, but only for one year. Then Sandy stayed on, lucky lad, while the others were apprenticed to my father. That's Rory and Jack, too, the three of them were friends from their first day there. I suppose Jack and Sandy must have known each other as boys, but I don't remember him from before that time.' She set her sewing aside, and gave Murray a more thorough examination than she had previously. 'Do you know something of this matter, then, sir? I find I am talking easily to you about it, and yet I have no idea of your standing in the case!'

She managed to make the challenge sound more friendly than it might have done, and he smiled.

'I beg your pardon. I was unfortunate enough to be there when Mr. McArthur was found yesterday: as you say, I am acquainted with the Shaws, and Professor Shaw is much distressed. I have some experience in such cases, and Constable Round has asked me to help him a little.'

'I see.' She straightened in her seat, taking the conversation more seriously. 'Then can I be of assistance?'

'I had called hoping to see your father or your brother, but of course you knew Mr. McArthur, so I should be very grateful for your impressions of him and of his circle.'

'My father and brother are at the shop: my father still dreams of luring his son back into the business, I believe, though there is little hope of that! Perhaps if you will allow me to fetch my shawl and bonnet I can take you to see them, and we can talk on the way.'

'That would be very kind of you,' Murray acknowledged, and she left him alone in the solar, feeling that his investigations were progressing in a very pleasurable fashion.

Chapter Eight

'Shall we go the long way round, past the Cathedral?' Miss Bogue asked as they left the old sandstone close and entered South Street. 'My father's shop is not far: if you want to ask me about Rory and the others before we reach it we should have to walk so slowly it would arouse comment on our eccentricity, if nothing else!'

'If that suits you, then by all means,' said Murray. 'I should hate to be thought to be any more eccentric than I already am.'

She smiled, and turned right to the east. The ruined Cathedral with its twin spires and the monumental block of St. Rule's Tower dominated this end of the small town, though with its low walls and the broad green sweep of kirkyard about it, it was a peaceful spot, partially at least sheltered from the sharp winds off the sea close by. Murray had walked there many a time. The road curved towards it then bent right back on itself to become North Street: the end of Market Street, the middle of the three parallel main streets, was tucked into a jumble of houses within that sharp bend. To their right, as they approached the Cathedral, a steep path led down through strange ecclesiastical arches to the harbour – the Pends, it was called – but they crossed that and continued until they came to the Cathedral gates. Murray opened the nearer one and ushered Miss Bogue through.

'I'm afraid,' she said as he drew level with her again, 'that I have been building you up for some great revelations about Rory and his friends, but it will be no such thing!'

'Any information will help. I only saw him once, at the recital, but I should very much like to find out who killed him and why, and if possible bring them to justice.'

'Goodness: no small task, then. Well, what do I know of Rory? Roderick McArthur.' She considered, tucking her hands firmly inside her muff. She had forsaken a shawl in favour of a warm red spencer in a very fine wool, but then she was the daughter of a cloth merchant. 'I first met him I suppose a week or so after Sandy began at the college, so that would have been in the autumn of the year '13. Sandy brought him and Jack home to play music together: it's about the only thing that Sandy is truly enthusiastic about, for everything else in Sandy's life can ebb and flow and Sandy will remain entirely unconcerned.' She spoke with the habitual fond criticism of an older sister for her brother. 'Rory and Jack were both more serious than Sandy, though that would not be difficult. Jack perhaps not so much – he and Sandy would have a laugh, and indeed several drinks, but Rory did not often join in. Yet he was a gentle man, I have always thought, kindly: he just took life much more seriously. He was never as easy with money, either. And I have the impression he had to work harder than either of the others to keep up with them, too, though I may be wrong.'

'Not as bright?'

'Not academically,' she amended. 'In terms of understanding other people and their needs, perhaps much brighter – but then young men can be a little like that, can't they?' she asked, with a teasing glance in his direction.

'It's a long time since I was one – it's hard to remember,' said Murray with mock sorrow. 'You must have spent quite a lot of time with them, all together.'

'My parents like having guests, of all kinds – you'll have seen that. The two boys often ate with us, for – well, you know what the food in the college is like, and Jack's mother is dead so housekeeping there was not always reliable, either.'

'Did Mr. Swanson dine with you, too?'

She considered.

'Very rarely. I'm not sure he and Father get on. Not that there's any particular animosity,' she added quickly, 'but they just don't seem to have very much in common. Mr. Swanson is not musical, for one thing.'

'Yet Jack is.'

'I think he must have that from his mother. I don't remember her. Well, anyway, there they were playing and so on, and then at some point they found that artist, Cosmo Gordon, and he joined them to play string quartets, which is what they all really seem to enjoy.'

'Did he fit in well?'

'He's a little older,' said Miss Bogue, her head tilting. Her hands seemed to want to express themselves even inside the muff. 'He's not really one of them. He's very talented, though.'

'He seems to be,' said Murray, without emphasis.

'Well, anyway,' said Miss Bogue with renewed briskness. 'At the end of their bejant year, Jack and Rory quit the college. Jack, I believe, never intended to do more than a year or two, and Rory's parents died. I believe he's from Perthshire, did I mention that? So he had to leave, with no money to go on, and I think Jack just took the opportunity to go at the same time. Father enjoys having apprentices to train, and he had space, so he offered them both posts as clerks for a couple of years. I don't think either of them was formally indentured, but there was some agreement for it. Anyway, the three of them carried on much as before. Jack and Rory were always a bit competitive, though, there in the same office each day. They were always seeing which of them could write better, or faster, or please my father more in some way: it meant there was more of an edge to them. It was much pleasanter when they came to visit separately then, for Jack would tease Rory and sometimes Sandy would join in, and Rory would go red and sort of swell up, trying not to lose his temper, and he was hopeless at teasing back which of course would have been much better. Jack and Sandy tease each other half the time, and neither of them loses his temper. Well, Jack does sometimes, but I'm not sure Sandy would know how to. But they kept on playing, and of course Jack and Rory competed in that, too.

'And then everything changed again.'

'Rory married.'

'Well, first of all their agreements with my father came to an end. There was some talk of him keeping one of them on as a more senior clerk, but when it came to it he could not choose between them knowing that they were so competitive: it would cause bad blood, and there was little between them in reality in their skills.

Jack is cleverer, but Rory works harder. Then just as he had taken on someone else as another apprentice, Rory announced he was leaving and going back home. Well, Jack had his nose put out of joint for my father would not – was not in a position to – take him back, and it left them short of a violin for the quartet, too. Sandy started training Wee Dod – you saw him the other night – to take Rory's place. Then the next thing we knew Rory was back, and married.'

'He had never mentioned a sweetheart?'

'Never. In fact, I thought there was someone here in St. Andrews and he was just biding his time until he was in a secure position to make an offer for her, but no: he arrives back with this lassie from Perthshire.'

'What did you think of her?'

'I've only met her ... twice? Mother asked them to tea when they first arrived: she hardly spoke, looked to Rory for every word and action, and they left early. Then Mother and I called after the baby was born.' She made an odd little twitch of her eyebrows, as though there was more to be said there if she could say it. 'Sweet little thing – actually, both she and the child are sweet little things. But there's not much else to her that I could see, apart from nerves.'

'But Rory must have been enamoured.'

'You know I never saw it? You'd think he would have been as proud as punch bringing her back here and setting up home, and being invited to tea with her, but no, not a sign of it. A duty undertaken, that was what crossed my mind. Just a duty.'

'Curious.' A possibility was crossing Murray's mind, too, but he was too delicate to say it to a woman he had only just met. He cleared his throat. 'I have had two suggestions put to me already concerning this tragedy, and I should like, if I may, to ask your opinion on them.'

She nodded, a woman not unused to having her opinions consulted.

'The first is that Rory, angry at Jack for missing the recital, attacked him in some way and in defending himself Jack killed Rory.'

'No!' She was shocked. 'Jack would never ... yet if he were defending himself?' She tried to picture it, and amended her statement tentatively. 'Jack might, if he were indeed defending himself. I should say he is a strong man, and in that he and Rory would have been well matched. But would Rory ever attack him? Physically, I mean?' She thought hard. 'I cannot imagine it. Maybe. I know Rory had a bad temper, but I have never seen him hurt anyone, or even threaten to. As I think I said, he was a gentle man, at heart. And Jack would never attack him unprovoked,' she said with certainty, then gave a little laugh. 'I don't know if I have helped you there or not. What was the other suggestion?'

'That someone had followed the McArthurs here from Perthshire with the intention of doing them harm, that that was why Mrs. McArthur spent most of her days in hiding in their house, and that possibly she is in fact their prime target.'

Miss Bogue stared at him.

'Well,' she said after a moment. 'That is simply extraordinary. Someone has been reading too many novels, I think!'

'You think so?' Murray smiled. 'Then perhaps I can set aside that theory. Thank you, Miss Bogue, for bringing common sense to bear on it!'

'You are teasing me now, Mr. Murray. I shall take you to my father and be rid of you.'

'No more than I deserve, I am sure,' he agreed, nodding sadly, and followed her with a happy grin out of the kirkyard.

Indeed it was a short walk to Mr. Bogue's cloth warehouse, which stood to the south side of Market Street at the point where it widened and spread to accommodate the actual marketplace. Most of the buildings there were elderly, but Mr. Bogue's was a smart new construction, with good tall windows to make the most of the northerly light, both facilitating customers' choices inside, and tempting them with cunningly arranged goods from the outside. Murray wondered if Mr. Bogue had been much in Edinburgh or Glasgow for the whole enterprise had a modern, energetic feel, and the cloths inside were rich and bright with the latest dyes and prints. The place smelled of wool and wood, but also of lavender, a pleasing touch that was no doubt practical, too: an outbreak of moths in a cloth warehouse would be exceptionally bad for business.

The atmosphere of sweet fragrances and soft cloth, however, was rather dispelled by shouting going on somewhere in a rear office.

'Always check the coins before you accept them!' a man was instructing in a tone that implied this was something he had said a few times previously. 'Particularly from a stranger! You know we've had trouble before!'

'Aye, sir,' came a faint acknowledgement. Miss Bogue paused and cocked her head to listen, a little frown on her face.

'It's no damn' used you standing there like a piece of damp ravelling and saying 'Aye, sir', is it? Who's going to make up that shilling?'

'Ah, me, sir,' came the faint voice, accepting the inevitable with sorrow. Miss Bogue's lips twisted in a faint smile.

'And what do you ken about this stranger, eh?'

'I think it was a fellow, sir,' said the other, with a sigh. Miss Bogue looked at Murray with widened eyes and a shrug, and led the way through boldly into the back offices of the shop.

Murray recognised Mr. Bogue from the recital: a man giving the impression of melting from his head down, his eyes sagging and his jaws lugubrious. His interlocutor was a lad of about fourteen, colourless of hair and eyes, prominent of tooth and ear, and generally failing to give the impression of one who would go far. Mr. Bogue, however, turned and beamed a smile at both Murray and his daughter as soon as they appeared.

'It was Mr. Murray, was it not?' He bowed readily, requiring, Murray supposed, some rearrangement of the layers that surrounded him. Murray returned the bow.

'It is indeed. Thank you again for your hospitality on Wednesday evening, Mr. Bogue.'

A frown was poured over Mr. Bogue's face.

'Aye, well, no doubt you'll have heard it didna end well for one of the musicians, I'm afraid.'

'Mr. Murray found poor Rory, Father,' put in Miss Bogue quickly. Bogue eyed him with new interest.

'Did you? Did you now, sir? That must have been a distressing thing altogether, I'm sure.'

'It was certainly not very pleasant,' Murray agreed smoothly. 'As I have already explained to Miss Bogue, I have some experience in matters of this kind, and Constable Round has asked me to assist him to find the murderer. Of course as I did not know

Mr. McArthur, this will only be possible if I can build up some kind of picture of him from those who knew him well, such as you, Mr. Bogue.'

Bogue drew up his lips, fighting gravity.

'I see your point, sir, of course. And you want to ask me about him?'

'That's right, if you'll be willing to afford me the benefit of what must have been some years of careful observation.' There was no harm in a little flattery, and Murray had the feeling that Mr. Bogue might be a little more susceptible to it than some. Mr. Bogue considered.

'You'll be wanting a word in private, then. Sarah, take this young fool home for his dinner and see if you can worm out of him any more about the fellow that gave him the bad coin.'

'Of course, Father.' Sarah Bogue laid a kindly arm across the lad's shoulders and guided him out of the shop. 'No doubt we shall meet again, Mr. Murray!'

'I hope so!'

'That's what comes of employing a country lad, Mr. Murray: they just don't have the breadth of experience you or I would have had at that age, begging your pardon, sir. He took this in today,' he laid his hand out flat, showing Murray the silver shilling in his yellow-white palm. 'False as the fifteen of spades, of course. See? Feel the thing.' He handed it to Murray. The coin was indeed a little off: perhaps a fraction heavier than it ought to be, perhaps a fraction thinner. It was hard to tell without a real shilling to hand. Mr. Bogue, as if he knew the problem, produced one from a box on the counter beside him.

'Here's a proper 1817 shilling: see? That one has the motto from the 1816 coin, but the date 1817.'

Murray studied the two coins: the sound one had 'GEOR. D:G:' then 'BRITT: REX 1817' on it, while the one Bogue said was false had 'GEORGIUS III DEI GRATIA 1817'.

'It's hard to remember what is right and what isn't, these days,' he said, 'with all the new coinage. You were quick to spot the fake.'

Mr. Bogue took the false coin back with a satisfied look.

'Trouble is, the lad's new in from the country. He says a stranger gave it to him but they're almost all strangers to him yet.'

He sighed. 'Ah, well: I don't suppose I'll stop the whole amount from him. Not the first time.' He put the good coin back in the box and the bad one on a shelf nearby. 'I'll take that to Constable Round later, no doubt. Now, Mr. Murray: would you like to take that stool, or would you be more comfortable standing, the height you are, sir?'

Murray smiled.

'I'll stand, I think, thank you.'

'And you want to know about Rory McArthur. Well, I dinna ken rightly what to tell you. He was a solid clerk but no good as a salesman.' Murray waited a moment, but Mr. Bogue appeared to have come to a stop.

'In what way was he no good?' he prompted.

'Ah, well, he had no great feel for the cloth, first of all,' Bogue went on happily enough. 'You need a feel for it to be able to sell it: you need to know what will work for this or for that, and what someone will like, and how to sell them something a wee thing more expensive than they came in for,' he stopped briefly with a sideways glance at Murray, hoping he had not noticed this indiscretion. Murray's face was bland. 'Or to sell them not quite what they came in for but what they could afford that would do nearly as good a job,' he added, assuming a more angelic expression.

'And that was not something McArthur could do?'

'Nah,' said Bogue wearily. 'He just didna have it in him. Nor did Jack, come to that, but Jack could pretend. Jack's a salesman, all right, no question about that. He has a great way of getting alongside the customer, making them feel he knows them better than they know themselves. Rory would never go that far. He was too – well, maybe reserved? Maybe shy? I dinna ken. Jack doesna have the same problem, anyway.'

'But you didn't keep him on after the apprenticeships were ended?'

'No, not him either. See, Jack could sell anything, but he was never here on time and when he was he idled about the place all the time he could. Rory, now, he was reliable: a deaf man could tell the town clock was striking if they saw Rory walk in the door for work. And he was a good clerk, always neat and steady, if not quick. Jack was quick, but he made a gey lot of mistakes, and that's no good for a businessman.'

'Of course not.' Murray pondered for a moment. 'I gather they were friends, though, despite their differences.'

'Oh, aye, they were that. They and my own lad, Sandy, they enjoyed the music together, always had since they started at the college. Sandy loves his music!'

'Sandy and Jack must have known each other before college, surely, both living in the town?'

Mr. Bogue's liquid eyes slid back towards Murray again for a second, and away, looking up at some fine tweeds on an upper shelf.

'I dinna ken that they did, at all.'

'Well, these things happen. But they all remained friends, once they had met?'

'Oh, aye, indeed. See, in here there was always a bit of an edge to them, the two of them. My boy had no quarrels with either of them, but sometimes they just rubbed each other up the wrong way. Jack likes to be best, ken, always has, though he runs at it and doesn't do the job properly. Rory was steadier, as I say, but sometimes Jack could just rile him. I mind twa three days I came in here and Rory was just standing there, thumping his fist into a bale of cloth, over and over again, his face the colour of that broadcloth there –' He nodded to a roll from which Miss Bogue's red spencer could have been cut.

'But at least I suppose he was hitting the bales, rather than whoever had made him angry,' said Murray reasonably.

'Oh, it'll have been Jack, nae doubt,' said Mr. Bogue with a sigh. 'But worse was the day I came in and found Rory on his own, sitting on that very stool. See that dent there in the wood of the desk?' He pointed to a gouge, relatively freshly made. 'Feel that, feel how deep it is. There was my lad with his penknife, just thump, thump, thump into the wood. I took a shilling off his pay for that damage. Mind, I didn't have the nerve to do it at the time, not with him holding a knife and that look on his face. I did it later, when he'd calmed down.'

'What did he say?'

'Och, just that he was sorry. I didna ask him why he was angry, and he didna tell me.'

Murray considered, feeling the depth of the gouge through his gloves. He could picture the scene.

'How long ago was that?'

'Och, ages ago. Before he left here, of course. Before he married, and all.'

'Of course. Well, thank you very much: that has been enlightening.'

Bogue straightened, nodding affably.

'Aye, well, you have to get to know your employees, to get the best out of them,' he said, quite satisfied with himself and his workplace. Murray pushed himself away from the bench on which he had been leaning.

'One more thing, Mr. Bogue, if I may. Two possibilities have been suggested to me for the solution of this crime, and I should like you, as one who knew Rory McArthur well, to tell me how they strike you.'

'Of course.'

'I have no attachment to either theory,' Murray reassured him, 'so please speak as you find. The first is the idea that Rory, angry over Jack's failure to come to the recital, attacked him and Jack killed Rory while defending himself. How does that sound to you? Likely at all?'

'Well, I've tellt you about Rory's temper ... But I've never seen him hit Jack, or anybody else, I have to say. Yes, he punched the bales and yes, he made that hole in the desk, but I always thought that was enough for him to calm down. What does Jack say?'

'Jack has not been accused yet.'

'He'd likely tell the truth if you came out with it to him,' said Bogue, but he did not sound entirely sure. 'What's the other notion, then?'

'There is some idea that someone from Perthshire – Rory was from Perthshire, was he not? – had come to St. Andrews to harm either Rory or Mrs. McArthur, someone from their past, with a grudge, perhaps.'

He waited for Mr. Bogue to dismiss this fantasy as quickly as his daughter had done, but the clothier pondered the idea for a little.

'D'you know, that doesna sound that unreasonable to me?' he said at last. 'I always thought to myself that Rory was a man with a secret. He never spoke of his family or his friends at home. It was as if his life had only begun when he came here as a student. I dinna think he ever even said the name of his village – or town, or whatever it was he came from, though I had the idea he was a country lad. It wasna that he refused to answer questions, he just had a way with him that made you think he would if you tried, so you never bothered. When he said he was away home, after the end of the apprenticeship, you could have knocked me down, I was that taken aback.' Murray tried to banish from his mind the sudden image of trying to haul Mr. Bogue to his feet again, had he been knocked down. 'It was as if the fellow had said he was away to – I dinna ken – some mythical place. The Land of Faerie, maybe. But he still didn't say where it was he was going home to. And when he came back again, with the wee wifie and all, I half thought he'd have aged a hundred years or some such. Hi! Listen to me! Daft, that's what it is. But to think someone might have come away out of such a place, to do him harm – that seems as likely to me as anything else, and more than some.'

Chapter Nine

'I had hoped to speak to your son Sandy, too, Mr. Bogue,' said Murray, about to take his leave. 'Miss Bogue thought he might be here.'

'He was, indeed,' agreed Bogue, 'but I sent him to take a few yards of cloth to a particular customer who favours him. Sandy knows his cloth, though I say so myself, but he has no interest in the business. Aye, well, it comes and it goes,' he added obscurely, 'and maybe I'll persuade him yet. He'll be away home for his dinner, no doubt. We eat early: we dinna keep very fashionable hours, you'll be thinking, Mr. Murray! But it's easier with the trade.'

'I'm sure,' said Murray politely. 'No doubt you'll be heading back yourself?'

'Aye, aye, in a wee while. Go on ahead and welcome if you want to talk to him. No doubt he'll be willing to help all he can. He was gey upset when he heard the news.' He nodded to emphasise his point, as he walked Murray back to the front door of the shop. 'He'll want to catch the fellow that did it, whether he's from here or from Perthshire – or from Faerie!' he added, chuckling at his own notions.

The old house, when Murray reached it, was full of the scents of some complex end-of-the-week dinner made of the oddments left over during the week. Murray was made painfully aware that it had been a long time since breakfast, and he hoped his stomach would not rumble as he spoke to Sandy Bogue. It diminished one's authority, somewhat.

This time the maid was happy to acknowledge that Sandy was at home, and that he was awaiting dinner in the parlour. Rather to

Murray's surprise this did not mean the cosy solar where he had spoken with Miss Bogue: instead the maid meant the impressive barrel-vaulted drawing room where the recital had taken place. The room was brighter than Murray had expected in the daytime, a row of arched windows facing east allowing the last of the morning's rays to spill butter-yellow light on the stone floor. With its high ceiling and unlit fireplace, it was a chilly enough room on a cool March morning, but Sandy was seated at the pianoforte, playing Mozart with his eyes shut, and did not even hear, apparently, Murray being announced. The maid gave a minute shrug, curtseyed, and left Murray alone with Sandy and the music, a situation which Murray was only too happy to enjoy. Sandy Bogue was an excellent pianist.

At last, however, the music came to an end, and Sandy sagged back on the stool, and opened his eyes. When he saw Murray, the eyes widened a little further, and he pulled himself to his feet.

'I beg your pardon, sir, I did not hear you come in.'

'The maid did announce me, but then she left: I think she feared to interrupt such a splendid performance. I was at the recital the other evening, too, along with my friends the Shaws: my name is Charles Murray of Letho.'

'Alexander Bogue,' said the young man, bowing. He had the same toffee gold hair as his sister, but his expression spoke rather less of an intelligent engagement in his surroundings. In a servant Murray would have had him pegged as lazy, and sent him to Robbins for correction. 'If you're looking for my father, I believe he'll be back shortly. We'll be dining soon,' he added, with a deprecatory smile.

'I've just come from speaking with him, actually. I should like a conversation with you, too, if we can manage to avoid your dinner time.'

'Oh, yes?'

'Concerning Rory McArthur.'

'Oh.' The young man gestured Murray to a padded upright chair, and took another himself. The furniture was chilly, and they could almost see their breath.

'I have been asked to help investigate his murder, Mr. Bogue, and so of course it is most helpful to talk to those who knew him and who saw him on the night of his death, to find out what might have been happening to him around that time and therefore why he might have died.'

'You mean you want to find out if I killed him?' There was a half-smile on Sandy's face, but only half.

'Well, did you?' Murray responded, acknowledging the smile.

'No, of course I didn't. He was my friend. But I suppose even friends kill each other, sometimes.'

'I'm afraid they do, yes.' Murray paused, but Sandy was gazing into the black fireplace and said nothing. 'Tell me about your friend, then, if you will.'

Sandy sighed.

'Well, Rory was a dull fellow, to be honest, but a good fiddle-player.' He gave himself a little shake. 'I'm trying to be honest. And he was dull, but I liked him, all the same. And not just for the fiddle-playing, though in my book that can take you a long way.' He tried another half-smile. He was used, Murray thought, to charming.

'You met at the college?'

'Aye, we did. We got on well enough: he was a hard worker, though, and had not much money, and he took everything gey seriously. I suppose we teased him a bit.'

'"We" being you and Jack Swanson?'

Sandy grinned.

'That's right. But we meant no harm by it – or I didn't, anyway.'

'He seemed pretty angry that Jack did not turn up for the recital the other night.'

'Oh, aye?' Sandy blinked, as if reminding himself why they were having this conversation. 'Aye, I suppose. Rory could be bad-tempered enough, if something riled him.'

'What kind of thing riled him, then?'

'Well … people not doing what they said they would. He didn't like someone saying they would turn up, and then not doing it.'

'He went looking for Jack, didn't he? Do you think they would have fought?'

'Fought?' Sandy looked uncomfortable. 'I dinna ken. I don't think they ever fought, not with their fists. I mean, they argued, because Jack liked annoying Rory and Rory would get angry, he couldn't seem to help it, but he never punched Jack, never that I heard. And I'm sure Jack would have said if he had.'

'You didn't by any chance go with Rory to look for Jack on Wednesday night? I mean, you must have been curious as to why Jack didn't turn up, weren't you?'

'I suppose ...' Sandy considered, then grinned. 'I suppose I left that to Rory. I mean, Jack hadn't turned up, but Wee Dod played, and everyone was happy, so why bother trailing after Jack to find out what had happened? I went to my bed,' he said, as if that were the only logical thing to do.

'You graduated A.M. last summer, didn't you, Mr. Bogue?'

'Aye, that's right.' Sandy relaxed, though to tell the truth he had not been very tense. Murray wondered if he knew what tension was.

'And what are your plans now, if I might ask?'

'Och, well, who knows? I might look for a parish, maybe: maybe one in Edinburgh where I could get to some concerts and such. Or I could teach, I suppose ...'

'The world is your oyster?'

'Aye, pretty much.' Sandy slid him another grin, happy with his lot.

'Oh, that's another thing:' Murray had been about to rise. 'What do you know about Rory's wedding? And his marriage?'

Sandy sat up sharply, making the chair legs bang on the floor.

'His marriage? Why's that? Is Mrs. McArthur all right?'

'Yes, yes, she is,' said Murray hurriedly, taken aback. 'She's staying with friends. There was some talk that whoever killed Rory might be someone from Perthshire, perhaps with a connexion to his wife.'

'A connexion to his wife? Is she in danger, then?'

'Have you seen much of her?'

Sandy appeared to calm himself, by force.

'Much of her? No, not really. Maybe a dozen times?'

That's more than anyone else I have asked, Murray thought.

'Did you visit them at home?'

'Aye, I did. They had a nice wee house there: she made it fine and comfortable for him.'

'Was that you on your own that Rory invited, or was it Jack as well? Or other people?'

'I don't remember any other people ever,' said Sandy, considering. 'Aye, Jack was there a few times. With me,' he added, for emphasis.

'Did you form the impression that Mr. and Mrs. McArthur were – that they were happy together?'

Sandy's head tilted back, and he gazed at the barrel vault for a moment.

'Happy ... Aye, I think they liked each other well enough. They were easy together.'

'But they were newly married: was there not more to it than that?'

Sandy gave a sudden, surprising laugh.

'Well, there's times when you're newly married for love, and times when you're newly married to, ah, correct a mistake, isn't there?' he asked, flashing an odd look at Murray.

'You mean they may have been required to marry?'

'Well, the bairn came along mighty quickly, did she not?' He beamed, shuffling in his chair. 'Mind you, Rory was the last person I would have expected to make a mistake like that: that would mean he might even have acted on an impulse for once in his life.'

'Sometimes, when one meets a particularly enticing girl, perhaps ...?' Murray suggested.

'Even then ... and I always thought there was someone that he had his eye on in St. Andrews. But there, he made his bed and being Rory that was the only bed he lay on. Shame, though,' he finished, thoughtfully.

'A shame?'

'Um, I mean, if they weren't really happy with each other. But Rory would always do the right thing by her, of course.'

'Of course.' Murray drew out his watch and opened it. 'I should leave you to your dinner, Mr. Bogue. May I return if I think of further questions to ask about Mr. McArthur?'

'Oh, aye, of course.' Sandy kicked himself out of his chair as Murray rose. He turned as the door opened behind them.

'Mr. Sandy, it's dinner time.'

It was the boy Wee Dod who had played so well at the recital. He started apologetically when he saw Murray, and nervously flicked his fringe out of his eyes.

'Aye, I'm coming,' said Sandy. 'Will you see Mr. Murray

out?'

'Aye, sir.'

Sandy bowed farewell, and disappeared somewhere else in the house. Wee Dod displayed a tendency to scuttle on his sturdy little legs, possibly anxious for his dinner, and Murray tried to slow his own striding pace to make a little time for conversation before they would reach the front door.

'That was you the other night with the fiddle, wasn't it?' Murray asked as an introduction. 'You played very well.'

'You're very kind, sir,' said Wee Dod, over his shoulder.

'How long have you been playing?'

'Och, since I was a bairn.'

That could not have been very long, Murray reflected, but it might have been a few years.

'Someone told me you were not so keen on playing in front of people.'

'Aye, well, I'll hae to get used to it. We're a man down now altogether, no just for the night.' He nodded to himself, rather grown-up for his age.

'It'll have been a dreadful shock about Roderick McArthur, I should think.'

Wee Dod's shoulders hunched instinctively.

'Aye, sir. It was that.' He rounded a corner, waited for Murray to catch up, then paused. 'And there was us thinking it would be Mr. Swanson found – dead.'

'Mr. Jack Swanson? The one you replaced?'

'Aye, him.'

'Why's that, then?'

Wee Dod's eyes flickered around the passageway, perhaps checking for eavesdroppers.

'We thought – well, the family thought – Mr. McArthur would do for him.'

'Just because he had missed the recital?'

'The what?'

'The music. The concert.'

'Oh, aye.' Wee Dod hesitated. 'Aye, that.' He may have felt he had not said enough, for he added quickly, 'The master and Mr. Sandy went out after him, to see was he all right. I dinna ken if they found him, though, because they werena back for hours. I was away to my bed,' he added with virtuous emphasis.

'And that was the night of the concert? Two nights ago? They went looking for Jack Swanson, to make sure he was safe?' Wee Dod looked uncertain, so Murray reassured him, 'That was good of them, particularly to take so long over it. I wonder if they found him quickly but stayed to talk, or if they took a long time to find him.'

'Aye, well, that I dinna ken, sir,' said Wee Dod, shaking his head sadly. 'You'll have to ask the master. Or Mr. Sandy, a course.'

'Of course. Thank you for telling me, Dod. I'm trying to help find Mr. McArthur's killer, so if you remember anything that might help I'm staying at the Shaws' house – do you know Professor Shaw?'

'Aye, he allus comes to our decitals,' said Wee Dod, proud of his new word.

'Well, that's where I'm staying, or where I can be reached, if you think of anything useful.'

'Aye, sir, I'd be happy to. Mr. McArthur was kind to me, times. He let me borrow his bow once when the dog had got at my own.'

'Yes, that was good of him.' Despite their speed they had at last reached the gate on to South Street, and Wee Dod politely opened it to show Murray out. 'Thank you for your help, Dod. I hope to see you again.'

'Sir.'

Murray strolled back down South Street, thinking over what he had learned. Jack and Sandy had seen more of Mrs. McArthur than anyone else, which at least implied that Rory had trusted them if there was indeed a threat to Janet McArthur. But Sandy and his father had gone after Rory, or gone looking for Jack, after the recital, apparently to see that Jack was safe and that Rory had not 'done for' him – but Sandy had told him quite calmly that he had gone straight to bed after the guests had gone. Why hide their concern? After all, Rory had not done for Jack in the end. Had Jack done for Rory? Mr. Bogue and his daughter did not think it likely – or so they had said.

And there was another thing he had learned: he would not at

all mind having another excuse for a stroll with Miss Bogue.

On his way along South Street he chanced on Constable Round, who agreed to walk with him to the Shaws' house. Taking the path that circumnavigated the rambling structure, they came upon Professor Shaw, once more disconsolate in the garden. He was seated on a stone bench and staring into the fishpond in which Rory McArthur's head had been submerged. He was not so deep in his reverie, though, as not to hear them approach: he turned, and smiled weakly.

'All my fish are dead, Charles!'

'All of them?' Murray was taken aback.

'Well, the ones in this pond. My poor little rudd!' He sighed.

'Rudd are not particularly hard to come by, are they?' Murray was an occasional fisherman, in his own streams.

'No, no. But of course I do not want to put more in here until I find out what killed these ones.'

'A heron?' suggested Constable Round, his mind no doubt running on violent death.

'Walter has been watching from the bushes,' said Professor Shaw, nodding to a small shrubbery. Murray glanced over and to his surprise saw that Walter had made himself a little nest inside it with his notebook and pencil. He waved the pencil at Murray, but maintained his watchful silence. 'He has not reported a heron. And the fish are not gone, they are dead. And anyway, why would a heron take the rudd, at the bottom of the pool, and not the minnows and sticklebacks which seem to be thriving higher up in the water?'

'Some kind of contamination, then,' said Murray. 'Perhaps you need to flush out this pond and downstream.'

'Perhaps – but then what will I be flushing downstream? What else might I kill that way?' Poor Professor Shaw was deep in gloom. 'I should find some way of examining the water, I suppose.'

'Well,' said Murray, seeing Constable Round shuffling his feet, 'I brought the Constable here to discuss what we have each discovered so far about poor Rory's death. Would you like to be a part of the discussion, sir? Or shall we move out of your way, perhaps into the house?'

'No, no, here is perfectly all right,' said the Professor, putting his worries to one side to concentrate. Constable Round looked mildly relieved: he seemed to Murray to be an outdoor sort of person, not one for parlours. Murray joined the Professor on the stone bench, and once again Constable Round arranged himself around his staff.

'Why don't you start, Constable?' said Murray. The man nodded solemnly.

'Well, I havena been able to do much in the business since you left yesterday. We've had twa-three incidents in the town – it's been gey busy,' he admitted.

'What did you think of our talk with Mrs. McArthur, though, now we've both had time to reflect?'

'Aye, well,' said the constable. 'I been thinking about that. What if some fellow in Perthshire was jealous of Roderick McArthur? Yon lassie's gey pretty: what if some fellow was chawed and followed them here to get rid of Roderick and take her?'

'They'd need to be very jealous. And why now? Why not before?'

'Maybe they didna ken where she was.'

'If she married Rory and left their home village, St. Andrews strikes me as a good place to start,' said Murray, unimpressed by the deductive powers of this hypothetical person.

'Aye, well, all kinds of things can cause delays,' said the constable, standing his ground. Murray acknowledged it.

'You're quite right: who knows what might have detained them. That's part of the problem, though, isn't it? No one seems to know much about where Rory came from, or why he suddenly went back there. I put the idea of a Perthshire murderer to Mr. Bogue and to his daughter: Miss Bogue dismissed it as a fantasy, but Mr. Bogue thought it might fit as Rory was so mysterious about his background.'

'Oh, aye? You've been to see the Bogues?' The constable smiled and nodded. 'I'm glad you did that, sir: Mr. Bogue is getting a wee bit up in the buckle to talk to a carlie wee constable!'

'His business seems prosperous,' Professor Shaw put in, anxiously defensive of anyone. 'And his musical evenings are just lovely.'

'Aye, I suppose,' conceded the constable, who had probably never attended one of them. 'And yes, he's doing affa well in yon warehouse of his. Oftimes I've caught my ain daughter with her neb up against the glass there, admiring the clouts. And I've heard tell he's generous with his hospitality, and all.'

'Maybe he should invite some more people from other ranks of society,' said Professor Shaw, worried now. 'Perhaps if I mentioned it to him – not that he has any need to listen to me, but he's always so kind ...'

'I'm sure he'd listen all right, sir, if it would be anything to improve his trade,' said the constable.

'Well, anyway,' said Murray, drawing both of them back to the matter in hand, 'he did not think it likely that Jack Swanson killed Rory in self-defence. No one seems to think that likely, principally because although Rory was well known to have had a bad temper, he had never been known to hit anyone. Things, yes,' he added, remembering the nasty gouge on the desktop, 'but not people.'

'Something might have provoked him. Pushed him just that wee bit further,' said Constable Round.

'Surely that would have to be something more than simply not turning up for an ordinary recital, when there was someone else who could take his place,' Professor Shaw observed.

'You would have thought so, wouldn't you?' Murray agreed. 'However ... Apparently Mr. Bogue and Sandy were so concerned about Rory going off to look for Jack Swanson that they headed out after him – or to look for Jack.'

'Did they indeed?' asked the constable. His fingers performed a little trill on his staff. Professor Shaw frowned.

'That seems strange. Unless they just wanted a walk before bed and that was an excuse?'

'Well, maybe,' said Murray. 'What makes me wonder about it, though, is that Sandy Bogue claims to have gone straight to bed after the recital. I never challenged him, for it was only afterwards I was told they went out. Wee Dod mentioned it, and I cannot see why he would have lied.'

'Now that is peculiar, indeed,' agreed Professor Shaw. 'Though he may have misremembered.'

'Maybe,' said Constable Round, but he sounded as dubious as

Murray felt.

'I could go back and make sure,' Murray said. 'I could ask Mrs. Bogue, or indeed Miss Bogue ... Or even Mr. Bogue – after all, it was only Sandy that claimed he had gone to bed. He may have had some reason to say so, while his father might be quite open about the expedition. Except - since I was asking him about that evening, you would think he would think to mention it.'

'Aye, you would,' agreed Round heavily. Professor Shaw said nothing, shaking his head sadly.

'Is there a reason why Bogue and Swanson might not be friendly?' Murray asked suddenly. Both the constable and the professor looked surprised.

'No, I don't think so,' said Professor Shaw.

'I canna think of a'thing,' agreed Round. 'They've just never much moved in the same circles. Different guilds, ken.'

'Of course.'

'What now, then, sir?'

Murray frowned, thinking.

'We need to find someone who was about that night and might have seen something. Really we need to track Rory McArthur's movements from the time he left the Bogues' house until he ended up in the fishpond. If the Bogues will admit to being out and about, maybe they can help, at least with telling us where he was not. And according to Wee Dod they were out for hours: did they find Jack quickly and spend time talking with him? Did they have trouble finding him – and if so, then where was he, for he says he was at home? or did they do something else entirely? Where were they for all that time?'

'That's going to depend on them talking to us,' Constable Round pointed out.

'It is, yes. We need to find out more about where the McArthurs came from: surely Mrs. McArthur can at least tell us the name of their village, or town, or estate, or something.'

Constable Round emitted a small snort of disbelief, with which Murray sadly agreed.

'What else, then?'

Round and Shaw considered.

'I dinna ken, not just yet,' admitted the constable.

'I need to find out why my fish are dead,' added Professor

Shaw sadly.

'Can you think who might have been about to see anyone?' Murray asked Round. 'There's a night watchman, isn't there?'

'Aye, I'll talk to him.'

'Good. I'll try to put together a list of the people who were at the recital. Some of them left the house ahead of Rory, and some after. Perhaps one or two of them saw at least the direction he was taking.'

'And I'll try to find out why my fish are dead,' said Professor Shaw again. Murray patted his shoulder, and went to see the constable off.

At the front gate he decided to go back into the house, rather than return to the garden and the question of the dead fish. He pushed open the front door without troubling to bother the manservant with the bell, and considered what to do first. The hall was quiet, the only sound a bracket clock ticking on the wall. It was as if the house were holding its breath, and for a moment he did not move a muscle. Then he heard it: a sob, breaking out after being held back. It came from the parlour. The door was ajar, and he reached out long fingers and pushed it gently open.

The room was dim, the fire unlit. But curled up in a ball of misery in the corner of the sopha was Flavia, her face soaked with tears.

Chapter Ten

'Oh, Miss Flavia – I beg your pardon,' said Murray, seeing that he was not going to be able to pretend he had never been there.

'Mr. Murray!' she cried, obviously resigned to the same realisation.

'May I be of any assistance?' He had not seen her since her flight up the garden when Rory McArthur's body had been identified: it was just possible she had seen something that everyone else had missed, for she was not a stupid girl. He allowed her a moment to answer, then tried again. 'These events have been very upsetting, even for a strong constitution like yours.'

'Oh, but I had particular reason –' she broke off. 'I thought …'

'You and Mr. McArthur were friends?' Murray suggested encouragingly. He crouched down in front of her, not too close, but enough that she could talk down to him without having to raise her head. She pulled herself up, uncurling her legs from her skirts on the sopha. Her lashes dropped over her plump cheeks.

'We had an understanding. It seems a long time ago, now.'

'Before he was married, I suppose!'

'Oh! Yes, of course!'

'Did your parents know?'

The question produced no guilty looks: there had been nothing clandestine here.

'I think they guessed, but there was nothing official, you know. But we were both still very young,' she added, with all the condescension of a sixteen year old just out.

'Would you like to tell me about it? About him?' He made his voice even more gentle. She smoothed her skirts, gulping down another sob, then wiped her eyes with the backs of her hands, batting her hair.

'He was so handsome! He was Father's student, you know, he stayed here just like Walter is doing. For a month or so, anyway, then he went into the college when he matriculated. Father was interested in trees at that time, mostly fruit trees, and I used to help – help with collecting the blossoms ...' The tears welled up again and her voice broke, but she managed to pull it back together. 'I was only a girl, but he was so kind! Just as kind as handsome. Then he went to the college, but he would come back for supper sometimes, and he would play his fiddle for us, and when he left the college I was so pleased he took the post at Mr. Bogue's and would still be here.'

'Did he ever speak to you of an understanding?'

'Yes!' Flavia's eyes challenged him, then seemed to defeat themselves. 'Well, not exactly. No, not really. But I could see it in his face. He was really fond of me, I know he was. And when he said he was going home, he came to say goodbye – to Father, of course, but he seemed to say it to me, too, and to say he would not be long.'

'He intended coming back? He had not just decided to go and use his clerical skills at home?'

She stopped, frowning.

'I'm sure he gave the impression he was coming back. But he didn't say he was coming back with a wife!'

'That was certainly a drawback. You must have been terribly shocked.'

'Oh, I was!' She turned wide eyes on him. 'It was awful! And her such a bitty wee thing: I couldn't see why any man would marry her!' She wriggled her plump shoulders: the new fashion for puffed sleeves certainly enhanced the breadth she already had. 'But I don't think he was in love with her, you know. I'm quite sure he wasn't. And I just thought – well, maybe if I hang on ...'

'Hang on and what?'

'Well ...' she had the grace to look a little shamefaced, 'she didn't look very strong, and people die, you know. In childbed, and so on ...'

'Flavia!'

'I know! I'm not proud of how I feel, Mr. Murray! Honestly, I'm not. But I was very fond of Rory, and I know he was fond of me, I know it.'

Was Flavia the person behind Miss Bogue's impression that Rory had a sweetheart somewhere in St. Andrews? He did not seem like a flighty person, from all Murray had heard. Yet even to appear to encourage Flavia and then run off to marry Janet did not seem entirely in character, if everyone had portrayed him accurately. And no one so far claimed that he and Janet gave any impression of being in love: it certainly had more of the air of a couple forced to marry because a child was on the way. Yet again, Rory had not seemed like the kind of person who would allow himself to fall into that predicament: he seemed exactly like the kind of person who would face up to such responsibilities afterwards. Had he perhaps taken on the sweetheart of someone else, someone at home for whom he felt he had an obligation to make amends? A younger brother? Someone absconded? Someone dead? That made more sense – but then what was this threat that Janet feared so much?

Flavia had for the most part recovered from her sobbing fit, though her face was still desolate. There might not, in truth, have been much hope for her, but she had not seen it that way: perhaps now when the mourning was over she could leave the thought of Rory McArthur behind and look elsewhere for a suitor.

He was about to rise, feeling his knees had stiffened, when another question occurred to him.

'If you knew Rory well, did he ever say anything about where he was from?'

'Perthshire,' she said straightaway.

'More specifically?'

She raised her eyebrows.

'I don't know that he ever said. And Father wouldn't know: you know that usually he takes students on recommendation from someone – like Walter – when he's preparing them for the college, but I remember that Rory was unusual, for he just turned up in St. Andrews and asked about, and Father took a liking to him and agreed to take him. Why do you ask?'

'He never seems to have spoken about his home with anyone. It's a little odd, don't you think?'

'A bit.' She shrugged. 'Oh, it was somewhere near Aberfeldy, though. I remember he mentioned going to the market there.'

'Aberfeldy? Are you sure?' It was not particularly specific, but it could help.

'Definitely Aberfeldy. I remember it because I said 'the birks of Aberfeldy', you know, from Burns, and he seemed surprised I'd heard of it.'

'Somewhere near Aberfeldy. Well, it's a start,' said Murray. 'Did you hear anything that night? You sleep facing the back of the house, I think?'

'I do, but I didn't hear anything. I sleep very deeply, you know.' She sighed, as though a restless night would have been more suitable for her unhappy thoughts.

'Well, thank you, Miss Flavia: I know it's a terrible shock now, but the pain will pass, I promise.'

'Oh!' She looked more closely at his mourning clothes, as if suddenly remembering. 'Of course. Thank you.'

She gazed up at him gratefully, with the kind of concentrated compassion on her face of a young person who does not yet quite comprehend grief, but knows they ought to feel it. Murray bowed and left, a guilty nag at his heart. He felt no grief for the wife for whom he wore the mourning, and would be more than glad when his two years was done. But he knew grief, all the same.

It was not yet dinner time in this establishment, but sweet smells of cooking were wafting from the kitchen and he was already famished. He decided to return to the garden to see if he could work out, with Professor Shaw to start with, a list of those who had been at the recital on Wednesday night and might or might not have seen something as Rory McArthur had left the Bogues' house. He went to his room to find paper and a pen, then headed back to the garden.

It was quite a large garden, and of course neither plain nor straightforward, but after ten minutes or so he was fairly sure that Walter and Professor Shaw were no longer in it. He wondered where they had gone, and was about to tour it again to make sure when he heard his name called. Looking about he could see no one at first: then it occurred to him to look up, and he found a face peering over the wall from the Swansons' garden. Mr. Swanson must have been standing on a ladder, for Murray could not quite picture the man climbing a tree.

'Mr. Murray!' called Thomas Swanson. 'Are you busy? Will you come round? I think we have found something that may interest you!'

'Of course,' agreed Murray at once, starting up the garden.

'It's quicker if you go by the bottom gate,' said Swanson, waving his hand down the slope towards the rills and fishponds. 'If you can,' he added.

Murray made his way carefully over the little stone-slab bridges and found himself at the bottom wall of the garden, where a gate stood closed near the point where the diverted stream left by a culvert to return to the mill lade. He tried the gate and it opened easily, only latched with a wooden latch. Outside, he found himself on a broad and well-worn path between the garden walls and the mill lade from which Professor Shaw was drawing his rills: the land here was flat after the gentle slopes down from South Street, and on the other side of the lade a sweep of farmland – partly, he thought, owned by St. Mary's College – lay between the lade and the Kinness Burn. A cowherd was amongst his cattle, seeing to one heavily pregnant cow, and a ploughed field was tinged with green. There was a decent cottage, more a gentleman's fancy than a labourer's hovel, amidst the farmland, with a carriage drive running to it as if it were a park, and a boy sweeping the gravel. People passed up and down the path with more regularity than he would have expected. Upstream were trees, not quite enough to constitute woodland but more than one or two, and further downstream where the lade and the burn headed for the harbour he glimpsed the ruins of what had been the college's observatory. He could see that beyond the Swansons' garden the common close down which the two houses were accessed continued this far and crossed the mill lade on a little bridge. Turning in that general direction, in a moment he was at a stronger-looking gate in the Swansons' wall. It opened with a clank – no wooden latches here on the silversmith's house – and Swanson himself ushered Murray in to his own garden. Victor the bulldog sniffed his knees in what Murray hoped was welcome. Another figure was standing near Swanson, and Murray was surprised to find that it was the artist, Cosmo Gordon.

'I know, sir, you found some signs that poor Rory had climbed the wall out of our garden up there,' said Swanson at once, pointing back to the tree which Murray had climbed earlier. There was indeed a small orchard ladder next to it. 'But I think we may have found where he entered the garden. See here!'

'It was the hat that caught our attention,' Cosmo Gordon explained.

'An artist's eye, you ken, sir: he saw a colour that did not fit with its surroundings and was off at once like a dog after a rat!'

Victor twitched his ears with interest. Swanson was a little breathless after this colourful description, and stopped at a place beside the back wall of the garden. Now Murray knew how the land lay behind the gardens, and the busyness of the path, he looked with interest.

The ground beside the wall had not been worked for some time: the grass extended almost to the bricks themselves, and was long-established, the earth hard and compacted beneath it. There was, however, a long scrape down the brickwork, as if the heel of a boot had caught as someone jumped, and a little of the mortar had been knocked out with a spray of powder around it. The grass did look slightly crushed, though that may have been by Gordon and Swanson examining the wall, but in the tangles of a bramble next to it was, indeed, a black hat. Murray looked first at how it lay in the bramble, upside down and half-hidden, then picked it out and examined it carefully. It was a man's hat, of course, of a type entirely compatible with being worn by a young clerk of limited means but some respectability. It had not benefitted by being out of doors upside down for a couple of nights, or being pulled through a bramble bush, but on the whole it was in good condition.

'And you think this is McArthur's?' Murray asked, his long fingers examining the lining.

'I'm sure it is,' said Cosmo Gordon at once. 'He was wearing it when he left the Bogues' house after the recital.'

Murray thought back to McArthur's departure. He had indeed been wearing a similar hat: he himself would not have been able to swear to its being this one, but Cosmo knew him better.

'Do you think,' said Swanson, with a tragic expression on his face, 'that he climbed in here for refuge, but was too closely pursued?'

'That is certainly a possibility,' agreed Murray, looking about him. 'Did you find anything else? Signs of a struggle, perhaps?'

The two men shook their heads solemnly, casting their gazes about the garden again to reassure themselves.

'What did you do after the recital, Gordon?' Murray asked after a moment.

'I went home. I bunk near the top of Market Street. Swanson here called in to see me later on, didn't you?'

Swanson agreed, smoothly.

'I believe I told you I was at home all evening, Mr. Murray,' he said before Murray could comment. 'I had misremembered: all my thoughts about the silver dish were clear, but I had forgotten that I went to discuss them with the artist himself.'

'You designed the dish? The pattern is lovely,' said Murray sincerely.

'Thank you,' said Cosmo Gordon, accepting the compliment graciously.

'And how long would you have been there together, then?'

Gordon looked at Swanson, trying to remember.

'You arrived just as I was letting myself in the door, didn't you?' he said. 'My bunkwife is away at present,' he added in explanation. 'And we opened that flask of wine ... A few hours, I should say,' he decided, and Swanson nodded.

'I'm not used to that much wine,' he put in. 'It's not my normal way to spend an evening, I assure you, sir!'

'But no doubt a very pleasant variation in your routine,' said Murray, not wanting him to think him critical. Sometimes, Murray thought, he would be able to question people more effectively if he were a servant: they would be less likely to want to impress him. Cosmo Gordon, on the other hand, did not seem to mind what impression he gave of himself to his current employer: perhaps he felt that artists had greater liberty.

'Which way did you walk home?' Murray asked, hoping that Swanson had not been so drunk he could not remember.

'Oh ... let me think.' Swanson frowned and his wig shifted slightly on his forehead, making itself obvious. 'I would have walked down Market Street to one of the closes near the town kirk and crossed through there, then crossed South Street and down the common close to here, as usual.'

'You didn't walk along the mill lade, perhaps from one of the more easterly closes from South Street?'

'At night? Of course not, sir! I was not so inebriated as to risk that!'

'Quite so,' agreed Murray. As a student he had rarely walked down about here himself. 'Which close did you take between Market Street and South Street?'

'One of the ones near the town kirk,' Swanson repeated patiently.

'Yes, but which?'

'I honestly can't remember, sir, I'm sorry,' said Swanson. 'It's a path I walk so often I cannot call to mind this specific one. I know it was this side of the kirk, though, for I came out near to the top of the common close.'

It could easily have been the close where the McArthurs lived, then, Murray thought: or it might not.

'I assume you didn't see McArthur,' he said, 'but did you see anyone you knew?'

Swanson frowned even more heavily, closing his eyes to concentrate, but it was no use.

'I can't remember, sir. I'm sorry,' he said again. 'I was in a hurry to get myself home, see, and I just walked fast till I was here.'

'Well, thank you. I assume you didn't go out again that evening, Gordon?'

Cosmo Gordon gave a short laugh, which shocked Victor. The dog laid back his ears at the artist in reproach.

'After that wine? If I did I don't remember!' Then he sobered. 'To be honest, Mr. Murray, I feel bad about that. Maybe if I'd gone after him – after McArthur – to look for Jack together, this wouldn't have happened.' His gaze flickered over Swanson for a moment, then back to Murray: it seemed that Cosmo had not abandoned the notion that Jack Swanson had killed Rory in his own defence.

There was nothing more to learn here for now, Murray thought, and he thought he had heard the Shaws' dinner bell in the distance. His stomach growled, fortunately silently.

'May I take this hat back to Mrs. McArthur, then? You are quite satisfied that it was his?'

'Aye, of course,' said Cosmo Gordon, and Swanson nodded

sadly.

'I don't like to think of him climbing that wall, thinking he would be safe, and then – and then not being safe,' he finished. 'I wonder if he called out for Jack or me? I should have been here! He would have expected me to be here – och, the poor lad!'

Swanson's face was contorted, and Cosmo met Murray's eye, laying a hand on the silversmith's broad shoulder.

'I'll look after him,' said Cosmo, nodding to let Murray go. The dog was about his feet but he shoved it out of the way, steering Swanson back up the path towards the house. Feeling himself dismissed, Murray bowed at their retreating backs and left by the gate to the mill lade, latching it firmly behind him.

The cooking scents had not lied to him: dinner included not only a deliciously balanced curry, but also two of Mrs. Shaw's famous puddings, the first a fragrant stuffed cabbage and the second sweet with the end of the winter apples, and served with custard. It was no wonder, Murray thought, leaning back a little in his chair to aid digestion, that all the Shaw family were comfortably upholstered: he wondered how long it would take Walter, who liked his food and even more his sweet puddings, to grow as large.

The boys had been dismissed to their studies and the ladies had retired to the parlour, leaving Murray and Professor Shaw at the table with the brandy and a dish of dried fruits at which they picked lazily, no longer remotely hungry. Murray had made sure his paper and pencil were still downstairs, and fetched them from the hall.

'Let's see if we can remember who was at the recital, shall we? Though you will have to help me with the names, of course.'

'Of course,' Professor Shaw agreed readily, trying to sit straighter in his seat. 'I should like to be of some assistance, if I can. I feel so responsible.'

'By the way, I was in the Swansons' garden again just before dinner,' Murray said, realising he had not mentioned it. 'It looks as if poor McArthur was trying to escape someone or something by the mill lade.'

'Goodness – what was he doing down there at that time of night?'

'That I don't know. It seems a much-frequented path.'

'Yes, but not so much at night, that's the thing, Charles. Though Mr. Binny's pretty cottage lends some air of respectability, to be sure. But he does not live there very much: I cannot think that Rory could have been going to see him.'

'He could have run down there from somewhere further along South Street, or who knows where? I don't think we'll have any idea until we try to find out as much as we can about where he went after the recital.'

'You're quite right, of course, Charles.'

'Well, we were there,' Murray began for the sake of thoroughness with a list of the Shaws, Walter and himself. 'And the Bogues were there – Mr. and Mrs. Bogue, Sandy and Miss Bogue.'

'A lovely girl.'

'Indeed.' Murray did not meet his old tutor's eye. 'Mr. Bogue and Sandy went out later but not immediately McArthur left the house, and may not have seen him at all, not even in the distance. I'll have to ask them.'

'There were the other musicians, don't forget,' said Shaw. 'Wee Dod, and that artist.'

'Yes: Cosmo Gordon left after him, and went home to Market Street. He certainly didn't mention seeing McArthur after that. Nor did Wee Dod: perhaps I should have been more thorough in my questioning.'

'We have to start somewhere.' Professor Shaw listed five families he had recognised, abruptly, as if he needed to say them before he forgot them again. Murray scribbled quickly.

'Any other university people?' he asked. Professor Shaw considered, and shook his head. 'Clergy?'

'Oh! The town kirk's minister, of course, and his daughter.'

'Right ... any others?'

'I don't think so.'

'Tradesmen?'

Shaw counted three out on his fingers, and tried to remember what family members they had had with them.

'And I think – I think there were several more people in the – er, the left hand corner of the room behind us. I know I didn't much look there – getting stiff in this shoulder,' he explained apologetically. 'I don't like to turn that direction any more than I have to!'

'Well, if I ask these people what they saw, then I can also ask them who else they remember being there, and between all of us we should be able to account for all the guests.' Murray reread his list, making sure he could decipher the names he had written so quickly. He glanced at the little mantel clock above the table. 'I could easily fit in a few now. Who lives closest?'

They went down the list family by family, Shaw giving the addresses or as close as he could to them. Murray pushed himself up from the table, feeling still the weight of the delicious puddings in his stomach.

'I could do with a walk: I shall see how many of these I can find. They should at least be in at this time of day.'

Indeed, most of them were, and some he found at the houses of others he sought, having been dinner guests. Some were hospitable, offering him negus and a seat by the fire while daughters played to entertain their visitors: one or two found his curiosity distasteful, but gave him what information they had quickly, to rid themselves of him. With several he was already acquainted and enjoyed a gossip; with some others he was very happy to make their acquaintance and looked forward to increasing it. All enthused about the talents of the string quartet and the kindness of the Bogues in hosting the musical evenings, though one or two hinted at Mr. Bogue's being a little above himself in presuming to invite them – of course they themselves had been far too generous with their time to refuse the invitations. Feeling lighter with every step he kept going, house after house, until he had completed the list and added the few people Professor Shaw had not been able to identify, and visited them, too. All who had seen Rory McArthur leave the Bogues' house agreed that he had turned left outside the door and headed west along South Street. Some, who had been before him in leaving the house and were already some few paces down South Street were fairly sure he had crossed Eastburn Wynd and continued west, and one girl, a little young to be out and quite excited at the whole turn of events, declared that she was sure he had passed the university library by St. Mary's College gate. But no one had seen him after that, no one had spoken to or with him after his departure, and no one had any idea if he was going home, to Jack Swanson's house, or somewhere else entirely.

Chapter Eleven

On Saturday morning, after breakfast, Murray reluctantly assumed his black neckcloth again, instead of the grey half-mourning he had been allowed since October. The reception for Rory McArthur's funeral was to be held at Professor Shaw's house, ostensibly because there would be more room for the number of guests expected than in the McArthurs' own tiny house, or indeed in Mrs. Loudoun's home across the close. It appeared that while Murray and the constable had struggled to speak to Janet, and had then left her alone, negotiations had been taking place between Mrs. Loudoun and Professor Shaw's worthy wife. It was they, and not Janet, who had gone to the police office in Market Street, arranged for a coffin, laid out the body and seen to its transport to the Shaws on the Friday night when darkness would deter the curious. They, too, had sent out the notices, and Mrs. Shaw and Flavia and their small staff had arranged the funeral meats, all without much reference to the men of their acquaintance. Professor Shaw, probably the man who had received the most warning, was also the most bewildered: Murray after breakfast found him under a brown silk umbrella in the garden, dejectedly counting fish.

'She was quite right to suggest it, of course,' he said, as if Murray had been arguing against it, 'quite right. Though it is disruptive, having so many people in the house, so many strangers! But it is for poor Rory. I have not been to his little house, but my wife says it is very small.' He raised the umbrella to accommodate Murray, but their height difference was so great that Murray gestured him to lower it again, propping himself against a stone bench to allow them to carry on a conversation.

'Did Mrs. McArthur take much persuasion to have it here, do you know? You would imagine she would have liked her husband home for the last time.'

'Mrs. McArthur? I believe she agreed very readily. I think she told my wife that in having the funeral here she feels safer, because then no one would know where she was hiding. She is a nervous creature, from all I hear. Do you believe, Charles, that she really is in danger from some person from Perthshire?'

'It sounds extraordinary, doesn't it?' Murray agreed. 'Yet no one seems quite to know what their background was in Perthshire. We have been told that Rory's village was near Aberfeldy, but we do not know its name. We don't know why Rory suddenly returned to St. Andrews with a new wife, with whom he was never, that I can make out, very affectionate.'

'I assumed,' said Professor Shaw, a little ashamed, 'when the child came so quickly, that poor Rory had fallen into sin with the girl. Do you not think so?'

'When you thought of that, were you surprised?'

'I'm not sure,' said Shaw, pondering it. 'I suppose there were other boys I would have expected it of before Rory. Jack Swanson, for example. But if Rory had fallen from grace, he would never have abandoned the girl to any kind of disgrace. He would certainly have married her – and there he was, married.'

'It feels too simple,' Murray objected. 'There is something not quite right.'

'Accidents happen, dear Charles!' said Shaw, demonstrating the kindness with which he would have run his parish, had he been allowed the liberty.

Murray sighed.

'And yet, if it is not some mysterious body from Perthshire, who killed him? So far Jack Swanson is most people's favourite, but the Bogues' movements after the recital are unaccounted for. Mr. Swanson was with Cosmo Gordon, so he is in the clear: I wonder if he lied about being at home so as to vouch for Jack? Or was he just ashamed of being drunk as he says he was?' He toed the stone by the fishpond thoughtfully. The breeze was cool this morning and bore the drizzle that casually drifted under Professor

Shaw's umbrella, and he was growing chilled. 'The mourners will be arriving soon: I suppose we had better go in.'

'Of course.' Professor Shaw gave one more longing glance at the fishpond, and turned to follow Murray up the damp garden, folding the umbrella with a slap at the back door.

The funeral notices had gone out broadly, as would be expected with the death of a young person with a fair acquaintance, and they were widely accepted, as would be expected with such a tragic and mysterious end. By eleven o'clock, when the ceremonies were scheduled to begin, the drawing room was quite packed with people. It was a room rarely used by the Shaws, a little too grand and draughty for a cosy family little inclined to elaborate entertaining, so the fire had been lit for the last couple of days and the curtains and cushions brushed down and aired. Murray had never been in it, to his recollection, and he looked about with curiosity, as much as he was able, in the crowd, at the unfashionable furnishings and mismatched family pieces that sat in uneasy companionship about the room. The earliest-arrived guests had just about dried off in front of the fire, and were moving to make way for the later comers, when the first service of food and drink appeared and the minister of the town kirk coughed for silence to say the grace.

For want of young male relatives to take on the privileged role of serving the funeral meats, Jack Swanson and Sandy Bogue did the duty, under Cosmo Gordon's guidance, the string quartet performing together for the last time in its original formation. The minister relaxed for the moment and accepted a fresh bannock and ale, and the guests followed his example with a will. Mrs. Shaw's cooking enjoyed an excellent reputation, and certainly the fact that the funeral was to be hosted at the Shaws' house would have been an extra attraction for any who might have felt a delicacy at attending. If anything, the Shaws' unaccustomedness to large gatherings had made them even more generous than was necessary, and in a very short time the company was at ease, eating and drinking to their appetite's desire, while Mrs. Shaw anxiously watched from the door to see that everyone had all they required. She had been in the dead room, the parlour downstairs, with Janet McArthur, and had little Rosina perched on her hip. Rosina had a mangled hunk of bannock in one small fist.

'Mrs. Shaw, you have nothing to worry about!' Murray heard Cosmo Gordon reassure her. 'All is well: everyone is content. There is no rush to the fourth course until they have at least consumed this one, if not digested it.' He smiled at her, and his charm seemed to work, for she allowed herself a smile, too.

'Thank you, Mr. Gordon: it is a great comfort to have reliable helpers at a time like this.'

'We'll all do our best for Rory, Mrs. Shaw. To be of assistance to you as well is an extra privilege.'

Mrs. Shaw blushed, not quite sure how to deal with such compliments.

'There, I am sure Mr. Cardno has an empty glass, Mr. Gordon. Do you go and offer him to refill it!'

'At once, Mrs. Shaw!' Cosmo bowed, teasing her, and swept off through the crowd.

'All well, Mrs. Shaw?' Murray asked, as she gazed after him.

'Oh, Charles, yes, I believe so! Mr. Gordon is being very charming today, and the boys are so helpful. Just as long as we can keep washing glasses between courses all will be well, I'm sure!' She blinked up at Charles, used to sharing minor domestic trials with him.

'Is Mrs. McArthur all right downstairs?'

'She is bearing up quite well, in the circumstances. She does not like to be left long alone, though: I should go back to her at once, really. She is a nervous lass.'

'Then I should go and speak to the Bogues, if you do not need me.'

'Go, of course! I'm sure you have questions you need to ask,' she added with a slight sigh: in an ideal world this occasion would be one of seemly grief and appropriately sympathetic society, rather than a place for interrogation. Murray made an apologetic face, and bowed himself away from her. Little Rosina made an appreciative noise and waved the bannock, but Murray dodged it adroitly. He knew from experience that any substance mixed with a small child's saliva could easily be used as a strong adhesive.

The Bogues had been early arrivals and were now gathered at a window, watching Sandy perform his duties with the ashets. Mr. Bogue was grand in the very best black cloth, and Miss Bogue wore a delicate black muslin with white about the bodice – black was not her colour, sadly, Murray thought, and hoped she would not have to wear it too much in her life. Mrs. Bogue, whom he had met only briefly before, was stiff with bombazeen, and Murray half expected her to crack when she moved. Mr. Bogue presented Murray to her with aplomb, and they gestured him to sit next to them.

'Thank you,' he began, with a smile at Miss Bogue. 'A very sad occasion, is it not? But well attended.'

'Our little musical evenings had helped to make Rory a popular figure about the town, no doubt,' said Mr. Bogue comfortably.

'And the tragedy of his death,' added Mrs. Bogue, 'is the kind of thing that always attracts a good crowd.'

'My dear!' murmured Mr. Bogue almost inaudibly. Miss Bogue blushed a little.

'It was good of the Shaws to have everyone here,' she said quickly, trying to cover her mother's words with something less offensive. Mrs. Bogue, Murray noticed, seemed to realise what she was doing, and blushed in her turn. She had fair skin and reddish hair freckled heavily with grey, and had probably, Murray thought, been pretty, though she looked strained and tired and threaded with wrinkles. Murray decided to turn the conversation a little.

'Mrs. Bogue, you will have known Rory well as your guest over the years, from when he was just a lad at the college. Have you any light to shine on the sad manner of his death?'

It was too broad a question, he saw at once, and it confused her. After a moment's thought, she pressed her lips together and said,

'Rory was a nice lad, always, and very good manners at the table.'

Her speech was awkward, and for a moment Murray thought she might be fighting some impediment.

'Did he say anything to you before he left on Wednesday night?'

'No, not at all. I heard him say he was going to look for Jack, and then out he went intill the nicht – I beg your pardon, into the night was what I meant to say.' She folded her lips together again, and let her gaze drop to her lap. Her husband patted her on the shoulder, though whether he was congratulating her, comforting her or warning her, Murray was hard put to decide. It felt almost cruel to push on with her, she was such a little bit of a thing, but he did not know when he would see her again, even though he felt she would speak much more naturally with him away from her husband, and away from a large social gathering.

'Did he ever talk with you about his home? About Perthshire, or his village, or his family?'

'Och! Well, now, I cannot say that he ever did, sir. He was not one for chattering, you ken – you know.' It was like watching her words being wrung through a cloth: she was increasingly self-conscious, and he knew he would have to be merciful for now.

'He does appear to have been very reticent, doesn't he?' he added generally to Mr. Bogue and Miss Bogue. 'I think I have discovered that he was from somewhere near Aberfeldy, but his widow will not speak of it and no one else seems to know.'

'I suppose she does know?' said Miss Bogue suddenly. 'I mean,' she added with a smile, 'we have only Rory's word that he went home that time, and actually he never said that Mrs. McArthur was from his home village. He may have found her – oh, dear, that sounds bad! Met her, he may have met her somewhere on the way, or on the way back. She may not know anything more than that.'

'True,' said Murray, reluctant to acknowledge the possibility of another complication in his quest. 'Though surely he would have had to have the banns read in his home church, and it would be natural to mention it to her then. But she could at least tell us where she is from, I suppose, which would help to discover whether or not there is really someone from there who threatens her life, and who may have killed Rory.'

'I don't know how you have any hope of finding out!' said Miss Bogue with a smile. 'You have set yourself an impossible task!'

'You could well be right,' said Murray, though he had not lost hope yet. 'Mr. Bogue,' he said, turning to the man, 'I gather you were out that night after the recital. Did you perhaps see which way Rory McArthur went when he left?'

'I was – out – was I?' Mr. Bogue asked hesitantly, his eyes jerking away from Murray's gaze as if looking for a hiding place.

He had no wish to lose his freedom to a respectable wife. 'It would seem sensible, if you wanted to pass false currency efficiently, to start in Edinburgh or Glasgow where the trade is greater and the mass of people more confusing. But there were rumours in Edinburgh of a different source, all the same: I heard it from a man at my club, and in a couple of the – coffee houses,' he ended, apparently changing what he had been about to say. Murray did not press the point.

'What was the source?'

'An odd one, for such a thing. Several people thought the coins were coming from Perthshire.'

'From Perthshire? Anywhere in particular?'

'I don't remember hearing anywhere mentioned.' George smiled. 'But what good,' he added, misquoting mischievously, 'ever came out of Perthshire?'

It was a fine thing, but strange, to be back in familiar old Letho Kirk in the morning. A great deal had happened in one week: last Saturday and Sunday they had had the Easter Communions and a generous helping of preaching, mostly of a very high standard, and then after that had been all the strange events in St. Andrews and far too much traipsing back and forth along the road in between. Murray feared that he would be charged extra road tax at this rate.

The minister preached well, refreshed by having had a week off from his own pulpit, and the members of the Kirk Session, among them Mr. Baird with his cautious greeting, were well satisfied that all their work for the Easter Communions had gone well: there had been other years when despite their rigorous questioning and checking and planning, there had been incidents of an unwelcome nature, in the kirkyard if not in the church itself.

As he had no guests in the house to accommodate, Murray had chosen to walk from Letho House to the kirk with his household, trying his best, stiff in his best black coat, not to feel like an officer leading a rather mixed regiment. Though he wanted to chat with some of them, particularly Robbins and his wife, he was always expected to stride out ahead, followed in neat battalions by the household servants, the gardeners and the stablemen (two squads who constantly vied for priority), and the outdoor servants in the supper, and the moment he was gone, leaving the shilling behind on the mantelpiece, Robbins appeared with the supper dishes borne by Daniel and William. Murray ushered the Georges over to the supper table, and encouraged Miss George to pour the tea for them all. She took over the duty with her usual stately poise.

'I could take the coin to Cupar if you like,' George suggested, helping himself to potato pie as the servants left them alone to informality. 'I have nothing pressing to do on Monday.'

'I'd be most grateful if you would – and you could tell him about the Edinburgh rumours, if he has not already heard,' said Murray. 'I am involved in the investigation of a death in St. Andrews at the house of my old tutor, and would rather not leave it for long.'

'Oh, the lad found in the fishpond? Yes, we heard about that,' said George.

'Mr. Murray, you seem to attract such things, though!' Miss George objected with a shudder.

'I certainly don't try to,' Murray objected. 'But it does seem that if they happen near you once or twice, you become a kind of magnet for them – and then, of course, people get into the way of thinking of you when they do happen, and asking your advice.'

'It's quite a reputation to have,' remarked George with a grin. 'I'm glad mine is only for good horseflesh.'

It was not quite, but Murray chose not to dwell on Mr. George's other reputation. Miss George clearly had it in mind, too, to judge by the narrowing of her lips.

'I don't think either horses or murders will do you gentlemen much good in the search for wives,' she commented, with a governess-like air which only her long familiarity permitted her. 'Little Augusta needs a mother, Mr. Murray.'

'She does, I suppose, but I am in no particular hurry,' he admitted. His mind darted briefly to Miss Bogue, but the sudden panicky urge for female companionship that had followed the death of his wife seemed to have subsided, and this time he was keen to take his time and make no mistakes. Thoughts of Miss Bogue instead took him back to her father, and the false shilling.

'I imagine, then,' he said, 'that the counterfeit coinage is coming up from Edinburgh.'

'I suppose so,' said George, grinning at the change of subject.

brother's arm.

'One of the warehouses on the South Bridge had had one. I was there looking for that cherry-coloured gros-de-Naples, remember?'

'Oh, yes?' George frowned.

'But on the other hand,' she added, 'the other place someone mentioned hearing of one was at the fruit market at the Tron Kirk.'

'Well, there's no cloth sold there, is there?' asked Murray, sure he could remember none. 'I have seen two others, one in St. Andrews at the warehouse of Mr. Bogue,' he went on, and Baird's eyebrows rose in both recognition and surprise.

'Yon's a well-respected tradesman, sir,' he put in.

'Yes, indeed,' said Murray. 'His young clerk had not noticed it being paid over, and had not recognised any of his customers, being new to the job. When I was there Mr. Bogue was quite cross. The other, too, I believe was paid over in innocence: the new physician, Dr. Lindsay, was paid it by Francis Yule, in Letho village.'

'Oh, aye, that man would be dazzled by the sight of the silver and never look at the wee words,' said Baird, dismissive of the careless.

'The weight is definitely wrong, isn't it?' George remarked, comparing it with one he had drawn from his own pocket. 'Presumably it's mostly lead, with a silver coating.'

'Well, what should I do with it, sir?' Baird asked, already resigned to having to lose a shilling's profit.

'Best take it to the sheriff next time you are in Cupar,' said Murray. Baird looked wary, and Murray decided to help him out. 'Unless you'd like me to take it and explain.'

'It might sound better coming from you, sir,' said Baird frankly. 'The sheriff's no always inclined to think tradesmen innocent in matters like this, even if they come and tell him of their own free will. If a gentleman tells him he'd more likely take you at your word, sir.'

'Well, all right, then: I'm not sure when, for I'm due back in St. Andrews on Monday. But I'll try to do it soon: and I'll tell him about the others.'

'Thank you, sir.'

Baird was keen to leave and let the gentlefolk get on with their

Chapter Thirteen

'Let me see that, please?' Murray held out a long hand. Baird leaned forward to set the coin carefully into it, and stepped back. The silver shilling was a little used, but still quite clean, very much as one would expect from a coin minted only last year. The trouble was that the inscription, just as on the coin Mr. Bogue the draper had shown him in St. Andrews, was right for 1816, not for 1817.

'You'd have been selling cloth at Cupar market, I suppose?' Murray asked, making one connexion.

'Aye, sir. Though the kind of cloth we're getting these days, well, I dinna like to sell it for the old prices. I tell my customers not to expect too much from it, for it doesna wear at all well and the colours are no fast.'

'But business was brisk, you say?'

'That's right – some people will no be told.' The thought clearly caused him internal pain.

'May I see?' asked Mr. George, leaning forward to look. In the candlelight the greying hair on his temples shone a little, making him look more distinguished than his character would allow. Nevertheless he was a sound judge of many things. Murray handed him the coin. 'Interesting,' he said, his sharp eyes taking in all the details of heads, tails and edges. 'There was some talk of these, or something very like, in Edinburgh. All the recent new mintings have made people less cautious: they are not as familiar with what is the right inscription for a year.'

'But that one is for 1816,' agreed Murray.

'While the coin is dated 1817.' He showed it briefly to his sister, who nodded. 'I can't remember any particular link with the clothier trade, though,' he added, and Baird ducked his head as if acknowledging his support. Miss George put a hand on her

He opened the hand which had been in his pocket, and displayed a coin.

'A silver shilling,' said Mr. George, squinting at it in the candlelight. 'What's wrong with that, man? Or are you going to tell us,' he said with a laugh, 'that it's a fake?'

'Well, that's it, sir: I believe it is.'

susceptibility to the charms of the latest fashion plates. This evening she wore a gown so heavy with ribbons about the hem and the sleeves that Murray feared it would slide off her entirely: he hurried her to a seat by the fire, to stem the effects of gravity. Robbins brought negus and little cakes, and they talked vaguely of a hand of cards but instead sat comfortably chatting over the Edinburgh season and local matters, awaiting the arrival of the supper.

Before it could appear, Robbins opened the parlour door and bowed.

'Mr. Baird from the village is here, sir, with something he wishes to say to you. I told him that Mr. and Miss George were present, and he said that if you would be willing to hear him he thought it good that they too should hear the matter.'

Murray raised his eyebrows at the Georges, who nodded.

'Let him come in, then,' said Murray, interested. Baird was a respected villager and an elder of the kirk: if he asked to interrupt their evening it was likely to be for a very good reason. A moment later a thin, lugubrious man made his appearance.

'Baird! Good evening,' said Murray, standing politely. 'Will you take a seat? A glass of negus?'

'No, no, Mr. Murray, I'll no take up any more of your time than need be.' He bowed to the company, and stuck a hand in his coat pocket, then removed it again with something hidden in it. 'I was at the Cupar market, and business was brisk, I'm happy to say, though to be fair there was women there would just buy a'thing without consideration.' He was disapproving: Baird owned the drapery in the village, and more often talked people out of purchases he thought they might regret than allowed them to buy anything. It was a minor miracle of the county that he was still in business.

'I'm glad you're doing well,' said Murray encouragingly.

'You have a very fine range of ribbons at present, I noticed especially,' added Miss George. He flashed her a quick look.

'Aye, I suppose, but you'll no want to be buying that quality, ma'am, you'll need something frae Edinburgh for your ain use. Onywyse, I say it was busy because that was why I didna notice till I came to count up at the close, and I saw that someone had gived me this.'

join her.

'And what do you think of the pictures?' he asked. The pictures, in various stages of completion, were lined up against the wall one by one. Iffy's was nearly complete: Daniel's looked finished, while Carlisle's was only sketched in, the face cloudy and indeterminate against a more detailed background. Cosmo must have taken the chance to paint the hothouse, even when he could not catch the gardener. Mrs. Mack's had more detail about the face and muscular hands, but the rest was vague still.

'What do I think? I think he's wonderful, sir!'

'He's quite a talented painter, I believe: though there's something not quite right about Mrs. Mack's ears, there.'

'Oh, aye. But I always thought there was something funny about Mrs. Mack's ears – oh.' She stopped, wavering, forgetting to whom she was talking. 'And he really looks, so he must really see ... Och! When he looks at you, it's like he's looking straight through your skin! Och, those eyes!'

'Right ... perhaps you'd better pop back to the kitchens, Iffy, and have a nice cup of tea if you can manage one.'

Iffy looked at him in the candlelight, her eyes stretched out.

'Oh, aye, sir. Sorry, sir.'

She scuttled off, holding her arm steady. Murray watched her go, smiling, and turned to look at her portrait on the floor. Yes, Cosmo had caught that daft, panicky look very well, as well as a hint of adoration aimed at the artist. Murray hoped that Cosmo had more sense than Iffy had, or there could be trouble. He looked along the row of paintings: none of Robbins yet. Well, he supposed that the artist had not had a lot of time, what with travelling back and forth to St. Andrews for recitals and funerals. He hoped that Gordon would now attend a little more strictly to his work here, and finish it before the Blairs arrived with his daughter: if nothing else, he did not want Isobel Blair to meet the artist and fall into an argument with him over the work, for Isobel was as opinionated as she was artistic.

Dinner passed pleasantly in the parlour, and Robbins tidied away quickly so that the room was ready for the Georges arriving. They were prompt: Mr. George, a handsome gentleman with a reputation amongst the local girls, was nevertheless good company, and his sister was sensible enough except for a pulled himself back up on to the seat, deciding to turn the gig the easy way by driving up to the church at the top of the triangular village green and then back down on the other side of the triangle to the inn again. At the top he stopped to look back: at least Walter had vanished inside the cottage, and would not run the risk of getting lost: with Walter it was always a worry.

Murray grinned to himself, and set off down the hill to the main road which would take him to his own front gates.

The thought of another silent dinner and lone evening made him unaccustomedly melancholic, but as he handed the reins over to his groom at the front door, Murray was struck with an idea. Finding Robbins, he asked for a note to be sent over to Dures House, to ask the Georges if they would like to join him for supper. The weather had improved and it was not far, and he had not seen them for a while: it would make a pleasant change. By the time he had finished bathing and changing for dinner the reply had appeared borne by Daniel: they would be delighted, and would see him around seven.

There was still a little time before dinner, and he wandered across the hall to the dining room to take a look at the paintings so far begun by Cosmo Gordon. He was surprised to find a candle lit and perched on the edge of the bare dining table, and for a second thought that he had disturbed Cosmo at work, but instead a squeal told him that Iffy, the kitchen maid, was in the room. Iffy could be made to squeal by almost anything.

'Iffy, what are you doing here?' he asked, holding up his own candlestick to see her better. 'And how is your arm?'

'Och, it's affa sore, sir!' said Iffy, with a nervous giggle, touching it automatically and squeaking again as the touch hurt.

'It'll take a while, no doubt: it was a deep cut,' said Murray. 'But what are you doing in here?'

'Mrs. Mack says I was getting in her way seeing I canna cut a'thing straight and I canna lift a heavy ashet so she sent me off to sit somewhere I wouldna do any harm, and I thought I could maybe slip in here and see … and see the pictures.' She drew a deep, alarmed breath. 'I never thought you'd be back already, sir!'

Murray dismissed the thought of Mrs. Mack's opinion as to the harm Iffy could do in the dining room, and rounded the table to shoulder. 'It belongs to the doctor in Letho.'

'He must be visiting St. Andrews, then: I'm sure I should not lend that horse out if I had it, nor let it far out of my sight!' said Walter, impressed.

'I'd heartily agree with you, Walter: the horse is a beauty. No mention of horses in Ausonius, though, I think?'

'Not that I can remember, sir. Equus, though,' Walter contributed, keen to prove he knew more Latin than there was in Ausonius' travels.

'Well done. You're enjoying your studies, then?'

'Aye, well enough. I like looking after the fish and the trees an' all. And Professor Shaw lets us do some things with chemicals, though Mrs. Shaw's not so keen on having the smells in the house, right enough.'

'Do you get on well enough with James? He seems a lively lad.'

Walter made a noncommittal face.

'Aye, whiles he's gey funny. He makes jokes, like.'

'Good jokes?'

'Aye. When they're no at my expense, anyway, sir.'

'Does he do that often?'

'Och, whiles he hides my slate, or moves the fish from pond to pond, you ken the kind of thing. My auntie sent me a cake from Letho and he hid it. I'd like to think of something to do to him, sometimes, to make it fair, but I can never think of anything.' He sighed. 'But most of the time he's good enough company. And he's no bad at the Latin and the Greek.'

The conversation turned to Walter's studies, and the journey passed quickly enough for both of them, particularly when Walter discovered that Murray had actually visited some of the exciting and exotic places about which he was reading so enthusiastically.

At the inn at the foot of the village, Murray pulled up the gig to let Walter hop down, so that he could go to see his aunt. On reflection, he told Walter to stay in his seat and drove up into the village, stopping outside Mrs. Fenwick's cottage. Walter had been known to lose his way even on shorter journeys. He jumped down to help release Walter's pack from the rack, and handed it over.

'Well, no doubt I shall see you later up at the house,' said Murray. Walter waved goodbye at the cottage door, and Murray confidentially close to Murray, and seized both his hands in hers. 'You know how anxious he becomes over all these things – he feels dreadfully responsible for poor Rory. You're doing your best, aren't you, dear Charles?'

'I am, Mrs. Shaw, I promise. I don't know if my best will be good enough, but I will do it.'

'I know you will.' She gave his fingers a final squeeze, and stepped back to raise her voice again a little. 'And the Professor hopes Walter will find all his family well and have a pleasant rest, and come back refreshed, as do we all.' She smiled at Walter, who nodded dutifully.

'Well, climb up, then, Walter,' said Murray, seeing that his own small trunk was tucked under Walter's pack. He gave Walter a leg up, then greeted the horse and clambered up on the other side, taking the reins. 'See you all on Monday!'

The common close was too narrow for a gig: Murray guided the horse with extreme care along the tight-walled lane that took them from the Shaws' and Swansons' houses to Well Wynd, where they could emerge into the traffic climbing up to the West Port. Once up the hill it was only a moment before they had crossed Argyle Street and were once again descending, this time along Cow Wynd to join the Windmill Path that lead between pleasure gardens and gentlemen's properties out into the farmland again down by the links.

Murray was just about to steer the horse to the left towards Cupar when he noticed a loop of the reins rubbing on the horse's back. He reined in and slipped down to readjust it, hopping back up quickly. Walter was staring over the wall beside them.

'That's a nice horse, sir,' he stated, as Murray set off.

'Thank you, Walter – though I'm sure you've seen her before.'

'No, I meant that one, sir.' He pointed over the low wall to their left, into a little parkland where a horse was grazing nonchalantly, though it did not look like the kind of land where a horse would be left to graze unsupervised. The horse, however, seemed to accept it as his due: he was as fine a black stallion as Murray had ever seen.

'I think I know that horse,' he said, gazing back at it over his

'Was this before or after his father was seen?'

'Before, he says. See, the night watchman has a sweetheart near enough to the West Port, or at least a lassie he's sweet on. South Street must be the best patrolled street in the town, just now: if you have any criminal intent,' he added, 'I'd suggest maybe Market Street, if you dinna want to be seen at night.'

'I'll bear it in mind,' said Murray absently. 'So before midnight some time, Jack Swanson was out and on South Street, and possibly heading home about what time?'

'Say eleven of the clock.'

'Eleven. The concert finished about half past nine, and the Bogues came out after everyone had gone – say maybe ten – to look for Jack or for Rory. Even if they were later that would give them plenty of time to reach the Swansons' house before anyone came home, assuming both the Swansons went out earlier. I suppose,' he went on, considering, 'I suppose Jack would also have had time to kill Rory and go out afterwards.'

'That he would, sir, if we assume that Mr. McArthur was killed soon after he was last seen.'

'True. Oh, well, Round, I'm off back to Letho for the Sabbath tomorrow, but I hope to return on Monday: if there's any sign of Jack Swanson, can you send me word? I'd like very much to ask him a few more questions.'

'Of course, sir: so would I.'

Back at the Shaws' house, Murray found his horse already harnessed to his gig, with Walter's pack tied to the luggage rack and Walter himself pulling on his hat. James Shaw was at the front door, exchanging with him some dubious Latin phrases which Murray was fairly sure had never been taught in any class, judging by both grammar and content.

'I'm a very inconstant guest,' said Murray apologetically to Mrs. Shaw, who was examining the rose bushes in the front garden.

'Not at all, dear Charles,' she said warmly. 'We shall look forward to seeing you again on Monday: you know you are always welcome here! My husband has gone to have a little lie down to recover his nerves, but he says to tell you he's sorry to miss saying goodbye, and he'll see you on Monday.' She moved more

'Well, indeed.'

'Do ye think he's away, sir?' asked Round quietly.

'I don't know. Maybe.' He sighed. 'But if he is, I don't think it's straightforward.'

'You think McArthur attacked him, and he fought back?'

'I don't know,' repeated Murray. 'There's something we don't know, I'm sure of it.'

'I'm sure there's plenty we don't know, sir,' Round agreed in resignation.

Murray straightened after a moment.

'Was the night watchman able to tell you anything useful?'

Round considered.

'He doesna go as far south from South Street as Professor Shaw's house: he'd maybe take a wee jook down the common close with his lantern, but that would be as far as it would go, ken. And he wouldna come on duty till after most of the guests for the wee concert would be at home. Late on, nigh midnight or after, he says he saw Mr. Swanson in South Street, though.'

'Walking in a straight line?' asked Murray with a grin.

'No showing signs of drink, onywyse,' Round shook his head.

'He's maybe more used to it than he made out before,' Murray admitted. 'He was certainly making himself familiar with it today. Did the night watchman say which way he was going?'

'He was crossing the street by the well, heading towards the common close.'

'Just as indeed he would be if he were heading back from Cosmo Gordon's lodging in Market Street to his home. Well, it proves he was out and about as he said, anyway. Anything else?'

'Aye,' said Round, pausing for effect, 'there is an' all: he seen Jack Swanson too.'

'Jack? Jack said he was at home.'

'Aye, I ken. But the night watchman was dead sure.'

'Where did he see him?'

'Round about the same place, near the well, crossing South Street to the common close. It must just be where they're accustomed to cross.'

'We're all creatures of habit ...' Murray thought. Could this be why there had been no answer when the Bogues had come looking for Jack at home?'

No, he must have gone on his own account, and for want of a better explanation, that looked like guilt.

He glanced up at the mantel clock: Professor Shaw's house was well-provided with clocks, though some had been taken apart for various experiments. This one seemed to be running to time, and said that the hour had gone two. He intended to be at home in Letho for dinner, to be in the village for the Sabbath.

'I think I'll go to see Constable Round before I leave,' he said to the Shaws. 'He'll have to be told that Jack is missing, though I'm not sure what he can do about it just yet. Walter,' he called across to where Walter and James Shaw were feeding off the last of the bannocks like starved scavengers, 'I'll come back for you in less than an hour. Please be ready, eh?'

'Sir.'

The damp walk to the town house did little to clear Murray's head. He was not entirely satisfied that Jack had killed Rory, yet there was something going on which Jack was hiding, he was sure. And who had been telling the truth about the state of the Swansons' house after the recital – had there been anyone at home or not? Had Swanson lied about being at home because he thought he needed to defend Jack, and if so why had he then admitted to being out drinking with Cosmo Gordon? Or was he more used to being in his cups than he wanted Murray to think?

'He's disappeared?' asked Round in surprise. 'When did that happen?'

'At Rory McArthur's funeral,' Murray explained. 'No one has seen him since just before the kisting.'

'Have they gone to his house?'

'Well ...' That part of the hunt had not gone particularly well. Swanson, still muddled by drink and his abrupt departure from the funeral party, had been quite aggressive to those who had tried to search his house, even to those who had tried to explain that they were concerned about his son. 'All I can really say is that he was not seen going there along the street, and there was someone looking out of the dead room window at that time. But he could,' he suddenly remembered, 'have gone round the back.'

'Aye, but it'd be an odd thing to do, would it no, running away hame like a babbie when he's expected to bear his pal's coffin.'

Mrs. Shaw gave a little laugh.

'There was talk, as I heard, of a gentleman who had bought cloth from Mr. Bogue and admired his daughter too – foolish rumours! And they may have encouraged Mr. Bogue to hope. But I believe Miss Sarah will make her own choice, though, don't you, dear?' She leaned forward to touch her husband's shoulder gently with her own as they sat side by side. It was an endearing gesture, and Professor Shaw smiled. They had married for love, anyway. Murray tried not to sigh. He sat back, idly watching the women in the room. Mostly their menfolk had returned from the interment and they were simply postponing the moment when they would have to leave this warm drawing room and go home in the misty rain. Janet McArthur sat with Mrs. Loudoun at the window where the Bogues had gathered earlier, looking fretful: every now and then she glanced out of the window, as if she feared her potential attackers were advancing on the house. She certainly seemed convinced of their existence. If only she would have the courage to tell someone who they were, or even why they might be dangerous, it might help to prevent another attack – assuming she was right, and they had killed Rory. Why would anyone want to kill Rory?

From what he had learned of Rory's character, it seemed more likely that someone would attack him in frustration at his stolidity. Or indeed would defend themselves against his anger – but no one had ever seen him violent against another person in his anger. Yet there was that gouge on the desk ... was it only there because the desk was not a person? Who had annoyed him so much that he had made that cut? Was his anger then related to his reasons for leaving St. Andrews for his Perthshire home?

And then there was the question of Jack – where had he gone? He was a grown man: however ashamed he might have been of his father's behaviour, or his own accident with the tray, he should not have run off and left his friend's coffin a bearer short. Murray had had to step in, and as he was half a head taller than the rest of the bearers it had not been an easy walk to the burying ground. Could Jack have had another reason for disappearing? Guilt, perhaps? Surely he could not have been abducted: with everyone around for the kisting, that would have been difficult for anyone to achieve, and he was a strong young man. He would surely have struggled.

Chapter Twelve

The interment, somewhat delayed, took place in a light drizzle in the shadow of the Cathedral ruins, and after a tot of whisky which in many cases could well have been done without, the mourners dispersed. Neither Swanson nor Bogue had attended, and Jack was nowhere to be found.

Back at the Shaws' house, the carpet in the drawing room had been cleaned and the ladies of the party, with the exception of the Bogues, were sitting around thoughtfully, taking it in turns to hold and play with little Rosina and drinking fresh tea. Murray and Professor Shaw accepted cups gratefully, and sank down by the fire to dry out.

'Still no sign of Jack?' Professor Shaw asked his wife.

'No, dear, nothing at all. I think he was too embarrassed by the accident with the tray – which of course was nothing, really, but young people feel that kind of thing so much – and then his father and Mr. Bogue …'

'Is there some history there?' Murray asked, lowering his voice. He had asked Professor Shaw before, but sometimes he had found it was useful to leave a question for a little to sink in before a thorough answer emerged.

'No, not really, I believe,' said Professor Shaw with an anxious face. 'It's just, I think, that both of them would like to think of themselves as a little higher in society than they are, and that leads to terrible dissatisfaction.'

'Mr. Swanson mentioned his son and Miss Bogue, though.'

'Oh, that was nothing! Well, I believe it was nothing for Jack or Miss Bogue, anyway. It may have been an ambition of Swanson's, but Bogue I think would prefer a higher marriage for Miss Sarah.'

Lexie Conyngham

black cloth doesn't quite meet the wall. I saw him go past, alone.'

Several of the mourners nearest the door went out into the hall, and called Jack's name, and there were a few minutes of hurried searching and tentative knocking at the door of the privy, but already it was becoming clear: for whatever reason, Jack Swanson had vanished.

on the floor, and picked up one or two of them. Miss Bogue, Jack and Cosmo had vanished, presumably to clean off the sprinkles of brandy.

'Time to leave, Mr. Swanson, Mr. Bogue.'

'Aye,' said Bogue solemnly, 'we'll have to intend the atterment.'

'I think you'd be better to go home. Isn't Wee Dod downstairs?'

'Aye,' agreed Bogue. He was having trouble focussing on Murray's face.

'Then he can see you home. Mr. Swanson, back next door now, please, and if you're wise, off to your bed.'

'I'll no be sent to my hame by him!'

'You're not being sent home by him, Mr. Swanson: you're not well. Off you go. Do you need a hand to rise?'

Swanson shook his head again, and his wig departed completely. Murray plucked it fastidiously from amongst the brandy pools, and returned it to him, and Swanson rose and left the room with a rather meandering dignity. Murray helped Bogue from his seat as best he could, and led him down the stairs. From the parlour he could hear the minister stretching out the kisting prayers, perhaps waiting for the carpenter who might not have been quite ready to fasten the coffin so suddenly. Wee Dod was waiting in the hall: Murray handed Bogue over to his servant's custody, and slipped into the parlour.

He had been wrong: the carpenter was quite ready, and as soon as the minister nodded he slipped the lid over Rory and secured it.

'The bearers?' said the minister, looking about him. Sandy and Cosmo stepped forward, and another man of around their age. Everyone paused.

'Where's Jack?' asked Sandy.

'Is he still up the stair?' asked the other lad.

'He's not in the drawing room, or wasn't when I left,' said Murray.

'Could he have taken his father home?' Professor Shaw suggested meekly.

'I saw Mr. Swanson leave,' said Miss Bogue, who was standing by the parlour window. 'There's a chink here where the son, onywyes!'

'I would rather not discuss such matters here, if you'll forgive me, sir,' said Miss Bogue politely. Murray shook himself, glanced at Professor Shaw who was sitting by the fire with a look of flat panic on his wrinkled face, and stepped over to try to sort things out. Cosmo Gordon seemed struck by the same idea, and at the same moment Jack moved forward too, his tray of brandy glasses forgotten in his hand.

'I'll no take this,' came a low grumble from the window. 'You've insulted my daughter, you, you –' Bogue stopped himself, unable to find suitable words in keeping with his standing.

'Perhaps, gentlemen,' Murray began, but Swanson waved a hand back at him, shaking his head slightly more slowly than his wig was moving.

'He's no a gentleman! He'd like you think he is, though, is that no right, Bogue?'

Bogue swung round in his seat, amazingly quickly for a man of his size and shape, and his fist shot out. It connected with Swanson's generous stomach. Swanson doubled over, backing hard into Cosmo Gordon. Cosmo sidestepped, and Swanson, flailing, hit the tray of brandy glasses held by his son. The tray spun up into the air, spraying revolving brandy glasses as it went, scattering bright drops of spirit over Swanson, Cosmo, and Miss Bogue. Swanson sat heavily on a nearby chair, and glared at all about him.

'Right,' said the Town Kirk minister, rising magisterially from his seat, 'time for the kisting.'

Most of the company surged to their feet and hurried downstairs, leaving the minister to bestow a warning glare on Swanson or Bogue if they chose to follow. Murray went after the minister on to the landing and found Professor Shaw there, wringing his hands.

'What should I do, Charles?'

'Do you want me to put them outside?' Murray was not at all sure that he could shift Bogue without some kind of crane, but he had to offer.

'Would you, Charles?'

'Of course – I'll try.'

He returned to the drawing room, trying to avoid the glasses

'Yes, yes, at the front. In the room you saw.'

Then who was right, thought Murray: Swanson and Jack, saying he was at the front of the house, or Mr. Bogue, who claimed the house was in darkness? And anyone knocking at the front door would surely have heard someone playing the violin in that front room.

They bowed once again to Mrs. McArthur, and left so that Murray could show Swanson upstairs to the drawing room. The man wove a little as they crossed the hall, and Murray wondered if he had been sharing a cup of wine with his important customer from out of town: even if he had, he was probably not as far gone as some of the mourners already upstairs. He plodded slowly up each step after the silversmith, glad when at last they reached the landing and he could move past him to open the drawing room door, and usher him inside.

Conversation was brisk within, with the occasional spurt of laughter or an opinion voiced a little more loudly than seemed quite proper for a funeral. Catching sight of his father before Murray had the chance to call him, Jack hurried over with a tray of brandy glasses, and Swanson snatched one with a nod. He drained it swiftly, and Murray blinked: was there something about the merchants of St. Andrews of which he had previously been unaware? A flush rose at once to Swanson's cheeks, and he blinked heavily, making his wig shift downwards on his brow. Then his gaze focussed sharply.

'Is that man here and all?' he said, his voice carrying and clear.

Murray spun round. As far as he could see, Swanson had focussed on Mr. Bogue, and Mr. Bogue was entirely aware of his presence. Bogue stayed solidly in his seat, and made a great display of pointing out something outside the adjacent window to his wife and daughter. Swanson was not to be deterred, and before Murray could decide whether it was worth intervening, he had staggered across the room.

'I'd have thought all this was a bit beneath you, Bogue!' he snapped. 'I thought you only consorted wi' gentlefolk these days!'

'Mr. Swanson, please,' said Miss Bogue quickly, seeing that her father was still staring through the window.

'Oh, aye, all prettified are you, young lady? Too good for my

In the parlour, the coffin had been laid, open, on a board on the table, with cloths appropriately draped about, over the mirrors and across the windows. Professor Shaw's portrait had been removed. The candlelight showed Mrs. Shaw and Mrs. McArthur as wax-pale as Rory's cold corpse: black did not flatter Janet McArthur either. The child was not there – presumably Mrs. Loudoun had taken her this time.

'Janet, dear, you remember you've met Mr. Murray?'

'Oh? Oh, yes, I think so,' said Mrs. McArthur. She looked up at Murray in bewilderment as he bowed, then went to touch the body.

'And this is Mr. Swanson, Jack's father.'

'Oh!' squeaked Janet, and sagged against Mrs. Shaw's sleeve. Both men stepped backwards involuntarily, while Mrs. Shaw pulled her reticule from the bookcase and brought out smelling salts, holding Janet half-upright as she opened the vial with one hand.

'Not the first time today, alas!' she murmured. 'Poor lass, she's no strong.'

Janet came round with an odd descending moan, her eyelids fluttering frantically.

'Oh!' she cried again. 'Mr. Swanson, did you say? Jack's father?'

'That's right, ma'am,' said Mr. Swanson in best customer-serving form, making a low bow. 'I am sorry to have to make your acquaintance on such a terrible occasion. Your husband and my son had been friends for many a long year: we are both so very sad.'

'Thank you, sir,' said Mrs. McArthur faintly. Swanson turned to the coffin, bound in more black cloth.

'Och, poor lad, poor lad!' Swanson muttered. 'To think he could have called out to us for help, and us not there!'

'I thought Jack was there?' said Murray in surprise. Swanson stumbled.

'I mean – I mean within hearing. If Jack was playing his music, he'd never have heard anything – I mean, you wouldn't, would you?'

'And of course he would have been at the front of the house, wouldn't he?'

You knew Rory had gone looking for Jack, and you left your house a little after Rory had left. Surely the first place you would go would be the Swansons' house, to see if they were there?'

'Oh!' Mr. Bogue's face cleared magically. What had the man been thinking? 'Oh, aye, we were there and all.' He stopped again, then saw Murray watching him patiently. 'There was nobody in. Nobody came to the door, no lights, nothing.' He shut his mouth like a trap. Murray was not sure whether he was lying or not, and if he were, whether it was about visiting the house at all or about there being no reply at the door. It would bear investigation: he hoped he would be able to catch Sandy on his own before his father had the chance to speak with him and get their stories straight.

If Mr. Bogue was hoping for such an opportunity at the next service, he was to be disappointed: it was Cosmo Gordon who appeared at their sides in a moment, bearing a large ashet heaping with the rich fruit cake served at funerals. This example was sodden with brandy, and served with porter. Murray, taking it gently on his second day of Mrs. Shaw's rich cooking, was astonished to see Mr. Bogue gulp down two slices, then take a third glass of porter. He looked more closely: the clothier was slightly pinker than he remembered. Cosmo, with an amused look, offered him the ashet again – Murray thought he intended it as a joke, but Mr. Bogue happily pawed a third slice into his mouth. Murray felt his jaw begin to drop, and stopped it. No wonder the man was the shape he was.

Glancing around he could see several people in the room to whom he had not yet spoken, and he also wanted to pay a visit to the dead room before the kisting: he decided that propriety demanded that, first. He excused himself to the Bogues, still stunned at Mr. Bogue's consumption, and slipped out of the drawing room and downstairs.

On the doorstep he met Mr. Swanson.

'Oh, Mr. Murray, I am so sorry I am so late!' he murmured hurriedly. 'A customer from out of town – so difficult to turn them away!' It was not clear whether the difficulty was with the customer or with Swanson's enthusiasm for trade over social duty. He was here now, though, and at his request Murray led him into the parlour to see the corpse.

'Oh! Yes, I was. But I didn't see Rory: it was later than that.'

'You and Sandy, I believe, went to look for Rory, to make sure he was all right?'

'Who told you that?' Mr. Bogue tried hard to maintain his genial expression, but there was a sharpness in his eyes.

'Do you know I'm not sure I remember?' said Murray smoothly. 'I've talked to so many of your guests over the last couple of days – all unanimous in their appreciation of your hospitality and the quality of the music, I have to say.'

'Oh, aye, aye.' Mr. Bogue nodded acknowledgement of the compliment, and Mrs. Bogue looked pleased.

'But you were worried about Rory, I believe, as any good host would be.' Heavens, thought Murray, this is not exactly subtle flattery. Surely it won't work.

'Well, of course: he was angry with Jack Swanson for not turning up to play, and it crossed our minds – mine and Sandy's, that is – that somehow the pair of them might do themselves some kind of injury. To each other, I mean, or even to themselves in the – in the process.'

It had worked.

'So you went after Rory? Or to look for Jack?'

'Um.' Mr. Bogue was not quite clear. 'Both, I think.'

'And you went in which direction?'

'Well, down South Street, of course. And we went round by the Cathedral, and a wee bit down Market Street, and we took a look into North Street and all.'

'And you saw no sign of either of them?'

'Not a bit of it.'

'Did you happen to see Mr. Swanson, by the way?' Murray asked suddenly.

'Thomas Swanson? No: he wasn't at the recital, though.'

'No, he wasn't. And what about Swansons' house?'

'Swansons' house?' Mr. Bogue looked puzzled.

'Yes, their house. Next door to this one.'

'Well, aye, I know it's there. What about it?

'Well, did you visit it that night?'

'Visit it?'

Murray took a breath.

'You were looking for Jack Swanson, or for Rory McArthur.

laundry, dairy and attachments. The family and workers on the Mains Farm came next, trying their best to be taken for an echo of the big house: with the wives and children of the servants tagging along in their places it could all look, on a good day, like a travelling circus come detached from its animals.

To complete the set, Walter was at church with his aunt, and after the service was made much of by the Letho House staff, in their various ways. Murray tried to observe discreetly, and was fairly content with what he saw: he had been anxious that his actions in arranging for Walter's tutoring and later attendance at the college might have caused jealousy amongst the other servants, but neither Daniel nor William would have benefitted much from the study of Ausonius and could not have been trusted alone in St. Andrews with inns and girls – Daniel was quite bad enough in Letho, with its much more limited scope. In any case, Walter had been a terrible but occasionally devoted servant, whose life had been placed in danger more than once and who had probably done more in his short time on the Letho staff than anyone but the Robbinses: he deserved his reward, and Murray was sure he was the boy who would make the most of it.

'Mr. Murray,' came a voice near his elbow, and he looked about to see Mr. Helliwell, the minister.

'Good day to you again, Mr. Helliwell,' said Murray, having already shaken the minister's hand as he left the kirk door. Mr. Helliwell had adopted his stern look.

'A word, if I may: is your gardener Carlisle quite well?'

'Carlisle? Yes, I believe so: why?'

'He was at the Communions last week but otherwise has not been seen at church for a month or more. I hope he is not deserting us,' said Helliwell, his words mild but his frown sombre. As if to alleviate his effect, his wife popped up beside him.

'And he has promised me snowdrops, and soon it will be too late to move them!' she added with mock severity.

'In that case I shall certainly question him,' said Murray with a smile. 'But was he not questioned by someone else before he was given a token for the Communions?'

'He was,' sighed the minister, 'but it was Melville who did it, and you know he's always more eager to get back to home and family than to sit examining anyone's right to a communion token.

He could have been slaughtering the innocent in a greenhouse when Melville arrived, and as long as he told him he'd no desire to burn down the church Melville would have ticked him off the list.'

The alarming images the minister's words conjured up fortunately made Murray smile again.

'Carlisle is not the most sociable of people,' he conceded. 'I'll go and see him this afternoon and see what he has to say.'

'And please ask him about my snowdrops!' put in Mrs. Helliwell, grinning. 'How is little Augusta? Have you heard?' and to the minister's mild irritation, talk turned entirely to Augusta's progress and health and charms, for Mrs. Helliwell was almost as much of an enthusiast for Murray's daughter as Murray himself was, and therefore, in Murray's eyes, a woman almost without fault.

The pleasant chat having drawn to a close, Murray was about to summon his troops for the walk home when he found someone else had been waiting in grim politeness for the minister's wife to go. It was Walter's aunt, Grisel Fenwick.

'Mr. Murray, sir,' she began, as soon as he acknowledged her.

'Walter's looking well, isn't he? Do you think he is enjoying his studies?' Murray began. The woman always made him nervous.

'He says he's no got his flannels,' said Mrs. Fenwick flatly. Murray blinked, then remembered the little willow kist tied to his saddle.

'Oh! I'm sure it reached St. Andrews safely: it must have gone astray in the stables at Professor Shaw's.'

'I gived you that kist in good faith, sir,' she said, ominously.

'Yes, yes, of course. I am sorry for not seeing it through to its conclusion. I really am.' He found he was gabbling, under her hostile gaze, and managed to slither to a halt. 'I – I'll see to it as soon as I go back tomorrow. Tomorrow afternoon, as soon as I arrive at Professor Shaw's.'

'Aye, well, I'd like fine to hear it's arrived safely, ken, sir. It was a while I spent stitching his wee jackets and drawers, and he'll need a new set now the winter's through. I hear St. Andrews is a gey cauld place to bide.' She spoke as though it were Kamchatka, and about as distant.

'I'll find them, Mrs. Fenwick.' He tried to sound firm.

'Aye, well,' she repeated, and finally withdrew the spear of her gaze. 'I'll let you get on, then, sir.'

'Good day to you, Mrs. Fenwick.' He turned away as soon as he politely could, and hurried off to find the Robbinses. On his way he caught Walter's eye: it seemed to be pityingly sympathetic.

Back at Letho House, the servants dispersed to their various duties. It was usually a time when Murray retreated to the library with a pot of tea and a book, but as the day was fine and he had promised the minister, he decided to keep his boots on and go looking for the gardener, though how he might be able to persuade Carlisle, of all people, to attend church regularly if he did not feel inclined to do so was beyond him.

Carlisle was supposed to live in a cottage tucked inside the garden wall at the foot of the kitchen garden, shielded from prying eyes by brittle honeysuckle, just coming into bud in little shocks of green. It was a cottage designed more to be a bothy for garden lads, but when Carlisle's wife had died and his family had grown and left, he had asked to be moved into it to be nearer his beloved garden. The lads had happily shifted elsewhere and Carlisle had taken root about the little building, using it as a place to sleep and keep his most precious seeds, and not much else.

Nevertheless Murray chose to think that the gardener might respect the Sabbath by staying at home, at least, if not actually attending the kirk, so he made his way down the kitchen garden towards the bothy. The beds he passed were well worked and dark with rich soil, with copper markers gleaming at the ends of beds to mark the new sowings, and pea stakes were propped and clean by the hothouse, ready to be set up when the peas were planted. Fruit trees sprawled in tidy espaliers against the warm brick walls, arranged according to their delicacy, for chimneys directed the heat from fires laid to make the walls even more comforting to trees more used to southern climes. The place was set out and prepared to face the business of spring, and every branch seemed full of birds singing.

There was no reply at the low door of the cottage, and Murray took the liberty of pushing it open and popping his head inside, feeling like a giant. The fire was tamped down, the kettle cold, the bed made up and tidy. There was nothing much to be seen unless

Carlisle could have hidden under the table where he arranged his seeds by the window: Murray did squirm down to peer under it, but it, too, was stacked with wooden boxes for seeds and bulbs. Carlisle was definitely not in the cottage. In apparent reproach to the minister, though, Murray noticed that a Bible was laid open in the middle of the table, held open with a trowel. He smiled, thinking that at least the minister's wife would approve.

Murray straightened and left the cottage with relief, then scanned the gardens. There was no sign of movement bigger than a blackbird: the garden servants would be in their homes or at their new bothy for their dinners, not working on the Sabbath. But where was Carlisle? He had certainly not been on the path between the village and Letho House, for he had tramped that there and back at the head of his domestic army. The likelihood was that he had slipped into a hothouse to carry out some small task and had either become distracted and forgotten the time, or had met with some accident and was stuck, perhaps with a broken ankle, waiting for rescue. Murray drew a deep breath: Carlisle injured and impatient would not be pleasant to find, but better he did it than some hapless garden lad.

He began with the hothouse nearest to him, the one where he had interrupted Cosmo Gordon's attempt to persuade Carlisle to sit for him. It was surprising that that had even worked as much as it had, he thought, remembering the rough outline of Carlisle already in Cosmo's stack of paintings in the dining room. The hothouse, benefitting too from those cunningly devised wall-chimneys which heated the fruit trees, was sweet-scented and warm, the glass heavy with condensation and the stone floor damp. Murray looked up at the vines and fig, delighting in the rich planting, then glanced down as he stepped forward.

He saw the foot immediately.

Carlisle was lying under a rack of plants, face down on the stone-slabbed floor, his complexion, what could be seen of it, a nasty grey. But when Murray found his wrist and tried it, there was a faint throb still. He pulled off his coat as fast as he could, tucked it around his gardener, and turned and ran from the hothouse.

The new bothy for the garden lads was nearest, and the garden lads were young and fit. He interrupted them just as the oldest was ladling out thick meaty gravy on to their pewter plates for dinner, and apologised rapidly. In a moment the youngest lad was hurtling towards the village and the doctor's house, tugging his jacket and muffler about him as he fled. Murray, flailing a borrowed blanket, ran back to the hot house.

He tucked the blanket around Carlisle, noting that the gardener was in his Sunday best: he hoped he would live to tell the minister that he had fully intended going to church after all. But what had happened to prevent him? Murray wriggled along the stone slabs, and found that the back of Carlisle's head was bloody and dented. Could he have crawled under the rack for something then tried to stand up too soon, knocking his head on the rack above him? But surely Carlisle knew his own hothouse better than that? And when he bent to look at the underside of the racks, there was no sign of blood. Perhaps he had been hit by something falling nearby, and crawled under the rack before collapsing? Murray glanced around the hothouse. Nothing seemed to have fallen: nothing, indeed, was out of place except for a long, narrow spade. What was that doing here? It was not the kind of tool, Murray was fairly sure, that would be used in a hothouse: it was for outdoor beds and serious digging.

He reached over to it. The blade was clotted with dark blood.

Murray looked quickly from it to Carlisle and back. The spade's message was unmissable: Carlisle had been hit by someone, deliberately.

He checked Carlisle's pulse again: did he only imagine it, or was it fainter? He patted the gardener's shoulder, not wanting to move him much in case he caused more damage.

'Carlisle?' he called. 'Carlisle? Come on, man, wake up!'

Carlisle gave the faintest of grunts but at that moment it was the best sound Murray could have heard. He kept patting, hoping the sensation would catch Carlisle and turn him back from the deepest layers of unconsciousness. At least the hothouse was warm, though the slabbed floor was already chilling his own legs as he sat on it.

His legs were indeed quite numb by the time he heard footsteps on the gravel garden path outside, and a voice from the doorway of the hothouse.

'Mr. Murray, your servants seem to be particularly prone to accidents! What is it this time?'

Murray leaned back so that he could see if Dr. Lindsay was alone. The young garden lad was behind him, hopping with importance on the threshold.

'Thank you, Allie, off you go for your dinner,' he said, and waited a moment. When Allie's scampering footsteps had faded, Murray explained, 'Not an accident, but an attempted murder, I believe. This is my gardener, Carlisle.'

'Good Lord!' To do him credit, Dr. Lindsay hurried forward, flinging off his coat as he came the better to squeeze in under the rack and see what the damage was. He pulled off his gloves and touched Carlisle's head wound gently. 'Messy,' he murmured. 'Any idea what …?'

'That spade, I should think.' Murray nodded towards it. Lindsay looked carefully, and agreed.

'That would fit, certainly. It's not very clean, either: even if the man recovers consciousness there is a high risk of infection. Did you find him just here?'

'That's right: I haven't moved him, in case of making things worse.'

'We should get him to his bed. Has he family? Someone to look after him?'

'No, he lives alone. But the cottage is nearby, and someone from the house can come and take care of him.'

'Could we carry him between us, do you think?'

'He's short, and not heavily built – I think so. Shall I spread out this blanket?'

He eased the blanket off Carlisle's back, and laid it on the floor. With Lindsay at the head end and Murray at the feet, they gently rolled the gardener on to the blanket with Murray's coat over him. Dr. Lindsay paused to put his own coat back on, then they lifted the blanket with its burden between them and walked Carlisle at funereal pace over to his cottage, laying him down on his neatly made bed.

'Oh, my bag,' said Lindsay, testing to see if the kettle was warm for hot water. He began to poke the fire.

'I'll fetch it,' said Murray, and hurried back to the hothouse. Lindsay had set his bag down near where Carlisle had been lying and flung his coat on top of it: when Murray picked up the bag he saw a folded letter, which had presumably fallen from a pocket of either his own coat or the doctor's. He flicked it open casually, intending just to look at the address. 'Dear Brother,' it said, and opposite that, 'Invertally Castle', somewhere completely unfamiliar to him. It must be Lindsay's, so he folded it shut again and took it with the bag back to Carlisle's cottage.

Lindsay had the fire going and a kettle warming, and seized the bag to draw out dressings and an ointment made, he said, with honey against infection. There was little use doing anything until the water was boiled but see that Carlisle was as comfortable as possible, taking off his boots and loosening his stiff Sunday collar, and pulling the blankets up over him. Dr. Lindsay quickly surveyed his limbs but found no breaks, and then looked over Carlisle's bare hands.

'No defensive wounds,' said Murray, watching him. 'It looks as if he was taken by surprise.'

'That's what I was thinking,' said Lindsay. 'You know something of this kind of thing, then?'

'A little. Oh, here: you must have dropped this in the hot house: it's not mine.' He handed over the letter.

'Thank you.' Dr. Lindsay pocketed it again, shoving it down hard.

'Were you in St. Andrews yesterday collecting your mail, then?' Murray asked, more to make conversation than anything. He still found Dr. Lindsay oddly awkward.

'In St. Andrews? Not at all: not for several days,' said Dr. Lindsay at once.

'No? Then your beautiful black stallion has a twin brother!'

Lindsay stared at him, eyes wide, but said nothing, until Murray, taken by surprise, looked away, down at Carlisle and his bloody head.

Chapter Fourteen

Lindsay did not say much more as he delicately cleaned and dressed Carlisle's wound: Carlisle himself said less. There were two signs of hope, as far as Murray was concerned: the thrawn old man had managed not to die straightaway, hanging on till he was found, and while he was being tended to he did, just once, squirm under the doctor's hands and mutter something entirely incomprehensible. Murray was not quite sure why he was reluctant to leave Carlisle alone with Dr. Lindsay – it certainly was not for the enjoyment of Lindsay's company for its own sake - but he was pleased when he saw that the gardeners, released from their dinner table, were lingering just within sight of the cottage, presumably dying of curiosity. He stepped outside to summon one of them, and this time the eldest strode over, trying his best to look serious and responsible. He was a tall lad, with shoulder muscles made broad by digging, and a healthy, outdoor look to his face and hands.

'Tam Gunn,' said Murray, 'is any of you at the bothy a good nurse to an injured man?'

Tam Gunn was not prepared to say that any of them was.

'Then go to the house and find someone who will come here and tend to Mr. Carlisle. Tell them he has a head injury, but that Dr. Lindsay has cleaned and dressed it. You will be in charge of the daily routine in the gardens until Mr. Carlisle is fit again, all right?' He had nothing against Tam Gunn, but he hoped that his period in charge would not be a long one. He told himself that Carlisle was bound to recover.

'Yes, sir.' Tam's face, dismayed at the talk of head injuries, brightened irrepressibly. 'I can do that.'

'I'm glad to hear it. Now, before you go, Tam,' he glanced back into the cottage, but Dr. Lindsay had finished his work and was wiping his hands clean on one of Carlisle's well-kept towels, 'do you know anything of what has happened to Mr. Carlisle?'

'Well, sir, you said he had a head injury.'

'Yes.'

'That's all I ken, sir.'

'Oh.' Murray tried not to smile. 'Had you seen him at all this morning?'

'No, sir.'

'But you would normally expect to walk down to the kirk with him, would you not?'

'Well, yes, sir. But we went to chap at the cottage door here, and he wasna within, so we thought he might already have gone ahead,' he suggested this though he clearly had no faith in the idea, 'or that he might be busy somewhere.'

'The minister said he had not been very regular in his attendance recently.'

'That's right, sir,' said Tam, relieved that Murray had mentioned it first.

'Why was that, then? Do you know?' Murray was interested enough, for the minister could count it as his responsibility to see that his staff attended the kirk with all due propriety.

'I dinna ken, sir,' said Tam, primly, then could not resist adding, 'only that the minister said something about flower gardens being a waste of time in his sermon one week, and Mr. Carlisle took it bad.'

'Oh, I see.' This time Murray did smile: no doubt the remark had not been aimed at Carlisle, nor at any of the other gardeners in the congregation, but had derived from some quarrel with his wife who would spend her days in the garden and never enter the manse at all if she could manage it. 'So you didn't see Mr. Carlisle here, and you didn't go to look for him because you thought he might be avoiding going to church.'

'That's it, sir!' Tam Gunn looked pleased to be understood so easily.

'And he definitely wasn't within here? You looked?'

'Aye, sir. We always chap and then push the door in, and he wasna here.'

That ruled out the idea that Carlisle might have been sitting in his cottage with his attacker already, silent by his own will or otherwise.

'Did you see anyone else in the gardens this morning? Anyone, perhaps, who should not have been here?'

Tam's eyes widened.

'No, sir. Nobody at all.'

'Right, then: hurry along and find someone to sit with Mr. Carlisle, and then be about your duties. But I should like to speak to all the gardeners, one by one, before dinner. I mean before my dinner,' he added, remembering that they had eaten theirs already. Tam nodded briskly, and strode off towards the kitchens to find a nurse.

Tam did indeed send the gardeners one by one, as Dr. Lindsay left and Murray remained near the cottage. Mary Robbins, who had been an army wife and had nursed more injuries than he cared to think of, came to sit with Carlisle so he had no anxieties there: Carlisle would be well cared for, and anything he said would be noted, but Murray felt the gardeners might talk more freely in their own familiar territory than in the library or the parlour. However, none of them had seen anything strange or startling or the least bit useful, not even the boy whose job it was to stoke the wall fires and who had therefore been out earlier than anyone else. Murray was left to return frustrated to the house. He could think of no good reason why anyone would attack his gardener and leave him for dead in a hothouse on a Sunday morning – except that Carlisle had been in St. Andrews, and around the Shaws' house, on the night that Rory McArthur had been murdered there. Had he seen something? Or someone? And had that someone realised who he was, and followed him to Letho? If so, who could it have been?

It would not leave Murray's mind that Jack Swanson was, as far as he knew, still missing, and that he could easily have walked from St. Andrews to Letho by Sunday morning.

Cosmo Gordon arrived bright and early on Monday morning, and found for once that the subject of today's portrait was ready and waiting. Walter had resumed his Sunday best coat and his ferocious aunt had presumably seen to it that his chestnut cap of hair glowed with even more shine than usual. Cosmo had had Walter's situation explained to him, and had elected to paint the boy standing by a small table on which a few books had been arranged. The mistake had been in assuming that Walter would be able to resist trying to read them every time Cosmo Gordon's gaze left him. By the time Murray entered the dining room after breakfast to see how things were going, Cosmo Gordon was growling and Walter had assumed an air of self-righteousness that Murray felt sure he had already seen on young James Shaw.

'Settle down, Walter, and let Mr. Gordon paint your likeness,' said Murray firmly. 'I have undertaken to have you back in St. Andrews this afternoon, and if the painting is not done by then, then you will not be painted and that is that.'

Walter had the grace to look slightly subdued, and Cosmo Gordon swiftly took advantage of it. Reminded that time was short, he let his brush fly over the canvas more swiftly than usual.

'If you stay still long enough, I can fix your face in my head,' he explained to Walter, 'and then any finishing touches can be done after you've gone back to St. Andrews – or if Mr. Murray wishes it, I can finish the painting there.'

'That will depend on Professor Shaw,' said Murray. 'It was kind of him to allow you to take a couple of days to come here, Walter: not every student is allowed home halfway through the term.'

'Yes, sir,' said Walter dutifully. Cosmo worked on in silence for a few minutes, only the light scrape of brush on canvas tickling at the peace of the room.

'You are well established, then, in Fife,' Murray tried after a little while: Cosmo was not the kind of artist who disliked conversation as he worked.

'I am, I believe,' said Cosmo Gordon with some contentment. 'I find the society in St. Andrews quite congenial.'

'And there is your music, of course, too. It must have been pleasant to find yourself playing with someone from your part of the world.'

'What?' Gordon's surprised question was just a little sharp to be wholly polite. Murry looked at him, eyebrows raised.

'I believe you said you were from Perthshire?'

'Yes, but –'

'And so was Roderick McArthur, was he not? I forget the exact name of his village …' Murray tailed off, hoping that

Gordon might fill in the gap. He gave him an encouraging look, but Cosmo was frowning.

'I said my family was from Perthshire,' he said. 'I believe I explained that we lost our lands some years ago, the estate and the castle.' Murray could see the artist's spine straightening as he said the words, his shoulders going back. 'I don't think that we would have known the McArthurs.'

'Nevertheless he would surely have said –'

'I don't believe he did,' said Cosmo, 'And I would never have asked him.'

'Ah, well,' said Murray, trying to bring the temperature of the conversation back down from its unexpected flare, 'I daresay someone will know. His wife, probably. You said you didn't know her, I think?'

'That's right. Roderick made sure we never set eyes on her: anyone would think he thought we would run off with her.' It could have been a joke, but he made it sound surly, as if he really grudged Rory his protection of his wife. Murray decided to turn the subject a little. Walter had a resigned look on his face which would not flatter him in the portrait.

'I gather our new doctor – our temporary one, at any rate – is also from Perthshire. There is a positive invasion at present, isn't there? I think he said he was from –' he remembered the name from the letter Dr. Lindsay had dropped, and tried it - 'Invertally?'

'Invertally?' Cosmo Gordon paused, and stared at the canvas in front of him. 'Invertally, indeed? What did you say his name was again?'

'Lindsay. Archibald Lindsay.' Murray paused, watching Cosmo's face. It made an interesting picture: lips pressed tight, eyes deeply thoughtful, a little frown. Yet had not Cosmo seen Dr. Lindsay the other day, when he left Letho after attending to Iffy? Murray remembered the look of shock on his face then, but now Cosmo seemed more collected.

'And he's here in Letho, you say?' he asked almost casually.

'He's helping with Dr. Feilden's cases: you know the local man broke his leg.'

'I didn't, no. Well,' he said, pulling himself back to briskness, 'there's little enough to Invertally: if he's a gentleman living there then he's likely at the castle.'

'I believe he did say his brother was a laird, so presumably he's Lindsay of Invertally.'

Cosmo gave a deep sigh.

'And once upon a time it was Gordon of Invertally,' he said wistfully.

'Oh, I see.' Murray had already guessed. 'You must miss it very much,' he added gently.

'It was my family's home,' said Cosmo Gordon simply. 'Now it is theirs. I hope fortune favours them more than it favoured us.' Murray waited a moment, but it seemed Gordon had said all he was going to say on the subject. The air felt heavy in the room, closed down. Eventually Murray cleared his throat and spoke quietly.

'Well, Walter, come and find me when you're finished here and we'll head back to St. Andrews. I assume you're painting Robbins next, Gordon?'

Cosmo Gordon grunted, stabbing his paintbrush at the canvas. Murray nodded, and left the dining room for his desk in the library.

Amongst the notes he was making on the matter of Rory McArthur's death, he added a small paragraph on Cosmo Gordon's reaction to that name, Invertally. He wondered what the nature of his family's financial disaster had been: something recent, perhaps connected with the French wars? He had been lucky at Letho, but anyone who had had money laid out in schemes that were not entirely sound had suffered when the prices shot up after Waterloo. Could Cosmo be the person from Perthshire so feared by Janet McArthur? But no, surely not: he was in the string quartet with Rory: Rory would hardly have spent his leisure time with someone who was a danger to his young wife and possibly also a risk to himself. And Cosmo Gordon had denied knowing the McArthurs before – and he had said that Invertally was a small place (certainly Murray had never heard of it), so surely if both families had lived in the same village, however different their stations in life, they would know of each other just as he knew all the families in Letho.

He stood and walked about the library for a moment, rubbing his long fingers hard through his hair and pausing here and there to greet old friends on the bookshelves. So far his notes on this recent death were not going very well. He had to consider the possible threat from Perthshire, though with Mrs. McArthur too scared to speak and without knowledge of where the McArthurs had come from in Perthshire beyond somewhere near Aberfeldy, that was a difficult line to follow. He had to consider that if there had not been a threat from Perthshire, then someone in St. Andrews had had reason to kill him, and he would have to work out who that might have been. It seemed unlikely to be a casual thief out after dark: for one thing, it had not been particularly late in the evening when Rory had last been seen alive, and there had still been plenty of people about – in the town, anyway. For another, if Rory had climbed the wall into the Swansons' garden, dropped his hat in his haste, and carried on to scramble over the wall into the Shaws' garden, and his pursuer had chased him all the way, it spoke of something more desperate than a mere thief after a purse. And what casual thief would pursue Carlisle all the way to Letho, if that was what had happened?

Rory had left the recital, and had last been seen heading west along South Street at around half past nine. At some time after that, he had climbed into the Swansons' garden, possibly to seek help, then as no help was forthcoming he climbed again into the Shaws' garden, where his pursuer caught up with him and drowned him. They had no idea what time that had happened. Then into the night's activities came Mr. Swanson, returning to his house at some point in an unestablished state of inebriation, and his son Jack practising his fiddle-playing at the front of their house, then young Sandy Bogue and his father, trying to find Jack Swanson, and then indeed the Shaw family, returning home from the recital at a reasonable hour and retiring, all unaware of the dramas unfolding just outside their house. Or were they all? Did he need to look closer to home? Not to the Professor or Mrs. Shaw, obviously, but what about the manservant? What about Flavia, who knew Rory McArthur better than she had at first admitted? What about James Shaw? No, surely both the children were too small to attack Rory and drown him with so little struggle, and the same applied to Walter. And anyway, how did that fit in with Rory being chased into the garden? Either they were chasing him, in which case how long had they been missing from the house, or they happened to be in the garden and murderously inclined when he appeared over the wall, losing his hunter but falling by an astonishing coincidence into their waiting hands … no, it would not do, not for any of the children.

And then there was Jack Swanson. No one seemed really convinced that Jack would have killed Rory, unless it had been to save his own life at Rory's hands. Yet Jack had disappeared, which was not usually a sign of innocence in such circumstances. Murray had asked the constable, Round, to send him an express at once if Jack reappeared, but nothing had arrived at Letho since he and Walter had returned on Saturday. He was growing impatient to return to St. Andrews and see what progress had been made. Had anyone come forward to say they had seen Rory McArthur attacked or pursued by the mill lade that night? Could they fill in any more of Rory's movements after he left the recital? It had not been that late at night: surely someone had seen him, somewhere.

He sighed. He seemed to be going round in circles, and his head was starting to swim. He rang the bell for some tea: it would not be long now till Walter was ready to leave, and if he were to drive to St. Andrews soon he wanted some sustinence.

Robbins appeared, looking if anything a little gloomier than usual.

'Any news of Carlisle?' Murray asked, suddenly anxious. Mary Robbins had earlier reported a peaceful but unchanged night.

'Oh, no sir. Nothing new. Mary says he sighs from time to time, and he has made a few sounds like talking but she cannot make out any words, sir.'

'And the gardeners found nothing missing, or damaged?'

'Nothing, sir. They made a very thorough search – Tam Gunn is a reliable lad, and he's taking his duties very seriously.'

'That's what I thought.' He nodded, sighing.

Robbins frowned.

'Do you still believe that he was attacked because of something he saw in St. Andrews that night, sir?'

'For want of any other reason, yes. Don't you? They say he had not particularly annoyed anyone in Letho, though I know he could be a thrawn old man.'

'That was just his way, sir. The gardeners wouldn't work anywhere else.'

'Yes ... He had quarrelled with the minister, but I don't think the minister realised it, from what I hear.'

'I think he had several quarrels like that, sir. If he stopped talking to you, you just had to go after him and find out why – or leave it, but it could take years then for him to make it up with you.'

'Well, there we are: often annoying, thoroughly stubborn, but not the kind of man you would take a spade to and leave him for dead in his own hothouse on the Sabbath,' he could not help adding, as if that made it worse. In a way it did, for the gardens were quiet on a Sunday and it was pure luck he had been found as quickly as he had been. 'But he was in St. Andrews and he was looking for Professor Shaw on the evening when a man was murdered in Professor Shaw's garden. I have no reason to suppose he was connected with the matter in any way unless he happened to see something that someone wishes unseen, in which case someone, who has secrets to keep and probably murderous ones, followed him from St. Andrews to Letho and attacked him. Mary – Mrs. Robbins does know to be careful, doesn't she?'

'Yes, sir.' Robbins met his eye with his own pale gaze. They both knew that Mrs. Robbins was perfectly capable of looking after herself, and that she did not welcome excessive anxiety over her wellbeing. They both shrugged.

'Well ... Cosmo Gordon wants to paint you next, Robbins: he should have finished what he needs to do with Walter within the hour.'

'Oh, that's a pity, sir. I have a great deal to do this afternoon. Perhaps someone else could go instead.'

'William? Has he been painted yet?'

'No, sir, and he's looking forward to it: Daniel has been telling him what a fine, handsome portrait he has made, so of course William wants to do better.'

'As ever. Mrs. Mack and Iffy have been done, of course.'

'Yes, sir, and if the servants hear one more psalm of praise of Mr. Gordon's eyes or his hands from Iffy, I shall have to take action, sir, for there will be a riot.'

'And we're already too many servants down, so be careful, Robbins!' Murray grinned. 'No word on a housekeeper or maids?'

'Nothing yet, sir.'

'Miss Blair is keeping an eye open in Edinburgh for us.' And looking after Augusta, he thought to himself. He hoped she would be home soon.

'That's very good of her, sir.'

There was a calm tattoo on the door, and Walter entered, a small smudge of blue paint on his nose.

'Mr. Gordon says he's finished with me, sir, and would Mr. Robbins please step in?'

'I'll fetch William,' said Robbins hurriedly. 'Are you wanting to go now, sir?'

'Send in some tea for Walter and me, and ask for the gig, and then we'll be off.'

'Sir.'

Robbins vanished, and Murray gestured Walter to select a book and read until the tea arrived. He himself pulled out his father's atlas of Scotland and peered at the Perthshire page, concentrating particularly on Aberfeldy and its environs, but he could see no Invertally. He returned to his notes, shaking his head, and making no progress at all.

The journey back was pleasant with conversation about books and animals, once again. Walter's enthusiasm for his studies was clear, though it seemed young James Shaw was not quite so devoted. Murray hoped he would not prove a distraction. As they began to meet the beginnings of the day's traffic leaving the town, Walter started eyeing the various bundles and kists that were being borne on the backs of mules and ponies, and on handcarts. He fell into thoughtful silence, then as they were passing the West Port he drew himself up on his seat and said,

'Ah, Mr. Murray, I think maybe I did see that kist of flannels after all.'

'Did you? Where?'

'Ah. That I'm no so sure, sir. I think Pennie gave it to me when I was in the garden by the fishponds.'

'Pennie? Oh, yes, the manservant, of course.'

'And because I would have been in the middle of taking notes and making observations,' he liked the word, clearly, 'I maybe set it down where I was and forgot to pick it up again.'

Murray sighed: it seemed he was not yet entirely free of Walter's proclivities for losing things.

'Well, you'd better find it, Walter, and soon. For one thing I'm sure the jam ought not to be left in the garden, and for another, your aunt will do something savage to me if she goes on thinking I've lost it. Be so good as to save me from that!'

'Aye, sir, I'll do what I can.' Walter had a resigned air. He had always been well aware of his own limitations. They reached the Shaws' house as promised comfortably before dinner time. Walter scuttled into the house at speed, presumably intent on searching the garden for the kist before it slipped his mind once more. Murray took the gig round the side of the house to the stables with Pennie the manservant following: Murray had never been entirely convinced that Pennie was strong enough to manage a full grown horse and a gig. Pennie, however, began to unharness the mare with competence, having water and feed ready for her.

'Pennie, did you hear anything odd the other night? The night young McArthur must have been killed in the garden.'

Pennie shuddered.

'I dinna like to think of it at all, sir. That poor lad!'

'Where in the house do you sleep?'

'Och, down by the back. But I dinna think I heard nothing, sir. It strikes me cold, thinking he could have cried out – or that we could all have been murdered in our beds! And I'd have been the first to go, no doubt,' he added, nervously.

'There might not have been much noise,' Murray admitted. 'But you heard no one cry out?'

'Not a bit of it, sir, and I'll tell you I'm a gey light sleeper. The least wee noise has me awake. Mr. Swanson working late in his workshop, now, that often has me with my head under the pillow, crying out for peace!'

'Was he working that night?'

'He was indeed, sir, though it wasna the usual hammering and beating and thumping – you'd never believe it, sir, if you didna have to put up with it yourself in your ain bed.'

'So what was he doing, then, if he wasn't hammering? What could you hear?'

'Och, just shifting stuff, I think. Doors banging and suchlike. He never thinks other folk might want a decent night's sleep, ken?'

'What time would that have been, then?'

'I have a wee clock, sir, that my last master gave me in his will. It keeps grand time, a lovely wee piece it is, and it told me it was gone half past ten. Half past ten, and Mr. Swanson still working! I always think, sir, that it's a miracle.' He lowered his voice with some reverence, eyes wide. 'All that racket and catterbatter, and what does it produce? The most perjink wee rings and brooches, the prettiest ashets you ever did see, all swirls and flowery leafy oh! so fine! So whiles I canna take the noise, and whiles I think ah! but what'll it be this time?' He sighed wistfully, and Murray thanked him, coming away astonished at Pennie's sensibility. Where did Professor Shaw find his servants?

But on a more serious note, what was Swanson doing in his workshop on Wednesday night, when he said he was at Cosmo Gordon's flat, drinking himself silly?

Chapter Fifteen

'Any word of Jack Swanson?' Murray asked as soon as he found Professor Shaw. The parlour had been cleared of its black funeral hangings, and the Professor had quickly involved Walter in a piece of work he had set for his son. The boys already had their heads down at the parlour table, muttering Greek declensions fervently, while Shaw and Murray established themselves by the fire. Professor Shaw's portrait had not yet been restored to its former position.

'Not a thing, Charles, my boy. My dear wife thought he was embarrassed at the accident with the tray, but he did not run home and he has not reappeared. Swanson is distraught: he was in here yesterday for two hours demanding to know what he could do. Constable Round has had enquiries made at the harbour and at the toll gates in every direction, but as to that he could easily have slipped away if he had wanted to, over the fields or in a small boat.'

'Was he a boating person?'

'No, not that I'm aware of. Just … there are ways of going, easily enough, if he has gone.'

'Well, at least it's more likely that he is hiding somewhere than that he has become the murderer's next victim,' said Murray, a little tentatively. 'He seems at least to have vanished of his own accord, and not been snatched away.'

'Lured away, though?' Professor Shaw seemed in a low mood, and not much wonder with the past week's events. He sighed.

'Constable Round said he would come along this evening after dinner to speak with you, if you will. Though you must be tired with all this travelling back and forth to Letho. Is all well there?'

'My gardener was attacked and left in one of the hothouses yesterday morning,' Murray said, 'and I fear it has something to do with the same business.'

'Your gardener? Mr. Carlisle?' Professor Shaw had paled.

'Oh! I am sorry: I had half-forgotten you were acquainted.'

'The man so interested in my little experiment with the peas. Is he all right?'

'He was still unconscious when we left, but seemed not to be worsening. I am praying that his tough head and general stubbornness will see him through.' He smiled, trying to be reassuring, though he was still very worried himself.

'Is young Archibald Lindsay tending to him, then?' Professor Shaw asked.

'He did see to him to begin with, yes.'

'We have sent to ask him to dinner here tomorrow, so you may have more word of Mr. Carlisle then. It will be good to see my old pupil again! I am looking forward to it, after such a week. And my wife has asked the Bogues, too: all four of them are to attend.'

'Oh! Quite a dinner, then.' Murray's mind flickered between the possible advantages of more conversation with the Bogue menfolk and the distinct pleasure of more conversation with Miss Bogue. It was indeed something to look forward to.

If he had hoped that that evening's dinner would be a lighter meal in anticipation of the guests the following day, he was disappointed: once again he found himself filled to the brim with tasty but rich fare, and any energy he had in the parlour afterwards was focussed more on digesting than on thinking. Nevertheless Constable Round appeared promptly – Murray wondered if he had been waiting outside until he saw the candles lit in the parlour – and the rest of the family left Professor Shaw and Murray to their conversation in comfort. Round, nevertheless, pressed to sit and take his ease, selected a hard chair and sat to attention.

'The professor will have told you there is still no sign of Jack Swanson,' he began, 'alive or dead.'

'Yes: perhaps no news is good news.'

'Mmhmm. Aye. And there's little else to report, sir.'

'Tell him about poor Mr. Carlisle, Charles.'

'Of course.' Murray described once again the attack on his gardener, and explained why he thought it might be linked with the murder of Rory McArthur.

'Well, there have been no reports of violent attacks around the county,' said the constable thoughtfully. 'There was a highway robbery Crossgates way, but that's a different thing – a trader attacked and robbed. You say there was nothing stolen?'

'Not that any of the gardeners could discover. His cottage and his person looked intact, apart from the blow to his head.'

'Aye. That has the air of a personal thing, I'd say, sir.'

'Exactly. And no one about the place could tell us who might have had a personal grudge against the man: indeed, he is liked in spite of himself.'

'Yet he was in St. Andrews last Wednesday night?'

'He was, and he was about here for he was looking for Professor Shaw, but he saw the house in darkness and decided to come back on the Thursday morning, which he did. He would have had no reason to know Rory McArthur, I believe: he does not venture to St. Andrews often, and he has no connexion I know of in Perthshire. But he may have seen someone or something here that night when he was looking for the Professor – perhaps he did not even realise its significance.'

'Do you know what time he was here?'

'No. I have no idea. Presumably after we retired for the night, which would have been not long after ten. But I wonder if I have discovered something that would tell us when Rory was killed?'

Murray related what he had found out from the manservant Pennie.

'Swanson says he was out, and Jack Swanson stayed at the front of the house – or was out in South Street around eleven - so who was in the workshop at half past ten?'

'Wait,' said Professor Shaw, standing and going to the table, 'I feel the need to see this all on a piece of paper.' He found a pen and ink, and a book to lean on, and returned to his seat. 'The last time we know Rory was alive and in sight of others was when he left the recital, just about the time we did. When was that?'

'Around half past nine,' said Murray, 'though it took us a little while to leave, all of us.'

'Half past nine,' Professor Shaw repeated. 'At half past nine Rory was alive, and at the Bogues' house. At that time we don't know where Jack Swanson was, though we think he was at home, and we don't know where Thomas Swanson was.'

'Well, we think he might have been at home, too, but in his workshop,' put in Murray. Professor Shaw made quick, delicate notes.

'And the Bogues were at their house, too.'

'Yes, they did not go out to look for Rory, or Jack, or whatever they were doing, until later,' said Murray. 'I think probably about ten o'clock, from what Wee Dod said.'

'Ten o'clock, then, the Bogues set off, and the likeliest place for them to go first would be the Swansons' house.'

'Unless they went to McArthur's house on the way, sir, to see whether or not he was at home.' The constable's eyes were concentrated on the piece of paper. Professor Shaw's notes took the form of a grid, with times across the top and names down the side.

'True. When they did go to the Swansons' house –'

'Wait a second,' said Murray, 'we haven't thought about that. Would they have gone to McArthur's house? Janet McArthur has not mentioned seeing them.'

'Then presumably they went straight to the Swansons. And they found it in darkness: presumably again this was when Swanson had gone to visit Cosmo Gordon at the far end of Market Street. He was there soon after Cosmo returned home from the recital, so he must have gone out, if he went straight there, soon after half past nine. Between half past nine and ten, anyway.' Murray watched Shaw make another note in Thomas Swanson's row, then added, 'but we don't know where Jack Swanson went, or when. We only know he was seen in South Street around eleven, apparently heading home.'

'And Thomas Swanson the same, but an hour later,' the constable added. 'So if you're right about the noise Pennie heard from Swanson's workshop being something to do with McArthur's murder, then he was killed the back of half past ten, and Thomas Swanson is in the clear.'

'But Jack Swanson could have killed his friend, then gone out and still be heading home at elevenish.' Murray looked about at the other two. 'Does that all make sense?'

'Oh, aye,' said the constable, and Professor Shaw nodded.

'But does it actually get us any further?' Murray asked. The other two shrugged. 'What we want,' Murray went on, 'is some useful witness who was lingering about the mill lade between, say, ten and eleven on Wednesday night.'

'Well, Mr. Binny's away to Edinburgh for the season,' said the constable slowly, 'though we might find a servant there who would have seen something.'

'McArthur does seem to have come in from the path by the mill lade, over the wall at the bottom of Swansons' garden, and in a hurry, or he would have stopped to pick up his hat,' said Murray thoughtfully. 'But if I'm right about the noise, he then ran to the workshop – looking for help from Mr. Swanson, presumably. Swanson was out, so he ran again, this time climbing the wall to your garden, sir.'

Professor Shaw made an unhappy face.

'I wish he had called out for help, though goodness knows we might not have heard, or might have hesitated in confusion until it was too late. But I wish I knew he thought he could come here for safety … though of course he did not.' He let the book he was holding sag despondent.

'His murderer was clearly very determined, sir. I think that if you had heard something and gone out, you too might have come to serious harm,' said Murray, and Constable Round nodded agreement.

'Aye, sir, that could well have been you or your family, with your days ended in the fishpond.'

Professor Shaw swallowed audibly. Murray tried to change the subject.

'But anyway, who was chasing him, and why were they down by the mill lade? As far as we knew, Rory McArthur left the recital with the intention of going to look for Jack Swanson to ask him why he had not turned up. Could he have found Jack somewhere in that direction, and been chased by him?'

'Then why run to the Swansons? He might not expect sympathy from Thomas Swanson. Why not run up the common close to South Street where he might find the night watchman, or someone else who could help him?' Professor Shaw's point was fair, unless the common close was for some reason not an option.

'He could have been chased down the common close in the first place. What if he met his attacker in South Street, or even more likely outside Swansons' house? He might easily then flee down the common close, and turn right around Swansons' garden wall, then find he had nowhere else to go and tried to climb the wall to seek safety there.'

'Then it still seems unlikely to be Jack,' said Professor Shaw. 'If they argued outside the Swansons' house here, surely Rory would not have run round and tried to climb in at the back of the property?'

'Could Mr. Swanson,' the constable suggested tentatively, 'have barred his way to Jack at the front of the house, so McArthur ran down the lane to get at him from the back? Then he met Jack in the workshop and Jack turned against him, and chased him out of the garden?'

Professor Shaw and Murray looked at each other, trying to picture it.

'Would Rory have been that angry? So angry that he would run all that way, and not even stop to pick up his hat?' asked Murray. 'From what people have told me, his anger was a seething type, not a wild type. And even if he did, would Jack be angry enough not only to chase him out of the garden but to follow him and kill him?'

'And of course Thomas Swanson was not there, anyway,' added Professor Shaw, and Constable Round nodded.

'True, true. I was just trying it on for size.'

'Indeed, indeed,' said Professor Shaw sadly.

Murray wondered how best to use his time next morning: there was no point in visiting the Bogues if he was to see them at dinner, for example. He breakfasted alone, as Professor Shaw had taken the boys to some early morning class, and Mrs. Shaw and Flavia were already busy arranging the house for the dinner party. Murray noticed that Professor Shaw's portrait still had not been restored to the parlour wall, and wondered where it had wandered to this time.

After breakfast, having collected his hat, gloves, coat and

stick, he stepped out into the lane at the front of the house and considered. The first place his eyes fell upon was the Swansons' front door. He went and knocked, and almost at once heard eager footsteps inside. The door was flung open, but the anxious smile on the maid's face was immediately replaced by one of resignation.

'I'm sorry,' said Murray, 'I think you were expecting Mr. Jack Swanson, were you not?'

'Aye, sir,' said the maid, cast down. 'The master is within, sir, but I'm not sure ... He's no much use to a'body just now, if you see what I mean.'

'I understand. There has been no word at all of Mr. Jack?'

'Nothing, sir. We just dinna ken where he's away to, or if he went of his own accord or why he would do sic a thing.' It was clear from her face that she too had been crying, and had been asking herself the same questions over and over again. There was nothing he could learn here. He asked the maid to convey his good wishes to Mr. Swanson, and left, heading up the common close to South Street.

On the street a small crowd was clustered about the public steelyard, and there was some laughter. He stepped across to see what was going on. The long-armed scales were jerking up and down as if agitated, but what was on the end of the measuring chain he could not quite see until he was close to the crowd and used his height to secure a view. A merchant was stacking silver shillings on to a scale pan, while another held the pan steady. The steelyard master fiddled about adjusting the weights, designed for much heavier loads such as sacks of grain. He had a broad smile on his face. When the pan was ready, the merchants let it go, and it crashed to the cobbles, spilling shillings to left and right. The crowd chuckled, and several people crouched to help recover the coins.

'Far too heavy to be real!' the first merchant nodded to the second. 'It must be lead.'

'Where did these come from?' Murray asked.

'A pedlar found them, he says, on the road to Crossgates,' said the merchant genially. 'And now they're going off to the sheriff. There's not a proper coin amongst them.'

'May I see one?'

The merchant happily placed a coin in Murray's gloved hand, but kept an eye on it. Murray studied the inscription: it was indeed the right wording for 1816, but dated 1817. He handed the coin back.

'Have you seen any of these before?' he asked. The merchant laughed.

'Aye, a few, in these last twa three weeks. Someone somewhere has been a busy wee fellow, now!' He and the other merchant made a show of securing the false coins in a small box with a padlock, and climbed into a waiting cart, the one to drive and the other with the box on his lap. They set off to polite cheers, and the steelyard master reorganised his weights and settled back down to more ordinary business.

Across the road, Murray could see the little close where the McArthurs had lived, and wondered if he would be any more successful in his enquiries there than he had been at the Swansons. He crossed the busy street with care, and edged into the narrow alley mouth. The McArthurs' little house was still closed up, the shutters firmly secured, so he tapped on the door of Mrs. Loudoun's house across the close. After a moment, during which he was sure he was being inspected through some chink, the door opened about three inches, and Nathan Houston's unlovely face could just be seen in the gap, along with his shoulder. The black eye was now yellowy purple, and a study for any artist.

'What you want?' he demanded.

'I was wondering if I might have a word with Mrs. McArthur, if she is still with you.'

'Why?'

'I wondered first of all if she had seen Jack Swanson at all.'

There was a squeak from within the little house, and Nathan turned away just enough to utter the word 'Wheesht!'.

'Well?' he said, turning back.

'Was that a yes or a no?' Murray asked politely. 'Only, his father is very worried about him. He'd like to know at least that he is safe.'

Nathan glared at Murray for a second, then slammed the door shut. Without even pressing his ear to it, Murray could hear a swift, urgent conversation from within. The door shot open again to its narrow angle, and Murray surreptitiously slid his boot into the gap while holding Nathan's gaze.

'She doesna ken a'thing of where Jack Swanson is, and you can tell his faither that an' all.'

'I see. Thank you, that is very helpful.'

Thinking the visit was over, Nathan tried to slam the door shut, and bounced awkwardly against it in surprise when it jarred on Murray's boot. Murray was glad his boots were tough: he still had to school his face to hide the pain.

'I also wanted to ask,' Murray went on, 'if she feels ready to tell me what part of Perthshire she is from, so that we are better able to protect her from any attack from the people she seems to fear.'

'You dinna need to fash yoursel',' said Nathan. 'I'll be the one looking after her. I can protect her just fine, thank you.' He thudded the door into the side of Murray's foot again, though it seemed to be more absent-mindedness than malice. He glanced back into the room again, and Murray thought he even surprised the least look of tenderness on Nathan's ugly face.

'Is that with your pistols, Nathan?' Murray asked. 'Did you get them after you were robbed near Crossgates?'

Nathan's head snapped round in surprise, but any response he might have made was interrupted.

'Is that Mr. Murray?' Mrs. Loudoun's sensible tones could be heard from within. 'Why didn't you say, you foolish man? He wants to help her!'

'I'll do the helping around here, you auld carline,' Nathan declared, but it seemed that Mrs. Loudoun was the stronger of the two. The door was pulled fully open and Mrs. Loudoun stood on the threshold with a more welcoming nod. Little Rosina was in her arms, looking well fed and content.

'Mr. Murray. She's grand, really, but still not talking about anything from where they were before, or what she's afeared of. I'm trying to get her to say, and the minute she does I'll get word to you, I promise.'

'Thank you, Mrs. Loudoun. You know how important it is.'

She nodded, and Murray felt reassured: he himself was not sure how important it was, but he trusted Mrs. Loudoun's judgement where Janet McArthur was concerned. And oddly, he trusted Nathan Houston to protect her, if it could be done with dedication and a bit of well-placed violence.

'Young Jack Swanson's still missing, then, did I hear?'

'He is. We have no notion, as you know, that he did not go of his own accord, but that does not put him in a good light with the constable.'

'No, it wouldna at all.' She sighed. 'Well, I hope you find him, whatever he's done or not done.'

'So do I,' agreed Murray, and took his leave. He managed not to limp until he was out of sight, though he did wonder if Nathan's door had managed to break a bone in his foot.

After a few steps he thought it more likely that his foot was bruised, and that a healthy walk would ease it out. He strolled to the top of South Street, eyed the Cathedral for a moment with its whirling gulls, then turned to the right down through the Pends towards the harbour. The walk took him between the water and the old abbey walls, where fishermen busied themselves with boats and nets, then around the sharp corner of the abbey grounds and back up towards South Street as far as Dauphin Hill and the mill lade. Turning left there at the bottom of Eastburn Wynd he made his way back up the stream of the mill lade to the end gate of Professor Shaw's garden, passing the solidly latched gateway into the Swansons' grounds. There were few people about and none seemed interested in a strolling gentleman taking the air. If there were few at this time of the day, it would surely have been very quiet when Rory McArthur ran along here with his murderer flying behind him. Anyone who had been here would surely have remarked it – wouldn't they?

He let himself in through the Shaws' garden gate, and went to dress for dinner.

They were twelve for dinner: the Shaws, except for James who was thought to be too young (Walter was exempted on the same score, and both retreated content to the kitchens for their meal), Murray, the Bogues including Sandy and Miss Bogue, Dr. Lindsay and the young man with whom he was staying in St. Andrews, and to make the numbers even, for Mrs. Shaw did not much enjoy the responsibilities of a hostess and could not bring herself to complicate them further with uneven numbers, a couple of sisters, Playfair by name. They were a little older than Murray, unmarried and without much in the way of dowry, and were well used to coming out to evenings such as this one with no expectations of the company except for a good meal and a pleasant gossip. Murray had met them before and found them inoffensive if a little dim. Dr. Lindsay's host, a Mr. Hepburn, was a contemporary of his from the college and had taken a house for the summer: a single man of reasonable fortune, he was affable and possessed of a rounded, shiny appearance that spoke of decent food and no need for much exercise. Dr. Lindsay was the better-looking of the two, a fact that Murray noted Flavia taking in as soon as the gentlemen arrived. Flavia was evidently getting over her disappointment at Rory's death, then, he thought with a grin. He had overheard her mother telling her to look after young Sandy Bogue this evening, who would be suffering the twin distresses of one friend's death and another's disappearance, but Sandy Bogue was familiar and therefore dull: Dr. Lindsay and Mr. Hepburn were much more exciting by their novelty, at least.

Conversation was general at first, and then Professor Shaw cleared his throat.

'Mrs. Shaw and I thought it best to say that in the circumstances we should have no dancing after dinner – music, of course, if people wish to play, but out of respect for the dead, and for, er, the missing, no dancing.'

The Bogues all nodded sombrely, as did the spinster sisters, but Dr. Lindsay and his friend looked puzzled.

'Please forgive us,' said Lindsay, 'we were unaware that we were entering a house of mourning.'

'Ah,' said Professor Shaw, 'it is not quite that, or of course we should be in mourning, as you say. Unfortunately, a young man of our acquaintance – in fact a good friend of young Mr. Bogue here – was found dead in our garden less than a week ago.'

'Good heavens!'

'Yes: a most distressing matter. It seems likely that he did not die accidentally. And at his funeral, our neighbour's son, a friend of the deceased, went missing and has not been seen since.'

In the general noise of surprise and explanation, Murray glanced to his side. Miss Bogue was staring at him hard, as if she would say something but for some reason could not. She gave the faintest of nods, and looked away, just as Mr. Bogue was explaining that:

'Young McArthur and my son here were part of a very fine string quartet, you know.'

'I see – what a shame,' said Dr. Lindsay. 'A tragedy all around. Did this McArthur have any family?'

'A wife and small child,' said Mrs. Shaw sadly.

'A wife and small child ... dear, dear. But perhaps he left close family that will support her?'

Blank looks were exchanged about the table.

'It is strange enough to relate,' said Professor Shaw at last, 'but alas nobody knows. Rory McArthur was a quiet man: he did not chatter about himself and his concerns.'

'But his wife will know, of course,' said Dr. Lindsay.

Again, the looks bounced about.

'Ah, she is too distraught to speak of it yet,' said Murray, feeling inexplicably defensive, as though they had all let Rory down.

'Does she live in the town?' Dr. Lindsay persisted.

'She is staying with friends,' said Murray quickly, growing even more uneasy. He plunged into a change of subject. 'Mr. Hepburn, were you in Edinburgh for the season? Perhaps you saw that play at the Shakespeare ... oh, what was it called?'

And the conversation turned to drama and society, and for a while Rory McArthur was not apparently thought of.

A dinner presented by Mrs. Shaw had to be well-cooked and nourishing, and by the end of the second course, Murray felt he could move no more. Professor Shaw sat at the head of the table with his neck cloth askew, red in the face with the struggles of digestion, and how the ladies managed to rise and leave the room was beyond Murray. The gentlemen made a token effort to bow, then sagged back in their chairs while Professor Shaw fiddled with the brandy bottle. Mr. Bogue, who had been somewhat lost in conversation about Edinburgh plays, cleared his thick throat and introduced the topic of suitable professions for a young graduate, in the clear hope that his son Sandy might derive some inspiration from it. It was a subject on which they all had opinions, and they had a lively and good-humoured chat until they felt they could just about push themselves out of their chairs and stagger up the stairs to the grand drawing room.

Murray saw as they entered the room where Professor Shaw's portrait had gone, and why: Dr. Lindsay had been one of the students who had arranged for it to be painted, and so it had been moved to pride of place over the mantelpiece. Lindsay recognised it at once.

'I had never seen it finished: Gordon, the artist, sent us a sketch, and we had to hope from that. I hope you are well pleased with it, sir: I have to say I think he did a good job.'

'He is an artist of some repute here,' said Professor Shaw carefully.

'He's another in that string quartet I told you of,' added Mr. Bogue. 'A fine fellow.'

'He's doing some work at Letho. I'm very pleased with it so far,' said Murray.

Lindsay was still studying the picture, leaning to keep clear of the fire.

'His family hailed from the same village as me, I believe,' he said absently, 'though we were not contemporaneous. The Gordons of Invertally were attainted in the '45, and forfeited the estate, and my great grandfather bought the lands and the castle from the Government. Now my brother Robert is the laird,' he finished, turning away from the portrait, his thoughts apparently far away.

Cosmo Gordon's family pride must be considerable, thought Murray. He talked of his family castle as though they had closed the front door behind them a year or two ago, not in 1745. But many of the Gordons had been Jacobites, from the Duke down: he should have thought of it, had not the matter seemed so recent.

Miss Bogue had graciously declined to play the Shaws' little box piano, and Sandy had taken her place instead, with Flavia happy enough to turn the pages for him. Under the cover of the music, Miss Bogue manoeuvred her chair so that it was a little closer to Murray's, without looking too obvious.

'You do not play for us this evening?' Murray asked her, with a smile.

'Nor this nor any evening: all the musical talent in our family is Sandy's,' she explained. 'I shall not disgrace myself and offend your ears. But Mr. Murray, there is something that has occurred to me, and since you are helping to look into poor Rory's death, I felt I must tell you.'

'What is it?'

Her face was eager, but not excited: she had considered this carefully.

'I believe I know where Jack Swanson might be.'

Chapter Sixteen

He turned his chair quickly towards her.

'Where?'

'Sandy used to hide there as a boy,' she explained, 'and then he shared his idea with Jack and Rory. When they didn't want anyone to overhear them or just wanted their own company, they would go to St. Rule's Tower. I believe that is where Jack has hidden himself.'

'St. Rule's Tower?' The tall, square remnant of St. Andrews' first cathedral stood amongst the ruins of the later buildings: he had heard that the top used to be accessible only by wooden ladders, but someone had built stone steps inside it fifty years ago and in the summer it was a popular viewpoint for visitors to the town. 'Surely people have looked there for him?'

'I don't believe they have,' said Miss Bogue, keeping her voice low. 'There is all this talk about him fleeing the town, and guards on the toll gates and at the harbour, but no one has thought to search in the town itself beyond his own home, as far as I can see. But it makes sense to me: he would have shelter, and he would not be far from news if he wanted to know how the pursuit of him was going.'

'Do you believe him guilty of Rory's death?' Murray asked. The idea seemed more likely to him than the image of Jack rowing himself inexpertly out of the harbour in a stolen boat.

'No, I don't think I do: so I believe he is only hiding until the fuss dies down.'

'But he has contributed to that fuss, surely, by running away?' She made a face.

'I never claimed that Jack was particularly bright. Poor fellow, he must be very frightened.' Her eyes were tender for a moment.

She glanced around, making sure that no one was listening to them. 'Look, Mr. Murray, will you go there with me and see if he is there? He needs to come out of hiding and explain himself, and Sandy refuses to rouse himself and come with me. He says I'm being ridiculous.'

'Surely it would not take long to prove that to you by accompanying you.'

'That's what I said to him, but still he will not go with me.' Murray wondered why Sandy was so reluctant to look for his friend: was it his general unwillingness to put himself out, or was there something more to it? 'Will you please go with me? If it is that you are too busy looking for the real murderer,' she added, with some acidity, 'I can assure you it will not take long.'

'I know how far it is: I have been there many times,' said Murray. 'But I'm not sure that would be entirely proper, Miss Bogue, not at this time of the evening,' he went on, even as he was considering the possibilities. He noted that Mr. Bogue was watching them from across the room: he had no wish to be ensnared into a marriage. 'I'll go myself, though.'

'Will you? You aren't just saying that?'

He looked back at her. She must feel strongly, to be this impatient. Had she more feeling for Jack Swanson than she had previously admitted? Murray hoped not: he felt she could do better, as long as it was not him. He tried to reassure her.

'Of course I'm not just saying it! I'll go after supper.'

'After supper!' Miss Bogue's voice rose and she had to take two or three breaths to calm herself again. 'Not in much of a rush to find him, are you, Mr. Murray?'

'Well, I don't notice you hurrying there either!' he could not resist snapping back, then apologised. 'I know it is not easy for a woman on her own to do such things – and you should not go alone anyway, for your own safety.'

'I had thought more that he might be injured, and I should need help,' she said, 'but yes, it is not easy. That is why I asked you –'

'And I've said I'll go,' he interrupted. 'But if I suddenly stand up and go now it will attract attention. You say you believe he is not guilty: someone in this room might be, and if they find out where he is and perhaps reach him before me, they could turn that to their advantage – they could perhaps even kill Jack and make it look as if he had taken his own life out of guilt. And since I have just been seen talking urgently with you, you might be determined as the source of my information, and you too could be in danger. If Jack is in hiding, and of his own free will, a few hours are not likely to make much difference to him. I shall go after supper, as the guests disperse.'

She sat back, with a rather mutinous twist to her mouth, assessing his arguments, glancing around the room as though trying to identify the murderer there. Then her lips relaxed into a sweet smile, and he looked about to find Sandy approaching amiably.

'You two look as if you're having a quarrel!' he remarked. 'I shouldn't have thought you knew each other well enough to argue.'

'Music brings out such feelings, don't you think?' said Murray smoothly. 'Miss Bogue tells me that you have the only musical talent in the family, and I was insisting that she should pay more attention to the subject. I am very fond of music,' he added disingenuously.

'A waste of time,' said Miss Bogue, swiftly co-operating. 'You know my opinions on the subject, Sandy: you can have the grand piano all to yourself at home!'

'Do you play, Mr. Murray?' Sandy asked, dismissing his sister's opinions at once. 'I've brought my fiddle, if you would accompany me.'

'Surely, if the company wishes it.'

Murray was happy to play with a good musician, and pleased enough to have anything to distract him until supper was over. Miss Bogue might think him too patient, but he was itching to see if Jack Swanson really was in St. Rule's Tower. She might reckon Jack innocent, but if he was not he might well fight his corner. Should he fetch Constable Round to go with him? He was not sure where the constable lived, and he would probably not be in his office by the time they had had supper. He concentrated on the delights of the music, and later on the conversation of the company, and tried to ignore the occasional glare from Miss Bogue.

No one could manage much supper, still bulging after the

generous dinner, but yet it was after dusk by the time everyone gathered their things and made their farewells. The Playfair sisters were determined to make the most of their gossip, and Mr. Hepburn and Flavia were deep in conversation about books, and Miss Bogue was reduced to drumming her slippered feet on the hall floor, eager to be away and let Murray have no further excuse to wait. At last all had gone, and Murray, who wanted to change his footwear, hurriedly explained to Professor Shaw that he meant to go for a walk and work off a little of his dinner: he feared that if he went into further detail, any of the guests might be lingering outside and overhear. The last of them must only have been a few minutes gone when he, too, slipped out into the lane and took the mill lade path towards the harbour, in case, again, any of the guests might see him in his haste. They might indeed have seen him as he staggered to a halt, propped himself against a wall and removed one boot to shake out a stone: it had been pressing precisely where Nathan Houston had caught his foot with the door, and needed urgently to be removed. He pulled his boot back on, and after a few tentative limps carried on.

At least the walk did his digestion some good: he felt almost lively as he turned up the Pends from the harbour, disappearing into the shadows of the high arches over his path. He remembered, with a grin, a number of ghost stories he had heard as a student, about nuns on the Pends, but his main concern was Jack Swanson and he strode rapidly up the steep path between its high walls, too fast for any casual ghost to bother. At the top he found himself by the wall of the Cathedral grounds, and paused for a moment. The street was quiet, the kirkyard apparently empty of all living beings, except the occasional late gull crying high above, pale as any ghost. The great archway of the cathedral ruins could only just be perceived in the cloudy-dark sky: St. Rule's Tower beyond it was visible only in his memory. He slipped along to the gateway, glanced around and passed inside.

Kirkyards at night held little fear for him, but he walked with caution: the ground was uneven, he knew, and he had no wish to spend the night here with a twisted ankle. Aside from that, he did his best to listen hard for any other persons who might be lingering here. The wind, here above the harbour, was lively enough to block much in the way of noise, but he was well aware that there were plenty of places to hide, for anyone who wished either not to be seen or to attack an intruder. He proceeded with caution, and when he reached the solid rectangular building that formed the base of the tower, he noted the door, which was ajar, and then paced noiselessly round the whole little edifice. There was no sign of anyone, for all he could see. He completed his circuit, and was about to check inside, when he heard a breathless 'Mr. Murray!' from behind him. There was a rapid rustle of skirts, and he turned in resignation.

'Miss Bogue! I said that you should not come with me!'

'Well, I didn't come with you,' she replied with some asperity. 'I did not quite think that you would come here on your own, so I decided to venture myself.'

'But now you find I did come here, would it not be best if you went back home?'

'I need to see for myself!' she hissed. 'I'm here now: properly, having found me in a dangerous situation, you should escort me back to my home, but then questions would be asked, wouldn't they? And any discovery would be delayed still further – though perhaps that won't bother someone who could sit so calmly through supper before coming here.' He opened his mouth to object, but she carried on regardless. 'So it would be simpler if we just looked now, and made sure, wouldn't it?'

'Oh, for pity's sake,' Murray muttered. 'Well, then: come on. Let us investigate.'

He seized her firmly by the hand, so that he knew where she was, and walked ahead of her into the tower.

There was one little room inside. The staircase was off-centre: the only place really to hide, though someone tucked into a dark corner might not be noticed, was behind the stone steps. He drew her forward into the gloom, and called out quietly.

'Jack? Jack Swanson? Are you here?'

There was a moment of silence, underswept by the sound of the wind around the tower. Then the quality of the dim light changed, there was a soft rattle, and the door was shut behind them.

'Jack?' cried Miss Bogue, suddenly less sure of herself. Murray stepped back and grabbed the door handle, rattling it hard. The door would not move more than half an inch. From the sound, it was chained on the outside.

'Oh, wonderful,' said Murray, when he could trust himself to speak. 'I don't suppose you mentioned to anyone where you were going?'

'Of course not: I slipped out the back door as soon as I could fetch a dark cloak, and ran.'

'I thought as much.' He reflected on his own rushed conversation with Professor Shaw: he would probably have been perfectly safe in telling him. Perfectly safe? Well, someone had wished them harm. Had Jack seen them coming and slipped out to trap them?

'Is Jack behind the stairs, there?' Miss Bogue asked, and he could hear the effort she was making to keep her voice calm. He edged his way around the staircase, using his gloved fingers for guidance and being most careful not to knock his head on anything he could not see. He completed a round of the stairs.

'No, he isn't, either conscious or unconscious.'

'Oh.' He heard her shiver. To judge from the silky fistling of the cloth, she was probably still in her light dinner gown under that cloak – but at least she had the cloak. He had his dinner clothes, his boots, gloves, hat and stick – useful for all kinds of things, but none of it a cosy cover for a night in a cold stone tower. He sighed.

'I wonder if the top is open?'

'Do you mean we could try to signal for help?' she asked quickly, a little too eagerly.

'I'm not sure anyone would see us at this time of night,' said Murray with regret. 'But I'll see what I can see.' Using both hands and feet he climbed the stone steps, feeling his way. At least outside there might be a little residual light to see by: and if they could shelter from the wind against the balustrade it might not be any colder than in the chilly tower itself. He was going so slowly that when he reached the trap door to the roof, by bumping the crown of his hat on it, he barely felt the impact. He pushed at the trap door gently at first, then harder.

'What are you doing?' called Miss Bogue from below.

'Trying to open the trap door. I think it's bolted – just can't find the bolt,' he explained. He had been up here many times, but of course had never particularly had cause to notice the position of the bolt. 'Oh, here it is.' He felt the shape of the heavy metal, angled it to slide, and pulled it open. The trap door opened easily enough, and in a moment he was outside on the roof.

The wind had been busy: the soft rainclouds of the evening had been tidied briskly away, and the night was full of stars and the dented circle of the waning moon.

'You've opened it!' said Miss Bogue, her voice much closer than a minute ago. 'Thank heavens: I felt suffocated down there.'

He turned and helped her out, then moved back to allow her to stand freely. Almost at once he tripped on something in the dark corner under the balustrade. It was soft. He crouched down.

'It's Jack!' he snapped. 'Jack, can you hear me?' He shook Jack's shoulder. He was slumped, half on his side, against the wall, and Murray could not see any more of his face than a pale blur. He felt around Jack's head and neck: there were no apparent injuries, but Jack's collar was turned up, as if against the cold. A quick inspection down the front of his shirt and the back of his coat indicated no bloody wounds, but it was so hard to tell in the dark.

'Is he alive?' Miss Bogue's voice had a squeak to it. Murray felt Jack's throat, and his forehead.

'He's alive, yes, but cold, and I can't rouse him. I think ... I wonder how long he has been out here?'

Miss Bogue crouched down beside him in a flurry of silk skirts, anxious hands feeling Jack's chilled fingers.

'I wonder if he has been out here all this time?'

'Surely not,' said Murray. 'He would be dead, I should think. He has no blanket: look, I believe he is still in his mourning clothes from Rory McArthur's funeral.'

'Jack! Jack!' She shook his shoulder, then began rubbing his hands.

'And who bolted him up here?' Murray thought aloud. He had been about to close the trap door in case one of them fell down it, but now he was not so sure he wanted to block that possible exit. Anyone could sneak back up those stairs and slide the bolt home again, and then they would be trapped, too. 'And who locked us in?'

'He needs warmth,' said Miss Bogue decisively. 'Can we take him inside?'

'Not in the dark: it's hard enough climbing up and down those steps without trying to take a deadweight with us.'

'Don't say deadweight,' she snapped.

'You know what I mean. We'll need to wait till morning.' He rose to his feet and stepped over to the balustrade to gaze out at the town below. From here the triangle of its three long streets was very clear, as was their near emptiness at this time of night. Lights shone in many of the houses, but no one would be looking up at the square tower in the dark. He sighed.

'Well, perhaps if we sit closely, one each side of him, it might at least keep him going until we can move him,' he said at last. 'Oh – and I have a flask of brandy.' He had slipped it into his pocket at the last minute, as it was slim and there was little else of use he could carry in his evening clothes. He brought it out, and delicately dabbed some on to Jack's lips. Gratifyingly, Jack murmured something. It reminded Murray of his gardener Carlisle: how was he doing, he wondered? There was too much happening, and he could not fit it all together: he felt suddenly very tired.

'We could put my cloak over him,' Miss Bogue was saying.

'What? No: you are less warmly clad than he is. I don't want to have to carry both of you down the stairs. Keep your cloak around you, and sit up as close as you can there beside him, and I'll get behind his back here.' He sat on the cold stonework, with the smooth wool of Jack's black coat against him. 'And take a sip of this,' he added, passing her the brandy flask. She sipped precisely, and passed it back. He swallowed some, too.

'Doesn't this prove he is innocent?' Miss Bogue asked after they had made themselves as comfortable as the circumstances allowed. 'Surely if someone is keeping him prisoner here, it must be to incriminate him and safeguard themselves?'

'Maybe: we'd need to find out who did. Who knew he was here?'

'Could anyone have overheard our conversation this evening?'

'Dr. Lindsay?'

'The handsome doctor? Surely he can have no connexion with this! He would never have known Rory McArthur!'

'Well, he is from Perthshire – and he was asking rather too many questions about Rory, didn't you think?'

'He was just being polite, surely. And his friend Mr. Hepburn: well, I think he was too interested in Flavia Shaw to be listening to us.'

'Perhaps.' Well, thought Murray, without speaking, her brother Sandy could have heard them, too. And Sandy was the one who had refused to come with her to look for Jack here. And Sandy was the one who might have thought of the tower as a hiding place in the first instance. And there was a thought: if Jack had been here since the funeral, stuck up on the top of the tower, why had he not called for help during the daytime? Would Sandy have been able to persuade him, somehow, that staying here was the safest thing he could do?

'I think his pulse is a little stronger,' she said, after a while.

'Good.' He was on the edge of sleep. Should he allow himself to doze? He was not sure: not while that trap door was open, and someone inclined to do them harm had the key to the outside door. With Jack unconscious, he was the only person fit to protect Miss Bogue. No, he should stay awake. He stared up at the sky, naming the stars in his head.

'This will be the end of me,' murmured Miss Bogue, drowsily. 'One of you had better marry me, for no one else will take me after tonight. Two men!' she exclaimed softly. 'What will Papa say?'

'One man sick and you're nursing him, and the other man here as chaperon,' said Murray reassuringly. Indeed he was not at all sure how Mr. Bogue was going to take the event. If they had just found Jack, or even not found Jack, she could have slipped away home safely, leaving him to deal with the situation. Now they were trapped it was inevitable that the gossips would pounce. He sighed, then worried she would ask him what was the matter, but she seemed to have drifted off. He settled his shoulders more comfortably against the cold stonework behind him, and tried once more to piece together the parts of the puzzle.

Several times during the night he dozed a little, and woke with a jump, but nothing disturbed their peace. Miss Bogue breathed gently, wrapped up in her cloak against Jack's chest, and Jack himself just about held on to life, it seemed to Murray. Every now and then he roused Miss Bogue to make sure she did not slip into a dangerously deep sleep, and every time she woke she chafed Jack's face and hands vigorously, while Murray rubbed the unconscious man's back till his hands burned against the wool. Then they checked the pulse in Jack's throat, and held their breath, sure that this time it had ceased. Then there would be the least movement, and they would both breathe again. He wondered how Carlisle was, if he had surfaced yet, if he ever would. Mary would look after him, he knew. If anyone could bring him round, with skill and discretion, it would be Mary. He allowed himself a moment to think of her, tall and proud with her wild dark hair and angular brows, then banished the thought before it could grow, as he always did. Poor Carlisle: if he came round, would he even remember what had happened, or who had attacked him?

At last he was sure that the least light of dawn was beginning to creep over their little battlements. Gulls spun, lamenting, catching the low dawn light, as if their glittering feathers could make up for the fading stars. He made sure Jack was steady, and stretched his long legs before gently rising to stand and look out over the waking town. To the east the long finger of the pier pointed towards the sunrise, misty but promising a good day. He could see one or two figures down by the shore, but they were far too far away to be of any use to him here. The west was a better hope: doors were opening, lamps were being lit, smoke began to trickle from chimneys, slipping up through the breeze, and that very breeze would be more likely to carry his voice over to any passengers he saw on the road past the cathedral.

He slipped carefully down the steps into the tower. Before he began shouting at random passersby he wanted to make sure the door was indeed still chained and locked. It was: it had not just been intended as a temporary hindrance, though their assailant must have known they would be able to escape when day came.

Back on the roof, he roused Miss Bogue with a firm hand on her shoulder. She sat up, blinking, but at once aware of where she was.

'Thank goodness for thick woollen cloaks,' she said at once.

'I'm about to try shouting for help. I didn't want to wake you that way,' he explained, and she nodded, then turned to check Jack's condition once again.

'I want to believe there's a change for the better,' she said thickly, 'but I'm not at all sure that there is. Are you staying up here for the moment?'

Murray blinked, wondering where else he would go, then understood.

'Of course. I'll close the trapdoor over if you like.'

'No, I might need the light.'

She managed the stairs well for one in wide skirts, and he turned back to the wall, discreetly, surveying the town. He waited until a few people were about, to make the most of his shouts, then with as much strength as he could summon he cried out,

'Help! Help up here!'

Chapter Seventeen

It was fortunate that the first person who heard him was a journeyman carpenter, passing on his way to work. The carpenter was bright, awake, and clear of hearing: he detected Murray's shouts and located the source, and ran across the kirkyard to assess the problem. Having done so, with a few exchanged shouts up and down the tower, he then went and fetched his friend, a blacksmith. The blacksmith was, though substantially less bright and awake, better equipped than the carpenter to deal with a keyless padlock and chain. With the carpenter dancing excitedly around him, the blacksmith arrived, grumbling about student pranks, and Murray was pleased enough to be flattered that the blacksmith thought he was still young enough to be a student – though gratified, too, when the blacksmith met him close up, saw the state of Jack Swanson, and realised the gravity of the situation. Miss Bogue fled for home to raise the alarm and comfort her parents. The carpenter poked his friend into place on the stone stairs and the two of them took the weight as Murray lowered Jack down towards them, his knees creaking: Jack was no lightweight.

In the daylight they were better able to assess Jack's condition, and as he had apparently no injuries they carried him as he was off to the Bogues' house, the nearest friends. Mrs. Bogue, warned by Miss Bogue, met them at the gateway and ushered them quickly inside. Forgetting her need to impress, she lapsed into broad Scots and practicalities, overseeing the removal of Jack's mourning clothes, damp with several days' dew, the arrangement of hot bricks around him, the tucking in of clean, soft sheets and blankets, the provision of broth for when he might need it. Murray was ushered away to have his broth immediately: the carpenter and blacksmith left with some coins apiece, and Wee Dod was sent scurrying down South Street to let the Shaws know that Murray was alive and well and safe, and to bring Mr. Swanson to his son's bedside.

The broth had a prodigiously restorative effect, as did the fire by which Murray ate it. Mrs. Bogue bustled in and out, and after a little while Miss Bogue came to join him, wearing an old wincey gown which looked both warm and comfortable. She met his eye.

'I'm not sure I want to wear an evening dress again for at least a month. They were not designed for prolonged wear out of doors,' she stated firmly.

'I'll happily exchange these for a day coat and breeches,' Murray agreed, waving at his own stiff evening clothes. 'I'm only glad I stopped to put my boots on.'

Mrs. Bogue poked her head around the parlour door, her gaze flicking between the two of them. Murray wondered what her daughter had told her of the previous night, or whether she was looking for evidence of an intimacy between them.

'Mrs. Bogue, may I go to sit with Jack? I am anxious he might have some useful information for us.'

Mrs. Bogue blinked, and glanced again at Miss Bogue.

'For the constable and me,' Murray clarified, 'and for all those who wish to see Rory McArthur's murderer brought to justice. May I also send for Constable Round? He will wish at least to know that Jack is found.'

'Oh, aye, indeed – the minute Wee Dod comes back,' said Mrs. Bogue, her head busy. 'And away up the stair with you and sit wi' Jack: likely he'll come round all the faster if someone talks to him, ken.'

Murray set aside his empty broth bowl, and left Miss Bogue to enjoy hers. Upstairs, Jack was a much better colour than he had been when they left him, and his skin had a healthy warmth to the touch. Murray once again counted his pulse: it was stronger, and a little faster, but not so fast as to suggest a fever. Murray sat back in a chair by the bed, and regarded the young man in front of him. What would cause such a man to be locked for four nights on top of a tower? Who bolted the trap door against him, and why did he not call for help? And was it the same person who had locked the bottom door, and imprisoned him and Miss Bogue?

Jack stirred, giving a soft moan. Murray could see his fingers wriggle even under the blankets.

'Jack?' he said. 'Jack, can you hear me?'

Jack's eyes flickered under his grey lids, but they did not open. Murray sat back again. Doubtless his father's voice would have a greater effect, when he arrived, but it did look as if there was some hope.

There was a sound at the door of the bedchamber, and Murray looked around to see Wee Dod balanced on one leg, wondering how to attract his attention. Murray beckoned him over.

'Yes?'

'Sir, I been to tell Professor Shaw you was safe and here, and he says to ask you if you want a'thing sent along or if you'll be back to dinner. And he sent you this, sir – says it comed for you this very morn frae Letho, or some such.'

'Thank you, Wee Dod,' said Murray. 'I believe your mistress will send you now to fetch Constable Round, but if you could in the same run let Professor Shaw know that I need nothing, but hope to return before dinner, that would be most obliging of you.'

'Aye, sir. Sir?'

'Yes?'

'Where's Letho, sir?'

'Between here and Cupar, a village just off the toll road.'

'I've never been there, sir. When I'm older, I have hopes to travel.'

'Perhaps you will, Dod: there's a good deal to see.'

'Aye, sir, so I've heard tell. Thank you, sir.' He nodded briskly, and departed. Murray cast a glance at Jack, who had not moved, and opened the note from Letho House. It was from Robbins.

'Dear Sir,' it began, 'Mrs. Robbins felt it would be useful to you to know what is happening with regard to Mr. Carlisle. He is somewhat improved, I am pleased to say: the wound on his head shows no sign of infection, and though he is not fully awake he moves and speaks a good deal: nothing, though, which can be made out yet. Yet each day he seems a little better.

'Mr. Gordon is to return this morning, I understand, in order to paint the head groom. All else is as you left it. There is no word as yet regarding a new housekeeper or maids.

'I remain your obedient servant,

'Henry Robbins'.

The head groom, thought Murray: there was still no word of Cosmo Gordon painting Henry Robbins.

'What?' came a voice, and for a moment Murray thought he must have spoken out loud. 'Who's there?'

It was Jack, eyes still firmly closed, hands struggling under the covers. Murray hastily freed one of those hands, and held it fast.

'Jack? Jack, can you hear me?'

'Who's there?' Jack demanded again, though there was a edge of panic in his voice.

'It's Charles Murray. Remember? I'm staying with the Shaws, next door to you. I was at Rory McArthur's funeral.'

'It wasna me!' Jack snapped at once. 'I didna kill him! He was my friend!'

'That's right, Jack, that's right.' He hoped it was, anyway.

Jack's eyes shot open, then he winced at the sunlight. Murray let go of his hand, setting it back down on the blanket.

'It is you,' he said, slightly surprised. Then he frowned. 'Am I at the Shaws', then?'

'No, you're at the Bogues'. It's thanks to Miss Bogue that you were found before it was too late.'

Jack just looked confused, not even sure which question to ask first. He wriggled in the bed, as if he was checking to see that all his limbs were there, and which clothes might be missing. Then he tried to sit up a little.

'You'd be better to stay under the covers and stay warm, for now,' said Murray. 'Though I could recommend a bowl of Mrs. Bogue's broth, if you feel ready for it.'

'Broth!' Jack breathed with reverence. 'Oh, michty! I could eat a barrel of it!'

Murray laughed. It sounded as if Jack was going to be all right.

'Before I rouse the household to your consciousness, though,' he said, 'can you tell me quickly, while we're on our own, who it was that locked you into St. Rule's Tower?'

'Into the Tower?' Jack's eyebrows rose. 'I have no notion. What was I doing there?'

'When we found you, lying unconscious on the roof. Were you hiding in case you were arrested over Rory's death?'

Jack's face fell.

'I didna kill him.'

'Yes, that's what you said. But were you worried that the constable might think you did?'

'That's right. At the funeral ... I realised that everyone thought it was me. I mean, apparently he left the recital to come looking for me, to give me laldy for not turning up, and the next thing anyone knows is that he's dead. Even I can see that looks suspicious, doesn't it?'

'It's circumstantial,' said Murray, non-committally.

'I miss the man,' Jack admitted. 'Whiles I was driven mad with him being so ... so serious, but he was still my friend. He was like a balance to Sandy Bogue to me,' he said frankly, 'for Sandy's so relaxed he would slip down a crack in the pavement and never bother, and Rory was the other way round: he was like a hurcheon in a hole half the time. But he'd never have raised a hand to me, and I never killed him, in my own defence or out of anger or anything else.' He drew in a long breath. 'I wish I knew who did kill him.'

'So you ran away from the funeral,' said Murray, trying not to sound accusing, 'but presumably you didn't lock yourself into St. Rule's Tower.'

Jack scowled.

'I didna see who locked me in. I heard a rattle at the door and that was me. Och, could I no have that broth now?'

'Very nearly. Did you run to the tower straightaway when you left the funeral?'

'No, I didna. I went down about the mill lade for a while, wondering where to go and what to do. I sat in the trees up the stream for a wee bit.' His gaze fell on to the blankets, seeing not them but something back by the mill lade. 'I thought some friendly soul might help me, but that turned out to be a lost cause.'

'Any particular friend?' asked Murray. Jack shook his head.

'I'd better no say.' He flicked a wary glance at Murray, who assumed a bland expression. 'And I couldna go home: my father was bleezin and I couldn't depend on him. So – well, it was cold, and getting dark, and I thought I'd best find some shelter. I knew the tower would be open, and I didn't think many would be looking in there after dark, or much at all at this time of the year.

So I went the quiet roads to get to the cathedral, and it took me a while because I was careful, and then I slipped inside when I thought no one was looking. Though just as I closed the door behind me, I did see someone ... I canna think why he might have locked me in, but he was the only person I saw around the place.'

'And who was that?' Murray could feel his pulse quicken.

'It was a fellow who trades up and down to Edinburgh: he lives near Rory's house. His name's Houston, Nathan Houston.'

'Mrs. Loudoun's brother?'

'Aye, that's the fellow. But why would he do that? I mean, I've never had much to do with the fellow. When my father has pieces for assay in Edinburgh he usually takes them down himself, or sends them with another silversmith he trusts. Nathan Houston's not that kind of trader. And if he was the one who locked me in, why did he wait? I mean, I had been in there a while when the door was locked.'

'I see – yes, that's odd. But then how did you end up on the roof? For when Miss Bogue and I came along, you were locked up there and the bottom door was ajar.'

'Let me think: it's all a bit confused.' He considered for a moment, counting days on his fingers. 'I would have gone in there on Saturday night, and the bottom door was locked. The floor was damp and I thought I'd be just as warm, and drier, on the roof. When I woke up in the morning and went down inside, there was food on the bottom step but the door was locked again. So that was Sunday – and not much food either,' he added. 'Please can I have that broth?'

Murray leaned over and rang the bell by the fireplace.

'So on Sunday the bottom door was still locked. Did it not occur to you to call for help from the top of the tower?'

Jack's face took on a hunted look.

'I was trying to avoid being arrested, not trying to attract attention to myself. I thought that if someone was feeding me and I was safe inside there, maybe they were there to protect me.'

Murray considered. Surely a protector would make themselves known to the person they were protecting? Or was Jack simply as dim as Miss Bogue thought he was?

'What happened next?'

'I slept up on the roof again on Sunday night. I mean, if it had rained or snowed of course I'd have come in, but the weather was fine, and I was fairly comfortable. Next morning there was food again so I ate that and on Monday night I went back up on to the roof. On Tuesday morning – how long ago is that, then?'

'Yesterday.'

'I was really stiff and cold when I woke. In fact, I think I slept late, and didn't rouse till the sun hit me. I was starving, so you can imagine how I felt when I went to open the trapdoor – I'd closed it in case I fell down the hole in the night, you ken – and the trapdoor was locked. On the other side, ken.'

'Aye, sir?'

Wee Dod had appeared at the door. His eyes widened slightly at the sight of Jack Swanson half-sitting up and awake.

'I believe Mr. Swanson is ready for some of your mistress's fine broth now, Dod. Could you fetch some for him, please?'

'Aye, sir.' Wee Dod disappeared about his business.

'And you were locked up there then from Monday night? With no food?'

'Aye, I suppose. It was gey cold and wet all day – yesterday, then. It was getting that I felt so sleepy, and I must have fallen asleep before dusk, even. I don't remember how you came to find me and bring me here.'

'Miss Bogue remembered that you and Sandy and Rory had used the tower as a meeting place, and thought it had not been checked. Fortunately she was quite insistent that I went to look for you, and here you are.' He decided to leave out the cold night when the three of them had huddled together up on that roof: it was up to Miss Bogue to tell him that if she wished to.

The broth had been kept warm: in a moment Wee Dod was back, carefully balancing a tray with a spoon and a fragrant bowl on it. Jack seized it with eager thanks, and Murray dismissed Wee Dod with a smile. He waited until Jack's initial appetite was satisfied and he scraped longingly round the empty bowl.

'Where were you the night that Rory McArthur died, Jack?' he asked. Jack glanced up at him.

'I told you, I was at home.'

'Were you? Only it all seems a bit vague.'

'I was practising for the recital, getting my nights wrong,' Jack insisted.

'But it's a funny thing, then,' said Murray. 'Rory went looking for you straight from the recital. Then less than an hour later, it seems the Bogues went looking for you, too. Surely the first place Rory would have looked would have been your house, yet you say you never saw him. The Bogues say the place was in darkness and silence – if you were practising in the parlour, you would have heard them knocking and they would have heard you playing.'

'They must be mistaken,' mumbled Jack.

'Someone saw you in South Street, heading back towards your house, around eleven o'clock, Jack.'

There was silence. Jack trailed the spoon slowly around the bowl, and sucked it clean, not meeting Murray's eye.

'Well ... maybe I went out for a wee while.'

'Did you? Did you see Rory?'

'No, I didna. I never saw Rory that night or had anything to do with his death, I give you my word.'

Murray nodded.

'Then where were you?'

Jack's shoulders squirmed.

'I was with a friend.'

'A female friend?'

'Aye.' The single sound came out in a reluctant burst. 'Aye, a female friend, indeed.'

'And who is she?'

The silence was longer this time, but Murray could be patient. He sat motionless, watching Jack. Jack was still, too, but you could almost hear his mind ticking over like the works of a clock. Murray prayed they would not be interrupted. At last, Jack drew in a long, long breath.

'Look, it's not what you think it is, honestly.'

'Mmhmm?'

'I can think of a reason why Nathan Houston might have wanted to lock me up, even maybe to do me harm.'

'Oh, yes?' Murray was quietly encouraging. Every sentence seemed to need squeezing out.

'He's always fancied her, but she's never been interested in him, that's what it is. Maybe he thought if he locked me away she would be able to ... but it's all so difficult. Or it was, until Rory died.'

'Wait,' said Murray, suddenly taken aback. 'Do you mean you were out meeting Janet McArthur? Is that who you mean?'

'That's right,' said Jack, a glint of something that might have been love appearing in his sorrowful eyes. 'Nathan Houston has an eye to her, but she and I were out that evening together. He won't have liked that, not at all.'

Chapter Eighteen

Though Murray would have liked to talk a little longer, he had no chance: word of Jack's return to consciousness had reached Mrs. Bogue, and she was soon there, bustling around him, as caring as if he were her own son. Murray stood, easing the pressure on his evening breeches, but standing again made his feet remember to hurt. He had to go and change.

He took his leave of Mrs. Bogue and found his way down the stairs, but before he could head for the passage that would lead to South Street, he was waylaid. Mr. Bogue, enormous and sagging, had been waiting for him.

'Lucky I caught you, Mr. Murray: I was just on the point of departing for my warehouse,' he said grandly, though Murray suspected he would have lingered a good while longer. 'Come in, come in, sit down. A strange business, is this not?'

He led Murray into a room that passed for a gentleman's study, with a broad desk against the wall, some aesthetically-filled bookshelves and a small globe on a stand. At the desk was a broad chair with a hard back, which Murray suspected had been specially made for Bogue's abundant figure. Bogue took it, and waved Murray to a better-cushioned, but awkwardly low, chair nearby. It would have been amusing, Murray thought, if he had not been so tired, to observe how the merchant aspiring to the gentry treated a gentleman whom he wanted to put in his place.

'Strange enough,' Murray agreed, reluctantly perching once again. His breeches creaked, and he regretted rebuttoning his stiff waistcoat. His back ached.

'I do not think I understand it yet,' said Bogue, assuming an anxious frown that was not quite genuine. 'How did young Jack come to be on top of St. Rule's Tower, and how did you and my daughter come to find him there?'

'He was there because someone persuaded him that hiding was his only chance of avoiding arrest,' said Murray, 'and Miss Bogue your daughter was clever enough to remember that her brother had shared the secrets of his childhood hiding place with his student friends, and that no one had thought to look there, intent as everyone was on believing that Jack had fled, or would attempt to flee, the town. I believed she could be right, but unbeknownst to me she too had decided to find out for herself, and we met there by chance.' He hoped he was not ladling too much emphasis over this, but he had no wish for Mr. Bogue to believe that he had planned an assignation with his daughter, for whatever reason. 'Jack had, by his own account, been locked in the tower for several days, almost since his disappearance, by someone he thinks was protecting him. Whether it was the same person or not, someone locked Miss Bogue and me into the tower as soon as we stepped inside to look for Jack. We saw no one, by the way: it was already dusk. Realising we were trapped, we then went out on to the roof to see if we would be able to attract help, but it was already too dark. No one was about, and if they had been they would not have been able to see us. Anyway, there we found poor Jack, who was already chilled into unconsciousness, and we managed - within the boundaries of propriety,' he added, trying not to sound too ironic, 'to keep him living until the morning when I was able to attract the attention of the carpenter and blacksmith who helped to bring him here. We were most grateful to them.'

Bogue sat back in his wide chair, though he still seemed to overflow the sides like an article of confectionery left too long by the fire. He considered a little in silence, in which Murray half-expected to hear the drip of melting ice.

'I think, by your words,' he said, just as Murray was beginning to believe he could escape, 'that you now consider Jack to be innocent of Roderick McArthur's death?'

'I think I almost do,' Murray acknowledged. 'He pleads very convincingly that he misses his friend. Now, a friend killed in the heat of the moment may indeed by missed most sincerely even by his killer, but in this case ... I find him at present quite persuasive.' Yet, he thought, had Jack himself not just given him a very good motive for his own murder of Rory? Visiting Mrs. McArthur behind Rory McArthur's back might place him high enough up indeed in the rankings of suspects. Yet he had no wish to share that with Mr. Bogue just at present: he was still not sure that Mr. Bogue had told him the whole truth about his own movements that evening.

'Well, then, it is hard to see who might have killed the man,' Mr. Bogue was saying ponderously. 'Now, to other matters: it is of course my duty as a father to investigate the absence of my daughter through the course of a whole night, particularly when I find that she spent it with two young men. Now, I know you are a gentleman, Mr. Murray, and would not see her reputation come to any harm: what do you say?'

Murray could feel his heart beat faster, though he had been expecting something of the sort. In Mr. Bogue's eyes he could see a look he was familiar with amongst the matrons of Edinburgh: a calculation of the income of the lands of Letho, with here, as an additional pull, his rank. Mr. Bogue wanted a gentleman for his daughter: the Shaws had said so. Murray found he had no particular wish to be that gentleman.

'All I can say, Mr. Bogue, is that during the course of a very cold night Miss Bogue tended to Jack, who was unconscious, while I attempted to keep him warm and tried to plan an escape of some sort. I don't believe Miss Bogue and I had any contact at all, and I urged her to make sure she was well wrapped up in her cloak at all times against the cold. It is not, I agree, a promising situation, but it is an innocent one.'

Mr. Bogue sighed, a sound like layers shifting.

'Very well,' he said at last, though Murray could sense that he had not quite lost hope of a match. He was a good enough businessman to know when not to push a deal too hard. 'Well, you must excuse me, Mr. Murray: I must go to see what my fool of a clerk is up to this morning. We have had a delivery of the finest French silks and lace – I should hate to go and find that he has been selling them for the price of a bolt-end of winsey!'

'And I must go and change out of these clothes!' said Murray, adopting the same cheerful tone and letting the advertisement pass over him. 'I can tell you that evening dress is not the ideal costume for a night out in the cold, on a stone floor.'

'I'll make sure and tell my customers,' Mr. Bogue nodded, in a momentary show of humour. It almost made Murray warm to him.

Murray was almost at the front door once again, Mr. Bogue hurrying off ahead of him at a dangerous speed for one so heavy, when he heard his name called. He was tempted to pretend he had not heard, but turned to see Sandy Bogue waving at him from the garden end of the stone passage. He lifted a reluctant hand in greeting, and followed Sandy into the garden.

It was a little, enclosed space, pretty with the yellow blossoms that spring favours, the frosty dew just lifting off the grass where the sun angled to touch it. To judge by the marks on the grass, Sandy had been pacing a little, and his boots were damp.

'You found Jack!' he said. 'He's well, I gather?'

'He will be, when he is warmed and fed.'

'Sarah says he was locked into St. Rule's Tower!'

'He was. He believes it was done by someone trying to protect him: food was left for him for the first couple of days.'

'But then not?' Sandy was quicker than Jack. 'That's strange, to feed your prisoner and then to starve him.'

'I wondered if you might know something about that?'

'Me?' Sandy's open face became wary. 'Why should I know about it?'

'The tower was a bit of a haunt for you when you were small, wasn't it? And then you showed it to Rory and Jack?'

'Well, yes, but that doesn't mean I'd lock my friend in it and starve him!'

Murray tried to ease his back, knuckling his spine.

'Did you speak to Jack at Rory's funeral?'

'Yes of course. We were doing the service together.'

'I mean about the possibility that he would be arrested.'

'No! I don't think so.'

'You didn't offer to help him? To meet him after he left? Down by the mill lade, perhaps?'

'The mill lade? No! That would be a stupid place to meet anyone. For goodness' sake, anyone can walk along there. Anyone at all. What a stupid place to meet.'

Murray's head was buzzing as he strode quickly down South Street, then darted through to Market Street to collect Constable

Round from his office. After a night of lying on a stone floor and a morning of sitting and waiting and talking, he took considerable pleasure in walking fast to shake off his stiffness and stretch his back and legs, and he was most eager to change. He jostled the constable to the Shaws' house then callously left him with Professor Shaw without telling either of them anything, while he himself ran upstairs, washed his face in cold water, and changed blissfully into a clean shirt, warm woollen coat, comfortable corduroy breeches and thick stockings, pulling his boots back on with much greater ease. He leapt back downstairs with renewed energy, apologising as he reached the garden where the constable and Professor Shaw waited with much-provoked patience.

'Any news, Constable?' he asked first.

'Nothing, sir. I have been trying to find anybody that might have seen something by the mill lade that evening, and I have been looking for Jack Swanson or reports of him, and have no news whatsoever.'

Professor Shaw looked anxiously to Murray when the constable mentioned Jack Swanson.

'Did you not say …?' he began. 'I thought …'

'Yes, indeed, but I had not yet told the constable. Jack Swanson is found, safe and if not well then soon, I believe, to be so.' He told the others about Miss Bogue's deduction and the resulting night in St. Rule's Tower.

'You were locked in?' said the constable, fixing first on the probable criminal act. 'But who would have done such a thing?'

'Presumably the person who locked Jack in. I think he has suspicions as to who that was: he has a lingering belief that the person was trying to help him to escape you and arrest, and it has not yet struck him, as I believe, that he was left up there to die. Miss Bogue and I must have interrupted that process: perhaps the person panicked when he or she saw us arriving, and locked us in too until they could decide what to do. I don't know. I challenged Sandy Bogue, thinking he might have been doing it to help his friend, but he denies it – and denies offering to meet him on the mill lade where Jack went when he fled the funeral. Jack says he just lingered there a little, but my impression is he had hoped to meet someone. I just don't know who.'

'Who else would be likely to go out of their way to help

Jack?' asked Constable Round.

'His father?' suggested Professor Shaw.

'But Swanson was roaring drunk,' objected Murray.

'Could he have been pretending?' asked Professor Shaw, a little surprised at his own thoughts of others' deviousness.

'I don't know. He did it well, if he was. If he thought Jack had committed murder, would he defend him?'

They all considered that for a long moment. Would Swanson have been loyal enough to Jack to protect him, or would he have considered it bad for business? From their silence, it was evident they could not decide.

'So he's at the Bogues', then?' asked the constable at last.

'Thank the Lord that he is alive and safe,' murmured Professor Shaw. 'Thank the Lord: that is one good thing in all of this.'

'No' if I have to arrest him for murder,' said Constable Round glumly. The little professor began wringing his hands again, and Murray twisted his eyebrows at Constable Round. The constable's face fell.

'But by the sounds of things,' he added hastily, 'Mr Murray here thinks he might not have done it at all, at all. Is that right, Mr. Murray?'

'Certainly at the moment I believe him to be innocent,' said Murray. 'But he did tell me something very interesting. On the night when Rory McArthur was killed, Jack was out with Mrs. McArthur.'

'Out?' Professor Shaw stopped wringing his hands, confused.

'What might that mean?' asked the constable.

'I'm not sure yet,' said Murray. 'He wouldn't tell me: he told me to ask Janet McArthur. On past experience I'm not going to learn much there, either, but maybe this is a way into the whole thing.'

'But if …' Constable Round glanced down at Professor Shaw, calculating what might or might not upset him, 'if Jack Swanson was … er, seeing Mrs. McArthur behind her husband's back – and that was a grand time to do it, while McArthur was off at his wee music thing – then is that not a good reason why Jack might want McArthur out of the way?'

'It is,' Murray sighed. 'I know. He did say it wasn't what it looked like … but he would say that, wouldn't he, if he wanted me to think he hadn't killed Rory?'

'Aye, he would,' said Constable Round, nodding solemnly.

'The thing is,' said Murray, 'while I don't think that killing Rory McArthur required a great deal of intelligence, I believe that covering up any guilt would require more brains than Jack Swanson has been granted. He's simply not bright enough and not deceitful enough to hide his own involvement, if he had been involved. I mean, the Bogues say they were at the Swansons' house and saw no one, but there's something wrong with their story, too: if Jack had simply stuck to his account that he was at home playing his fiddle, and had maybe wandered out for a breath of air about eleven o'clock to be seen by the night watchman, I would probably have believed him. But Jack goes and admits to seeing Mrs. McArthur without even seeming to realise that that shows him in an even worse light than before.'

'How could he?' asked Professor Shaw, and his eyes were damp. 'How could he visit his best friend's wife behind poor Rory's back? Rory would have been heartbroken.'

'Would he, though?' Murray asked experimentally. 'From all that I've heard, Rory and his wife were not particularly attached.'

'Nevertheless ... Rory perhaps was just not very open about such things ... a quiet boy, always. Who knows how attached they might have been, in private life?'

'It is true that no one outside knows what goes on within a marriage,' Murray agreed, trying not to think about his own ill-fated one.

'Well, it seems to me we have good reason to try again to talk to Janet McArthur,' said Constable Round with resignation. 'If anyone knows what was going on inside that marriage, it must be her.'

'Yes, if she'll talk at all.'

'Poor woman, poor woman!' murmured Professor Shaw, blowing his reddened nose.

Murray and the constable decided to go forthwith and try to persuade Janet McArthur to talk: both were impatient to find out her side of the story, if they could. They strode up the common close to South Street, finding it busy enough, and crossed to where the little lane slipped off the street to Mrs. Loudoun's house. Both the constable and Murray had to twist a little sideways to enter it comfortably.

Constable Round chapped smartly at the door. The McArthur house was still shuttered and dark, but there was no answer at Mrs. Loudoun's, either. The constable hammered the door again.

'Odd,' he remarked. Murray shielded his eyes to peer through the window. Inside, the fire was low, and all was in order, so far as he could see.

'Is it locked?' he asked. Constable Round tried the latch, and the door swung open.

'So much for keeping her safe,' he said.

'Maybe they have taken her somewhere else.'

Round stepped into the small parlour: there was no sense in Murray entering too when between them they would take up half the space. He stayed at the door and watched as Round examined the box bed and the press, and peered around the child's damp clothes hanging above the fire. Murray wondered briefly what it was like to have several children in a house like this, with hardly any space outside to dry the inevitable laundry, and not much more inside. When Augusta was brought to him she was almost always clean and dry, but he had glimpsed the lines of napkins on the drying green behind Letho House, and been in awe of the labour even one small child required.

'Well, they're no here,' said Round obviously, backing into the lane and pulling the door shut behind him.

'We'll have to try again later,' said Murray, and led the way back to South Street. In the street again they could walk side by side and did so, keeping their voices low.

'What now?' asked Constable Round.

'I think I want to talk to Thomas Swanson again, but not just yet,' said Murray. 'He'll be at the Bogues', seeing to Jack, no doubt – oh, no, there he is!'

Swanson, on the other side of South Street, was walking beside a small donkey pulling a cart, in which Jack was sitting hunched under a blanket, pink with warmth and mild embarrassment. Swanson, too, was a little red in the face.

'It looks as if he has reclaimed his son from the Bogues' – forcibly, perhaps,' Murray suggested.

'Jack looks healthy enough,' the constable remarked.

'He's a solid young man: it would take more than a couple of nights outdoors without food to defeat him completely. Oh, good morning, Mr. Gordon.'

Cosmo Gordon had almost bumped into them as they stood watching the Swansons' progress towards the common close.

'I beg your pardon, Mr. Murray. I hope I find you well?'

'Very well, thank you. You may already know Constable Round?'

Cosmo bowed stiffly, clearly uncomfortable, then turned back to Murray.

'The Bogues want to have another recital soon, in memory of poor Rory, Mr. Murray, and we are to meet and discuss what to play. We have always tended to prefer more cheerful music, so a suitable programme will require some thought: though perhaps that is fitting. Rory was a thoughtful man.'

'Then I wish you well for it,' said Murray sincerely. 'From what I can make out of the man, it sounds like a gesture he would have appreciated. Who will be invited?'

'Oh, all his friends and acquaintances. We hope perhaps even to be able to draw his widow out to join us: then I think we would feel we had truly made him a fitting tribute.' He smiled a little ruefully, already aware that drawing Janet McArthur out would be a challenge. Yet where was she today?

'How was the painting going when you left Letho?' Murray wanted to know.

'Exceeding well, I have to say,' said Cosmo. 'Several are complete: I have a little more work to do on your head groom and of course on your gardener, Carlisle.'

'And Robbins?' Murray asked quickly, almost knowing the answer and wanting to return to the subject of his gardener.

'Ah. No, he's a very busy man, that one.'

Murray nodded. He was not going to have a portrait of Robbins, he was fairly sure.

'How was Carlisle when you left? Any news?'

'No, nothing that I was told. I'm sure they would have let you know if there had been any change: he was still incoherent, I believe, and he had not opened his eyes.'

'The longer that goes on, the less chance, it seems to me, that he will make a recovery.' Murray sighed, and the constable and

Cosmo nodded sympathetically. Carlisle had been at Letho since before Murray was born: even for him to be ill was unsettling. If he died, it would be an earthquake.

'I must go on, I'm afraid,' said Cosmo. 'I am expected at the Bogues' house.'

'Of course.' Murray pulled himself back from such melancholic thoughts. 'Good day to you.'

Cosmo bowed to Murray, nodded at the constable, and strode on up South Street.

'He seemed less than pleased to see you,' Murray remarked, thinking back.

'I think it was you introducing me, sir,' said the constable. 'Mr. Gordon does not think of himself as a tradesman, you ken: more in the line of a gentleman.'

'He does, doesn't he?' Murray reflected, thinking of his exchanges with Gordon at Letho. 'A gentleman fallen on hard times.'

'Oh, he makes plenty,' said Constable Round. 'I dinna ken what he charges for his wee pictures, but he's never short of the cash, sir.'

'He's a busy man.' Murray considered what Cosmo Gordon was charging him for the paintings of his staff: it was not so much. He was fond of his staff, but he would not have paid Henry Raeburn's prices for portraits of all of them.

'Mr. Murray!' a voice called.

'Michty,' remarked Constable Round, 'can we no walk three steps together without another acquaintance, sir?' But he was smiling. Murray looked ahead and found Dr. Lindsay with his friend Hepburn, smartly turned out and brisk in the sunshine.

'Good day to you, Mr. Murray!' Hepburn, his whiskers glinting and his cheeks baby pink, bowed to him with a bounce of enthusiasm. Dr. Lindsay was slightly more restrained. 'Have you just come from the Shaws' house?'

'Well, in a round and about way, yes,' said Murray. It was hard not to smile at Hepburn. 'Is that where you are bound?'

'Well, we just thought …' He glanced a little plaintively at Lindsay, who raised his eyebrows hopelessly. 'We just thought we would have a little pop in before dinner, and see if Miss … if the Shaws were in so that we could thank them for such a lovely evening yesterday.'

Good heavens, that dinner had only been last night. For Murray, it seemed a week away.

'Well, they are in: I'm sure they would be delighted to see you,' said Murray. He thought that young Flavia, at least, would be happy.

'Then we'll take our leave – perhaps we shall see you later? We don't want to be too late and detain them from their meal.' Dr. Lindsay bowed with a hint of apology as his friend bounded off towards the common close.

'Miss Shaw has a suitor, then?' asked the constable, straight-faced.

'Dear me, was he that obvious?' asked Murray, grinning. 'It might be a good match, indeed. Time will tell. But look! Isn't that Janet McArthur?'

He pointed across the street. The slight figure, clutching her child to her, was outside the university library – not a remarkable thing in itself, but the look of dismay on her face certainly was. She seemed pressed against the sandstone wall, eyes wide and darting from side to side.

Murray and the constable crossed the street quickly.

'Janet?' Murray called. 'Mrs. McArthur?'

Her jaw dropped as she saw him. She met his eye, shoved herself away from the wall, and fled.

Chapter Nineteen

Janet McArthur's turn of speed, carrying a child and encumbered by skirts, was impressive. She nipped through the crowds on the other side of South Street, flashing in and out of view as they followed parallel on the north side. She darted amongst the students at the gateway of St. Mary's College then slithered past the bank office as they on the north skirted the bulk of the town kirk. Round was concentrating so hard on not losing her that he almost toppled a woman swinging her bucket from the well there, but Janet was oblivious, not even glancing back, fixed on her goal, running to as well as running away. But where was she going? Murray was sure she was heading home, but that meant that she would have to cross the road towards them. He slowed, not wanting to end up ahead of her. The close where she and Mrs. Loudoun lived was very near now. He waved an arm at Constable Round, causing him to stop, too. They watched. Janet was hesitating, and at last glanced back. Whatever she saw, it was almost as if someone had shoved her in the small of the back. She started, and ran into the street.

If she had been a second slower, she might have been all right. A second slower, and she might have backed away when she saw she was in the path of a lumbering timber cart, instead of darting forward. She missed the cart, but flung herself straight into the path of the town kirk minister's gig – and the minister was anxious for his dinner.

Murray was in the midst of it before he realised, and found that the child Rosina was already safe in his arms. Janet, though, was in a tumbled heap on the cobbles, the horse prancing and shaking its head in bewilderment with hooves a touch too near for comfort. The minister was still in his seat, clutching the edge of it with both hands and letting his jaw fall slack. Constable Round, not far behind Murray, seized the loose reins while Murray, balancing Rosina on his knee, crouched beside Janet.

Blood was beginning to ooze from a deep cut on the side of her face, and another on her upper arm where her shawl must have slipped. She was white as a sheet, her red hair startling against her skin, but she was at least partially conscious.

'Mamma!' squeaked Rosina, and began to cry. Murray hugged her against his shoulder.

'I think Mamma's going to be all right, but she'll have a sore arm, don't you think? Now, we need to find some nice people to help carry Mamma home.'

'Oh, let me, let me,' came a voice, and Murray turned to find that the minister had managed to descend on wobbling legs from his seat on the gig. 'How did that happen? I was going too fast, far too fast. Is she hurt? Is she – is she alive?'

'She's alive, but she is hurt.' Murray managed to pull off a glove and ran his long fingers delicately over Janet McArthur's skull. She was wearing no bonnet, only her married woman's cap. 'I don't think her head is broken, but that wound to her cheek is going to be very painful. Mrs. McArthur! Can you hear me?'

'Ugh ... ow,' said Janet unhelpfully. There was a scraping and clattering as Constable Round guided the gig to the side of the street. With a practiced eye, he sorted out the traffic and cleared the less useful bystanders, leaving Janet with her attendants in a little island in the middle of the cobbles. 'Mamma cuddle?' asked Rosina, emerging soggily from Murray's coat shoulder.

'Not just yet, though I'm sure she'd love one later, pet,' said Murray. 'You save it up for her and make it a prodigiously good one, eh? Constable, can we get a board to carry her on?'

'Aye, the steelyard fellow usually has the like for his work. I'll go and fetch a couple.' Rosina found her thumb was a very ready comfort for a time like this, and began to suck it industriously, staring down at her mother. The minister sat down suddenly on the cobbles.

'That was an affa shock! Do you think she's going to be all right?' he asked, still needed reassurance.

'Mrs. McArthur! Don't fall asleep now, eh?' said Murray, prodding her gently. 'We're getting a board to carry you home.'

'It's a gey long way ...' said Janet vaguely.

'What was that?'

'It's a gey long way hame ...'

'It is, isn't it?' Murray said encouragingly, 'but no doubt we'll make it. What's that your village is called again? We don't want to miss our way.'

'Invertally,' she murmured. 'Invertally, by the Tally river. Take the Aberfeldy road, and ask again. You'll be grand ...' Her voice faded, and Murray poked her again, uneasy lest she slip further into unconsciousness. He looked about for the constable, but instead found an even more welcome sight: Mrs. Loudoun was bearing down on them with a face full of horror.

'What has happened here? Has someone attacked her? In broad daylight in the middle of the street? What's going on?'

'I struck her, ma'am,' said the minister wretchedly. He rose, head bowed, as if to accept his punishment.

'You? Are you frae Perthshire an' all?' demanded Mrs. Loudoun. She had been about to throw herself on her knees beside Janet, but stopped herself and spun at the minister. Her fists were clenched.

'Janet ran out into the street and the minister accidentally ran into her in his gig,' Murray called out quickly, not wanting to see the minister down and bloodied too. 'I think she thought someone might be chasing her.'

'Then we have to get her home, straightaway!' Mrs. Loudoun now did crouch down beside Janet, taking her hand gently. 'Has she spoken at all?'

'A little, and nothing to the purpose,' Murray reassured her, though part of his own purpose had been nicely fulfilled. 'Constable Round is bringing boards – here he is, in fact.'

Janet McArthur was small and light, and it did not take long to lift her on to a couple of rather dusty boards. The minister, making his penance as fervently as any Papist, joined with the constable to carry her along to her close. Mrs. Loudoun hurried ahead to open the door, and Murray followed, still carrying Rosina. The child seemed settled now, and happy that her mother was in safe hands. She wiped her nose firmly across Murray's shoulder.

'Mamma sleep now?' she asked.

'For a little, I think. Mrs. Loudoun will look after her well, won't she?'

'Aye. Look after Mamma.'

Someone certainly needed to, thought Murray. For a woman in fear of her life, she had been straying far enough from home and safety. What had she been up to?

In her small house, Mrs. Loudoun was already laying Janet McArthur on the box bed and telling the minister in no uncertain terms that he was worse than useless at a woman's sickbed.

'You're taking up valuable space, sir. Away hame with you and I'll make sure to tell you later what occurs. Mr. Murray, give me that bairn.'

But Rosina was not to be separated from her comfortable perch on Murray's arm.

'I like man!' she explained succinctly, making small fistfuls of his lapels.

'I'll just sit down here out of the way,' said Murray hurriedly, tucking himself into a corner as far from the box bed as he could be. He rearranged Rosina on his lap, and drew out a clean handkerchief for her to play with, making it into a hat for her. Mrs. Loudoun gave him an assessing look, then dismissed him from her immediate concerns. Constable Round offered to stand outside in the lane while Mrs. Loudoun saw to Janet's injuries, an offer that was met with a brisk nod. Already Mrs. Loudoun was plumping up the fire, whirling the kettle on to it, and beginning to loosen Janet's laces to ease her bodice free of the cut on her arm. Murray's mind wandered, trying not to watch too closely, trying to keep Rosina's attention away from her injured mother. He slipped the handkerchief hat on to his own head, and made a silly face. The child chuckled and stuck an exploratory finger into his nose. If Mrs. McArthur had been wearing more fashionable wide sleeves, would she have been better protected?

He gently discouraged further nasal exploration, and began to fashion the handkerchief into a little mouse puppet, a trick he had learned in his own childhood. Rosina took to it at once, squealing with delight.

Invertally, he thought. How big was it? How big a coincidence was it that there should be three people in St. Andrews all at once who had a strong connexion with a village in Perth so small he had never heard of it? Mrs. McArthur – and presumably Rory, if they were right in thinking that Rory had gone home to fetch his wife – Dr. Lindsay, and more distantly but still strongly, Cosmo Gordon. And, Murray thought suddenly, making the mouse puppet jump unexpectedly in Rosina's damp fingers, both Dr. Lindsay and Cosmo Gordon had been in South Street, not far from Mrs. McArthur when she had suddenly made a panic-stricken dash for home. Which of them had caused her flight? Or was it something else altogether?

'Her arm is broken,' Mrs. Loudoun announced without looking around. 'I think a hoof hit her.'

'Nasty,' mumbled Murray, running the puppet mouse along his knee. He remembered receiving a similar injury when he was a boy, when his brother George had illicitly tried riding their father's flightiest mare, and he winced in sympathy. A sharp gasp made him look quickly towards the bed, but it was Mrs. McArthur reacting to a hot cloth touching her slashed cheek. Even from his spot on the floor Murray could see that her eyes were opening.

'What are you doing?' she objected. 'That's affa sore!'

'You were knocked over by a horse,' said Mrs. Loudoun, 'right in the middle of the street. Do you no remember?'

Janet hesitated.

'I'm no sure,' she admitted. 'What was I doing in the street?'

'Now that I dinna ken,' said Mrs. Loudoun, somewhat sternly. 'What were you doing out of the house at all?'

Janet McArthur shifted uneasily, and let out a squawk as Mrs. Loudoun inadvertently jabbed her face with the hot cloth.

'I only left her half an hour,' Mrs. Loudoun muttered, half to Murray, half to herself. 'I told her I'd be back soon. A woman has to go out and get flour and butter once in a while.'

'Of course you do,' said Murray, as soothing as he could be. 'Is your brother not around?'

'Nathan?' Mrs. Loudoun cast him a glance accompanied by sardonic eyebrows and a tut. 'Rarely when he's needed. He's away down the harbour, I believe.' She turned back to her work on Janet's face. 'Whiles he buys a load in Edinburgh, in frae Holland or the like, and has it shipped up here by sea. You ken it's cheaper than the roads, but he'll still go and argify it out with the shipmaster, nae doubt.' She fell silent again, concentrating, and Murray let it be. There were plenty of little coastal brigs, he thought, flitting up and down with all kinds of cargoes. He was glad he could afford to pay the difference and go by road: his stomach felt uneasy at the very thought of coastal brigs. There was another groan from Janet on the bed.

'Is it bad?' she asked nervously.

'Nae doubt you'll have a scar down your face, anyway,' said Mrs. Loudoun, brisk with the bad news. 'You're lucky it didn't get your eye. Dinna move your arm or you'll ken all about it.' Inevitably Janet twitched her arm, and cried out. Mrs. Loudoun's lips tightened in grim satisfaction. 'I tellt you.'

There was silence again for a little, as Mrs. Loudoun swabbed and bandaged with more tenderness than her expression would lead anyone to expect.

'I went out for an apple for the lassie,' said Janet eventually. 'She wanted an apple, and there was none in the house.' Then the thought struck her. 'Where is she? Where is she? Is she safe?' She struggled to sit up, gasping at the pain, but Mrs. Loudoun pushed her gently back down.

'Look over there in the corner: yon Mr. Murray's playing nursemaid. Are you fine, there, Rosina?'

'Man has a wee mousie, Mamma!'

Janet's head had already been turned so that Mrs. Loudoun could work on her cheek, but she had to angle her gaze to see them in their corner. She tried hard to smile at her daughter.

'A wee mousie? I hope it's no a real one!'

Rosina frowned at the mouse, wondering. The mouse twitched, making its ears wiggle, and she giggled again.

'What are you doing here, Mr. Murray?' Janet asked. She could speak more clearly now: her face was bandaged as if she had the toothache, and Mrs. Loudoun had moved a little to work on her arm. She was still white as a sheet, but her eyes looked less dozy.

'I was there when you were hit,' he explained. 'I looked after your lovely daughter while the constable and the minister carried you in.'

'The constable and the minister? My!' Janet was enough herself again to be flattered at such attention.

'The minister was very sorry he hit you, but he couldn't help it,' Murray went on, hoping to stimulate some recollection. 'You ran out into the street, dodged round a cart, and came out in front of him, and he was going too fast to stop.'

'I ran out into the street?' Janet sounded perplexed. 'What would I do that for?'

'I had the impression,' said Murray carefully, 'that something frightened you.'

Mrs. Loudoun emitted a gentle snort.

'She's frightened of any wee thing, though, this one,' she vouchsafed. Murray ignored her.

'Can you remember anything you saw or heard that might have made you frightened?' he persisted. Janet considered, eyes wide. 'No one, perhaps, from your home village? Invertally, is it not?'

Janet shrank back on the bed, making Mrs. Loudoun tut again.

'How – how did you know that, sir?'

'Someone told me. Now, look, there are people in St. Andrews at the moment from Invertally: did you not see them? Either of them?' Janet pressed her lips together hard, eyes fixed on him like a small animal waiting for the moment it would be safe to run. 'Dr. Archibald Lindsay? Cosmo Gordon?' She shook her head very slightly, wincing at the pain, but her lips were sealed. Murray sighed, trying to stay even-tempered. He was sure Rosina on his lap could sense the tension, and he tried to make the mouse play and distract her. 'It's difficult to help you when you won't tell us anything,' he said, allowing his voice to become sorrowful. 'And I'm not sure I understand what was going on, anyway, in that house of yours across the close. For I'm told that when your husband was out playing in his string quartet, you were off walking with another young man.'

'What's that?' Mrs. Loudoun demanded, spinning on her heel. 'That's no right, is it, Janet? You tell him.'

'Where did you hear that?' asked Janet, unsteadily.

'From the young man in question,' said Murray, keeping her gaze.

'Some limmer, nae doubt, trying to bring down a good woman's reputation!' snapped Mrs. Loudoun. 'Who was the braisant gallow-breid, then, eh?'

'You know, don't you, Mrs. McArthur?' said Murray.

'I – I dinna ken ...'

'I don't believe he was lying: he had no reason to be. What

were you doing out walking with Jack Swanson on the night Rory was killed?'

'Jack Swanson?' Mrs. Loudoun was breathless. 'Jack Swanson? But that was Rory's best friend! Why would he say such a thing?'

'Because it's true,' whispered Janet.

'What?' Mrs. Loudoun turned and sat down heavily on the end of the box bed. Rosina, oblivious to the atmosphere in the room, and to Murray's trying to ease the cramp in his leg, slipped slowly into sleep against his shoulder, clutching the mouse he had slipped off his finger. He waited.

'I've met him a few times,' said Janet softly. 'I took the bairn and went to the end of the close, and he walked along and met me, and then we would go for a wee wander up and down or down to the mill lade or up to the cathedral – though I dinna like kirkyards much after dark. I didna want you to see us,' she explained to Mrs. Loudoun.

'I should think you didn't,' muttered her friend, though without her usual force.

'He's affa nice to me, and he's grand with wee Rosina there,' said Janet, a little smile playing on her bandaged face. 'I couldna see no harm in it.'

'Harm?' snapped Mrs. Loudoun, gathering her strength again. 'Harm? You a married woman and him your husband's best friend, dallying ahint his back when he's off playing his fiddle – and worse,' she added as an afterthought, 'being murdered! What did you think you were doing, lassie?'

'Aye, well, Rory was always out working here or playing there. He would never let me leave the house, always telling me to stay at home out of harm's way, out of sight of anyone who might come frae – frae Perthshire to find us. But I wanted some diversion, too! I wanted to go out and meet people and go to things and do my own marketing, and he wouldna let me. Why should I no slip out for a wee wander with a friend?'

'But you're a married woman!' Mrs. Loudoun cried again.

'No, I'm no.'

The silence that met this statement made Janet suddenly nervous. She blinked, breathing unsteadily.

'You're no?' said Mrs. Loudoun eventually.

'I was no supposed to say…' Tears rose in Janet's eyes.

'I should think no. Living out of wedlock in a respectable close! Whyfore did you no wed, the pair of you? And a bairn and all – och, the poor wee thing! A taint on her frae birth, and the pair of you living in sin with no thought to her! How could you do that to the wee one!'

Murray, not wanting to interrupt the flow of the conversation, stroked Rosina's back as she stirred at Mrs. Loudoun's raised voice.

'We couldna marry -' began Janet, sobbing.

'You couldna marry? Is one of yous already wed? Is that it? Absconded from your ain husband, are you?'

'No, I'm no wed,' said Janet firmly. 'And nor was Rory. He had notions of a lass here in St. Andrews, but – well, that went by the wall.'

'Then what were the pair of you up to? Why could you no wed?' Mrs. Loudoun demanded.

'We could no wed,' said Janet, wiping her eyes on her sleeve and struggling up to glare at Mrs. Loudoun, 'because Rory was my brother.'

Murray found it quite satisfying to watch Mrs. Loudoun's jaw drop quite that far, and the silence allowed him, too, to gather his thoughts. Even so, it was Mrs. Loudoun who spoke first.

'And the wee bairn …?' she breathed, the possible full horror of the situation sweeping over her.

'Och, what on earth?' Janet was almost as shocked. 'That's disgusting! Dinna think that! Och, my!'

'Then what's going on? What's the truth of the matter? For pity's sake, lass, out wi' it!'

Janet took a deep breath.

'Rory's my brother, and that's all. He came home and found that I was expecting a babbie, and he said the best thing to do would be to go back to St. Andrews where we would be safe, and pretend we were husband and wife. Well, Rory's always been the one with the brains, ken, so I did what I was told.'

'Have you no mammy and daddy?'

'Och, they're long dead. I lived whiles with my grannie, but she'd not long died, which was why Rory said he would come home and try to find clerking to do maybe in Aberfeldy, ken. But then he found out what had happened.'

'But what did happen? Lass, you're making very little sense here.'

'I've told you it all – what do you mean?'

'I mean why could you no just marry the faither? Or if he was already married, get him to say before the kirk session that he would support the bairn? That's the usual way – here, onywyes. Maybe it's different in Perthshire,' she added sourly, as if Perthshire was another country.

'Aye, but see ... well, the faither didna want to marry me, but he wanted the bairn. And we didna ken if he wanted the bairn dead or alive, to be honest.' Now she was telling her story, she seemed to have brightened: she was enjoying her role as tragic heroine.

'But ...'

'And the faither was the laird, see, so he wasna just a wee man with no power in the matter.'

Murray blinked. He was a laird, but he did not think he would have the power to kill a child and get away with it. Perhaps indeed Perthshire was another country: or perhaps Invertally was simply a little further from sheriff's officers and law courts.

'But surely ...' Mrs. Loudoun was not accustomed to being speechless. She was floundering.

'I heard tell he said he was going to kill me and the bairn, for see, I was going to tell the kirk session that he forced me. I didna want to go with him: big hairy fellow like a Highland cow. There were plenty men I liked better, even in Invertally.' She finished with a tiny coquettish nod of the head: Murray was fairly sure that the laird had not been her first suitor, and Jack Swanson might not be her last, either. But that was no reason for the laird to assume he had rights in the matter, and if he had forced himself on her, he might indeed fear her statement to the kirk session – or at least her confession to her brother. The laird of Invertally ... was that not Dr. Archibald Lindsay's brother?

'So Rory said this way would be safer, and he told all his friends he had married and we found the wee place across the close. But I don't think Rory was thinking straight, all the same. He trapped us, see? He couldna court the lassie he wanted, and I couldna court a'body at all.'

'Och! Och, lassie,' Mrs. Loudoun's face was suddenly full of dread. 'You dinna ken a'thing about his death, do you? You and Jack Swanson, you didn't ...?'

'No!' Janet was definite. 'Jack wouldna do such a thing. He was gey fond of Rory. And me – well, he drove me wud half the time, just like a brother should, but I'd never harm him. My poor Rory: he tried to protect me. Who'll protect me now?'

'Jack Swanson?' Murray could not help suggesting. Janet gave him a little scowl for spoiling her tragic moment. 'Listen: I know the laird of Invertally is a Lindsay. His brother is in town, and he was on South Street just now. Is that who you saw? Is that who frightened you?'

Janet took a deep breath.

'It was him, then, was it? I thought it was. I've only seen Dr. Lindsay the once, but aye, he's the laird's wee brother. He's been away at the university a long while, now. But I thought I recognised him when I saw him. Do you ken, Mr. Murray, has he found out where I am?'

'I don't think so,' said Murray. 'But if you fear him as much as you say, you're going to have to stay in the house until we sort this out. No more running out for apples, understand?'

Wide-eyed, she nodded.

'I'll do my best,' she said. But she was so flighty, flirting one minute and terrified the next, that he was not sure that her best would be good enough.

Chapter Twenty

'Did you hear any of that?' Murray asked, when he had handed back the still sleeping Rosina and found Constable Round still lingering in the close outside.

'Some of it,' the constable admitted, 'but whiles their voices got gey quiet.'

Murray quickly summed up what he had discovered, edging the constable towards the street the better to avoid eavesdroppers. In South Street he found his gaze was already darting about, looking for any sign of Dr. Archibald Lindsay.

'He was off to Professor Shaw's, so that Hepburn could visit Flavia,' he muttered half to himself. 'We'd better go straight there, unless we see him in between.'

'Do you think he's our man, sir? I mean, he seemed a very gentlemanly character, I thought.'

'He might be: it's certainly worth trying to find out more about his movements. I know he was not at the recital, and claims to have been drinking copious quantities of claret with Hepburn that night, but he could have allowed Hepburn to drink the claret and slip out to kill Rory.'

'But what would be his reason?'

Murray stopped on the edge of the street.

'Do you know, that's a good question?' He thought for a second, his mind half on watching the road for any more impatiently-driven gigs. 'Come on, let's get into the common close and discuss that.'

The close was quieter than the main street, and they slowed their pace. Murray considered before replying to Constable Round's question.

'We know that Lindsay and Rory were from the same village.

We know that Lindsay's older brother is the laird. According to Janet McArthur – McArthur, apparently, to her own name, and not Mrs. at all – and I agree she is not the most inspiring of confidence amongst witnesses I have met – according to her, the laird, Mr. Lindsay, is the father of her child Rosina, whether by assault or by seduction, but certainly out of wedlock.'

'Aye, from what I heard I wasna clear whether she encouraged him or no,' Constable Round agreed.

'I suppose at this stage that is immaterial,' Murray conceded, 'for the more important thing is that, according to her, either her life or the child's is in danger from Mr. Lindsay – and that makes Dr. Lindsay's presence in St. Andrews, and his whereabouts on the night of Rory's death, a matter for enquiry.'

'But sir, that still does not explain why he might have murdered Rory McArthur.'

'His brother's revenge for taking Janet away? Or perhaps he came upon Rory, recognised him, and tried to get him to tell where Janet and the child were hiding? And matters went too far.'

Constable Round pursed his lips, and for a moment the only sound was the solemn tapping of his staff on the beaten earth of the path.

'You're not convinced, Constable, are you?'

'Well ...'

'Well?'

'It's just a bit of a leap, sir.'

'He was in Letho when Carlisle was attacked.'

'And where was he when young Swanson was locked in St. Rule's Tower?' asked the constable. Murray reflected.

'In St. Andrews: he had been at dinner with the Shaws as I had been.'

'Aye, that was when you were locked in, sir, but what about the time of Rory McArthur's funeral when Jack Swanson was locked in? Where was he then?'

'I'm not sure ... I'd have to think.' He tried to remember. Had Lindsay been at the funeral? No, he had not. Constable Round heaved a weighty sigh.

'I agree, sir, that he needs to answer a few questions, for there are altogether too many coincidences in all this for my liking, and there's no doubt that Janet McArthur was scared enough of him when she saw him. She's a flighty wee thing, but to run out into the street like that carrying her bairn an' all – well, we need to talk to him.'

'Well, then, back to Professor Shaw's.'

They had walked almost the length of the common close and were now at its foot, where it opened on to the path by the mill lade.

'What would Dr. Lindsay have been doing down here, when his pal lives down by the links?' Constable Round mused. 'If he saw Rory McArthur by chance, where was that? Did he just chase him down here?'

'Dr. Lindsay couldn't have convinced Jack Swanson at the funeral that he should run away, because he wasn't there,' said Murray, gazing upstream at the small stand of muddled trees where Jack Swanson said he had hidden and waited that day. 'Could he have sent him a note?'

'But why would he do such a thing?' asked Constable Round. 'As far as we ken, he wouldna even be acquainted with Jack Swanson.'

'He might have heard that he was suspected of Rory's death, and want to make him look more suspicious. Oh, look, the night of Professor Shaw's dinner, Dr. Lindsay was asking all kinds of questions about Rory, what family he had, who was nearby, all that. He was still hunting for Janet, of course! I don't believe he deliberately killed Rory: I think Rory died while Dr. Lindsay was trying to make him tell where Janet was.'

They stood silent for a moment, watching the stream patter past, listening to the fall of water leaving Professor Shaw's experimental garden beyond the Swansons' back wall.

'Why,' Murray wondered absently, 'did Rory climb over the wall, when there's a gate?'

'Maybe Swanson locks it by night.'

'Maybe so.' Murray stared at the gate without really seeing it, then pulled himself back to the present. 'Right, let's go and see what Dr. Lindsay has to say for himself.'

'Aye, sir.'

The Shaw household was quiet when they let themselves in by the front door: from vague sounds from upstairs Murray deduced that the boys had been sent to make themselves presentable for dinner – the aromas emerging from the kitchen areas were enough momentarily to distract him from any thoughts of Dr. Lindsay – so probably Professor Shaw was engaged in the same business in his own quarters. There was, however, a soft murmuring from the parlour, and Murray, nodding at Constable Round, tapped softly on the door and went in.

The parlour presented, as it was accustomed to doing, a happy domestic scene. Mrs. Shaw, looking more settled than Murray had seen her for a while, was stitching something more practical than pretty at one end of a sopha, while her daughter Flavia sat at the other end. It was where Murray had found her curled up and sobbing after Rory's death, so today presented a pleasant contrast: Flavia was already dressed for dinner in a lilac confection with lemon gloves and slippers, and her little round face was rosy with smiles and content. In a chair by the fire sat Mr Hepburn, as rosy himself, eyes shining behind his round spectacles, pudgy hands comfortably folded in his lap. He flung himself into a standing position when he saw Murray come in, showing his little teeth and crinkling his eyes in a happy grin.

'Mr. Murray! I had no idea when we met you earlier what a terrible night you must have had! I am very glad to see you restored to – well, ground level!'

'Thank you, Mr. Hepburn. As you see, I have suffered no ill effects.'

'Mr. Hepburn has graciously accepted an invitation to stay to dinner,' said Mrs. Shaw admitting a little smile to her face.

'We are only awaiting the arrival of his clothes,' said Flavia, and blushed, batting her hair self-consciously.

'Then I must change, too,' said Murray, though the thought of resuming his evening clothes in which he had already spent so much of the last twenty-four hours was not appealing.

'Constable Round, will you stay, too?' asked Mrs. Shaw, never one to worry over-much about mixing classes around her dinner table. The constable, however, was more sensitive to such things.

'You're very good, madam, but I've had my dinner already.'

'Oh, of course!' For a moment Mrs. Shaw descended into an abstraction, but then she focussed on her sewing.

'Has Dr. Lindsay not stayed to enjoy such good company?' Murray asked, sitting on one of the hard chairs by the table. Constable Round stood by the door. He contrived to look as little as if he were on guard duty as possible, but it came hard to him.

'Dr. Lindsay merely walked me here and stayed a few minutes,' Hepburn explained. 'He was eager to return to his duties in Letho: your gardener, I believe, sustained a serious injury on Sunday morning?'

'Oh!' Murray was aghast, and tried not to show it. What if Lindsay returned to see Carlisle at Letho, and found him waking and remembering who had attacked him? He would have to get an express to Robbins straightaway. 'May I ring for Pennie, Mrs. Shaw? I have suddenly remembered an urgent message I have to get to my household.'

'Oh, what a shame: Archie could have taken it for you, if we had only known!' said Hepburn innocently.

'Pennie has gone down to Mr. Hepburn's house for his dinner things,' Mrs. Shaw explained.

'I'll go for you, sir, an you wish it,' murmured Constable Round. 'Will you put something in writing, and I'll take it to the express office?'

'Of course – thank you, constable. Excuse me.' He seized the writing paper that the Shaws kept in the parlour, wrote 'Robbins. Do not allow Dr. Lindsay alone with Carlisle until I can explain. C. Murray', and handed it, folded and with Robbins' name and address on the front, to Round. The constable bowed and left forthwith, meeting Murray's eye with concern. The same thought had obviously crossed his own mind.

'Nothing too serious, I hope, Mr. Murray?' Hepburn enquired politely.

'Not at all, only a delivery I meant to leave word about. I believe it may arrive today, and they need particular directions. Do you have a property somewhere, Mr. Hepburn?'

'I am not settled just yet.' He turned to smile at Mrs. and Miss Shaw. 'As I said, I have taken the house by the links just for the summer, to renew my acquaintance with old St. Andrews. My plans thereafter are not fixed. Not as yet fixed at all.' His nose wrinkled in another smile: his face did little else, it seemed.

'It is delightful to return, is it not? And it must have been particularly pleasing for you to be able to invite a fellow alumnus to stay, so that you could reminisce together.'

'Oh, yes! Lindsay was very keen to come. In fact, he suggested I take the house: I had been thinking of somewhere about Cramond, perhaps, but he said why not St. Andrews? And then, of course, he was asked to help your village doctor, so it all worked out beautifully. And I'm so glad I'm here and not at Cramond,' he added, directing yet another toothy smile straight at Flavia. Murray thought she might melt on the spot.

He would have to return to Letho again after dinner, he thought to himself, though travelling after one of Mrs. Shaw's meals was a daunting prospect. What if Lindsay reached Letho House before the express? An express was fast, but when had Lindsay left St. Andrews, and had it been on that fine, fast black stallion? He had no particular reason to be in a hurry – unless he had had word that Carlisle was conscious. But did that mean he had at least not seen Janet, despite her conspicuous accident in the middle of South Street? Was she at least still safe? Or was she just less urgent than silencing Carlisle? Murray could feel his heartbeat quicken, but for the moment there was nothing he could do.

Then a thought struck him.

Lindsay had left his friend Hepburn here, then, presumably, walked all the way back down to Hepburn's rented villa to fetch his horse and ride on to Letho by the coast road.

What if he had not left St. Andrews at all?

For a few seconds he was torn between sprinting after Constable Round or running to the little close off South Street to make sure that Janet McArthur and Rosina were safe. The few seconds were enough: there was a modest sound at the parlour door, and Pennie appeared to announce that he had deposited Mr. Hepburn's dinner accoutrements upstairs in a spare room and would be pleased to show him to hot water and a razor when he was ready. Murray slipped quickly into the hallway after the manservant, seizing a piece of paper and the pen as he went.

'Pennie, could you go quickly – or send someone quick, if you have someone – after Constable Round and give him this? He is gone to the post office to send an express.' He scribbled some words on the paper and directed it to the constable.

'Aye, I saw him up the top of the common close,' Pennie admitted, taking the paper from Murray and giving it an extra shake to dry the ink. 'I'll go and send the boy up the lane, if that's all right, sir: I did say I'd see to Mr. Hepburn just now.'

'Of course. Thank you, Pennie: and here is something for the boy.' He handed Pennie a few coins, popped back into the parlour to excuse himself, and went to change for dinner, happily well used to dressing himself.

By the time he was ready, Pennie knocked on his chamber door and handed in a reply. Constable Round's hand was laboured but clear:

'I shall see at once if the person is safe,' he wrote, 'but it is possible that N.H. is already on guard duty.'

N.H. ... Nathan Houston, of course. Yes, he seemed inclined to protect the fragile Janet McArthur: no doubt she would be safe. He sighed, feeling that events were slipping away from him, and went down to dinner.

By the time they had eaten all they could of Mrs. Shaw's delicious dinner, and listened to about all they could of Mr. Hepburn's relentlessly cheery conversation – made, Murray was sure, all the more nervily positive now that Hepburn was seeing Professor Shaw in the shape of a potential father-in-law – it was dark outside, and once they had rejoined the ladies it was debatable whether Hepburn would leave before midnight. Murray could see that his old professor was becoming edgy again, and suggested that they might take some air in the garden.

'The stars are likely to be fine again tonight,' he added as a temptation, though he felt he had seen enough of them last night. Professor Shaw gathered himself into the appearance of a teacher, and looked to Walter and James.

'Boys, yes indeed, you should come and learn some more constellations,' he said.

'Oh, Father, do I have to?' asked James, who had his head in a book at the parlour table. 'It's freezing out there!'

Walter was already on his feet, though, so the three of them, with hats, gloves and mufflers, ventured out into the whitelit garden.

'Did you find your flannels, Walter?' Murray asked, his grin hidden in the poor light.

'Not yet, sir,' said Walter stoically, 'but I'm making do with the old ones.'

The moon, waning from its fullness at Easter, was yellow-white and sagging in the sky, dimming the stars around it, but across the arc of darkness there were hundreds of pinpricks of light, even more if you concentrated. Walter stopped and gazed up at it, nodding now and again as he recognised constellations he had already been taught. Murray wondered if he could find his way around the night sky any better than he could find his way around the earth beneath it.

'I did not see you earlier, Charles, my boy, and in any case that man Hepburn seems to have taken up residence, for some reason.'

'I think he might possibly have succumbed to the charms of Miss Flavia,' Murray said lightly. Professor Shaw turned in surprise.

'Oh! Good heavens, that cannot be it. She is only just out, you know.' He frowned, then dismissed the idea. 'What progress has been made, Charles? Do you know anything more?'

'Well, yes, some more. Prepare yourself for something of a shock: Rory and Janet McArthur were brother and sister, not husband and wife.'

'What?' Professor Shaw sat down heavily, fortunately on one of the stone benches. The cold of the stone caused him to rise again almost instantly.

Murray explained how the ruse had been worked for the protection of Janet and her baby.

'And she admits at last that the person who so frightened her was Dr. Archibald Lindsay, the brother of the laird she says is the father of her child.'

'Dr. Lindsay? My old student, who was here last night? *That* Archibald Lindsay?'

Murray began to regret telling Professor Shaw so much at once: the onslaught of emotional information was clearly upsetting him. He laid a hand on Shaw's little arm.

'There is no evidence that he means to do her harm, or even knows where she is,' he said gently. 'It may just be a coincidence – after all, Cosmo Gordon's family also comes from the same tiny village.'

'Cosmo Gordon, the artist?'

'That's the one.' They had wandered further, Walter trailing behind them still staring upwards, and Murray's gaze lit on a tree on the Shaws' side of the garden wall that was close to the one Rory McArthur must have climbed on the Swansons' side. He had a sudden urge to look at the Swansons' garden again: something about the trail Rory seemed to have left in there bothered him. His evening clothes could hardly cause much more dismay to Robbins than they already would: he reached up to the branches and began to climb the tree.

'Didn't he say his brother was a laird somewhere, too?'

'Not his brother, his family,' Murray corrected. 'Lairds of the same village, it turns out, but Gordon's family were attainted at the '45, and their lands forfeited.'

'To hear him speak you would have thought he himself was the laird, or something greater,' Professor Shaw remarked, with a little more acid than was usual for him. Cosmo had treated him very rudely. 'It is hard to think of him coming from a village so small we had not even heard of it.'

'He walks through Letho as if he was scared it would stick to the soles of his boots,' Walter suddenly put in.

'What was that, Walter?' Murray asked. He was concentrating on securing his foothold, before he would survey the Swansons' garden.

'I was coming back from my other auntie's on Sunday night,' Walter explained, watching Murray's progress unconcernedly. 'I saw Mr. Gordon on his own at the top of the village, and he looked as if he'd wipe his feet the minute he left. I'm no sure I fancy the gentleman much, sir.'

'Noted, Walter,' Murray murmured. His feet were steady, and he shifted his gaze to the garden below him. The workshop to his left had a light on, and over its roof he could just see further lights in the house on the ground floor. Presumably the maid was clearing up after their dinner, or perhaps having her own if she ate there. The rest of the garden was almost in silence, the still twigs and blades of grass steadying themselves for another frosty night. Rory had climbed out here, had jumped into the Shaws' garden. Over there, by the back wall, he had landed after climbing the wall outside, by the mill lade. Who was pursuing him? And why did he climb the wall, rather than using the gate? He should ask Swanson whether or not he locked the gate at night, and if Rory would have known that. He peered through the pewter moonlight at the back wall, then allowed his gaze to run along to the gate. It looked bleached in this light, though solid still. That latch was heavy, he remembered, staring. And it moved.

It was probably Swanson or Jack coming back from somewhere, he told himself. Yet he held his breath as the gate swung half-open, creaking only a little on its well-maintained hinges, and a figure slipped through the gap. Murray clung motionless to the tree, staring down the garden. The figure was bulky, in a broad-brimmed hat and dark coat, but then both the Swansons were large men. The brim cast a shadow and he could not see the man's face, but he had the clear sense that whoever he was, the new arrival was on soft-footed business that was not strictly honest or honourable.

He watched, praying that Professor Shaw and Walter would not call up to him – he could hear them murmuring behind him somewhere, about stars or trees or fish, no doubt. His hands were growing cold, and he tried to wriggle them inside his gloves without moving the branches he was holding. The figure advanced up the garden, staying on the narrow gritty path but pacing carefully, making little sound, hands held out to his sides as though he needed to balance – or did not wish even to make a sound rubbing his sleeves against the sides of his coat. He drew level with Murray, and finally he managed to see just a little of the man's profile. It was enough: it was Nathan Houston.

Murray drew breath, but then wondered what to shout. He decided to wait: what would Nathan do next? To his alarm, Nathan reached the top of the path and turned left, towards Murray. Again he held his breath, but the big man's attention was fixed, he could see, on something much lower down than Murray up his tree. What was he looking for? Something, evidently, near the foot of the garden wall. There was a moment's delicate shifting and scuffling, as if he were searching as quietly as he could amongst whatever plants might be down there. Then there was the least grunt of satisfaction, and he straightened up, holding something smallish and squarish in his hands. He stood and fiddled with it briefly, then something must have made him look up. At once he saw Murray: he could not fail to. He let out a yell of astonishment.

There was an answering cry from the workshop, and Murray heard the door open and slam, then trotting footsteps as Thomas Swanson emerged from its dark shadow into his garden

'What's going on there? Who is that?'

'It's Charles Murray here: there's a man acting very suspiciously in your garden, Mr. Swanson, and it's Nathan Houston.'

'What's that?' The words came simultaneously from Swanson, in his shirtsleeves and waistcoat, and from Professor Shaw on his own side of the wall. 'Is that Mr. Swanson?' Professor Shaw added, padding over to the tree.

'Nathan Houston?' demanded Swanson. 'What are you doing in my garden, man?'

'I was just ...' Nathan Houston glared up at Murray with a filthy look.

'He took something from down there, at the foot of the wall,' Murray went on, as Swanson neared Nathan Houston warily. 'That's it in his hands.'

'The foot of the wall?' Swanson seemed bewildered. 'What would have been there?'

Nathan, rather stupidly, was trying to tuck the square thing he was holding into the breast of his coat. There was no chance that it would fit, and in a moment Swanson was next to him, hands out for the object.

'What is going on, Charles?' Professor Shaw called. Walter, in a flash of initiative, scrambled in a most un-Walter-like fashion up into the lower branches of Murray's tree to see what was happening. Murray felt the tree swayed by Walter's enthusiasm.

'Nathan Houston, the man whose sister is looking after Janet,' said Murray, keeping his voice as low as possible in case they might be overheard by some unseen listener – or even Mr. Hepburn, friend to Dr. Lindsay. 'He's in Mr. Swanson's garden and has found something down by the wall here.'

Professor Shaw rose nervously on tiptoe, though it still brought him nowhere near to seeing over the wall.

'Do be careful, Charles! Be careful, Walter!' he murmured, agitated.

Swanson had taken the object from Nathan's reluctant hands.

'What's this?' he asked generally.

'I don't know,' said Murray, after Nathan had had his chance to reply, 'but he headed straight for it. What could it be?'

'Well, it's a kist, sir,' said Swanson, holding it up into the moonlight. 'Only a small one.'

'What's in it?'

'It's gey heavy, for all its size!' Swanson balanced it on his arm, while he fidgeted with the straps. Nathan stood helpless, though Murray had an eye on him in case he decided to run. Swanson tugged the strap free, and opened the lid of the kist. Nathan made a movement as if to stop him, but let his arm fall, helpless. Swanson peered inside, reached in a finger, and drew out something soft, which unfolded itself as he lifted it into a distinctive, familiar shape.

'Sir!' cried Walter in delight, 'it's my flannel drawers!'

Chapter Twenty-One

'These are yours?' Swanson squinted up at Walter in surprise. 'What are they doing in my garden, then?'

'I don't know, sir. There should be jam in there and all, though,' added Walter, keen to take care of the essentials.

'It's certainly heavy enough.' Swanson stepped forward delicately and handed the kist up to Walter, who struggled to hold both it and the tree. Murray took it from him while he slithered down to the ground, then reached it down with a finger in its leather strap. 'Well, I'm not sure there's anything more to be said here, sir, is there? I doubt Mr. Houston was here to steal young Walter's flannel suiting.'

'Nor yet his jam,' muttered Nathan Houston, and Murray had the sense that he was struggling to contain laughter.

'Well, then, off you go, man,' said Swanson heartily. He tapped Nathan Houston on the arm. 'Away home out of harm's way.'

'But …' said Murray, not sure what was going on. Swanson was taking this all too easily, and already Nathan Houston was heading down the path to the garden gate. Yet if Murray let him go, the chances were he would head back to his sister's house and that would mean some protection for Janet McArthur. Should he talk Swanson into detaining him, or not? For whatever Houston had been looking for in the shadow of the wall, Walter's flannels were not what he had expected.

'Good night, Mr. Murray,' said Swanson, quite as if nothing untoward had happened at all. He waved and with an audible shiver, in his shirtsleeves, he made his way back to his workshop. Murray watched him go, and saw that Nathan Houston had also disappeared. The Swansons' garden was silent again, and Murray, after a moment, slid down out of the tree to explain, as well as he could, the whole event to Professor Shaw.

'He was in the garden when he shouldn't have been, and he was looking for something he expected to find there,' Murray finished. 'Yet Swanson was perfectly happy to let him go.'

'He can be a generous man, on occasion,' Professor Shaw offered doubtfully.

'Nathan Houston didn't want him to open the kist.' Murray thought aloud. 'I'm sure he didn't, but Swanson was quite content to open it – does that mean that Swanson somehow knew it was not the one that Houston was expecting? But what does that mean – did Swanson leave something there for Nathan Houston to find?' He considered, watching Professor Shaw's open, confused face. Then he sighed sharply, exasperated. 'I don't believe anyone is telling us the truth at all. What time is it?'

'Between half past eight and nine, I believe,' said Shaw. Murray glanced at Walter, who, with an air of profound concentration, was carefully rewrapping two stone jam jars in layers of fresh flannel.

'I think I shall see if Cosmo Gordon is at home,' said Murray. 'It was very convenient for Swanson when Cosmo remembered that Swanson had been drinking at his house. I wonder if Cosmo's memory could be jogged a little?'

On the way up South Street Murray resisted the temptation to drop in to the little close and see if Janet McArthur was all right. While he had no idea where Dr. Lindsay was, he should try not to draw any more attention to the place than was strictly necessary. He deliberately waited until he had reached Logie's Wynd by the town kirk before he cut through to Market Street, emerging just at the end of the town house where Constable Round had his office. No lights could be seen in the building: the good constable was either keeping guard on Janet McArthur or away home for his well-earned supper. He turned east, and in a moment on his right was Mr. Bogue's cloth warehouse. The shutters were firmly closed, but he thought he could distinguish the least chink of light around them. Mr. Bogue was presumably still sorting out his new deliveries of fine French silks and laces. Perhaps, Murray thought in passing, he should buy something pretty for little Augusta – or something for Isobel Blair for looking after her.

In the more eastern reaches of Market Street, before it met Heukster's Wynd, the street narrowed but the houses became broader and more spacious – nothing to North Street's fine terraces, but still comfortable. Cosmo's bunkwife apparently owned a white house on the left, about halfway along this narrow part of the street. Murray hesitated, nodded a reassuring greeting to an old woman sitting by a candle in the unshuttered window opposite, then opted for the palest house he could see. It was the right one: in a moment, Cosmo himself opened the door.

'Mr. Murray! Come in, sir! What can I do for you?'

He ushered Murray into a small but cosy parlour, with a rag rug or two on the stone floor, panelled walls and a lively fire. The remains of a pie lay on a small blue and white ashet on a round oak table, a pewter plate and knife sprinkled with crumbs beside it: Murray was suddenly visited by the notion that that corner of the room had not changed in two hundred years.

'My bunkwife is still away and I have to fend for myself in the food line,' Cosmo Gordon explained, seeing where he was looking, 'but there is claret aplenty if you would care to take a glass.'

'Thank you, that would be most welcome.'

Cosmo ushered Murray to one of the two modern chairs by the fire, dispelling the feeling of undisturbed history in the corner. The claret was very fine.

'I like to keep a good cellar, even in these straitened circumstances,' Cosmo said, settling into the other chair.

'Yet your business seems brisk,' said Murray. The ambiguity of Cosmo Gordon's position seemed to allow him to make a comment which would have been impertinent to another gentleman, but Cosmo recoiled a little.

'It is as nothing compared with where my family was,' he said stiffly. Murray nodded, mouth twisted in sympathy.

'Have you spent much time in – Invertally, wasn't it? I imagine it's a beautiful spot.'

'I have visited,' Cosmo conceded. 'It is indeed picturesque in the extreme. The present laird, Lindsay, seems to be a tolerably good landlord and not actively disliked locally.'

Damned with faint praise indeed, Murray thought. Yet not quite Janet McArthur's hairy attacker, either.

'His family acquired it straight after the – misfortunes which occurred to your family? There was no intervening owner?'

'No: as I understand it – and I have been paying attention, I can assure you – Lindsay's great grandfather bought it directly from the Government in 1748.'

So if Janet McArthur spoke truthfully about the laird of Invertally being the father of her child, it was certainly a Lindsay that she meant.

'A sad case,' Murray murmured. 'Did you know the Lindsays at all? Were they a local family originally?'

'I believe this branch hailed from the Borders somewhere,' said Cosmo dismissively. 'Probably some businessman who had prospered enough to look for somewhere in the country, and timed it well. Your own family, I take it, were unaffected by the forfeitures?'

'Oh, we are far too unimportant!' said Murray blandly. 'Only the more prominent families, as you well know, were constrained to forfeit their lands!'

'True, true,' Cosmo allowed, accepting the level of superiority Murray had granted him. Murray wondered when the Jacobite uprisings would fade into history once and for all.

'Anyway, how is your work at Letho going?' Murray asked, shifting in his chair to emphasise a change of subject.

'No progress since this afternoon,' said Cosmo with a slight grin. Murray smiled too: he had completely forgotten that he had met Cosmo on South Street before the whole incident of Janet McArthur and the minister's gig. 'Though I should be glad of any hints you might have for pinning down your manservant, Robbins. He claims to be busy but I have seen such things before: I believe he has no wish to be painted, and is avoiding me.'

'Knowing Robbins, that is entirely probable. I must have a word with him, for he is one of whom I should particularly like to have a portrait.'

'What will you do with them after they are framed?' Cosmo asked curiously. 'Not every gentleman wants a gallery of his staff on open display.'

'I had thought to line them on the corridor down to the servants' wing,' said Murray, 'so that they can each see themselves, but so that they are not too far from the main house and I can see them, too.'

'You have no housekeeper just now, and only the one maid?'

'That's right.' Murray had no wish to discuss the painful circumstances that had led to that. 'I have friends in Edinburgh who are seeking new staff for me, but they are very particular on my behalf and it is taking some time. I am in no hurry, though. While I am alone at Letho it matters very little.'

'And is there word about Mr. Carlisle?'

'No progress, as far as I am aware. Poor man: he has been there for longer than I can remember.'

'It's unsettling, isn't it?' Cosmo agreed, then fell silent. Murray glanced at him, then remembered something Walter had said. Cosmo had been in Letho on Sunday night: Murray had thought he was only to travel from St. Andrews on Monday morning to paint Walter. Could he have been there on Sunday morning, too? He was about to frame a question when Cosmo went on. 'But I suspect you did not come here to ask me about the paintings at Letho. How can I be of service to you, Mr. Murray?'

'Well … It's a little awkward. It concerns Rory McArthur's death.'

'Oh, yes? I still cannot quite believe it, you know. I keep thinking of things to play at our next meeting – though whether Jack will be with us still or not is another question. Is it Jack you want to ask about?'

'No … But there is something suspicious about that household, and Jack and his father are not, I believe, telling me or the constable the whole truth about their movements that night. Now, I know that Thomas Swanson was seen crossing South Street towards his home around midnight that night, so he had been out, indeed, as he said. You told me that he left here around that time, but what I wanted to know was are you quite sure about the time of his arrival? You said that he appeared just as you came home after the recital. You might perhaps have misremembered? Or you were delayed for some time on your way home? Or … perhaps Mr. Swanson asked you to help him in some way? A favour for a friend?'

For a long moment, the only thing that moved in the little parlour was the fire, oblivious and lively. There was no other sound: Cosmo stared into his claret glass, the light refracting bloody but motionless through the wine. Murray waited, praying he had not pushed too far. Cosmo's pride was hard to calculate. At last, Cosmo heaved a slightly uneven sigh.

'Yes, that's clever of you,' he admitted. 'And it's a difficult thing to admit.'

He hesitated, but Murray said nothing, patient and still.

'I need his business: I do patterns, you see, for silverware. Not everyone wants their portrait painted, or can afford it.' He glanced at Murray, who nodded: he remembered seeing the ashet in Swanson's workshop. 'He asked me – he told me he had told you he had been at home that night, then he remembered that he had seen the night watchman as he crossed South Street heading home. So he asked me to say that he had been here.'

'And was he, at all?'

'No, not at all. I don't believe he has ever spent an evening here. And I have no idea where he was. But Mr. Murray, to be honest, I can see no reason why Thomas Swanson would have killed Rory: and the idea of Swanson scrambling over garden walls after anyone is just laughable. Besides, Rory climbed into the Swansons' garden, remember? Why would he have done that, if it was Swanson chasing him? No: if you ask me, Swanson was off doing something he doesn't fancy people knowing about – a woman, maybe, something innocent enough - but not murder.'

Murray looked at him, his long face full of concern in the firelight, eyes anxious. He was still keen, it seemed, to protect his friend – but where had Swanson really been that night? It was clear that Cosmo Gordon could not, or would not, say.

He closed Cosmo Gordon's door behind him with a sigh, and nodded again at the woman in the window across the street. She was evidently one of those gatekeepers to whom some kind of social due is paid as a toll for passage: she smiled and waved at him, making her candle flame flicker. If she had not been there he might have hesitated a moment longer, but as it was he turned west and set off back down Market Street, the way he had come. At Heukster's Wynd he turned left, and in a moment was back in the upper reaches of South Street, lingering thoughtfully.

Everyone was lying, as far as he could tell. Jack had claimed to be at home, and now he said he had been out walking with Janet

McArthur. Janet had not been married to Rory at all, which presumably she had told Jack, as he seemed happy enough to be courting her. If Jack knew that Rory and Janet were not married, he had no reason to kill Rory out of jealousy.

And if Jack were out with Janet and Thomas Swanson had been seen returning at midnight, then perhaps the Bogues had not been lying when they said they had found the Swanson house in darkness. Had Rory already been dead by then? If Pennie's report of the noises in the workshop were anything to go by, Rory died just after half past ten. He could not remember how accurate the Bogues had been in their account of the time they were at the Swansons' front door.

Yet he was still not happy with the Bogues' story. If they had been worried about Rory and Jack, they might indeed have gone out to look for one or other of them, and they might have delayed an hour or so, too, while they talked it over and their anxieties grew. Yet it seemed to Murray that if they had been sensible in their search they would have gone to Rory's house and to Jack's house, one way round or the other, and would have remembered that clearly: that did not seem to be the case. Had they really been looking for Rory and Jack, or had they some other reason for being out at night? Or had they some reason for killing Rory themselves? Rory had been Bogue's clerk: was there something about the business that Bogue was worried Rory would not keep secret? And could that be why Jack's life was threatened, too, on top of the tower? But it was a while since they had worked for Bogue: why suddenly worry now? That did not make sense.

And then there was Nathan Houston: what had he been looking for in the Swansons' garden, and had Swanson left it there for him? And how had Walter's flannels ended up in their hands instead? Murray grinned to himself: that seemed like a lesser mystery, and not even Walter was likely to pursue that now that his jam had been restored to him unharmed.

He wished that Carlisle would improve, not only for his own sake but also to say what he could remember. It must have been something he saw that night when he came looking for Professor Shaw, and found the Shaws all retired for the night. It had to be something worth pursuing him to Letho for. He sighed, and sent up yet another silent prayer for Carlisle's recovery. But for now, he thought, it was time to talk to Jack Swanson again. He had been co-operative that morning: he might have some clue as to where his father might have been that night.

The town kirk clock struck the half hour as he began once again to walk down South Street – half past nine, not too late to call on the Swansons. There were still quite a few people about, walking to friends for supper, indoor workers finishing late, students slipping back from discreet sessions in alehouses. One was singing, in a voice fit for the chapel choir, a song very much unfit for the chapel choir, and his friends laughed raucously. Murray smiled, feeling old. Even the song had not changed much since his day.

And even the shouting took him back to various student scuffles of his young days, and he was lost in memories when he realised that the shouts were not those of students. He had reached the town kirk, and ahead of him he could hear a woman scream. Two figures lurched into the street from a close ahead of him, one yelling ferociously at the other, while the screams persisted, surging with anger as much as with fear. The man not shouting stumbled across the cobbles, pursued by the other, but righted himself and swung a practised punch at the shouting man. The victim fell silent with a whoosh of breath, doubled over with his arms clutched around him. The assailant, lighter on his feet for all his height, kicked out for good measure at the injured man's kneecaps, but the man, recovering, dodged and caught at the assailant's boot, trying to unbalance him. The assailant hopped, windmilling his arms wildly, and the punched man took his chance, charging forward from his hunched position and seizing the tall man about the waist, shoulder in his stomach, driving him backwards. The tall man took a few desperate steps backwards, then managed to turn, letting the smaller man's momentum spin them both around in the middle of the street. Confused, the smaller man let go with one arm, flapping his hand as if seeking a support. The taller man broke free, still spinning, then righted himself and sprinted up the street, past Murray. Lamplight from a window caught his golden hair. It was Dr. Lindsay, and the man he had shaken off, temporarily, was Nathan Houston. Nathan had gathered himself together, pushing himself off a wall, and shot up the street after Dr. Lindsay. Murray blinked, and followed.

Dr. Lindsay was built to sprint, light and tall as he was. Nathan Houston was more of a charging bull, shoulders down and snorting in pursuit, built for staying power rather than for speed. If he caught up with Dr. Lindsay at his current rate, though, Murray thought, it would be like being hit by a mail coach in full flight.

Lindsay must have tried an attack on Janet McArthur, he thought, as they reached the top of South Street. Which way would he go – round to North Street, through the cathedral kirkyard or down towards the harbour by the Pends? He could almost feel Lindsay trying to decide as the choice neared him rapidly. He made for the cathedral gate. Nathan followed as he darted into the kirkyard, and Murray, slipping on the cobbles, ran after them. Another night in the cathedral, he thought with revulsion – and he was in his evening clothes again. He would have to speak to his tailor.

They were not going to spend long there, though. Lindsay dodged about the headstones for a little, and around the crumbling walls of the ruined cathedral, but Nathan kept close to him and Lindsay eventually panicked, making for the gate to the cliff path by the side of the precinct. He was tiring, Murray could see – rather to his relief, for he was starting to breathe heavily himself. Nathan swung through the little arched gateway, glared left and right, then set off right towards the harbour. Murray, not far behind, followed.

The sea was in darkness to their left, hissing and surging by turn at the foot of the rocks below. To their right the precinct wall of the cathedral rose, the sandstone dusky in the moonlight. Lindsay was just about visible as a tall shadow ahead of them, and beyond him the pier that marked the harbour's boundary could be seen, pointing out sternly into the silvery sea. They began to slither down the path to the harbour in Lindsay's wake, skirting the dark hillside where the cathedral loomed in the blackness above them.

At the foot of the hill, Lindsay hesitated again. Clearly he had not spent his time as a student lingering at the harbour: Murray could sense that he was unfamiliar with its geography. He made a move towards the pier, realised the folly of being trapped there, and turned right along the harbour's edge. Nathan, however, seemed to know the harbour well, and was experienced enough a brawler to take advantage of Lindsay's moment of doubt. He hurtled forward, head and shoulders hauling him forward, and belted into Lindsay just at the water's edge.

With a cry of shock, Lindsay shot sideways, arms and legs flailing. Before he had even hit the water, Nathan was clutching a bollard, panting, and watching in satisfaction. Murray jogged up beside him.

'Why did you knock him into the water? Now we'll have to fish him out.'

'Let him drown,' growled Nathan with satisfaction.

'No, we can't do that. I want to know if he murdered Rory McArthur.'

'Him?' said Nathan in surprise, but Murray was already pulling off his hat, slippers and coat, trying to keep Lindsay's position in his eye. He had dragged people from the water before. Sometimes he had saved them. Once, tragically, he had not.

The water was icy, and he gasped as his head surfaced then dived into the mucky water of the harbour. In a moment he had found an arm, struggling against his grasp, and he managed to follow it to find Lindsay's head. He looped his arm around Lindsay's neck, and slipped him up out of the water, making sure he could breathe. Lindsay slowly realised what was happening, and calmed down.

'I can't swim,' he cried.

'It's all right: there are steps over there. I'll help you, if you stay still.'

'He'll push me in again!' Lindsay had caught sight of Nathan on the harbour edge, watching them with some interest.

'He'd better not, or he'll have to fish you out himself next time,' said Murray grimly, and back-paddled to the steps by the harbour wall.

Lindsay had recovered enough to pull himself out and up the steps, and Murray followed, shivering. At least his coat would be dry, he thought, then looked down at his evening breeches. They were tastefully adorned with bits of fish head and seaweed. That really was the end of them.

'Right,' he said, seeing that Lindsay was shuddering with the cold, and Nathan was regarding him with deep hostility, 'let's get somewhere warm, and sort this out. And then I very much want a change of clothes.'

They attracted a little attention on their squelching way back down South Street, though perhaps not as much as they had as they had chased after each other on the way up the street. Nathan kept a firm grip on Archibald Lindsay's arm, looking self-righteous. Murray let him know he was under surveillance himself, in case he decided to dispose of Lindsay on the way. Where did Nathan stand in all this: a thief, a conspirator, or a valiant protector of Janet McArthur? Or all three?

Well, for now it was time to focus on Dr. Archibald Lindsay, and find out what he had been up to this evening, when he had claimed to be leaving St. Andrews for Letho.

Chapter Twenty-Two

Murray might have been anxious about leaving Lindsay in the parlour, dripping, with the Shaws, but Nathan Houston was not going to leave him alone to do anything the least dangerous. When Murray came downstairs after a rapid change out of the stinking rags that had once been his best evening clothes, he found Lindsay sitting on a hard chair in the centre of the parlour, wrapped in a very elderly blanket, dripping mournfully on to a sheet of oilcloth, while Nathan stood grim by the door, eyebrows a ferocious hedge, with his arms folded in a manner that said they would easily spring free if occasion required it. There was a strong aroma of fish heads. The Shaws and Walter sat as far away as possible in a line about the edges of the room. Mr. Hepburn, sensing awkwardness, had offered to return to his house and bring dry clothes for Lindsay, thus saving him from having to decide whether to sit with Flavia or with his friend.

When Murray returned, Mrs. Shaw rose to her feet and did her best to bustle about, offering hot drinks, but Professor Shaw put a hand on her arm and suggested gently that she and the children should leave the men to themselves for now. In Shaw's anxious eyes Murray thought he detected a wish to follow his wife far away from the difficult scene in the parlour, but curiosity, as well as duty, kept him there. He poured some hot brandy for Murray, and returned to his perch on the sopha, jiggling his knees nervously.

'Constable Round should be here soon,' Professor Shaw told Murray. 'I sent Pennie for him. I should offer the poor man a room here, for he must spend as much time here as at home just now …' He tailed off, as if he had lost interest in what he was saying. He could not really take his eyes off Archibald Lindsay. Murray smiled at him, sorry that he had brought Lindsay here, but there would not have been room to talk properly at Mrs. Loudoun's house and he had desperately, selfishly wanted clean clothes and a warm fire. He took a welcome draught of the brandy, and sat down opposite Lindsay. The physician tried to straighten his back under the blanket, an odd expression on his face. Murray considered: if he asked Lindsay for his version of events first, Nathan Houston would likely explode and the conversation would go nowhere. He sighed, but relaxed a little when Constable Round slipped into the room, nodding to the company. Murray could begin.

'Houston, will you tell me what happened this evening, before the point where you and this man ended up brawling in South Street?'

Nathan looked surprised at being asked to speak first, but stood upright, enjoying the privilege.

'Aye, I will an' all,' he announced. 'We were sitting down to our supper like any honest folk, that's my sister Maggie, Janet McArthur and the bairn and mysel', when this gentleman –' the designation was not used respectfully 'chapped at the door, and then walked straight in like he owned the place. Which he doesna,' he added, for the sake of clarification. 'It's the college owns that close.'

'All right,' said Murray. 'Go on.'

'He comes in all fancy and says he wants to talk to Janet McArthur, and is that the bairn that was born to her nine months afore? Well, I was away to ask him what business of his it might be, but Janet stood up at the table and just keeled over in a dead faint. She knocked over the bowl of brose an' all. Well, my sister Maggie – that's Mrs. Loudoun, ken – she starts skrauchin' and skirlin', and whiles she's bending over Janet, seein' is she all right and takin' the bairn from her and the bairn's greetin' an' all, and it's a wonder the constable didna appear that minute with the noise goin' on in the place. And Maggie, she cries that that's the very man that Janet says was coming to kill her and the bairn, and that he killed McArthur, too, and that fella –' he jerked his head again at Lindsay, 'he looks like he's been slapped, so I tellt him he'd better go, and I maybe helped him a wee bit on his way, an' all.' He stopped, smacking his hips together with finality.

'When you say you helped him a wee bit,' Murray sought clarification, looking at Lindsay's bruised face and raised eyebrows, 'that would have been with your fists?'

'Aye, maybe so,' agreed Nathan after a moment.

'And then there was the chase up South Street, for which no doubt we have any number of disinterested witnesses.' Murray considered. He exchanged looks with Constable Round. 'Well, Dr. Lindsay, would you like to give your version of events?'

Lindsay rearranged the blanket about his shoulders, playing for time. Murray waited, though he could sense Nathan twitching by the door.

'Yes, I visited their little place this evening, looking for Janet McArthur and her child. I had no intention of doing either of them any harm: I had my own particular reasons for wishing to speak with Janet and see the child, and I saw no reason to share this reason with strangers. Would you want your private business generally known?'

'Of course not,' Murray agreed, 'but I think Nathan Houston and Mrs. Loudoun felt they had a good reason for trying to protect Janet McArthur, and after this evening's events you can be sure you are not going to be allowed to meet her at least unless your reasons are made more widely known. If you have her welfare at heart no doubt you will understand this: so I suggest you tell us why you wanted to speak with Janet McArthur.'

'It's complicated,' said Lindsay at last. He was frowning, his mouth twisted. To Murray, more than anything else he looked embarrassed.

'I'm quite clever,' said Murray mildly. 'There's a chance I'll understand, if you speak clearly enough.'

'Sorry.' Lindsay looked at Murray. 'I meant no offence.' He pressed down with both hands on his crossed legs, stretching his shoulders up and back, then relaxed. 'Look, I think I've mentioned my brother to you – he's laird of Invertally.'

'He has come up in conversation, yes,' agreed Murray.

'My brother,' said Lindsay hesitantly, 'is ... a gomerel scatterwit.'

Nathan gave a little snort, as if he had all lairds in the same box. Murray stopped him with a glance.

'And as far as I can tell,' Lindsay went on, a pinch of bitterness in his voice, 'Janet McArthur is not much better.'

'Hi!' That did not please Nathan so much. Again, Murray

glared at him, but Lindsay gave him a look over his shoulder.

'Don't tell me you're another victim of her limited charms. If you listen to my brother, Janet McArthur is Aphrodite and the Queen of Sheba in the one parcel.' He stopped, reflecting, perhaps, on conversations with his brother where they had not seen eye to eye on the subject. Murray could not resist a little prompt.

'So the child is his?'

'Aye, the child is his, so far as he knows. Certainly that's what Janet told him, and even my brother can count, on his day. And he wants to marry her and make all right.'

'Does he, indeed?' Murray was not convinced. How could an offer of marriage be mistaken for a threat of murder? It was generally only further down the line that marriage and murder became confused.

'He does: he made her an offer, he told me, and Janet said she'd think about it – she's a bit of a flirt, from what I hear around the village – and then her brother appeared home and the next thing anyone knew, they had flitted.'

'So you traced them here?'

'Eventually,' said Lindsay with a grunt. 'Janet had lived with her grandmother, who had never quite grasped where Roderick had gone to college, and Janet's daft. I tried Glasgow first, and then Aberdeen. If I'd thought to come back to my own college first, I'd have saved a few months.'

'Why didn't your brother come himself?' Nathan growled unexpectedly. Lindsay jumped.

'He broke his leg falling off a horse,' he said, twisting in his chair. 'I was summoned home to tend to him, for he took a bad fever and for a while his life was feared for – and all the while he was calling for Janet, and I had no idea who he meant. But then he recovered, and I began to look for her – told him, as his doctor, to stay put and make sure his leg healed or he would be no use to her when I found her.' Despite his gruff tone, Murray thought he could detect a hint of fondness – exasperated fondness, but fondness nevertheless – for his hapless brother.

'So why does Janet think you're here to kill her and steal the child?' Nathan demanded.

'I have no idea,' sighed Lindsay. 'The last thing my brother wants is to harm her or their child.'

'But you?' asked Murray. 'How do you feel about the possibility of his marrying her?'

Lindsay met his eye.

'If you think I'm after my brother's fortune, you can think again. It may not be so gentlemanly, but I make more as a physician than he is ever going to make from Invertally. If he wants to roam the hills and marry a village girl and bring up a quiverful of children, it's up to him. I'll go back to Edinburgh, prosperity and civilisation, thank you very much. I love my brother.' He sighed, as if it were a painful thing to admit. 'But we are cut from different cloth, the two of us.'

'And what if Janet doesna want to go back? What if she has a suitor here?'

Or two, thought Murray, but he chose not to say. He did wonder, though: Nathan's black eye the day after Rory's death. Had he met Jack out with Janet, and come to blows over her?

Lindsay sighed again.

'That's up to her, though I think my brother would like to talk about the child, at least. It's a girl, is it?'

Nathan and Murray looked at each other.

'I think we're still not quite sure we can trust you,' Murray admitted.

Lindsay began ferreting somewhere beneath the stinking blanket, then remembered.

'Give me my coat, will you?'

It was drying nearer the fire. Murray reached over and handed it to Lindsay. Lindsay felt in the pockets.

'Here,' he said 'here's something to the purpose, anyway.'

It was a damp sheet of paper, wrapped, Murray saw, in the letter he had inadvertently picked up in the hothouse the day Carlisle had been found unconscious.

'Extract of a minute of the Kirk Session of Invertally, 10th. October 1817. Sederunt –' a list of the elders followed, along with the minister. 'Janet McArthur having been summoned on a charge of fornication failed to compear. Mr. Lindsay the laird nevertheless asked to address the meeting, which being granted he stated that the child Janet McArthur was carrying was his own, and that he intended if he could find her to marry her. He paid the fine for antenuptial fornication and was absolved from further corruption.

Signed a true copy of the minute, Al. McDonald, A.M., Minister of Invertally.'

'You'd better let this dry out properly,' Murray remarked, laying it on the table. 'It's true that Janet might have received other offers here in St. Andrews, now that she is thought to be a widow, but that's between her and your brother. What was your business with Roderick McArthur?'

'With Roderick? None whatsoever.'

'And the night he died – where were you?'

'I said before. Regrettably drunk with my friend Hepburn, reminiscing about college days.'

'And the day I saw your black horse here, and you said you were in Letho?'

Dr. Lindsay scowled.

'I didn't want the laird – you – to think I was shirking my duties as the village doctor. But yes, I was in St. Andrews, trying to track down Janet McArthur – and not doing particularly well at it. I thought I could follow Janet home from the funeral, but something odd happened at the funeral and there was a great deal of toing and froing around this house, and I lost her in the confusion.'

'Looking for Jack Swanson, I suppose,' put in Professor Shaw. Murray had almost forgotten he was there, but turned to him now.

'Well, Professor, do you believe Dr. Lindsay, sir?'

Professor Shaw's face wrinkled, a little anxious frog.

'Well, yes, I believe I do.'

Lindsay gave a wry smile.

'Your pardon, sir, but you are well known for believing the best of everybody! That does not prove my worth, though I am pleased to have your credit.'

Murray smiled too.

'It's a very good start. Anyway, I think I hear Mr. Hepburn returning with your clothes: go and change, and then we shall see what Janet herself thinks.'

Janet cried a good deal during Lindsay's plea before her: her soft heart was touched by the laird's predicament, and she seemed genuinely distressed when Lindsay described his injury and illness.

Nathan glowered throughout but managed to keep his mouth mostly shut, and Mrs. Loudoun watched the whole conversation attentively, cradling the sleeping Rosina on her lap. Lindsay had asked to see her, but sensibly had not wanted to waken her and said he would call again, if permitted, to make his niece's better acquaintance. Once he was sure that everything was at least peaceable, Murray retreated to leave them to their talk. He was thinking of Jack. How would he feel about a rival suitor with an estate, however poor, in Perthshire?

Jack was in his mind, along with Thomas Swanson, all the way back down the common close. Even if he had not been, the sight of the lit window in the Swansons' house and the sweet sound of the violin from within would have attracted his attention. He was sorry to disturb the music, but he knocked on the door nevertheless. The violin was silenced immediately, and in a moment the door was opened. It was indeed Jack.

'Oh!' he said in surprise. 'Come in! Mr. Bogue explained about you rescuing me from St. Rule's Tower: I was too stupid to realise earlier. I find I have much to thank you for, sir.'

'Not at all,' said Murray. 'We were stuck, too. I hope you are feeling better?'

Jack led the way into the parlour, which they had to themselves. A very fine violin lay gently cushioned on the table, its bow by its side. Jack automatically reached out a hand to it, then stayed himself.

'Much better, thank you. Though I should have been happy enough to stay at the Bogues', for Mrs. Bogue's broth was very fine and she and Miss Bogue were giving me every attention, but Father came and brought me home. Which I suppose was sensible. Can I offer you some punch? Our maid is away home, but there is brandy and water here.'

'Thank you, that would be most welcome.' He sat on the uncomfortable sopha, wanting to stretch his legs out to the fire and fall asleep. Jack busied himself with the glasses, and handed one to Murray. 'Your father and Mr. Bogue are not quite friends, is that right?'

'Aye, true enough,' said Jack ruefully. 'I sort of feel responsible, in a way.'

'Why's that? You and Sandy Bogue are friendly enough, are you not?'

'Oh, aye, Sandy's fine. Well ... Aye, he's fine.' He decided against whatever second thought he had had. 'He's in the same boat with me: his father would like him in the business with him, and Sandy has no notion of it. But that's not it: it's his sister that's the problem.'

'Miss Bogue?'

'My father thought it would be a grand idea if Miss Bogue and I wed, bringing together two good merchant houses in the town. Well, of course as I say I didn't want to be a silversmith: I'm sorry, but honestly, I haven't any artistry in me, and half the stuff in that workshop is poisonous. I don't want to be bald before I'm thirty! But I was keen at the time – she's a bonny lass, and we get on well. This was before – well, Miss Bogue was out of the picture before I found myself another distraction.'

'Janet McArthur?'

'Aye, maybe.' A grin flashed over Jack's face. 'But Mr. Bogue stymied the whole thing: he said he was looking for a gentleman for Sarah, and nothing less would do. Now, it's not that Father has a'thing against gentlefolk, particularly as his customers, but to marry one! He thought that Mr. Bogue was getting above himself, and said so, and they quarrelled. And it's a shame, for it's true that Sarah is a very pretty girl, and if pressed ... Well, I could do a lot worse. An awful lot worse.' There was a thoughtful look on his face, and Murray wondered if his rescue had painted Sarah Bogue in a new light for him.

'You're turning away from Janet, then?'

'Oh, Janet's a fine lassie, too. I just ... Well, I don't feel I'm ready to decide just yet, eh?'

Part of the decision might be taken from his hands, Murray thought.

'By the way,' he said casually, 'the night you were out walking with Janet: you didn't by any chance come to blows with Nathan Houston, did you?'

'With Nathan Houston? No. Why?' He looked thoroughly bewildered.

'Nathan had a black eye the next day, and I haven't been able to find out who might have done it. Not that I've asked him yet directly!' Murray drew to a halt at the look on Jack's face. He had clearly just thought of something, but the something was evidently not entirely good. 'What is it?'

Jack said nothing, his brow screwed up with the effort of thought. Murray gave him a moment, but nothing emerged from the mental struggle. He decided to try the other question he wanted to ask.

'You say you were out for part of the evening on the night that Rory died.'

'With Janet, yes,' said Jack eagerly, happy to change the subject. 'Father was in the workshop, and I slipped out to meet her, as soon as it was any way dark. To keep her safe, you ken?'

And yourself from prying eyes, thought Murray, but said nothing.

'And when you came home, where was your father?'

'Well …'

'We know he went out,' said Murray, briskly, as if he expected Jack to agree with everything he said. 'We know he was seen by the night watchman about midnight, coming back in this direction. We don't know, though, where he was.'

Jack was puzzled.

'But he was at Cosmo Gordon's. Isn't that what he told you?'

'No, he wasn't. Cosmo says that your father asked him to say that he was there and they were drinking together from just after the recital ended, but Cosmo has no idea where he was.'

'Oh,' said Jack, and slow though he might be his leaping thoughts were clear in his eyes. Yet he was still confused.

'Are you saying you think my father killed Rory?' he asked unsteadily.

'I'm not sure. I'm just trying to find out the truth, if anyone would tell it to me.'

'But why? Why would he kill Rory? That makes no sense.'

'I don't know. I'm not sure anyone had a good reason to murder Rory McArthur.'

'I ken one place my father was,' said Jack suddenly, then looked as if he would take the words back at once.

'Where was that?'

Jack pursed his lips, staring at him, then gave up.

'He was at Nathan Houston's place, across from the

McArthurs'. I dinna ken what he was there for, but he was arguing with Nathan Houston, so it's a wonder he wasna murdered himself.'

'What time was that?' asked Murray, tensing at a new piece of the puzzle.

'What time did the night watchman see me?' Jack countered.

'Eleven or so.'

'Then a few minutes before that. I heard the voices, and jooked out the window, for I'd just walked Janet home. I couldn't believe it when I saw my father heading in to Nathan Houston's place, and I thought I'd better slip home fast before he saw me. I bade good night to Janet and nipped away. Well, maybe it took a wee bittie longer than that …'

'As much as half an hour? An hour?'

'No! Certainly not an hour! Maybe half an hour …' He had the grace to look a little embarrassed.

'Did you see Nathan Houston clearly?' Murray asked. Jack's face once again twisted in concentration.

'Aye,' he said eventually, 'aye, I did. He brought a candle to the door when he opened it. It was surely him.'

'Did he have a black eye?'

A look of startled joy passed across Jack's face.

'Aye, he did an' all! It was all closed over and sore looking! Well, my father couldna have done that. He'd only just arrived, surely.'

'It seems unlikely, indeed. Does your father have business dealings with Nathan Houston?'

'I told you no before, I think. He ships things and carries things – he's not a carrier, more a trader.'

'Ships them to the harbour here?'

'Sometimes, I think. Or if it's small he'll bring it by road.'

'He seems to have been at home a lot recently. Business must be bad.'

'Or good.'

'True: he could be resting on his laurels.' Murray thought for a moment, then said, 'What about you? Your clerking: is it doing well enough for you to consider marriage, just yet?'

'Well, it's fair,' said Jack, taking the new subject in his stride. So many young men were regularly asked about their prospects.

'Now that there's no one else for the burgesses' work I should be doing well ... oh. Poor Rory,' he said sadly. 'He would have liked that post fine. And truth to tell, he'd have been better at it that me. Maybe I'll just have to take myself in hand, and make a good job of it, for him.' With moist eyes, he straightened, an unaccustomedly determined look on his face.

'Well, I should be getting on, and not keeping you back from your practice,' said Murray, rising from the horrible sopha. 'Tell me: have you been into your father's workshop lately?'

'Me?' Jack came back from his dreamy ambitions. 'No! Not in a long while. I canna stand the smell of the place. But I'm sorry,' he added again. 'I do feel sorry for my father. He needs to find an apprentice, who'll really love it the way he does. I just wish it was me.'

'We can't all please our fathers, however hard we try,' Murray assured him – after all, he had never managed to please his own. 'I'm sure he's proud of you anyway.'

'Ha! I don't think so.'

'Is he in his workshop just now?'

'Aye, I think so: do you want me to take you there?'

'Oh, no, it's fine: I'll go through if you don't mind. I remember my way, and you can go on with that lovely music.'

'Oh! Thank you,' said Jack, and even as Murray was leaving the parlour his hand was already reaching out for his violin again.

Murray walked softly through the rear apartments of the Swansons' house and let himself out as quietly as possible into the yard where the workshop was. But instead of heading for the workshop door, he skirted the low building and slipped down the path by its side that led to the Swansons' garden, which he had overlooked earlier that evening. He hoped that no one would have had the opportunity to meddle with anything there since he had left.

He marked, in the darkness, the moonlit tree which he had climbed on the Shaw side of the high garden wall and the end of the cross path which Nathan Houston had taken in his search for – for something, and his discovery of Walter's aunt's kist. Murray crouched down in the shadow of the wall, and began a cautious examination of the low growth there, just as Nathan must have done. The border had the usual late winter consistency: rotted leaves, sharp shoots, bare, whippy branches, all of which had to be felt around delicately for whatever it might have been that Nathan had been searching for. And though it seemed to take an age, it was probably only a few minutes before his gloved hands brushed something not plant-like, something solid, with sharp corners. He felt along it: it was no more than nine or ten inches long, and less in height and width. He shifted it in his hands: heavy, anyway. He removed one glove and felt it. It felt like wood, a small wooden kist, not far off the size of the basket kist in which Walter's flannels had been packed. He took a look about the garden – still deserted, and he could hear no sign of movement. He lifted the wooden kist clear of the plants, and found a patch of moonlight. He set the box at the edge of it, and with bare hands quickly undid the binding straps. He lifted the lid.

The box was jammed full of silver shillings.

Chapter Twenty-Three

'Well, they're obviously fake,' said Constable Round with a sigh. 'And they look just like the ones I've had complaints about: I'm collecting a wee treasury to myself back at the town house. Excepting only the date's right on these ones: they must have realised their mistake, but the weight's wrong. Too much lead, I reckon. And these were in Mr. Swanson's back green?'

'Under the wall, where Nathan Houston was looking earlier.'

The constable tapped his teeth thoughtfully. His mind was clearly busy, but he was hesitant to speak his next thoughts.

'Do you think,' he said at last, tentative, 'that Mr. Swanson, being a silversmith an' all, might ken a'thing about these false coins?'

'Oh, no! Surely not!' Professor Shaw, dutifully attending yet another interview that was likely to cause him distress, was shocked. 'I'm sure Thomas Swanson is an honest man. Why, he's been our neighbour now for more than twenty years!'

'And if your own goodness were contagious, Professor, then no doubt he would be innocent,' said Murray, only half joking. 'But I think we need to find out. Do you think there would be evidence in his workshop, Constable?'

'You would think that would be where it would be, would you no?' agreed the constable, happier now that the idea was in the open. 'And from what you've described, it sounds as if Nathan Houston was to take the coins away earlier.'

'To distribute them, do you think?'

'Aye, why no?'

'It's just,' said Murray, considering, 'if I were issuing false coin, I think I'd want it distributed a little further away than my own fairly small town, wouldn't you? In Edinburgh, or somewhere.'

Professor Shaw nodded.

'It would be much safer, no doubt about it.'

'And Nathan Houston travels up and down to Edinburgh, by boat and road,' Constable Round said. 'Maybe Mr. Swanson did a bit of experimenting, and wanted Nathan to take the next lot down to Edinburgh as you say.'

'Wait,' said Murray suddenly, 'wasn't Houston attacked and robbed by Crossgates recently? That's why he bought the pistols.'

'I believe so,' said Round, frowning.

'The merchants who were weighing a stack of fake shillings at the steelyard – they said that the bulk of them had been found by a pedlar at Crossgates. What if Nathan was to take them to Edinburgh for distribution, but instead he was robbed and the coins were accidentally distributed much nearer home? On a road in the direction of Perthshire, as it happens?'

There was a thoughtful silence.

'Aye,' said Constable Round, 'nae doubt that would fit, indeed. But I'm worried about that box being here and not still in yon back green. Nae doubt if Mr. Swanson should happen to come out now and find them gone, he'll think only that Nathan Houston was able to come back for them, and has taken them away. But if Nathan Houston comes back and canna find them ...'

'I think he has his mind on other things tonight,' said Murray, remembering Houston's eager vigil with Janet McArthur. Which man will she choose, Murray wondered at the back of his thoughts – any of the three?

'So if – if, mind,' Constable Round added with care to Professor Shaw, '*if* Mr. Swanson is issuing false coin, could poor Rory maybe have found out?'

'Well, there was some evidence that he was in Swanson's workshop that night.' Murray remembered Pennie's complaints of a disturbed night. 'Or someone was, making a racket at half past ten. Surely Rory wouldn't have broken in: it would have been too difficult. If Rory were looking for some protection from his pursuer then he would have gone to the house – unless there were lights on and he knew someone was in the workshop.'

'And if he was in the workshop,' said Constable Round, 'and he saw Mr. Swanson coining, or saw the dies, maybe – Swanson might have attacked him.'

'Swanson would need to have been desperate to get over the wall into this garden,' Professor Shaw said sensibly. 'I cannot picture him climbing even quite a stout tree, can you?'

'And Swanson was apparently quarrelling with Nathan Houston at half past ten. And what about his pursuer, anyway?' added Murray. 'Isn't it too much of a coincidence to have someone chase Rory into the Swansons' garden and Rory to seek safety in the workshop, only to have Swanson then take over the chase and murder him? What did the pursuer do, shrug and go home?'

'Och, this is nae good,' said Constable Round with weary frustration, but Professor Shaw unexpectedly interrupted.

'Rory must have touched something in the workshop,' he said, his eyes wide.

'What kind of something?' asked Murray.

'I don't know: arsenic, maybe? There are all kinds of poisons in there, Jack is always complaining about them. But arsenic would fit. And then he came out and fell with his hand in my pond. And that's why all my fish were dead – the ones that graze the bottom.'

'Because arsenic is heavy, of course,' Murray added slowly. 'Well, that's another mystery solved – and Rory was definitely in the workshop.'

Constable Round wanted to gather together a few of his men to help with any search of the Swanson property, including its back green. Professor Shaw, relieved to have solved the issue of the dead fish, went off to find Walter and discuss how to clean out the pond for future use. Supper was not long off, but Murray felt the urge to get out and walk, and think, for matters seemed to be moving quickly but there were still many questions to answer. He gathered hat, gloves and stick from the hall stand, and slipped out of the front door. Then, pausing for a contemplative moment at the corner, he elected to continue down the common close, and in a moment emerged on the path that ran by the mill lade. A dark figure almost ran straight into him.

'Mr. Murray!' As if their discussion had conjured him out of the night, it was Thomas Swanson. Murray blinked in surprise, and managed to greet him in some kind of normal way. The moon was still high enough for it to be reasonable to stop for a moment and chat, and Swanson seemed easy enough, standing with his hands behind his back, broad chest spread with his usual confidence. Murray was less relaxed: could he find anything out from Swanson, or if he tried would he simply put him on his guard, so that he would hide any evidence before the constable returned with his men?

'I was glad to see Jack so much recovered earlier,' he tried. 'He seems to have suffered no ill effects from his nights on the top of the tower.'

'He was very fortunate you happened to look for him there when you did, though I understand you were then trapped yourself, sir? I hope you are also recovered?'

'I am very well, thank you.'

'I owe you more than I can say,' said Swanson, suddenly. 'It is only the two of us, as you know. If I had lost him ...'

'I'm sure. He is a fine young man,' Murray assured him.

'He is, isn't he? Though a father must always agree with such sentiments!' He smiled, and it was easy to see how sincere he was. Jack might feel he was a disappointment to his father, but his father evidently did not view the matter in the same way. His hands emerged from behind his back, were allowed for a moment to be expressive, then suppressed again, as if his moment of emotion had embarrassed him.

'Are you out for a constitutional?' Murray asked. 'The moon is very bright tonight.'

'Oh! Yes: I like a little walk before supper. And then I check all is secure, and set my mind at rest for the night.'

'Of course. You retire early, then?'

'Quite early: ten or half past, as a rule.'

'Well, I shall not detain you further: you'll want to be getting back to your fireside and your supper table. Good night, Mr. Swanson.'

'Good night, Mr. Murray! And thank you again!'

They bowed, and Murray turned towards the harbour end of the path, to the east. He heard Swanson's footsteps retreat behind him, and the garden gate open and shut, and the lock turn. So he did lock the gate at night: Rory probably knew that, and even as he was pursued knew he would have to climb the wall if he were to seek sanctuary with the Swansons.

But did he find sanctuary there? Could he have attacked Jack, and Thomas Swanson had tried to defend his son? His devotion to him was clear. None of this was making sense, and Murray's thoughts were in a complete tangle.

And what kind of constitutional did Thomas Swanson take, that brought him out by moonlight without his dog Victor, with no gloves on, and with earth all over his expressive hands?

Murray walked on, careful with his stick, not wishing to turn an ankle on the well-worn path along the mill lade. Around the end of Westburn Wynd there were some fine houses, homes for gentlemen, and he passed on between them, crossing the stream and turning to walk up the lade braes to the foot of Eastburn Wynd. There the houses were once again serried, built in terraces of bulging lumps of comfortable sandstone, most of the windows still lit at this time of night. He turned to the left, climbing gently back to South Street and emerging opposite the Black Bull Inn where a quiet rumble of talk and laughter still reminded him of student days and forbidden drinking with friends long gone. He stopped for a moment, staring over at it, for not all the memories were happy ones. Then he shook himself, and turned right, towards the Bogues' house, the Pends and the Cathedral.

There were lights at the Bogues' house, too, and he glanced up at the lit windows, but he passed on. He wondered if Mr. Bogue was home yet from his business in Market Street, and if Cosmo Gordon was still at home alone by his fire. He stopped at the wall of the cathedral kirkyard and stared out at the ruins, leaning against the gritty stonework and absently fiddling with the knop of his cane. He needed to straighten out his thoughts. He turned, and entered the kirkyard once again by the gate.

Inside, the moon still laid a path for him between charcoal headstones and silver grey rubble walls. He walked slowly, considering. It seemed to him almost certain now that Thomas Swanson was minting the fake silver shillings – who better than a silversmith? – and would suffer the consequences, and Murray would not be able to protect Professor Shaw against any upset that would cause him. Thomas Swanson would be hanged.

It made perfect sense that he might therefore be prepared to kill anyone who might have discovered his secret and threaten to betray it. Rory McArthur had been in Swanson's workshop that night, and had then been killed. But still – why had Rory fled into the Swansons' garden, and how had Thomas Swanson scaled the wall to pursue him? Something was not sitting easily there, and Murray badly wanted to know why.

Tense and irritable still, he paced silently through a deep, shadowy arch and entered what must have been the body of the ancient kirk. Ahead was the great double-spired screen that could be seen from miles off, skeletal and clear, a remarkable survivor. To the right, there was his old friend, St. Rule's Tower, the details of its block-like form lost in the odd light. And at the top, where his gaze was inevitably drawn, he thought he saw a movement.

An owl, probably, he said to himself: a barn owl, perhaps, catching the moonlight on its plumage, ready to swoop low over some hapless mouse or shrew. But even in the uncanny moonlight he could see that the shape was not quite right – and it was substantially bigger than most barn owls.

Only this morning he had had to be rescued from this building, and here he was, heading back for the doorway, albeit warily. He could see no movement amongst the monuments around him, though he could feel his eyes and ears wide and alert as if he might be the prey of that mighty owl himself. There were not many who would choose to be on top of St. Rule's Tower at this time of night, and he thought he might know which of them this was. The door was unlocked, and he could see the rectangle of light far above that showed that the trapdoor, too, was open: whoever was here just now was here of their own freewill. He began, softly, to climb the stairs.

If the person at the top, whoever it was, was disposed to be unfriendly, the most dangerous moment would be when he poked his head out at the top of the stairs, through the open trapdoor. He slowed as he reached the last few steps, trying to get a good idea of where precisely the figure was. A slight turn to his left, and at once he saw that the man was standing with his back to the trapdoor, apparently unaware of his presence. In fact, when he finally stepped out on to the roof and cleared his throat, the man leapt like a startled deer.

'Who's that?' cried Sandy Bogue in alarm.

'It's me, Charles Murray. Were you expecting anyone else?'

'No, I wasn't expecting anyone to be daft enough to be up here at this time of night,' said Sandy frankly. 'Except me.' He pushed his fair hair back out of his eyes and regarded Murray quizzically. 'So what are you doing up here, sir?'

'It's a fine night. I was taking a stroll through the cathedral, and thought I saw someone up here, so I came to see who it might be. Last night, after all, I spent the night up here as a reluctant guest of an unknown host: I have some interest today in the identity of those who like spending time here.'

'I feel bad about that,' said Sandy, with a little self-deprecating snort. 'If I had not introduced Jack and Rory to this place Jack might never have tried to hide here.'

'But it seems that someone else encouraged him: it was not all your doing. And I don't think he has taken any permanent harm from it. Though he might well have done: it seemed last night that he was in some considerable danger.'

'Poor Jack,' murmured Sandy.

'If you felt so sorry for him, why didn't you help him when he asked you?'

'Asked me?' Sandy glanced round, puzzled.

'He said that someone at Rory's funeral offered to help him to escape, sure that he was going to be arrested for Rory's murder.'

'Is that why he disappeared just then? Goodness,' said Sandy. 'I wondered if it might be something like that. Is that why you said just now that someone else encouraged him? But I had nothing to do with it, I swear. If I had, I'd have picked somewhere better to hide him – or at least given him a few blankets. I'd have ... I could have hidden him in some of my father's storerooms: they're warm enough, and a lot handier to take food to, and there would have been much less chance of someone locking him in by mistake, or finding him by chance.' He considered the possibilities, clearly annoyed that his abilities to hide his friend had not been used to their best advantage. 'Was it this other person who told him St. Rule's Tower was a good idea? I assumed it was Jack's own idea: he's sometimes not that bright, you know.'

'He's not saying much about it. He's sure the person tried to help him get away, so he's reluctant just now to name them.'

'As I say, sometimes not that bright.' He gave a mirthless, breathy laugh. 'But you and my sister saved him, eh?'

'As best we could, yes,' said Murray flatly. Then he sighed. 'Look,' he said, 'I have no intentions with regards to your sister. She seems a charming girl, but I don't believe either of us thinks we would be suited.' He had the growing impression that whatever their fathers said, Sarah Bogue was still interested in Jack, anyway, and last night could no doubt be reviewed as a romantic episode, with the right attitude.

'Father will be disappointed,' said Sandy at once, but his face was devoid of expression. He gazed out over the black and white kirkyard. 'He'd like to catch a gentleman for Sarah.'

'He appreciates rank, doesn't he?'

'He works hard for advancement,' said Sandy, and Murray was sure there was bitterness in his voice.

'He helped you gain a good education, anyway: that's usually the first step for a man's advancement.'

'Yes, if he would let me advance.'

'I thought you weren't sure what you wanted to do?' If Sandy was disposed to talk, Murray was happy to listen. He propped himself against the parapet he had grown to know so well last night, and stared out at the town, too. It would be no good looking at Sandy's face just now: it might discourage him.

'It's hard to make a decision when he's always drawing me back into the cloth business,' Sandy muttered.

'I've never seen you around the warehouse. Do you do much there?'

'I'm helping with the clerking at the moment, until the lad has a bit more practice. Father will never pay for a proper apprenticeship – he made sure he had Rory and Jack cheap, anyway. Rory had no parents around to sign the papers, and Jack's father wanted Jack to marry Sarah so he would take any deal. And I deliver pretty packages to nice ladies and smile and bow to them.' He paused. 'And I'm expected to go along and look – I don't know, as big and scary as I can? – when he needs to have urgent conversations with business contacts that he doesn't think are going to go well.'

There was an odd little silence. Murray realised that Sandy felt he had told Murray something important. His mind scrabbled for the answer. Meetings with business contacts ... who or when ...?

'Is that what you were doing the night Rory died?' he asked, praying that he had hit the right conclusion.

'Aye, that's right.' Sandy stopped, and Murray hoped he was not now having second thoughts about talking to him. He held his breath, and after a few seconds Sandy went on. 'He had ordered a shipment from – from abroad, and the fellow who had arranged the shipment was looking for more money than they had agreed.'

'Something from abroad? French silks and lace, by any chance?'

'That'd be the stuff.' Sandy nodded, pleased to be understood.

'The duty unpaid, perhaps?'

Sandy flicked a glance at him, over his shoulder.

'Aye. Straight into the harbour here, after dark.'

'So you were down at the harbour ...'

'No! No, it was already safe in the town, but the fellow wouldn't release it until the price had been, well, renegotiated. So we were by the mill lade, to meet him there.'

'By the mill lade ... behind the Swansons' house?'

'Aye, thereabouts. Well away from the warehouse, or our house, or the fellow's house, either. We went there after the recital, and waited for our fellow. And we left after our conversation with him – it would have been about eleven o'clock or more.'

Murray felt a tingle of excitement.

'You were down at the back of the Swansons' garden all that time? You would have seen anyone else around then?'

'We would, aye. We were in the trees just upstream, but I was watching carefully, waiting for the fellow.'

Murray took in the information, then drew breath.

'The fellow was Nathan Houston, I suppose.'

Sandy gave a little twitch of surprise.

'Aye, that's right. How did you – '

'Was there a fight between you?'

'No, no there was not: the conversation was – well, heated, but there were no blows exchanged. I was very keen to keep it that way, for I'm not the fighter my father thinks I am!'

'But his black eye ...'

'Oh, he had that when he arrived,' said Sandy. 'And a bloody nose. He was late, because he'd had a fight before he came to meet us.'

'An active man,' said Murray wryly. 'Any idea who it was he

was fighting?'

'Well, I do – that's the thing. He told us, because he was still furious. He said he was attacked by Rory.'

'By Rory?' Murray repeated, after what seemed like an age.

'Aye, that's right. He said he was at home, getting ready to come and meet us, when Rory burst in and demanded to know where Janet was, then laid into Nathan with his fists. To be honest, knowing Nathan, there was more to it than that, but he wouldn't admit to it. He said Rory had punched him a few times, then stormed out. Then someone else had arrived to talk to him, he said, delaying him, then he had come to meet us. He was very angry.'

Murray considered. Presumably Rory had gone home before looking for Jack, and had found his wife – his sister – not at home, and thought Nathan had something to do with it. Certainly it was difficult to keep up the pretence of a quiet married life, the pretence that would protect her, as far as they knew, from the threat from Invertally and the Lindsays, if Janet went out flirting with every man in the neighbourhood. Murray could feel Rory's frustration: it might be enough to drive a bad-tempered man to violence at last, or between him and Nathan violence had arisen. Then he slapped his forehead – of course Rory had gone home. He could picture him, leaving the Bogues' house, violin case in his hand. And where had Murray then seen the violin case? In Rory's own little house in the close. He cursed himself for an idiot. Sandy regarded him with baffled amusement, and Murray forced himself to shrug.

'Something I've just remembered. So you saw Rory by the mill lade before Nathan arrived?' he asked, pulling the conversation back. Rory must have been on his way again to look for Jack – or had Nathan pursued him?

'Saw Rory? No: just Nathan.'

'You didn't see Rory running by the mill lade? Near the Swansons' garden wall?'

'I didn't see him at all.'

'You're sure?'

'I was watching for Nathan. And then when he arrived, I was watching for anyone who might be listening to us. There was no one there at all, only the three of us.'

'But …' If Sandy had not seen Rory, then – then how could he possibly have entered the Swansons' garden over the wall after he left the recital and before the racket from Thomas Swanson's workshop that Pennie heard at half past ten? Murray shook his head hard. Nothing was making sense. If Rory did not climb the back garden wall … Something began to fit together in the back of his mind.

'Nathan was so angry we had to leave the negotiations for that night,' Sandy was going on, happy to natter. 'We had to arrange another meeting. We saw him here in the kirkyard the night of poor Rory's funeral and settled then – so you see, I wouldn't have sent Jack here to hide if I was going to be dealing with Nathan Houston in the same place.'

Murray nodded slowly. Jack had seen Nathan, but Nathan had not been there, presumably, to attack Jack out of jealousy over Janet McArthur.

'I think,' he said, 'I'd better go and see if Nathan Houston is still up and about.'

Sandy looked round in alarm.

'You're not going to have him arrested for smuggling, are you? My father … my father would be furious!'

'I'll think about that,' said Murray. 'It's not my first priority at the moment.' He made for the trapdoor, going carefully now it was darker. The moon was already slipping down in the sky, ebony shadows stretching. He was halfway through, feeling his way with his feet, when he looked back.

'You're absolutely sure you didn't see Rory that night?'

'Absolutely sure, sir. If we thought at all, we'd have expected him to go to the Swansons' front door, not down there to the back of the garden.'

'Then did you look at the house at all? You said you had gone there to see that Jack was safe.'

'It never even occurred to us. It was only when you found out that we went out after the recital, that was when Father said we needed a story to explain where we were or we would be under suspicion. I thought we would be better just to deny it, but somehow you found out we'd gone out and you're working with the constable … Please don't tell him about the French cloth and Nathan Houston!'

'It'll have to stop, anyway. I don't think Nathan will be travelling much for a while, when all this is sorted out,' said Murray, his mind bounding on ahead. He readjusted his hold on the trap door opening, his stick under his arm. 'I shall see you again soon, no doubt. Good night, Mr. Bogue.'

He hurried down the rest of the steps by touch, and quickly made his way out of the tower and back through the darkening graveyard. Things were just about beginning to make sense, but he had to talk to Nathan Houston as soon as possible, and make sure he was on the right track.

Chapter Twenty-Four

He was beginning to feel as if he had spent days striding up and down South Street, the sandstone buildings weaving back and forth on either side as the street narrowed and broadened, the dry cobbles gritty under his boots. Back past the Black Bull, quieter now; back past the shuttered windows of the stern university library and the dark gateway of St. Mary's College, back past the huddled bulk of the town kirk: things were beginning to make some kind of sense, but he knew he was still missing some of the most important facts. He ducked into the narrow entrance of the close where Janet McArthur was, he hoped, now safe, and rapped on the door. He pulled off his hat, and rubbed a gloved hand through his damp hair. Anyone offering him a cup of hot tea at this moment would have been absolved of any crime, he thought ruefully.

Mrs. Loudoun inched the door open, and peeked out, one intelligent eye assessing him round the frame. When she saw who it was, she pulled the door wider and let him in without question. There was a wry look to her weathered face.

'We're getting affa used to gentleman callers round here. She's fine,' she said, nodding to Janet nursing Rosina on the bed, a little awkward with a bandaged arm. Janet looked up with a brilliant smile.

'I'm going to marry Mr. Lindsay!' she said with simple satisfaction.

'Then I hope you'll be very happy,' said Murray sincerely. At least she would be out of sight of Jack and Nathan: they had that mercy. He prayed Jack at least would soon forget her and find that Miss Bogue was everything he desired: both of them would need something to sustain them in the days to come, no doubt. As for

Nathan, he had probably suffered enough, too. And no doubt in the days to come he would not have his troubles to seek.

'Would you take a cup of tea?' asked Mrs. Loudoun, making her his friend for life. She poured it quickly, well stewed but hot, and Murray could not resist taking the cup and an odd saucer. He knew he could not linger long. He sipped thankfully at the scalding liquid: he had been more chilled by his time on St. Rule's Tower again than he had realised. The monument had lost a good deal of its appeal. The room was smoky warm with the little fire and a couple of crusie lamps.

'Is Nathan walking Dr. Lindsay back to where he's staying, then?' he asked, wondering how long he would be able to wait for him.

'No! Dr. Lindsay's away this long time. Nathan's away out on some business – said he had to collect something. He'd tried earlier, he said, but he hadn't been able to, for some reason.'

The box of false coins. Murray turned to look at the shelf by the door. Nathan's guns were gone.

'Did he go armed?'

'Aye, right enough. He doesna like the things, but he said it was something valuable, and at this time of night, even in the town, you canna be too careful, eh?'

'How long is he gone, Mrs. Loudoun?'

'Ten minutes, maybe?' Surprised at his urgency, she looked across at Janet, who shrugged, still beaming. 'Aye, ten minutes or so.'

Murray gulped his tea with regret, and stood.

'I must catch him, if I can,' he explained ambiguously. 'Thank you so much for the tea, Mrs. Loudoun. Mrs. – Miss McArthur, I hope you sleep more securely tonight. Good night to you both – forgive me.'

In a moment he was back out in the close, and in another he had once again squeezed through the narrow entrance and out on to South Street. The cold night air slapped at him, rousing his weary head to work again. Nathan must have gone to collect the box of coins, he thought, and what would he do when he found out they were gone? He broke into a run, crossing South Street for the head of the common close. His very bones were tired. Would today never end?

He paused for just a second at the turning off the common close, where the fronts of the Shaw and Swanson houses were. Front door? No, Nathan would not go to the front door. It was too formal and his errand was too secret. He would go to the garden gate, as he had done before. Pushing himself off the corner wall, he ran on down to the foot of the close, and out on to the dark path by the mill lade.

There was no one in sight, but that was not surprising. Ten minutes' head start and Nathan would be in the garden by now. Murray slowed, wary on the rougher path. The cluster of trees was bundled dark ahead of him. The moonlight was still just good enough to see by even here along the back of the garden walls: good enough, for someone looking hard for it, to see a patch of recently dug earth some distance from the garden gate, even with trails of old bramble stems artistically arranged over it. He wondered what Swanson had been burying, though he had a feeling he could guess. Whatever it was, it could wait for now.

The garden gate that Swanson had so audibly locked earlier was now ajar. For a moment he did not touch it, but listened, keeping his breathing silent, praying not to hear a gunshot. But instead it was voices he heard, soft enough, but not whispering, coming from somewhere up the garden.

'I couldn't believe it!' The first voice was high-pitched, excited, and it took him a moment to identify it as that of Thomas Swanson. 'I had only just buried the dies, and there's Constable Round on the doorstep, asking to search my workshop! What an escape, eh?'

A mumbled reply, seemingly in agreement, came from probably Nathan. Presumably he had his back to Murray, and in any case was not so thrilled at the notion of only just evading the law.

'What an escape,' Swanson repeated, with something very like a giggle. Hysteria was not far away, Murray thought. He had not had an easy few days. 'A matter of minutes! Jack is just seeing them out now: of course he knows nothing. A good thing you didn't appear any earlier, either! What timing! And I don't know when you managed to pick up the kist, but I'm damned glad you did: my heart was in my mouth when they came out here with lanterns. I was ready to make a run for it – me! But no, all clear! It was like a magic trick: I couldn't believe it.'

'I didna collect the kist,' said Nathan, suddenly speaking clearly. 'I've no been able to get back till the now.'

Swanson's laugh was definitely unsteady.

'You what? What do you mean?' There was a thump, as of something being set down suddenly. 'You mean you're here now for the coins?'

'That's right. I've no had the best of evenings, either, so if you could just hand them over I'll be on my way. I want to get off to Edinburgh first thing.'

'But the coins are gone. They're gone. Look, here. That's where I put them, I know it.'

Murray could hear scuffling. Some source of distant light, yellower than the moonlight, shifted inside the garden. He was wondering whether or not to slip in and catch them in their hunt, when a sound from elsewhere attracted his attention. Soft footsteps - someone was coming down the common close. He could not be caught eavesdropping at someone's garden gate. He pushed at the gate, and disappeared into the Swansons' garden.

The gate alerted them to his coming with a peremptory creak. In that second, Murray could see them as a little tableau: Swanson held a lantern up above the place where Nathan crouched, feeling once again amongst the plants at the foot of the garden wall, the pool of amber light carving the two figures from the darkness around them. Victor the bulldog was a marble garden ornament, ears pricked attentively. Then they turned sharply at the sound of the gate, Victor barked and ran to meet him, and Swanson lifted the lantern high to see who was there.

'It's me, Charles Murray,' said Murray hurriedly. He had seen Nathan's hands twitch defensively, but at least they had not gone to snatch the guns. Murray assumed he had had them in his hands when he entered the garden, for he had laid them on a wooden table a yard or two behind him, in order to search for the kist. Reassured at Murray's voice, Swanson set the lantern down on the same table, and Victor escorted Murray up the path. 'I was passing and saw the gate was ajar, so I came in to see that all was well.'

'You are very careful of my security today, Mr. Murray!' said Swanson with another little giggle. 'I must thank you, sir.'

'Not at all: I know how important it is to you in your line of business.'

'My line of business – oh, yes!' Swanson grinned, eyes and teeth glinting wildly in the lantern light. Heavens, thought Murray, the man was a bundle of nerves. The constable's search and his narrow escape might even drive him to an outright confession, at this rate. The false coining was not in doubt, certainly – but what about Rory's murder? What could he tell them of that, if he would?

The gate creaking again made them all jump. Nathan was still at the garden wall, ready to carry on his search at the first opportunity, and Murray took the chance to step casually between him and the table where the guns lay. Nathan might not like using them, but Murray did not want anything persuading him. Swanson had again lifted the lantern to peer down towards the gate and Victor, his sigh almost audible, trotted back down to inspect the newcomer.

'It's me, Cosmo Gordon,' came a voice, unconsciously echoing Murray a moment ago.

'My, is the whole town to come to my back green this evening?' demanded Swanson, with another unstable little laugh, though his speech was very clear. 'Here's Mr. Murray, and Nathan Houston, and now you, sir!'

Cosmo advanced up the garden, the pale mask of his face in the moonlight drawing together into an expression of anxious greeting as he neared the lantern. Victor returned to sit on Swanson's foot, yawning expressively.

'I am glad to see you here, too, Mr. Murray,' said Cosmo. 'I have just heard – you should have told me earlier! - that Jack is found safe and well, and that you had a hand in it, sir! Swanson, you must be delighted! Well, at least that he is found safely,' he added, and Murray wondered if he imagined Swanson would be glad to have his son at home even if it meant seeing him charged with Rory's murder. But Swanson was smiling with pleasure.

'Aye, aye, he's back and well enough, for he's young and strong. I said to Nathan, he's just seeing some people off at the front door and no doubt he'll be through.' Swanson seemed to be sobering up from his state of heightened excitement: he was speaking even more slowly and carefully now. 'He's tired after the last few nights, though. He'll be off to bed soon, I should think.'

'I suppose he's told you all about his stay away,' said Cosmo sympathetically. 'Poor lad!'

'I gather he's having trouble remembering some of it,' said Swanson, lightly. 'I'd guess he has some pal he doesna want to get into trouble over it. Sandy Bogue, likely enough.'

'Aye, that would be likely,' agreed Cosmo. 'It's usually the two of them up to something!'

'Not so much nowadays, though,' said Swanson. 'They're growing into respectable young men.'

There was a certain weight to his words. In fact, as Murray listened, he was sure he could hear a warning in Swanson's voice – reassuring Nathan, probably, that these visitors would be gone soon, Jack would be safely off to bed, and Nathan could resume his hunt for the missing box of coins. There was need for reassurance, certainly: there was a tension in the garden, that sat oddly with the little night noises in the trees, the smell of fresh grass trodden underfoot, the warm glow of the lantern: for a moment no one spoke, and Murray felt as if everyone were waiting to see who would give themselves away first.

Well, since all the main players were here, except perhaps for Jack who might arrive at any moment, he himself might as well ask one of the questions he had come to ask.

'Oh, I discovered something this evening,' he said, as if it were a matter of little moment. 'Remember we discovered that Rory had climbed over your back wall there? And dropped his hat?'

'Oh, aye,' said Thomas Swanson after a moment. Cosmo said nothing, though Murray thought he nodded.

'Well, I met someone who was out at the back there that evening, from before the last time Rory was seen to after we think he was attacked, and they saw no one at all out there by the mill lade. Isn't that strange?'

'That's very odd,' agreed Cosmo smoothly, with a glance at Swanson. 'I wonder if Jack might know something about that?'

'Jack?' Thomas Swanson asked, but at that there came a voice that was not Jack's, from the other side of the garden wall.

'Charles? Charles, is that you?'

'Professor Shaw! Yes, yes, it's me.'

'I have some good news for you! I thought I heard your voice. Mr. Swanson, is it all right if I come round? Is your garden gate locked?'

'No, no!' called Swanson, adding, in a lower tone, 'come one, come all!'

'I'll just be a moment!' They could hear Shaw's little feet trotting quickly down the garden, over the bridges and around the various fish pools. His own garden gate squawked, then Swanson's gate objected once again. As Professor Shaw neared them and the lantern, reaching down awkwardly to pet Victor, it was clear he was almost ready to retire for the night: he wore a velvet cap and a dark green patterned dressing gown, but seemed not in the least abashed.

'How fortuitous!' he panted a little as he reached them, trying to bow and speak at the same time. 'Good evening, Mr. Swanson – ah, Mr. Gordon, Mr. Houston. Quite a party! I had no idea where you were, Charles, dear boy, so I took in the message myself, though as it was an express I hardly knew if I should or not, and of course I had to tell the messenger no answer as yet.'

'An express!' Murray exclaimed, running through the various awful reasons someone might send him such an urgent message – his daughter was the first thing on his mind, even just now.

'Yes, and then of course I came out into the garden to do the last few observations of the night – what a wonderful moon, isn't it? – and I was sure I heard your voice. And here you are!'

'But the express, Professor – do you have it with you?'

'Yes, yes, I do, because I put it safely in my pocket.' He felt in one dressing gown pocket, while Murray held his breath, and then in the other. The second attempt was more successful. 'Here we are!'

'It's from Robbins – my manservant at Letho,' Murray explained quickly to Swanson. 'Please excuse me a moment.'

'Here, use the lantern, sir,' said Swanson sensibly. He handed it to Murray, who moved a little away from the table out of politeness. Shadows lurched amongst them. Cosmo took a step closer to him just to say,

'I hope it is not bad news from Letho.' He stopped by the table, glancing at Nathan. Nathan tried not to look down at the plants under the wall, where the kist full of false coin might or might not still be. Murray, hardly aware of them, tore open the letter, squinted in the lantern light, read quickly, and breathed the deepest of sighs.

'Carlisle, my gardener, has come back to his wits at last!' he announced. 'Mr. Swanson, I should explain: someone attacked him and left him for dead in the gardens, last Sunday morning, and he has been unconscious ever since. I am more pleased than I can say.' He set the lantern back on the table. A puzzled frown slipped over his face and passed on.

'Then he should be able to say who it was who attacked him!' said Professor Shaw, anxiously.

'If he has, Robbins has not mentioned it. I imagine Mary – the person who is nursing him – has forbidden anyone to ask until he is more himself.'

'No doubt he will tell everyone soon enough,' said Cosmo. 'He's a strong-minded individual, isn't he? Such an interesting face to paint. Hers too – those eyebrows!'

Murray smiled, relief flooding him.

'And he's an excellent gardener. Your pea seedlings will continue in safe hands, Professor!'

'It was last Sunday morning he was so mysteriously struck down, was it not, Mr. Murray?' Cosmo went on.

'That's right.'

Cosmo seemed to have something on his mind.

'Rory's funeral, during which poor Jack – became temporarily absent. That was on Saturday, I seem to remember?'

'It was,' said Professor Shaw. He peered at Cosmo. The lantern cast an unaccustomed look of dislike upon his amiable face.

'Swanson, I'm sure you've considered … And your clever observation about the hat and the marks that made us all think Rory must have climbed into the garden that night, before he climbed out of it. Who might have had the opportunity to mislead us by leaving that little trail…?'

Murray felt things were going just a little too fast: there was something else he needed to ask before Cosmo put Thomas Swanson completely on the defensive. And where was Jack? How long could it take him to see Constable Round through the front door? Could he have lost his nerve and fled once again?

'Mr. Swanson,' he said hurriedly, 'on the night of Rory's death, you were not in your workshop at all?'

'No, I told you: I was out, to my shame, drinking at this gentleman's house.'

Cosmo shot a look at Murray that could be felt even in the lantern light.

'Only you weren't, were you?' he said. 'I'm sorry, Swanson, but Mr. Murray here asked me directly, and I had to tell him. You weren't there at all that night.'

Any colour that could be seen washed out of Swanson's face.

'I'm not sure I understand, sir,' he stumbled over the words.

'Were you, since you were not at Cosmo Gordon's, in your workshop between ten and eleven that night?' asked Murray. He could feel Professor Shaw, quiet as a shadow, slipping in somewhere behind him, seeking safety. The tension in the garden, dispelled by his arrival, had suddenly surged once again. Even Victor's ears were alert and sharp. Murray could hear Nathan breathing heavily to his right, near the garden wall: to his left, just beyond the wooden table where the lantern glowed, Cosmo Gordon stood with his hands tucked behind his back, intent on the scene, head up and confident.

'I was not,' said Swanson definitely. He waved a hand in emphasis: it trembled violently, and he quickly tucked both hands into his waistcoat pockets.

'But you have been in it since, have you not?'

'Well, yes, of course.'

'Did you see – any evidence that someone else had been in there in your absence?'

There was a long silence. They were so still that an owl, pale as a snowdrift, swept suddenly over them: Murray heard Professor Shaw yelp softly in shock, and Victor growled.

'Jack, for instance?' Cosmo suggested helpfully. Thomas Swanson flashed him a sour look.

'Jack doesn't go into my workshop unless he absolutely has to,' he hissed angrily. 'He doesna like it.'

'Well, it wasna me,' rumbled Nathan Houston, who looked as if the conversation was beyond his comprehension. 'Look, I need to be getting on, eh?'

'I think Rory went in there, looking for – something,' said Murray. 'Perhaps for Jack, but Jack was out elsewhere.'

'Then why would he go into the workshop? There'd be

nobody there, and the door would be locked – hey, are you saying he broke into my workshop? Rory McArthur?' Now Swanson was the angry father, whose son's friend had misbehaved.

'I don't think he broke in: I think he went in because there was someone already there, and he hoped it was Jack or you. But when he went inside, he realised it wasn't Jack – but it was someone else he knew. And he realised that that person was involved in a criminal activity: namely, making false coinage.'

'What makes you think it wasn't Jack?' asked Cosmo, still quite calm. 'Jack fits every part of the mystery, I should have thought: he was the one Rory was looking for, he was missing and could have been in Letho when your gardener was attacked, he could have made it look as if Rory came over the wall there. And he was fit enough to climb over this wall,' he pointed to the one between them and the Shaws' garden, 'and chase Rory in there – which, I regret to say, Mr. Swanson here is not.'

'Why are you blaming Jack?' cried Thomas Swanson in distress. 'There's no reason why Jack would have killed his friend! None at all! Why are you saying all these things?'

'Because they need saying,' said Cosmo, '- and because he's about to attack you, Murray!'

Quick as a flash, Cosmo whipped his hands out in front of him. He had Nathan's pistols.

The barrels pointed past Murray. He could see Cosmo's fingers, long, artistic fingers, tighten on the triggers.

He spun, grabbing Professor Shaw by his shoulders. He flung him to the ground, crouching beside him. There was a flash of movement, and a tremendous, double bang.

'Are you all right, Professor?' Murray snapped. He reached out a hand to Shaw's little face: it came away red. There was a tremendous howl close by. He swore, and turned. Beside him was a jumble of bodies, which he could not quite sort out. He could hear Nathan swearing, too, with force. But beyond the table, Cosmo Gordon held the two pistols loose in his hands and stared at what he had done. Then he turned and ran for the garden gate.

Murray found himself on his feet, running after him. The garden path was slippery with moss, but they scrambled down it. Cosmo reached the gate and whirled through, trying to slam it behind him. Murray caught the latch. It was torn from his gloved fingers, but the delay stopped the gate from shutting. He fumbled through it, and flung himself out on to the path by the mill lade. Something low and white shot past him, nearly knocking him off balance. Cosmo ahead tossed one of the guns down, ridding himself of the burden, and Murray almost tripped on it, dancing stupidly around the obstacle. He wondered how long he would be able to keep up the pursuit: Cosmo was younger than he was, and had not, presumably, spent such an exhausting day.

But the chase was not fated to last long. There was a cry from up ahead, an inhuman yell, then a curse more violent than any Nathan Houston had produced. Murray reached the point of action, and slithered to a halt, propping himself against a tree. Cosmo lay prone on the path, groaning with pain and frustration. Something plump and white had attached itself, growling, to his ankles.

Victor, it seemed, had settled his score.

Chapter Twenty-Five

'So the fellow'll no be hangit for uttering false coin, then?'

Carlisle had been allowed to sit outside his cottage for the first time, though Mary Robbins was attentive, her angular black eyebrows severe every time she saw him assessing the state of the garden since his absence. Murray was perched on a low stone wall: Carlisle had tried to free himself of the blanket over his shoulders but he was content to stay on the wooden bench outside his own front door, where the evening sun shone with unusual warmth for early April. The gardeners bustled about, anxious to be seen to be efficient but relieved to have their commander-in-chief at least back on the battlefield.

'Not when he's already dead, no,' said Murray, a little sadly. When he closed his eyes he could still see Swanson's large body, flung by Cosmo's double shot over his son's stricken form. Jack would take some time to recover, though he had no physical injury beyond a few bruises. Swanson had died instantly, defending his son.

'I mind that fellow, the artist. I didna see him hit me, if that's what you're saying happened,' Carlisle admitted, grudgingly. 'But I did see him nearby Professor Shaw's that night, just as you say. It was no business of mine what he was doing there, at all. But he was heading round the side of that house next door to Professor Shaw's. That was all I saw, for of course I was looking for Professor Shaw and the peas, and the Shaw household were all away to bed by then and I had no wish to disturb them. So I just came away, and forgot all about it.'

'But Cosmo remembered you, and knew where you lived, of course.' Murray felt apologetic, though there was nothing he could have done.

'He came to see Mr. Carlisle on Monday afternoon,' said Mary Robbins serenely. 'He said he wanted to draw him – said he'd be happy to keep an eye on him for me if I wanted a rest. Oh, he was very charming.'

'But you didn't go.' It was a statement: Murray knew she had more sense. She smiled, knowing it.

'Aye, aye,' said Carlisle. 'And Professor Shaw?'

'Well, he's still not recovered, but he's in good hands: his wife is gentle with him, and Walter is helping him with his work in the garden. He wasn't hurt, you know: but having someone's blood splash across your face is not a pleasant thing for anyone, even one of a strong disposition.'

'Aye, aye. That Walter's a canny lad, though, now. He'll keep him on his toes, nae doubt.'

'You're probably right.' Murray grinned.

'And he got back his flannels all right?' Carlisle asked, with a knowing look.

'James Shaw admitted to tipping them over the wall for a joke.'

'He'd no need to be doing that,' said Carlisle. 'Walter could have lost them all on his own. But he'll be glad enough to have them back before his aunt had a real tit over it.'

'Yes …' Murray agreed slowly. 'I shouldn't like to see Mrs. Fenwick in a truly bad temper.'

'What about yon other one? The fellow you said was helping them put out the coins?'

'Nathan Houston? Well, there's no firm evidence that he knew what they were doing. I doubt that the people who robbed him down the road a month or so ago are going to admit they stole false coins from him, and started using them around St. Andrews and Cupar. They probably didn't realise until it was too late. Swanson thought Nathan had been lazy and not taken the coins to Edinburgh where it would have been safer to start using them, so he went round to see him that night, and had a quarrel with him about it - Nathan's second quarrel that night, though at least this one didn't come to blows. That was why Swanson was very grateful when Cosmo suggested they give each other an alibi: Swanson thought Cosmo was being friendly, but in fact he was of course protecting himself – at least until protecting Swanson seemed likely to do him more harm than good.'

'So where was young Rory, then?'

'Young Rory had an eventful evening, I believe. He left the recital and went home, to find that his sister, whom he was trying to protect, was not there. He knew Nathan had an interest in her, and went round to accuse him of dallying with her: for whatever reason, this resulted in a fight, probably because Nathan likes using his fists. Nathan had a black eye and Rory split his knuckles. Then Rory went to find his friend Jack: by this stage it may just have been to talk with him, rather than to accuse him of missing the recital: we won't know, for he found the Swanson house in darkness, too. Jack was out with Janet, and Swanson was already out somewhere, possibly considering his visit to Nathan. Nathan, later, of course, met the Bogues at the mill lade.'

'My, the place was going like market day at Cupar!' Carlisle remarked drily.

'I'm glad I was in my bed,' Murray agreed. 'Rory decided to see if anyone was in the workshop, for of course the Swansons had no servant living in to answer the door. At the workshop he found, not Jack or his father, but Cosmo Gordon, working on his designs for the corrected coin dies. The ones with the right date on them.'

'Aye, indeed.'

'I'd say Rory realised pretty smartly what had been going on, and from what I've heard of him he would probably have said straight out. There was a fight in the workshop, during which he must have touched something poisonous. Then he fled into the garden: he would probably have known the back gate would have been locked, so he climbed over the wall. But Cosmo was fit enough and desperate enough to follow, and caught him.'

'Aye, poor lad, poor lad.' Carlisle reflected a moment.

'Cosmo seems to have decided quickly that it would be easiest to try to pin the blame on Jack Swanson. He talked to him at Rory's funeral, persuading him to run, and followed him to St. Rule's Tower. He left food there that night: he didn't want Jack deciding straightaway that it was a trap. Then he walked to Letho and dealt, he thought, with you.'

'Not taking into account my tough skull,' said Carlisle with satisfaction.

'Indeed. Walter saw him in Letho that evening but then he

must have returned to St. Andrews again to leave more food for Jack – or he paid someone to do it, but if he did, we don't know who. He was back in Letho to paint Walter on Monday morning, anyway, and had the air of one just arrived. He abandoned Jack, then, not expecting him to be found at this time of year until it was too late. It would have been useful to have Jack dead so that he could not deny killing Rory, but even when Jack was rediscovered in time he did his best to cast blame on him. A fine reward for Swanson's partnership.'

'And the constable has him soundly locked up?' asked Carlisle.

'He's gone to Cupar to the jail there.' Murray sighed. 'I think it was all his idea, you know. Swanson wanted advancement, but not as much as Cosmo wanted to be restored to his family's old status – Gordon of Invertally, a place no one has ever heard of, but a gentleman's designation.'

'Would the money have helped, sir?'

'He thought so. Maybe he thought he could buy the estate back one day.'

'Aye, a grand thing,' said Carlisle, 'being a laird and all.' His worn face had assumed an innocent look.

'Oh, a very grand thing, indeed,' said Murray. 'Except for the responsibilities, of course. I assume you'll be at the kirk next Sunday, Carlisle?'

'Oh, aye, sir, aye,' said Carlisle blandly. 'If I'm spared.'

'I'll do my best to see that you are,' said Murray.

Some Scots words in *Thicker than Water*:

Ahint - behind
Argify - argue
Ashet – serving dish
Bejant – first year student at St. Andrews
Bide – stay, live at
Bleezin - drunk
Braisant – brazen-faced, bold
Brose – oatmeal or peasemeal mixed with hot water or milk
Buckle, up in the – above oneself
Bunkwife - landlady
Carlie - common
Carline – hag, old woman
Catterbatter - row
Chap – knock (at a door)
Chawed - jealous
Clouts - cloths
Crud – (here) frogspawn
Dwam - daydream
Fash – trouble, upset
Gallow-breid - rascal
Gang - go
Gey – very
Gomerel - fool
Greet – cry, sob
Hurcheon – hedgehog (think sea urchin!)
Jook – pop one's head out
Kail ladle – tadpole
Keek – quick look
Ken - know
Kist – chest or box
Laldy – giving it laldy, putting some effort in
Limmer - scoundrel
Neb - nose
Peely wally – pale, ill-looking
Perjink - neat
Puddock's gener - frogspawn

Risp – a bar to rattle at a door, in place of a knocker
Screw – freshwater shrimp
Tertian – a third-year student at St. Andrews
Tit - fit of rage
Unchancy – unlucky, ill-omened
Water mouse – water vole
Wud - mad

About the Author

Lexie Conyngham is a historian living in the shadow of the Highlands. Her Murray of Letho and Hippolyta Napier novels are born of a life amidst Scotland's old cities, ancient universities and hidden-away aristocratic estates, but she has written since the day she found out that people were allowed to do such a thing. Beyond teaching and research, her days are spent with wool, wild allotments and a wee bit of whisky. Follow her professional procrastination at www.murrayofletho.blogspot, on Facebook or on Pinterest (Lexie Conyngham).

The Murray of Letho series:

Death in a Scarlet Gown
Knowledge of Sins Past
Service of the Heir: An Edinburgh Murder
An Abandoned Woman
Fellowship with Demons
The Tender Herb: A Murder in Mughal India
Death of an Officer's Lady
Out of a Dark Reflection
Slow Death by Quicksilver
Thicker than Water

The Hippolyta Napier series:

A Knife in Darkness
Death of a False Physician

Other books by Lexie Conyngham

Windhorse Burning
The War, The Bones and Dr. Cowie
Thrawn Thoughts and Blithe Bits (short stories)

Made in the USA
Lexington, KY
23 April 2017